Book cover by Ruxandra Tudorică

Methyss-art

©2017

## SPECIAL THANKS

To my wife, Claribel and my two boys, Logan and Connor
Your continued patience with this long and arduous process
makes me appreciate you more and more

# Books by Michael Timmins

## The Lycan War Saga

"The Awakening: Part One"

"The Awakening: Part Two"

"The Gathering"

"The War"
TBA

## Shards of the Coven Series

Prelude to the Shards Anthology
"Intellect"
"Race of the Witchguard"
"A Town Called Ghost"

"Starfall"
A Shards of the Coven novel
TBA

The Lycan War Saga

Book Two

# THE

# Gathering

## MICHAEL TIMMINS

# Appendix I:

Terms:

Lycanthropy- A common term used to describe someone who can transform into an animal or a hybrid, part animal, part human. Most commonly referred to werewolves, but it can also mean any were-creature. Also sometimes referred to as shifters

Trues- Refers to the original bloodline of were-creatures

Pures- Refers to anyone who is given lycanthropy by a True

Were- Originally delineated as someone who was given lycanthropy from a Pure, it can also be used generically in reference to someone who has lycanthropy

## Past people of import:

Sylvanis- Druidess from ancient Celt, reborn in this time. Believes in nature and civilization learning to live in harmony. With her rebirth, her four Trues have been reawakened.

- Clint Wallace- Sylvanis' True Werewolf
- Kat Cooper- Sylvanis' True Weretiger
- Hank Keller- Sylvanis' True Werebear
- Stephanie Boles- Sylvanis' True Werefox
  Jason Randal- Stephanie's Pure

Kestrel- Druidess from ancient Celt. Through magic placed her body and soul in stasis until current time. Believes that civilization is abhorrent to nature and needs to be destroyed. Sworn enemy of Sylvanis. With her reawakening, her four Trues have also been reawakened.

- Samuel Pitter- Once known as Syndor, he is Kestrel's True Weresnake
- Gordon Sands- Kestrel's True Werecrocodile
- Shae- Kestrel's True Wererat

- Blain Fouse- Kestrel's True Wereboar
  Taylor Westin- Blain's Pure Wereboar
  Joseph Clark- Blain's Pure Wereboar

  Officer Ben Charles- Police officer investigating a murder by a mysterious creature
  Beth Harristin- Best friend of Stephanie
  Mike Vinick- Best friend of Jason
  Cirrus- Son of Samuel

# Appendix II:

## New people of import:

Colonel Carl Simpson- Director of Homeland Security

Hector Garza- A man with a deadly secret that could change the course of the war

Zach Van Stanley- Leader of the eco-terrorist group, E.A.R.t.H or Earth Anger Retaliate to Heal

Eric Moran- Leader of the shadowy organization behind experimenting on Shae.

Jessie Brumfield- Ex-marine who has volunteered to join Sylvanis in her fight

# Prologue

The Roman centurions were already dead – they just didn't know it yet. Calin slammed into them like a battering ram, splintering them and breaking them apart. On either side, in contrast, Adonia and Katherine slid through their ranks like water after a rain, searching for the path of least resistance down a rocky hill. Not that the Roman centurions caused them much in the way of resistance.

When Calin, Adonia, and Katherine came across the patrol, they had been hunkered down in a copse of hardwoods, shading themselves from the afternoon sun. The Romans laughed and drank wine and rested. There had been no need for any heightened sense of concern, as the "conquest" of the isle had been all but assured as soon as the Empire turned its attention in full upon it. Mostly, the people capitulated and welcomed the Romans, adopting their ways and culture.

There had been a few holdouts, of course. The Druids had been recalcitrant to the Romans, and they had much sway over the people of land, though not as much these days. The Roman army had been systematically locating these Druids and "removing" them from their sphere of influences. The less control the Druids had, the easier it would be for the Romans to conquer the isle.

The patrol had been sent to remove the Druid. There had been word of an Elder Druid who lived in a village not far from the stand of trees they now lounged in, and they would arrive there early the next day.

For the centurions, there had been little cause for wariness, though the standard practice of putting outlying sentries was still upheld and a ring of them surrounded the impromptu camp. They died first.

As much as it grated on Calin, he barreled into the force in hybrid form. Normally, he would have fought the Romans in human form, as they were no match for him, even without his hybrid supernatural abilities. It had been agreed upon, by the three of them, any interaction with Roman centurions would be done in hybrid form, though. They couldn't risk the Romans learning their real faces. Calin would do this, grimacing the whole time.

The first eight centurions he killed in seconds. Arms out wide, he dragged his claws across open necks, spraying blood from the one on the left, nearly decapitating the one on the right. Turning his head, he opened his maw as he collided with a third, tearing out his esophagus by closing his fangs and allowing the impact to thrust the man away, leaving his throat a gaping hole. The impact with the centurion wouldn't have stopped him, but he allowed it to bring him up short as he brought his arms back to him. A mass of soldiers scrambled to their feet as creatures of myths and legends stalked among them, shearing them as effortlessly as a scythe through grain.

Five men converged on Calin; bronze swords held forward in fighting stances. They chose to not grab their shields for fear of being cut down before they could mount a true defense. It wouldn't have mattered either way.

Swatting the blades aside of the two immediately in front of him, he decided to show them how unfortunate they were. Claws extended, he punched forward with both hands, piercing their armor with such force, it folded in, piercing flesh with jagged metal, along with five incredibly sharp claws.

2

Ripping his claws out of the bodies of the two men, he turned his attention to the other three. Their fate dawned on them as they watched their compatriots collapse to the ground, red blood bubbling up from the holes in their armor, their hearts punctured. Clint snarled at them, bestial and full of menace. Running full speed at them, they barely had time to flinch before he launched himself— over and past them.

Ignoring the three in front of him, he sailed over their heads. Tucking his shoulder, he slammed midway up a tall hardwood, snapping it in half. The force of his blow slammed the top of the tree down on the confused and panicked legion, smashing and killing three more. Landing, he spun around to see how Adonia and Katherine fared.

Adonia, as usual, was a sight to see. Her long canine snout bared sharp fangs, tinted red with blood, sharp pointed ears, tufted black, turned down. The white fur of her throat and torso was stained as well, making a contest of dueling reds, blood marked fur next to the rusty-red of the rest of her fox coat.

Her bushy red tail, swished this way and that as she ducked and swung around scrambling soldiers, desperately trying to arm themselves and mount some sort of defense against the onslaught of three Lycan Trues.

Adonia slashed, clawed and kicked her way through, seldom stopping to kill. She maimed and incapacitated dozens in seconds, a violent breath of wind casually flowing through a landscape dotted with flesh and bone. She was effective and precise, her path carefully chosen to create the most discord and least resistance.

Katherine was a different matter. Where Calin was sheer brutality and Adonia precise violence, Katherine was fluid lethality. Her tiger stripes made her stand out among the soldiers as she pounced and sliced and gouged.

After slashing the throat of one soldier, she would leap on the next, boring him down with her weight, crushing his cuirass and caving in his chest. Before the man knew he was dead, she was gone, killing the next closest. She

3

moved with a quickness which belied her size. They all did, but Katherine made it look as if she wasn't fast, everyone else was slow.

Calin could spare them no more consideration. The centurions were gradually managing to gain control of their situation. Those remaining armed themselves with sword and shield and were trying desperately to form ranks. If he allowed them to set themselves, they would form a shield wall, which might hamper him — slightly.

Charging the centurions, as they began to form up, Calin noticed movement from either side. Straggling soldiers to his right and left had been effectively removed as a threat, as they were either dead or in no shape to join the fight. Katherine and Adonia converged on the soldiers from the sides as he made a frontal assault.

Several moments later, the Roman centurions were no more. Calin almost felt sorry for them. They should have brought more men. One hundred soldiers against three Trues? The moment Adonia had spotted them in the copse of trees, their fate had been sealed.

When they reached the quiet hamlet early the next day, only he and Adonia remained. Katherine took her leave to make her way to the next village. It was odd being back in this village, Calin thought. It hadn't been all that many years ago Adonia and he visited here with information about the end of the war. With the defeat of Kestrel, there had been a need to let villagers know they were safe now and the threat had been dealt with.

The village had grown some since last he had been here. The smithy, the storage hut, and the tavern were little changed, but there was a hint of expansion. The foundations of a church were half started on the rise beyond the town center, a foundation that would welcome the death knell for the druids. Several other homesteads, in various stages of construction, sprouted up around the foundation, as if the church grew followers from the very earth surrounding it.

Catholicism was a weed the Romans had sprinkled the seed of over the entire isle. This weed would kill everything else, till only it remained, a dangerous growth the people were starting to cultivate on their own, with little guidance from the Romans. They understood if they tried to remove the weed, it would fight back, and Calin knew which one was the strongest.

It hadn't always been this way. Before the war between Kestrel and Sylvanis, it would have been easy to push back the Romans. If they knew of the threat, they could have mustered their Lycan army to destroy these invaders before they had been allowed to take root in their soil.

Not for the first time, Calin cursed Kestrel and her quest for power. Her fear that civilization would destroy nature if allowed to grow unchecked, seemed all but certain now the war had weakened the druid's power in these lands to such an extent the Romans were all but unopposed.

Of course, Calin and the others did their best with what little resources were left. Their battles with the Romans had been lopsided. They destroyed legions of men, and only lost Weres. In recent months though, it changed. The Romans were no longer ignorant as to what they were fighting. They hunted Lycans as a hunter hunts deer. Calin knew their numbers were dwindling.

The Romans were too smart and too efficient at warfare. They used tactics to frighten the people into giving up the names of Druids, the names of Lycans. Then they destroyed them with overwhelming force, leaving nothing to chance.

The people were not to be blamed. All they wished to do was to live their lives, raise their children, and farm their land. Between the clergy making it a sin to harbor those of the 'old' religion, and the centurions threatening their

5

homes and families if they didn't inform on those who were considered a threat, what could a simple man do? No. Calin didn't blame them. The time of Druids and Lycans had passed — which found him in this village once again.

The Druid Elder still lived here and upon Calin and Adonia entering, he made his way to the grounds in the center of the village with the help of a youthful lad with chaotic hair. Surprisingly, the old man's beard had won the race and now stretched but an inch off the ground. Stark white, it looked as if the man had grabbed some passing cloud and convinced it to hang upon his chin, as it appeared light and fluffy. His hair, having deduced it would lose the race to the man's feet with the beard, had all but given up and began to recede in a silent pout. Much of the man's pate was absent of hair, leaving only the sides and the back of his head to carry on the task of hair growth.

The youth beside him, his student, or so Calin believed, was a stout lad. Short and stocky, he had a solid build. Bushy eyebrows nestled under hair defiant of the forces which naturally pulled things to the earth. Standing on end in some places, jutting out in others, forward and backward, it mattered not. His bushy brow furrowed as he helped his master pick his way over the uneven ground.

Adonia, as usual, took the lead when conveying the reason for their arrival. It wasn't that Calin couldn't do this, only, he didn't wish to. Words were something he never felt comfortable sharing with strangers. While he held a deep respect for the Elder, he had no desire to converse with someone he didn't know. At least, not when he had Adonia to do it for him.

The reason for their visit was clear, Adonia informed the Elder. The Romans were coming and were not going to be stopped. This battle, over before it started. The least they could do was let any and every Druid they knew to seek shelter and to run from this threat. The Elder didn't agree though, judging from the shaking of his head at Adonia's words.

A small crowd gathered now as word of their arrival spread. It was one thing you could always count on it these small villages. With little to do with their lives other than to eat, drink, sleep and work, when strangers arrive with news of the outside world, well, you went to find out what was happening.

A clergyman stood on the rise of his newly born church. Unable to protect itself as most babes, the priest stood defensively before it, arms crossed, brows furrowed, and eyes narrowed upon them, no doubt fearful of them, and the possibility of violence. Calin dismissed him. They were not there for him, and he had little to fear. He was a man of their god, and so deserved a modicum of respect.

As Calin surveyed the growing crowd he again rested his eyes upon the apprentice Druid. The boy stared at him. When their eyes met, the boy searched his eyes and face, and a look of concern rested there.

Calin looked away.

He knew the look. It was the same look everyone seemed to give him these days, like they took one look at his face and could read the immense sadness hiding behind his well-trained façade. As a soldier, he knew how to attach a blank look to his face — the look of unconcerned detachment soldiers had adopted for time immemorial. The look, apparently, never convinced.

He wondered how long his sense of duty would keep him alive. It was all he lived for these days. You would think, after all these years since Sylvanis' death, he could let it go; able to wash away the pain and regret and the immense sense of loss her death bestowed upon him. And yet, it still felt as if his heart had been drained of everything which made it the vessel of life. Oh, it beat still. Its motions had yet to betray him, but the feelings it granted someone to feel love — those fled.

Glancing back at the youth, the boy still looked upon him with tender eyes of sympathy. If Calin could dredge up an emotion long enough, he might have felt appreciation, or maybe anger. Alas, those were buried too deep to swim their way to the surface. In the end, he dismissed the boy, as he dismissed most that passed fleetingly through his life. The only ones he still clung to with any feelings, were his fellow Trues.

Adonia addressed the youth now. Apparently, the old man wasn't willing to flee. Not surprising given his age. He doubtless hoped the good people of this village would understand he was not long for this world, and to surrender him to the Romans had no point. The boy was another matter. He was young, and so would be a future threat in the eyes of the Romans. They would not hesitate to put an end to him. They were the most ruthless civilized people Calin knew.

He hoped the boy would listen. His death would be an unnecessary thing. A senseless death. Only time would tell, but honestly, they had other concerns. For the Romans, the Trues were the biggest threat. Not only were they powerful, but they could create more Lycans at will. They would not rest until all of them were dead. That could not be allowed to happen. They had a more important task to accomplish before they died. A task, even now, Calin loathed to address.

Having said her peace to the Elder and his apprentice, Adonia turned her horse and moved to join him. They traveled in peace for a bit. Neither wished to spend the night in the village. They were hunted and could only bring unwanted attention to the townsfolk. Attention which might lead to violence.

"The Elder would not listen to reason. He insists on staying," Adonia informed him after they were well on their way.

"The boy?" he asked, turning his head inquisitively to her.

Glancing over at him, she shook her head. "Varden? I am unsure. He listened to everything I said, but he seemed determined to stay with the old man. After speaking with him I glanced at the Elder and tried to convey the necessity of him leaving." Guiding the horse around a hole in the road, Adonia deftly moved back beside him. "The old man nodded at me at the end after glancing at the boy, so I believe he will do his best to convince the youth to flee."

"Good. We need to try and save as many as we can before we flee ourselves."

Adonia's frown gave him all the knowledge he needed about her feelings towards fleeing. It wasn't like she didn't understand the need for it, but she was a fighter, a hunter. She was not prey, to flee like a hare before a fox. She was the fox.

"We have only a few more villages to visit. Then, we will go through the Sundering." The words made her visibly shudder as she spoke them.

"It is necessary, Adonia." Looking at her with stern eyes, he continued, "We are doing a disservice to those who volunteered to become Lycans to fight the war. They are being hunted, killed, their fami . . .."

"I know, Calin," Adonia interrupted. "I don't need you to explain the reasons again. I do not wish to see them in harm's way, but the Sundering. I never thought we would be forced to take such action."

Nodding, Calin returned his attention back to the road. He had made this argument to Catherine and Adonia. Had made it long before it became apparent they would all be at risk from the Romans. He, unbeknownst to the rest, already performed the Sundering. Had already relinquished his control of those he granted lycanthropy to, and in turn, to those who had been granted lycanthropy by his Pures. They were all free now. Free of lycanthropy, and free of him.

It had not been a pleasant experience, and so, he knew not to judge Adonia's reluctance to go through with it. It just wasn't right to continue to put those good people at risk of persecution by the Romans.

They rode in silence for a bit, not wishing to breathe words into the quiet night and their discordant thoughts. Each of them battled with their own issues, Calin knew. He hoped Adonia would not breach hers tonight. He did not

9

wish to think of the future after the Sundering. Did not wish to think of the duty he and the others had yet to perform.

Adonia brought her horse a little closer to Calin's and his heart sighed in resignation, knowing she was going to ask again.

"Have you given any more thought to what we talked about. What we would do after the Sundering, Calin?"

His eyes closed upon her words. He knew what she referred to of course. In this past couple of years, her feelings for him became apparent. Her attempts at bridging the gulf between him and his heart had been worthy. But that chasm remained insurmountable. What's more, it flew in the face of his duty. His duty. The last thing he could do for Sylvanis—the one thing he had no desire to do.

"Adonia, you know I care for you. I do not wish to see you hurt . . . as I hurt . . . I . . . ." Words tumbled from him. He did care for Adonia, but he was no longer capable of love. She knew this. Why did she keep pushing him for something he was incapable of doing?

"It matters not, anyway. You know this Adonia. We have a duty. Sylvanis need us."

"Sylvanis is dead!" Her voice was harsh in its defiance.

Calin froze, though his horse plodded on as if nothing painful had been uttered.

Adonia lowered her head; a sigh whispered from her.

"I am sorry, Calin. I did not wish to say those words and wish I could take them back." A tear spilled from her beautiful green eyes. "It's . . . I love you, Calin. We have no idea what, if anything, will happen with Kestrel's spell or Sylvanis'. Do we forsake our own lives, our own feelings, for something which may never occur?"

"It is our duty." Calin's voice words were clipped and forceful. "It is *my* duty." He implored, "I know your feelings, Adonia, and I am sorry I do not share them. My love is for Sylvanis, and I owe her my life. Dead or not." Those last words came with a hint of bitterness. "We have one last task to accomplish for her, and I will not fail in it."

He looked at her, emotion visible upon his features. "Don't you understand, Adonia? This last thing, we must do? I despise it. I hate the idea of doing it!" Tears now flowed from his eyes. "The faith I keep for the love I have for Sylvanis, I must break it!"

"She needs Trues with her when Kestrel rises again. Trues only we can provide. Trues we can only provide with the continuation of our bloodlines." They both knew what that meant. While normal for people to get married and have children, it usually wasn't something one was honor bound to do.

"And those bloodlines must be pure, Adonia. You know this. If we were to be together. Have a family together. What would it do to our bloodlines? Would we be dooming Sylvanis to one less ally?" Adonia once again peered forward, unable to look at him, at the words she knew to be the truth. "Perhaps dooming her to the loss of two allies? We do not know what it would do, and for her sake, we cannot risk it." Calin looked forward as well, knowing this discussion was coming to an end. "I will not risk it."

Together they rode in silence from then on. One whose heart had long since broken, and another for whom the break was fresh.

# *Chapter One*

The office held little light. The sparse furniture were mere silhouettes in the gloom. A faint light, flickering, played across them before going dark again. A faint click of a mouse button, a sharp tap breaking the silence, and the light danced again. It played in full across the face of the man sitting behind the solid oak desk.

The desk itself lay as bare as the rest of the room. Few items rested upon it—a wire mesh basket with two shelves, one labeled in, the other, out, the latter filled with papers, while the other sat empty. A desk calendar, a tool most people seldom used anymore, relying more on digital reminders of meetings and appointments, lay flat upon the desk's surface. Writing covered almost every single square, a multitude of reminders of meetings and conference calls.

Resting near the front of the desk was a brass nameplate with a name etched upon its surface. Its face was dark, the name impossible to make out in the low light of the office. If one entered this office during the day, or when all the lights were on, they would have seen the name, Colonel Carl Simpson, Director of Homeland Security.

Colonel Carl Simpson sat behind the desk staring at the only other item which lay upon his desk, his laptop. The light from its screen bathed him in its pale light, disjointed by images flashing across it. Crow's feet bunched at the corner of his eyes as he watched dispassionately at the video, the second of two, he had been watching repeatedly for what seemed to be several hours. How long it had been, Carl had no idea. Despite there being a time stamp at the bottom of his screen, he had not yet taken the time to check it. His focus, *all* of his focus, remained upon the impossible images he watched, like some kind of horror loop.

As dispassionate as he had been at the start of this twisted movie marathon, worry and dread were creeping in. His earlier disbelief at the legitimacy of these videos, gradually turned to incredulity. Worry lines, a trademark of his, became more pronounced. The edges of his soft, fleshy lips turned down as he rested them against his steepled hands, tapping them lightly.

He was a stern man, tall and solidly built; it was often remarked he held a commanding presence, which suited Carl fine. If people looked at you like you were a leader, it made it easier to lead them. Remarkably, he still had a full head of sandy brown hair with barely a single gray one to mar its façade. Soft gray-green eyes darted around as he watched the scene play out on his computer screen.

The shaky video was one of many which recorded the events in Chicago. Despite its shakiness, likely due to the jostling crowd and the nervousness of the person who filmed it, it still provided the best angle and clarity of the fight. A fight, which apparently occurred between some sort of humanoid tiger, a humanoid wolf, and a humanoid boar.

When DHS agent, Yark, brought this to his attention, he reacted . . . poorly it would seem. The idea one of his best field agents would bring this obviously, he believed at the time, doctored video some special effects wiz put up on social media, as a legitimate concern for the Homeland Security Director, angered him.

That someone under his authority would bring this National Enquirer bullshit to his desk infuriated him so much, he fired Yark, then and there. Yark, who had been one of his brightest and most promising agents he had seen in quite some time, had the unfortunate luck of presenting a completely unbelievable video, long before anyone else could have understood the implications of it, especially Carl.

When another video had been brought to his attention, this video provided to him secretly, he realized his error. The video had been delivered into his possession so secretly, in fact, he still didn't have knowledge of which agency delivered it to him, or how or why they had known he had received this other video. It led to all sorts of questions. Questions, he didn't feel prepared to get the answers to.

This other video showed a disturbing scene. It was security camera footage from an office building. He had yet to discover where it was located. The lobby was all columns and tile. Large glass windows dominated one wall shedding sunlight deep within, making everything bright and full of color.

The video picked up at 3:26 pm. As the video progressed, people were milling about or sitting on the various benches lining the wall of glass or encircling one or two of the columns. Then chaos. A man could be seen running across the lobby, only to be overtaken by some humanoid rat, judging by its long pinkish tail and rat-like facial features.

The rat caught the man and held him. Security guards could be seen approaching, weapons drawn and aimed at the creature. The creature looked for a moment as if it would let the man go, but in one swift motion, slashed its claws across the man's throat, turned and tossed the man's body at the guards. Caught between helping the dying man and shooting the creature, they hesitated. While they remained uncertain as to what to do, the rat bolted through the door and escaped.

There had been a hunt for the creature, but it eluded capture. Later, they discovered a murdered family not far from where the creature escaped. A murder he only knew about because of the report he had been given. All attempts by him to find out where this happened, and who this family was, came up empty. He had been stonewalled and been told he would receive only information he needed.

Considering he was one of the highest-ranking people in Washington D.C., it surprised and rankled him to be kept in the dark about things threatening the country. This was indeed a threat to the country. What kind of threat, and how extreme, Carl didn't know.

The fight in Chicago ended on his screen. The humanoid boar tore through a formation of police officers, killing three. Two died from injuries. The other died from a heart attack later in the hospital. The wolf and the tiger disappeared into the crowd carrying away a young female—a doctor. She later disappeared after everyone on her floor at the hospital she was being treated at, was killed. Slaughtered really.

Rumors flew from the event like a thousand birds. The tiger and the wolf were seen at the hospital according to the rumors. The boar was also seen. There had been more than one boar. The tiger and the wolf fought each other. They fought the boars. What happened remained unclear. What was clear, 23 people died in that hospital. Twenty-three people lost their lives because, as far as he could tell, they were in the wrong place at the wrong time, and the ones responsible for this were evil, evil people.

The director clicked on the other file and watched the scene in the office building lobby again. Opening a drawer in his desk he retrieved a single folder. A folder designated as Patient 12. The folder he received came with the thumb drive containing this video.

The folder and the thumb drive were all he received, in a manila envelope, on his desk, when he arrived at his office one morning. There was no indication as to who dropped it off. No indication as to how it arrived on top of the desk of one of the most secure offices in government. No explanation. Just an envelope containing a video recording and a case folder.

While the video was disturbing to watch, the information within the folder was equally unpleasant. Why, whatever agency had been behind this, wanted to keep it classified, he understood completely. If word got out that one of the United States government's agencies was behind, essentially 'buying' a pre-teen girl, experimenting upon her in cruel and horrific ways, it would be the end of this administration. This would shake the government to its core, and it would erode what little confidence the American people had in the government protecting their civil liberties.

What they did to that little girl was beyond redemption. Regardless of her apparent ability to heal from almost any harm, the report indicated the patient still felt every ounce of pain caused by those experiments. It had been worse than torture and it disgusted Carl.

The report was detailed. It cited dates and times of each new and barbaric thing done to this poor girl. It detailed how they 'acquired' her as well. What happened to the girl prior to this which would have caused her to attempt suicide, he could only imagine. It must have been some sort of abuse, given the foster mother and her boyfriend had been found killed days after the girl escaped.

The report made it quite clear, the transformation the girl had undergone into the rat-like humanoid never happened before or during any of the experiments. It happened for the first time on that day. The scientist, Daniel Mathis, the one in charge of the study, the one who had his throat sliced open by the girl, disappeared. He survived the attack. Then, mysteriously, had a heart attack. He survived the heart attack and made a rapid recovery from his earlier injuries.

Shortly after being cleared to return to work, Daniel requested some personal time off, citing his near-death experience as the reason. The man disappeared, went completely off-grid. His bank account — emptied. His phone had been turned off, and he had not used a single credit card since he left. Carl hadn't needed the report to conclude what happened.

The report mentioned several times the supposed reason for what they were doing. The hope had been, they could transfer the rapid healing this girl possessed to someone else. While Carl lauded the idea, the means, and methods to which they were trying to accomplish this, were nothing short of immoral. The extremes to which this girl suffered led the Director to only one belief. Daniel Mathias enjoyed it. He was a cruel and depraved man, and despite his claims it had all been done for posterity, the claim rang hollow.

In an attempt to transfer this ability, Mathias tried blood infusions with a multitude of terminal patients, ones with nothing to lose and no one to notice they were gone. Mathias was nothing if not thorough. The patient's vitals were recorded, their prognosis described in detail. Every single one had been evaluated by an in-house doctor and their diagnosis confirmed. The level of detail in the first dozen or so patients sat in stark contrast to the later ones. In those, no prognosis was given, no description of what illness they suffered from. This led Carl to believe these later patients had been healthy, perhaps unaware as to what they were signing up for, if they signed up at all.

The security footage ended, and the screen froze on the image of the man, Daniel Mathias, lying upon the tiles of the lobby, clutching his throat surrounded by security guards and onlookers. Blood soaked his suit and covered his throat and hands. A dark inky-red halo pooled around his head. A fitting image, the Director mused.

Leaning back into his office chair, the Director sighed audibly. The file recorded the fate of each one of those blood transfusion recipients. Each one died. Each one died because of a heart attack. A heart attack, like the one

17

Daniel Mathias suffered after his attack by the girl. A heart attack which preceded a miraculous recovery from devastating injuries. A recovery, not unlike the ability the girl had.

It didn't take a genius to put two and two together here. It would, however, take a genius to figure out what the whole damn thing meant. What was sure, this wasn't some fabrication of some crappy tabloid. It wasn't some doctored video. These things, whatever they were, existed.

They were humanoid looking animals. Humanoid, because they had been, or still were, in some way, human. This girl, Shae, was proof. The fact they all but disappeared from the public radar, which would be almost impossible, given their size and appearance, could only mean one thing. Not only did they become these monsters, but they could change back into humans, at will. Worse, they, or at least, one of them, could transfer this ability to others.

Sighing again, he pressed his palms against his eyes to stall an oncoming headache. He would have to hire Agent Yark back. Hire him back and apologize. The man had been doing his job. Not only his job, but he foresaw the possible implications of what these creatures might mean. The threat they might possess. He should be commended.

Looking at his desk calendar, he made a mental note to call his secretary early in the morning and have her reschedule all his meetings tomorrow. The White House needed to be briefed on this. They needed to be aware of this new threat. A manhunt would need to be put together . . . if 'manhunt' was the right term. This girl needed to be found. Not only her, but the others needed to be found and dealt with before they could infect others.

"Infect," the Director muttered out loud. He hadn't considered the term before now, but the more he thought about it, the more the term seemed accurate. It would appear the CDC might need to be involved in this as well. He would leave the decision up to his superiors, though. They might wish to keep a tight lid on this for as long as possible. Keeping this quiet, he believed, was something they would have little to no control over for long.

# *Chapter Two*

The bus came to a rolling stop on the main street of Catemaco, a small lake-side town on the banks of a lake which shared its name in Mexico. Brakes squealed, their sharp whine, a painful cry cut off by the whoosh of the accompanying employment of the airbrakes.

The driver eased the mechanism closest to him, opening the door to let passengers vacate the bus, the driver, however, was the first one outside. Even with the dozens of windows open on the bus, the air still felt heavy and laden with humidity. Passengers idly attempted to cool themselves by fanning hats, folded newspapers or shirts they took off early in the ride.

Brown skin glistened with sweat on every person on the bus and Hector was no different. The heat hit him harder than most, he imagined, as it had been a long time since he found himself on the shores of Catemaco. For the past six years he had been living in Boston and attending Harvard. Boston is not known for its arid climate.

Glancing out the window of the bus, Hector took in the sights and sounds of the town. Pristine white buildings with red tiled roofs lined the road. Shops and homes mingled close like friendly neighbors, and the streets were bustling in the afternoon sun. Even with the lake a few streets over, a strong odor of fish floated on the wind, which wafted into the bus and assailed Hector's nose.

Hector turned to examine the people on the bus. Sweaty passengers, stinking from the long trip here on an overcrowded bus, gathered their things and filed out. Hector waited to begin the process of getting off as he hated those first moments when everyone felt the need to clog the only way out in a rush to get off the bus, only to slow the whole process down.

With a slight shake of his head at their foolishness, Hector returned to watching outside. He caught sight of the bus driver unceremoniously retrieving the passengers' belongings from the under compartment of the bus. Little care was taken as he grabbed them, and with hardly a second look, tossed the bags to the curb. He either didn't see or didn't care about the dirty looks some of the passengers gave him. Hector knew better and kept his only luggage, a worn, olive-green duffle bag, under his seat.

It was almost six years since he boarded a bus in this same spot. At eighteen years old, he had never travelled farther than the other side of town, and here he had been, getting on a bus, with his final destination, another country. He had been scared. More scared than he ever been, though he hid it from his mother and his grandfather. He returned only once, a year later when his mother died.

It had been his grandfather who arranged the whole thing. His grandfather, who after his father died, helped raise him, and taught him things no one else did. Who trained him and prepared him for what he called, 'his holy duty'. Not that Hector understood any of it, or believed it holy, but it had been his grandfather and he had always been taught to listen and respect his elders.

He worked hard, harder than any other child his age, or twice his age, in town did. The only playing he had been allowed to participate in was playing that would strengthen him in some way.

And strengthened him it did. He was a solidly built man, broad of shoulder, tall and fit. His muscles bulged along his arms and legs, visible as they were in his tank and shorts. His chest muscles were firm and defined, his trapezius visible as they rose to meet his neck. His broad flat face glistened with sweat which dripped from his wide flat nose, a trait of his heritage.

21

Peeling his tank top from his sweaty chest, he billowed it in an attempt to cool himself, with little actual effect. Reaching a hand up, he pushed a sweaty strand of hair off his forehead, allowing it to cling to the others which shared its current state. His dark brown hair, which typically held a slight curl, hung limp in the humid clime.

Hector's thoughts returned to his grandfather, as it was his grandfather's phone call which had him return home. The man had been cryptic, as he always seemed to be. A slight smirk grew upon Hector's face as he thought of his grandfather. He had been a hard teacher, but Hector loved him fiercely.

The man had not only taught him what he would need to know to do well in school, but he gave him lessons which helped him do well in life. There were few circumstances life could throw at Hector which he couldn't get himself out of or conquer.

All of that had been because of his grandfather. So, when his grandfather called him and told him he needed to return home, as something important had happened, Hector got on a flight the next day and flew home to Mexico.

Hector, of course, pestered his grandfather for more information, but the only thing his grandfather asked him was if he had continued his studies. Hector knew he hadn't meant for school.

His grandfather taught him how to be a warrior. To fight. To protect. He trained religiously, turning himself into a living weapon. He mastered countless fighting styles and was deadly in hand to hand as well as with a variety of weapons.

Many times, Hector thought to ask why his grandfather taught him these things, but when training was in session, his grandfather took on the role of master and he, student. And students didn't ask questions like those. They did what they were told and that was all.

The last of the passengers were making their way off the bus and Hector stood to follow. Grabbing his duffle from underneath his seat, he stood and quickly made his way off the empty bus and onto the sidewalk. Tossing his duffle over his shoulder, Hector started down the street, lost in thought.

Why his grandfather wanted to know if he kept up his studies had him curious. He had kept up, as best as he could. There were few places where he paid to train and few places which could teach him some new techniques, but American trainers were different than his grandfather, so it hadn't been the same.

Walking the streets of Catemaco brought back memories. The streets were busier than when he had left. There were more vehicles on the road as well as pedestrians. This out of the way town was a bit of a tourist stop on account of the brujas—the witches. The lake, it was said, held mystical properties and had once been the home of the Olmec, the early meso-Americans who lived in this region, and those who came before the Olmec.

Every spring, the council of witches would meet near the town and it became quite the spectacle. Hector went once, when he turned eleven, much to the dissatisfaction of his grandfather.

"Charlatans!" his grandfather had been fond of calling the council. Hector had to admit, after witnessing the congregation of the council, it looked more like a show than a meeting of actual witches.

Hector made his way toward the town center and the Basilica del Carmen. He would find a taxi willing to make the trip out to his grandfather's home there. His grandfather lived some distance from the actual town. He lived closer to the base of the volcanic hills of Mono Blanco, which visibly dominated the west.

His grandfather couldn't stand to live in town with all the so-called brujas. He, or so he claimed, was a direct descendant of not only the Olmec, but those who came before, whose names had been lost to history. He claimed to have real mystical powers, unlike 'those fakes' who lived in town.

Growing up, Hector had been fascinated with the idea his grandfather had been an actual sorcerer. As he got older, he realized magic didn't exist, only superstition and powers of suggestions. He never told his grandfather what he grew to believe. He figured it better to allow the old man his fancies. His grandfather had been so adamant Hector didn't want to make him feel like a doddering old fool who believed himself a mage.

The Basilica remained as beautiful as he remembered it. Twin white towers topped with crosses rose high on either side of the church, the massive arched doorway stood open in the midday sun, welcoming one and all into the shrine devoted to the virgin, Carmen.

Across the street from the Basilica were a row of taxis waiting for fares, and Hector crossed over to the crowd of drivers talking together. Their laughter filled the streets as one of the taxi drivers finished regaling them with a humorous story from his last fare.

As Hector approached, several drivers, who noticed him first, broke from the others to offer their services. Like sharks with the scent of blood in their noses, they quickly moved in for the kill.

Hector didn't wish to be inundated with offers from drivers who most likely wouldn't want his fare so instead he called out to all of them as he approached.

"I'm looking for a ride to Senor Garza's place out by Mono Blanco."

Immediately, most of the drivers quieted down and moved back to join the group. He didn't blame them; it was a long drive out to the place, and it was easier to pick up lots of short fares where you could pick up another at your destination. This would be a long drive, with little chance of a return fare.

One man broke from the crowd and moved to his taxi. He was an older man, older than most of the drivers, with graying hair and a legion of wrinkles.

24

As old as he seemed, he was still spry with a quickness to his step. Motioning with his hand to Hector, he quickly opened the back door of his cab for Hector to get in.

Hector smiled at the old man and nodded his thanks. The old man returned his smile, with a wide, almost toothless grin. If embarrassed by his lack of teeth, Hector couldn't tell, for his smile was open and put his gums on display.

Ducking into the cab, the old man shut the door behind him. Hector couldn't help but notice some of the other drivers shaking their head at the old man as he rounded the cab to the driver's side and got in. Without so much as a glance towards the other drivers, or Hector even, the old man started the taxi and eased out onto the road.

The white painted buildings of Catemaco sped by and soon they were on the road which led out of the town and onto the foothills to the west. The landscape appeared to undulate, like waves on a green sea, but Hector knew it an optical illusion, for he was the one moving.

Outside of town were plantations of coffee, the chest-sized bushes striated the hills in every direction. Hector stared out the window as the fields passed. Surprisingly, the taxi driver remained quiet, something Hector wasn't used to, as the drivers in Boston were talkative, too talkative for Hector's taste.

Gradually, the plantations gave away to empty hills, some dotted with livestock and others dotted with trees and bushes. It had been years since Hector had been home and yet the scenery remained unchanged. Time moved at its own pace here, unbeknownst to the rest of the world.

When they arrived at the entrance to his grandfather's home, the long driveway disappeared up and over a small hill. The house, as Hector remembered it, lay a short distance beyond it. Mono Blanco and the surrounding mountains rose as a backdrop to his grandfather's home; the dark green of the trees which blanketed it looked like a jade thunder cloud looming over them.

Hector indicated to the driver to drop him there and he would walk the rest of the way. The old man looked back at him and smiled his toothy grin and indicated the meter which registered the cost of the ride. Looking over the back seat, Hector took his wallet out and thanked the man and offered a sizable tip on top of the fare. Again, the old man offered him a generous smile as he took the money and Hector realized for the first time the old man had never said a word. *He must be mute.*

As the cab drove off, Hector hitched his duffle over his shoulder and began the long walk down the drive to his grandfather's house. The dirt road lay rutted and pitted from inattention and the scrubby looking grass covering the yard on either side of the drive encroached onto it.

He knew his grandfather was getting old, but he had always been a strong, fit man who took care of the maintenance of his home. From the looks of the drive, it would appear his grandfather's health had declined much since he left for the United States.

Hector's pace slowed as he went, unexpectedly dreading seeing his grandfather again. It wasn't he didn't wish to see his grandfather. He loved him, and missed him terribly, but his grandfather had always been a rock. A source of strength which by its magnitude imparted its strength on those around him. To see him in failing health would be devastating for Hector.

For the first time Hector began to wonder if this was why his grandfather had called him home. Perhaps, his health had grown so bad he wished to see Hector before it gave out altogether. The idea his grandfather might soon pass, drowned him in uncertainty and sorrow. With a heavy heart, he travelled the rest of the way to his grandfather's house.

The house was a sprawling villa, sparkling white, with the red tiled roof so many of the homes and buildings of the area sported. Flowers decorated the front of the home, their myriad colors in stark contrast to the white walls. Sounds of birds filled the air as they hopped around the home's garden, pecking at the ground snatching unlucky ants and other insects.

The house looked like he remembered it. For some reason, he expected it to look different. Perhaps, due to the lack of upkeep on the road, he imagined the house to have also fallen into disrepair, but it wasn't the case. The house looked in perfect condition, like it always had.

Hector's heart lightened at the sight of his grandfather's house, and his steps quickened. As he approached, the front door opened, and his grandfather stepped out.

# *Chapter Three*

In the six years of Hector's absence, his grandfather appeared to have actually grown younger. He stood more erect; his eyes blazed with an inner fire Hector could recall being there in his youth. Even the deepness of the man's wrinkles looked to have grown shallower as if his skin had grown younger, suppler.

The new youthfulness of his grandfather didn't spread to his hair though as it had turned grayer, shifting slightly toward white. Hector imagined in a few years it would be totally white. His grandfather was a bold looking man. He had been a handsome youth, or so his grandmother told him, before she died. With strong facial features—a square jaw, hawkish nose and full lips — he wore pride like others wore clothes.

In all the time Hector knew him, he'd never actually gotten to *know* him. Hector knew next to nothing of whom his grandfather had been, what he did growing up, where he went to school. It had all been a mystery. He knew his grandfather believed himself some sort of sorcerer, but that was all talk. Somewhere along the way, his grandfather learned to fight like a warrior and to somehow gain influence or prestige and finances to have sent Hector to Harvard — no small feat.

Seeing his grandfather now, standing there looking twenty years younger and exuding such a powerful presence, Hector was reminded of the many times his grandfather claimed to know magic. Seeing him now, Hector could almost believe it.

Hector approached his grandfather hesitantly, as the man gave no indication of his mood. Hector came to a stop a short distance from his grandfather, and looked at him expectantly, feet shuffling slightly, creating little puffs of dust which formed, drifted slightly and died.

Suddenly, his grandfather smiled. His smile was so full of love and light, Hector could feel wetness at the corners of his eyes.

"Mi niño!" His grandfather had called him that ever since Hector's father died when he had been three and his grandfather all but raised him.

His grandfather opened his arms wide to receive him and Hector quickly closed the distance to embrace his grandfather. They hugged for a while.

His grandfather pushed him back slightly.

"Let's have a look at you." Holding Hector out at arm's length, his grandfather took him in with his eyes, studying him.

"You have stayed fit. That is good. That is good." His grandfather nodded, his eyes straying off to the side, distracted.

"What is it, Grandfather?" He studied his grandfather. Something concerned the old man.

Turning, his grandfather eyed him appreciatively, and he nodded one final time.

"Let us go in. Are you tired from your trip? We can talk after you rest?"

Hector shook his head. He was tired but anxious to understand what caused his grandfather to summon him home. "No. I am fine. I would rather know what has you so anxious." Hector thought of the walk in. "Is this why the driveway looks uncared for? Have you been so distracted by whatever it is, you have let maintenance go?"

His grandfather, who turned back into the house, paused and turned back around, looking out over the driveway which stretched away from his home as if seeing it for the first time.

"I suppose it has, mi niño, I suppose it has." He clicked his tongue. "I didn't even realize I hadn't been taking care of it." He looked back at Hector. "No matter. There are more important things to worry about."

Hector raised his eyebrows at that statement, and his grandfather smiled a knowing smile. Hector could only shake his head. His grandfather had never been a showman, but he built tension like one.

His grandfather led him into his private study. It was a room in which Hector had scarcely been allowed to enter when younger. The few times he had been in this room it had been a wonder. Books lined the walls. Tomes ancient in origin, their rich, dark leather bindings spoke to their age. Seldom were books wrapped in such a manner these days, or in many generations.

An old globe stood perched upon a decorative stand made to hold it. The sweeping crescent arm which pinned the south and the north pole, allowed the globe to spin freely. The orb was dated as it showed countries which had long since vanished or been renamed, nor did it show any of the newer countries which came into existence in the years since its creation.

A large wooden chest sat in a corner. For years, Hector imagined treasure hidden in the chest, and he had tried to see what was inside, but his grandfather always left it locked, and never answered him when he asked. Leading a young Hector to believe even more, there was treasure in there.

His grandfather crossed the room and went to sit behind an old oak desk. The brutish furniture had beastly legs, thick and sturdy as if their job was to hold up the weight of the world and not simply a desktop. The top was thick by any desk standards and decorated with scrollwork; the flowing design swirled along the edge. Given the age of the desk, it would have been hand carved, and Hector didn't envy the crafter who worked on such a painstaking design.

His grandfather offered the seat across from him at the desk and Hector moved to join him. When he was seated comfortably, his grandfather studied him over steepled fingers.

The old man's eyes drilled into him, boring deep within to discover any secrets Hector might be hiding. It was an absurd observation, as he had nothing to hide from his grandfather, as he was sure his grandfather knew. It did, however, still make him squirm a little in his seat.

"Something has happened, mi niño," his grandfather began. "Something I thought would never happen, but which I had prepared for my entire life." He pointed at Hector.

"Had prepared you for, your entire life as well."

Hector stared at him. *What the hell was he talking about*?

His grandfather gave him a thin-lipped smile. "I know you have often wondered why I trained you the way I did. Why I taught you to fight and to be strong."

He paused, and Hector took it for something he needed to affirm and so nodded.

"To explain that, I will need to explain a little about our family's history and the history of the people we are descended from."

Hector couldn't help but smile. He heard enough of their family history all throughout his childhood. His grandfather loved to explain their heritage and had, at length, on multiple occasions.

"As you know," his grandfather began, "we descend directly from the Olmecs and those who came before them." Hector nodded. "There are very few of us left in the world. Most have died out over the years or have been bred out." His grandfather frowned, his lips barely forming a curl downward as sadness crept into his eyes.

"One of the main reasons we have survived when others have died out has been because we were entrusted with magic."

31

Hector stopped himself from rolling his eyes. The magic again. Did his grandfather truly expect him to believe this?

"I know you are skeptical," his grandfather said as if reading his thoughts, "but please, keep an open mind as I explain, and I assure you by the end you will understand."

Hector's lips turned down slightly as he studied his grandfather. He remained doubtful and the idea he would believe in magic afterward, highly unlikely, but he nodded anyway for his grandfather to continue.

His grandfather eyed him for a moment as if judging whether Hector would indeed keep an open mind. Satisfied, he continued.

"Our ancestors worshipped many gods. One of these gods, the rain deity, whose name has been lost, even to those of us who still follow the old ways, was often depicted as a Werejaguar. A half-man, half-jaguar."

Despite his skepticism, Hector was entranced by the story. His grandfather never spoke about this part of their history.

"The truth of the nature of our rain god is he is a Werejaguar. His story has been passed from generation to generation along our family line and I will tell it to you now.

"Ages ago, our rain god came to us and offered protection, protection at the cost of our worship. It was an easy trade in the eyes of our people's leaders, and we began to worship him." Hector's grandfather leaned forward and rested his arms on top of the desk.

"Other gods became jealous of our worship and they sent their servants to kill us. The servants they sent were lycanthropes. Were-creatures of deadly animals. As they rained down murder and death in our lands, we beseeched our rain god for his protection."

There was a twinkle in his grandfather's eyes as he told Hector this story and he could tell his grandfather was caught up in telling it as much as he was in listening to it.

"He answered our prayers. Appearing as a Werejaguar, he hunted the other lycanthropes and killed them without mercy. It wasn't long before the other gods retreated, taking their lycans with them."

His grandfather sat back in his chair, spreading his hands out wide as he explained.

"Before he left his people, we asked him how we could protect ourselves if those lycanthropes returned. Our god was pleased at our desire to protect our own, and in response, he granted us a boon."

Hector waited.

With a smile which creased his cheeks and grew crows-feet at the corner of his eyes, his grandfather pulled at a wire necklace which encircled his neck. It was a necklace he hadn't seen his grandfather wear before. As his grandfather tugged up the necklace, an old key, like those you see in movies with the exaggerated teeth and intricate head made of wrought iron or the like, became visible. The key swung back and forth as his grandfather held it out for Hector to examine.

"A key?" Hector said flatly, unable to hide his disappointment. An old key was the supposed boon of a god? Seemed pretty lame to Hector.

Shaking his head, his grandfather removed the necklace from around his neck and took hold of the key. Scooting his chair back, he bent down, and Hector assumed he was using the key in one of the drawers of the desk. The drawers, Hector knew, had always been locked for as long as Hector had lived, undoubtedly longer.

After a moment of fussing around and an audible click, his grandfather opened a drawer on the right side of the desk and retrieved something from within. What he brought forth left Hector in awe as it was the most beautiful thing he had ever seen.

Resting in his grandfather's hands was a long, wide-bladed knife. Easily over a foot and half long, the blade was carved from a dark piece of jade, its edge, a jagged piece, almost teeth-like. The knife held no cross guard, but instead was embedded in a round shaft of tarnished bronze. Raised, intricate images ringed the hilt. Circular stories told in the only written language of the age.

It was clear to Hector the knife was ancient, but when he considered the story his grandfather told him, if true, the knife was older than most relics in the known world. To be in such amazing condition after all these centuries left Hector stunned. When his grandfather held the knife out for him to take, he could do nothing but stare blankly at him.

"This is your birthright, Hector. This is your obligation and your duty." His grandfather's voice took on a solemn note. Gone was the earlier exuberance. Gone was the twinkle in his grandfather's eyes, replaced now by a hint of sadness. "I'm afraid your studies will have to wait, for you now have more important matters to attend to."

Again, his grandfather held the blade out to him, and this time Hector felt obligated to take it, though he didn't understand what his grandfather was getting at.

The moment the knife passed to his hands a feeling like he had never felt before flowed through his body. Heat passed from the blade to him, a heat barely contained, on the verge of breaking free and devouring him where he sat. It roared through his every nerve, his every fiber of being. As quickly as it had taken him, it fled.

Hector gasped, and his eyes widened as he looked upon the blade. The doubts he held before holding this blade evaporated in an instant. He felt as if he had been touched by a god — and perhaps that was what it was. Looking back up at his grandfather, the old man nodded in acknowledgment of what he felt.

"I . . . I don't understand what this means," Hector told his grandfather.

His grandfather didn't say anything in response. Instead he pulled out something else from within the drawer, surprising Hector for the second time this day. A laptop. As long as he knew his grandfather, he shunned computers. So, to see him now with not only a computer, but a laptop, was a bit of a shock. His surprise must have been written upon his face because his grandfather chuckled.

"I didn't not use computers because I couldn't, I didn't use them because I didn't want to get sucked into them like everyone else of this age." Setting the laptop on the desk, he waited a moment for it to boot up and Hector watched as he searched for something on the screen and clicked on it.

Spinning the laptop around he turned it to face Hector. On the screen was an open window with a video playing on it. The scene playing out before him left him cold. A boar-like man savagely attacked another man and a woman he was with. Just when it looked as if the boarman would kill them, a tiger-like woman entered the fight and saved them, briefly, before being all but killed herself. As the boarman was about to kill all of them, the man turned into a wolf-like man. A were-wolf, Hector realized. Which would make the others a were-tiger and a were-boar. Lycanthropes. Like the ones in his grandfather's tale.

Wide-eyed, he looked up from the screen at his grandfather.

"They're . . . back?"

His grandfather shook his head.

"These are not the ancient gods returned. These are aspects of a different . . . religion, let's say." His grandfather closed the laptop and put it back in the drawer. "Nevertheless, they are still subject to the knife's abilities, and so, are our family's responsibility."

Scrunching his forehead, Hector was confused. "What do you mean, 'the knife's abilities'?"

Drawing his lips into a straight line, his grandfather steepled his fingers before offering an explanation.

"Lycanthropy is caused when a person's totem animal is brought to the surface and linked with the person's . . . physiology. That is the best explanation that I can give you. Regardless, the knife severs that link between the person and their totem. Ending the lycanthropy."

The phrasing seemed final to Hector. "What happens to the person?" The words drifted out in like a whisper and the look his grandfather gave him was all the answer he needed.

Hector sighed and looked away "You are asking a lot of me, Grandfather."

"I know," his grandfather replied. "You are the only one who can put an end to them."

Shaking his head, Hector looked back at his grandfather. "This is ridiculous, Grandfather! They have guns! Bombs and missiles even! How can me with a knife stop them if they can't?"

"Hector," his grandfather began patiently, "these creatures are not of this time. The power which created them is old and unfathomably powerful." Standing up, his grandfather rounded the table and leaned back against it in front of Hector.

"From what I have been able to ascertain from the histories, these people, these . . . creatures, have incredible abilities to heal from almost any injury." His grandfather shook his head. "I'm afraid, guns and other weapons can only slow them, not kill them. Only you can do that."

Hector didn't miss his grandfather's shift from calling them people to calling them creatures. He was trying to dehumanize them so Hector could come to grips with the notion of killing them.

It wasn't working.

Hector set the blade on the desk in front of him and looked up at his grandfather.

"I'm sorry, Grandfather. I can't do this." Hector stood and searched his grandfather's eyes, hoping to find some understanding. "You are asking too much."

Hector moved for the door.

"Three officers died during that attack in Chicago."

Those words halted Hector at the door.

"If what I believe to be true, the Wereboar tore through an entire motel of people in London, killing all but two, who later turned into Wereboars."

Hector spun. "What?!"

His grandfather nodded. "Someone who survives an attack from a lycanthrope, becomes a lycanthrope. If someone doesn't stop them, we will have armies of lycans that are all but unkillable." He smiled wanly at Hector. "Unkillable, except for someone with this knife." He had picked up the knife at some point and now held it out once again for Hector to take.

Hector stood frozen by the door, staring at the knife as if it was the plague. This was not what he thought he came down here for. He didn't want this. He wanted to return to school. To graduate. This supernatural bullshit wasn't for him, regardless of how many people might be affected. It had nothing to do with him.

Hector lowered his head, turned and left his grandfather there with his knife.

Sleep took a long time coming for Hector, his mind restless, as it replayed the scene from Chicago, over and over. The ferocity of those monsters. The power. It left him rattled, seeing the Wereboar tear through those police like a hairy bowling ball knocking over pins as if they were made of paper. Except they weren't pins. They were people. People who died as a result. Good people who were simply trying to do their job of protecting innocents.

Flopping over in his bed, Hector tried to find a comfortable position to sleep in, as if somehow, if he rested, his brain would erase the horrors he had seen this day and his shame for choosing to not do anything about it.

Obviously, these monsters needed to be stopped. What wasn't clear was how he could truly do anything about it. Yes, he was a trained warrior. Yes, he apparently had a weapon gifted by an ancient god to deal with this type of threat, but he was still only a man. A man being asked to go to war with monsters. How he could be expected to accomplish this, he couldn't understand.

No. He had a life. He had responsibilities in the real world, not this fantastical world his grandfather wished for him to step into and to assume the role of lycan assassin.

As final as he felt his decision to be, doubts plagued him for hours before exhaustion at last wore him down and he slept.

When he found his grandfather the next morning, he found death had stolen in through the night to rob him of the last member of his family.

# *Chapter Four*

His grandfather sat behind his desk. The knife was in his hand before him, his eyes open and empty. Years had piled on his features in one night. Wrinkles, like crumpled paper, lined his face and arms where there had been none the night before.

Gone was the firmness of the old man's body; instead, what sat before Hector appeared to be a frail looking shell of the once strong man he had been. Hector's parents both died relatively young, and so, Hector had never seen an older person dead. He assumed some of what he was seeing had to be the result of death, but it still looked unnatural to him.

Hector collapsed into the chair across from his grandfather and stared at him. Anger flared up inside of him. Anger that his grandfather had been taken from him, but also anger because, in his mind, this left him with no other choice but to take the knife and do as his grandfather wished.

In a way, it had been his dying wish, though neither of them knew it last night. It was unfair, and Hector knew he had no right to feel angry at his grandfather, but he couldn't help it. He had made his decision last night. He was going to go home and the lycans were someone else's problem.

Now, he couldn't.

Standing and moving around the desk, he took the knife from his grandfather's cold hands and looked down at him. His grandfather still stared sightlessly at the empty place between his hands where the knife had been.

Reaching up, Hector closed his grandfather's eyes and kissed his forehead.

"Very well, abuelo. I will do as you asked. I will hunt down these lycans and end them." Tears welled into Hector's eyes, creating pools in their corners before filling and emptying in tiny rivulets down his cheek. His heart ached more than when his mother had died five years ago. He had loved his grandfather. Their training together created a bond stronger than family.

"Goodbye, abuelo. Te amo."

Tears flowing freely now; Hector turned and left the office and walked to the kitchen to the house phone. He made three calls. The first, to the family lawyer, who thankfully assured him his grandfather had taken care of everything in case of his death, and a coffin would arrive at the home in a day so Hector could hold the *velario*, the candlelight vigil.

"Your grandfather left you everything, Hector. The house, the land, his accounts." The lawyer paused and when Hector said nothing, the lawyer continued. "Do you know about the accounts, Hector?"

Hector didn't.

"Your grandfather was quite rich. Sooooo . . . now you are quite rich."

The amount of money his grandfather had, staggered Hector. He assumed sending him to Harvard had all but bankrupted his grandfather. Now, he knew it had been a drop in the bucket for him to afford Hector's tuition.

He had no idea how his grandfather accrued such wealth, and neither did the lawyer. The answer to that mystery might lie in his grandfather's belongings, the lawyer suggested. He seemed curious himself to discover the truth, and as much as Hector wanted to know, he knew he wouldn't have the time.

He left instructions with the lawyer to send some trusted people out to close up the house. The lawyer had been with the family for years and so

Hector felt, if his grandfather trusted him all these years, he could be trusted to do what needed to be done.

The second and third calls he made were to the cab company and the airline for arrangements to pick him up and fly him to Chicago the day after tomorrow.

# *Chapter Five*

The flight from Topeka to Chicago was short and they were on the ground and off the plane in a couple of hours. O'Hare Airport bustled with crowds of people going this way and that. Nameless faces passed by, like fleeting thoughts, momentarily there and quickly forgotten.

Sylvanis watched the people who passed. Their group got a few interested looks and she couldn't help but wonder what these strangers saw. She knew it couldn't be close to the truth. The truth of this group was hidden beneath the surface. There was no way for them to realize there were three of the most powerful people in this world walking among them. Four, if she was being honest. She was powerful too, if in a different way. Her power was still relatively unknown to her. She didn't grasp its limits. She feared to test them.

It was a subdued group who left the airport that afternoon. Clint hadn't returned to the house and they assumed he was on his way to Chicago. Kat was most affected as she knew Clint the most out of all of them, though the truth was even she knew little. Sylvanis watched her now. Straight-backed and tense, Sylvanis could see the muscles in Kat's cheek bunch in tension as she clenched her teeth.

Clint and Kat had been through quite a bit in Chicago and fighting for your life together tends to create a bond. Kat was worried for her friend. The events which transpired at the house last night, Clint's sudden departure, and the means in which he left them meant he was running straight for trouble.

He was no longer thinking straight and worse, Sylvanis had seen it happen to lycans before. Good people who allowed their animalistic nature of their lycan half take control. They went wild and although some were able to gain control of themselves, most had to be put down, for the safety of others. She prayed Clint would be capable of recovering his senses, for she feared for the group if they were forced to take that kind of action against Clint.

Sylvanis scanned the other members of the group. It included Hank and Sim, father and stepson, with twin olive-green duffels they brought with them slung over their shoulders, the only similarity between the two. Hank, broad shouldered and wide, had chosen to trim his beard and hair and no longer looked as bestial as the first night they met him with his shoulder length hair and long scraggly beard. He still looked fierce though.

Sim had also chosen to 'clean up' as well. He shaved his beard completely off after a teasing comment from Kat about how he appeared to have forgotten to glue some hair onto his cheek. He laughed about it but seeing him the next morning with it all gone let Sylvanis realize it stung a little more than he let on.

Sylvanis saw Hank notice her scrutiny and watched her with his bright blue eyes. She smiled warmly at him to let him understand he had nothing to be concerned about. He gave her a quick upturn of his mouth before returning to his straight lipped look. Sorrow haunted his eyes, a loss which constantly dragged on his soul.

Sylvanis managed to get their story from them both. Her heart wrenched to hear of the loss of Hank's wife and Sim's mother. The toll it had taken on the both of them, although completely different, had the unexpected effect of drawing the two of them closer. Sylvanis believed this bond was forged when Hank and Sim grieved her loss together and it saved Sim when Hank inadvertently passed lycanthropy onto him.

She felt a deep fondness for them both as the love they shared for each other, their bond, was infectious and inviting. Hank, a private person, who, despite his obvious reluctance, found himself the eldest in a group of misfits who now looked to him as an adopted father figure, due to his and Sim's relationship.

Even though Sylvanis was technically older than Hank, she was still younger in perception, and, if she was being honest, in her disposition and worldly knowledge. She found herself deferring to Hank in some ways, although she had brought them all together.

It didn't bother her. She had never been one to need control over every situation. That had been Kestrel. Sylvanis' thoughts strayed to her adversary, as much as she wished they wouldn't be on opposing sides, it seemed their twinned destiny. Once again, they had been set on the path to war, a war like nothing this world had seen before, a war for which they were woefully ill prepared. Conventional battles were one thing, but armies of almost indestructible warriors? Sylvanis feared for the world of men.

Kestrel, surprisingly, was the weak link in all of this. A powerful druidess, she still could be killed. She was more vulnerable than her lycan warriors, and while they might wreak havoc on the world for a time, without Kestrel's passion and direction they would most likely go their separate ways and could be destroyed individually. Together they are far more powerful as a force, and Kestrel is who will keep them together.

When they made their way out of the terminal, Kat stopped and turned to them.

"We should probably find a place to stay first. Get our bearings before we try to find Clint," her lips turned down in a frown, "and I guess, the others, if they are here."

The sun burned brightly, and the sky was crisp and clear, but the air was cool, cooler than it had been in Topeka. It occurred to Sylvanis, apart from the few places she had moved to for those short periods of time, she had never actually been anywhere else. In fact, given her father's penchant for keeping her inside, she hadn't truly been *anywhere*.

Shielding her eyes from the sun which looked to be resting slightly above Kat's head, she indicated her agreement. When it came to actions that would require money, she allowed Kat to take the lead. Or Hank. Both had accumulated vast wealth, though Kat was by far the wealthiest.

Her parents, who foresaw the potential need for money if their daughter needed to help fight this war, went about increasing their wealth early on. It helped her mother's family had also done the same throughout the years, knowing of this eventuality. Thankfully, at least one family had kept the knowledge safe and passed it on.

Kat arranged transportation to meet them at the airport. It wasn't long before they arrived at a hotel in downtown Chicago, one located near the street of shops known as the Magnificent Mile. It was the location in which Kat, Clint and the Wereboar fought and where they hoped to find either Clint, the Wererat, or both.

While Sylvanis was not worldly by any stretch of the imagination, and her understanding of expenses was limited to what she learned on her own, she couldn't help but flinch when Kat paid for three rooms at the hotel.

Kat saw her reaction and smiled at her. "Don't worry about it. It is a necessary expense, and my family has been planning for this for ages." Kat winked at her before continuing, "and besides, this isn't even an expensive hotel."

Sylvanis' eyes widened, and Kat chuckled.

Sylvanis invited the others to join her in her room as soon as they were settled in theirs. The room was a simple affair. It held two twin beds, a dresser, a TV and a fridge. A small round table with two chairs sat by the solitary window. Plopping down on one of the beds, she almost bounced off it because of its firmness.

She ran her hands across the bed sheets before standing and walking to the window. Pushing the curtain aside she looked out over the jungle of steel and brick. Soft, gray clouds had somehow blanketed the sky in the short time they took to get settled into the hotel. The effect on the landscape was sorrowful.

As much as she was a product of today, her heart and mind still lingered two millennia ago, in a land of rolling green hills and vast forests that carpeted the land. Oh, she knew there were plenty of places like that still here, but it was easy to forget when looking upon a vast city like Chicago.

She let herself reach out to the Earth, though only a touch for fear Kestrel would sense her if she did more. She reached out and found only faint whispers. She knew this was what men were capable of doing to the land; it was part of who they were, part of how they grew. It saddened her though. She hoped, when this war was over, if she lived, to help teach men to work with nature to preserve both.

A faint knock at the door brought her out of her questing and she moved to answer it. Hank and Sim were the first to arrive and she greeted them both with a big smile.

"I'm happy to see you both. Come in." She stepped aside, and they moved past her, each smiling back in return. Before she could shut the door, Kat came jogging up and caught her. She gave her a tight smile and Sylvanis was reminded of the urgency to find Clint.

Shutting the door once Kat entered, she turned to face the group. Hank and Sim had taken the two chairs at the table and Kat sat on the other bed in the room, so Sylvanis sat on the one she had rested upon earlier, facing them.

"I am open to suggestions as to how we should proceed from here. As you all know, I am not as old as I look and when it comes to getting around big cities, I am at a loss."

The anxiousness Kat exhibited was not lost on Hank and Sim and so they sat quietly knowing Kat would offer up what she thought would be the best thing to do. Sylvanis knew, if Hank and Sim didn't agree, they would make sure they were heard, but they were happy to wait and see what Kat had in mind.

"I'm going out to find Clint." The tone she spoke in left no room for argument, but Sylvanis still cocked her head in silent questioning of the idea.

"Look," she began, "it's like you said. You are a stranger to large cities. I am not." She gestured with a thumb back at Hank and Sim, "These two used to live in a forest as well, so they won't be much help."

"I didn't always live in . . ." Hank began in protest, but Kat didn't let him get far.

"Also, I have been in Chicago before. Have walked its streets for days before I ran into Clint and his girlfriend." She faltered a little. Sylvanis knew, even though Kat only briefly met Clint's girlfriend, she connected with the girl and she also felt guilty about leaving her to the Wereboar.

Kat stared off for a moment before returning her gaze to Sylvanis. "I know where the battle took place, I know everything I need to know about how I might find Clint. None of the rest of you do." A silent plea spoke in her eyes. "Let me do this."

Sylvanis sighed. While she didn't like the idea of Kat going off by herself when the possibility of other Weres were around, she couldn't argue with Kat's points. She was the best chance they had of finding Clint. She would still voice her concerns. Hank beat her to it.

"I don't feel comfortable sending you out there by yourself, Kat." When she turned on him, he held up his hands to ward off any verbal attack. "It's not that I don't think you are capable and can take care of yourself, but let's face it, if that Wereboar shows up, with his friends this time, and you are alone . . .?" He left the question hang between them and despite Kat's fierceness as a fighter, Sylvanis still saw the color drain from her at the thought of fighting three Wereboars by herself. She had been clearly defeated by one Wereboar, and if it hadn't been for Clint's shift and help, the boar would have destroyed them both.

Reluctantly, Kat nodded. "You have a point. However, I will not be in my tiger form. I will just be another human, walking the streets. So, unless I am really unlucky, the chances of them attacking me for no reason are slim."

Hank face scrunched up in hesitation, but he bobbed his head in reluctant agreement.

"Anyway," she continued, "someone should at least attempt to see if they can find those guys, and you three are much better equipped at dealing with them than I would be." Her eyes widened and sparkled with excitement. "In fact, I would love to see you go toe to toe with that piece of shit, Hank."

Hank's smiled back at her with an equal look of excitement. It was obvious to Sylvanis, Hank relished a chance to fight the Wereboar.

Sylvanis considered Kat. "When do you leave?"

Kat considered for a moment. "In a few hours. I will catch some rest and head out earlier this evening. If Clint is stalking around, he will probably be doing so at night."

Sylvanis nodded her approval.

"In fact," Kat stood up, "I will head off to bed right now, so I can be fresh for later." She nodded to Hank and Sim and left.

Turning to the two men, Sylvanis spread her hands wide. "That just leaves us. I for one have no idea on how to locate three Wereboars in a city. Do you?"

Sim snorted at the question. "Does anybody?"

48

Sylvanis smiled. She liked Sim's sarcastic humor, but Hank gave the boy a dry look, to which Sim smirked back. Ultimately, Hank shook his head at Sim and met her gaze and shook his head again. "It would help if we knew who we were dealing with. We know Kestrel, and of course Syndor? Samuel?" He gazed questioningly at her.

"He went by Syndor when I knew him. It appears he has taken the name Samuel now." She tapped a finger against her lips. "You are right though. We know of almost nothing of the other Weres. We don't know their names, where they lived before this. Nothing." The enormity of their task threatened to overwhelm her again.

Hank seemed to sense it and released a soft sigh. "My wife, Jennifer, used to tell me to deal with the task right in front of you first and worry about the tasks that come after when that one is done." He gave a reassuring nod to her. "Let us locate Clint and we will keep an eye out for anyone who might show an unhealthy interest in what happened here a few days ago. There is a decent chance the other Were . . . the rat . . . will show up. Whoever he might be."

Sylvanis bobbed her head in agreement with his assessment.

"Very well." Clapping her hands on her legs, she stood up from the bed. "We'll let Kat work the streets tonight, and tomorrow, we will work them during the day."

The other two stood as well, understanding they were being dismissed. They each offered her a slight smile before heading out.

"Hank," Sylvanis called out to him as he reached the door. "A moment."

Hank turned his head to peer at his son for a moment and a quick silent conversation passed between them, and Sim departed.

Closing the door as his son left, Hank turned to her and walked back into the room. Sylvanis sat back down on the bed and Hank moved to sit opposite her on the other. He waited patiently for her to get to what she called him back for.

She dreaded this conversation but knew it to be necessary.

"I need to speak to you about Clint." The words died on her tongue. She barely knew this man; she knew less of Clint and she was about to ask of him a difficult task.

Hank watched her intently as she struggled to put the words together to explain to him what he might have to do, if Clint couldn't be saved.

"You're worried Clint might become dangerous?" he offered, when it became obvious she wouldn't be capable of speaking the words aloud.

She nodded. "It would happen . . . sometimes. A Were would go 'wild' and would need to be . . ." Sylvanis lowered her eyes to stare at her hands, anywhere to look than into Hank's deep blue eyes, "put down."

This feeling of shame was unwelcome. When she had to order a Were to be put down before, she had done so with clarity of vison and purpose. This *youth* she was now, made making the hard decisions harder.

"It's all right, Sylvanis." Hank's voice was soft and understanding. "I will do what needs to be done." His voice took on a firm tone. "When, and only if, it truly needs to be done. Everything must be done to prevent that.

"I don't think our little group could take it," he muttered to himself, but loud enough for her to hear, and she couldn't disagree.

She forced herself to raise her gaze back to Hank. What she saw there warmed her heart. No recrimination, no anger, only sadness and sympathy.

"Let us hope we find Clint soon; for the longer he remains alone, the harder it will be for him to return to us."

Hank nodded understandingly and rose to his feet. Sitting still, he towered over her. He was an intimidating sight. Thankfully, he was on their side.

"Goodnight, Sylvanis."

"Goodnight, Hank."

He left, and she was alone with her self-doubt and a growing feeling of ineptitude. She was out of her element here, and afraid the others would realize it and abandon her. She knew it was a silly thought the moment it entered her mind, but it proved difficult to dismiss.

# *Chapter Six*

The room seemed to hold its own weight, a heightened sense of gravity pulling every occupant downward. The only one who seemed above it all, was Blain. Shae watched the man with wary eyes as he seemed unaffected by the mood in the room. Joseph radiated animosity, while Taylor sat in quiet unease. Sarah, who sat quietly next to her, held on to her strength, if only slightly. Her eyes darted around the room, a constant quest for a way out of this situation. Shae knew there was no way out. Not now. Not for Sarah.

It hadn't taken long for her to understand the dynamics in the room. Taylor and Joseph had been *infected* by Blain. So had Sarah. But, unlike the other two, Sarah had no interest in being Blain's lackey. Though, it appeared Taylor was reluctant in this as well. Joseph, as far as Shae could determine, hated Blain, but was more than happy to follow him as long as it allowed him to do what he wanted to do. Shae had an inkling of an idea as to what it might be.

Sarah, on the other hand, still fought, or, searched for a way out. Shae understood, there was truly nothing Sarah could do. She was caught in Blain's control. She couldn't help but think of Daniel and a sense of shame crept up on her.

Shae shifted on the bed she sat on and caught Blain's eyes snap toward her and she froze. Inwardly, she felt a flicker of satisfaction that she made the man's cool demeanor break, if only for a second. That he was, if for a moment, wary of what she did made her want to smile.

All of this she kept hidden though. She wasn't an idiot. There was little Blain could do to her permanently. She wasn't immune to pain though, and she learned early, pain was one thing Blain was effective at giving.

Her thoughts returned to Sarah. She felt a well of pity for the woman. She had been a doctor, well, Shae mused, she still is a doctor, but that life was over. She was pretty, successful and had been in love. Of course, that love ultimately brought her to this. Unfortunately for Sarah, she had been in love with a Were. A Were on the other side of some conflict with Blain, and as a result, she had been injured in a fight between the two and contracted lycanthropy from Blain.

Sarah's life had been blessed, and full of love and joy and it had been destroyed by lycanthropy. Shae's life had been dark, painful and full of horrors and had been saved by it.

Now they all waited in oppressive silence for the one Blain referred to as the 'Lady'. The one who would explain the purpose of all this. The reason behind Shae becoming what she had become, and more importantly, what would happen next. Shae was anxious to meet this woman. She needed answers. She needed to *understand* what was happening. But, as anxious as she was, fear clung to her as well.

Blain took up sentry duty by the front door. He leaned against the wall in the tight hallway. His attempt at looking unperturbed was almost convincing, but he constantly fidgeted and shuffled his feet in a vain attempt to look comfortable. Blain worried. He worried about what would happen when the 'Lady' arrived, and if Blain worried, Shae needed to be worried as well.

Time crept over them all. Each of them found their own way to pass it. Taylor, his tall, lanky form sat bent over a book at the kitchen table, spent most of his time avoiding the group. The few times he tried to engage Shae or Sarah in conversation led to a quick reprimand from Blain. Since it was clear he, Blain and Joseph were not companionable, he kept to himself.

Shae appreciated Taylor's attempts to be civil with them, but he certainly wasn't going to stand up to Blain. Not that he could, anyway, as had been demonstrated more than once.

Joseph sat slouched in a recliner. A look of disgust, envy and seething anger flittered across his face in varying degrees, depending on where his gaze lingered. When his gaze landed on Sarah, he would leer at her until she would meet his gaze. When she did, he would smile at her in a way that made Shae think of George.

She disliked Joseph, but not as much as she disliked Blain. When Joseph glanced at Shae though, it was a look of calculation and she could see him appraising her and whatever he thought, she could almost read it on his face. He saw her as an ally against Blain . . . or a tool. If he thought that, he would be sadly mistaken. She would not be used again.

Joseph seemed to relish in taunting Blain to the point of violence. it was like he enjoyed being hurt, knowing he would quickly heal himself of any wounds. He would constantly throw snide remarks at Blain, implying incompetence or stupidity. Shae had only been around them a short time, but she knew Blain was neither of those things. If anything, it made him even more frightening. Behind his size and cruelty, he was calculating and smart. You could lose sight of that given his brutish appearance.

Whether Joseph had not noticed these things about Blain, or if he chose to ignore them so he could continue to throw barbs at the man, Shae wasn't sure. If it was the first, then Joseph was the stupid one.

Blain sat up, and cocked his head towards the door, and everyone, including Taylor, who hadn't seemed to be paying attention, tensed. Someone approached the door. It could be the 'Lady' or, despite Blain's early insistence the Wolf and the Tiger couldn't find her, they had indeed, found the "Lady'.

The sound of a click and a hum caused Blain to relax. He had left a key card at the desk for the 'Lady' and so it must be her. Blain moved out of the hallway as the door opened and one of the most beautiful and regal women Shae had ever seen entered the room.

This, without any doubt, had to be the 'Lady' Blain talked about. She was tall, with long, lustrous, black hair parted to either side of her face falling to the sides, like ebony waterfalls. She had pale, white skin which appeared soft and yet chiseled from stone, with sharp angles and high cheekbones. She wore a long flowing black green dress. It was a dark, forest green and seemed to shimmer the same way the woman's hair did. The gown sported a deep V-neck, which revealed plenty of cleavage which the dress seemed to accentuate, along with the rest of the woman's figure.

The 'Lady' was as near perfection in looks as anyone Shae had ever known, and she couldn't help but stare, open-mouthed at her. There was a slight gasp from Sarah, whom Shae found to be a beautiful woman as well. Sarah paled in comparison to this woman, which of course left Shae feeling completely ugly in this woman's presence. As the 'Lady' entered the room, Shae noticed Taylor stand, and Joseph managed to get off his fat ass long enough to stand before this woman.

The imperious look the woman graced them with left no doubt as to who was now in charge. Blain acknowledged the woman's authority, if with great reluctance. When the woman's gaze rested upon Shae and Sarah, it softened. Gone was the look of superiority and it was quickly replaced with empathy and an apologetic look.

Gracefully she crossed the room and Shae felt obligated to stand up from the bed to greet her.

"Hello," the 'Lady' spoke with a strange accent. It was like Blain's, but she seemed more *uncomfortable* with the language. "You must be Shae? I have heard many things about you. Not all of them meant to be positive." She shot Blain a look who grunted and looked away. She glanced back at Shae and smiled mischievously. "But I took them to be."

55

Shae warmed inside. She had been afraid this woman would have seen Shae's earlier defiance and attack on Blain as a negative, something which needed to be punished. Instead, the woman liked that she stood up for herself.

"I am called Kestrel, and it is a pleasure to meet you, Shae."

She offered her hand and Shae stared at it for a long moment before inwardly chiding herself and taking the woman's hand in her own.

"Umm . . ." Shae still wasn't comfortable with people who seemed genuinely friendly with her and struggled with how to handle herself. "Thank you?"

The woman smiled at her and again Shae felt . . . something. Something she hadn't felt in a long time, not since first going to live with Anne before she was with George. When she had all of Anne's attention and was made to feel special and loved. That is how this woman made her feel. Special.

The woman's eyes moved to Sarah, who had yet to move from the bed and only stared daggers at the woman. Shae didn't entirely blame her. From what she had been able to gather, the 'Lady' sent Blain to attack Sarah's boyfriend, and because of this, Sarah became a Were and was now under the control of Blain.

The woman's features softened more, and she squatted down in front of Sarah. Something she managed to do while still appearing graceful. It was remarkable.

"You. You are named, Sarah? Yes?" Kestrel didn't wait for a response.

"I can understand . . ." That was all she got out, as Sarah moved with lightning speed. Grabbing Kestrel by the throat, she managed to not only gain her feet, but carry Kestrel up with her. Shae was so shocked by the sudden ferocity of Sarah's actions; she could do little except stare dumbfounded in their direction.

Just when it appeared Sarah was going to snap Kestrel's neck, Blain's voice cut through to her. "Stop!"

Sarah froze, Blain's will overpowering her. She still held Kestrel up in the air, with little to no effort. If the woman was startled or afraid by Sarah's actions, she revealed none of it. Instead, she stared down at Sarah as if she remained in total command of the situation. Shae had to admit, despite being held up in the air, she was.

The looks Sarah shot Blain and Kestrel were full of hate. Shae understood that hate. She had the same for George and Anne.

Sarah lowered the woman down without Blain having to tell her and stepped in close.

"Understand something, bitch . . ." Sarah bit off each word, as if it pained her to have to speak to Kestrel. "You may have me under your thumb now, but when Clint finds you . . ." She took her eyes off Kestrel for a moment and glared at the rest of the room, though she didn't look at Shae. "He will rip you all to shreds."

With that, Sarah let her hand fall from the woman's neck, turned and returned to her seat upon the bed as if the room hadn't just been on the verge of violence. The tension in the room eased— a little.

"Is everything alright, My Lady?"

It was a voice Shae didn't recognize and she peered immediately toward the door. Two men were just now entering. One was a tall, olive-skinned man with dark hair and exotic looking eyes, long limbed and slender. The other, was an attractive man of middling height, with sandy brown hair and tanned complexion. He had high cheekbones and a strong face. Green eyes rested under carefully sculpted eyebrows. He was a man who took pride in his appearance. Richly dressed, he had the look of a playboy, or at least, someone of wealth.

Upon seeing these two, there was two things Shae noticed right away. One, Sarah, for all her nonchalance a moment ago went stiff. She didn't look up at these two, but her eyes were the only thing which appeared to not acknowledge these new men. That told Shae all she needed to know. They were Weres as well, and given their lack of deference to Blain, or each other, they were different types.

The other thing Shae noticed immediately, was a change in the dynamics of the room when these two entered. Gone was Blain's posture of being the biggest bad in the room. With the inclusion of these two men, Blain's position of power had been challenged.

The tall newcomer continued to look at Kestrel questioningly and so Shae assumed he had been the one who spoke.

"Everything is fine, Samuel." Kestrel didn't turn but continued to look down at Sarah. "Just a misunderstanding that needed to be straightened out."

The lips of the man she referred to as Samuel turned down momentarily before he nodded and moved farther into the room, followed by the other man. That man held all of Blain's attention. These men couldn't be more different in Shae's eyes. Blain was a large, brutish, ugly looking man who wore his brutality like a second skin. This new man was attractive, classy and by all appearances, friendly as he offered up a smile to anyone who looked his way.

When he smiled at Shae, she smiled back, shyly. When the man looked to Blain, his smile slipped, but returned as quickly as it had fled. Blain sneered at the man.

"Boys," Kestrel spoke up, still looking at Sarah, "you will play nice. There will be no violence among you." How she knew of the quiet exchange between Blain and the newcomer, Shae did not know, but the woman spoke with utter command and left no doubt as to what might happen if they decided to go at each other.

In time, Kestrel turned away from Sarah and back to the group of men in the room who were all standing awaiting her command. Blain and Joseph stared daggers at the blond-haired man while Taylor stared toward Kestrel. The other newcomer seemed unaffected by the goings on and instead gazed contemplatively at Sarah.

Kestrel moved forward next to Samuel and rested a hand on his chest as she scanned around the room at everyone.

"At long last, we have all gathered." She patted Samuel gently on his chest and moved to the middle of the room, central to those attending her, like a queen addressing her followers.

"Some of you do not know why you are here," she indicated towards Shae and Sarah. "Others I have explained it already to." She motioned to the rest.

"A war is coming." Kestrel paused and regarded each in turn. "A war for the very soul of this planet. Man has ravaged this Earth long enough." She paused for effect. "It is time to take it back and return this land to its natural state."

This was not the way Shae thought this was going to go. She expected a speech calling for dominance, of taking control and ruling. She wasn't a fool. She understood with their ability to turn others into Weres they could create an almost unstoppable army. What else would you do with an army but take over?

"To do this, we must first wrest control from these fools who befoul everything thing they touch!"

And there it was. Shae wasn't surprised. It always came down to control.

Kestrel's voice reached a fever pitch. Regardless of what Shae may think about this being a play for power, there was no denying Kestrel believed in the righteousness of her cause. "We will take control from these men and we will ensure they never do what they have done again. We will force them to live at peace with the Earth. If they refuse, they will be removed for the safety of the Earth."

Shae shifted uncomfortably on her feet and noticed the others seemed equally as uncomfortable. The only one who seemed at ease with what Kestrel said, was Samuel. While she didn't see the same fires of passion she saw in Kestrel's eyes, it was obvious he was equally committed to her cause.

The uneasiness was not lost on Kestrel and she nodded as she looked around the room. "I know many of you do not share my concerns about the Earth, and care little for my cause." Raising her hand up, she pointed at each of them in turn.

"That is fine, as long as you help me win this war. I will reward you for your loyalty and your assistance. After all," Kestrel smiled cunningly, knowing all too well her audience, "I will need help to control this land. It is too vast for one person to control and so it will need to be split up between those who helped bring about victory."

Shae could see Kestrel's words were having their desired effect as there were quiet smiles around the room and a few small nods as the idea fully nested in their brains, to grow and mature. Kestrel held each of them now. They would do as she asked, if only for the promise of power and, Shae imagined for some, the violence it would take to win it.

That left Shae. She wasn't sure how she felt about any of this. She cared nothing about ruling the world. She did not wish to wage war on humanity. She came here for answers as what had been done to her, and why? What brought her to this point? Why was she a Were and what did it all mean? Was the only reason she had changed was to be this woman's soldier in a war she cared nothing about?

For the time being, the unmistakable tension in the air had left. They were all in agreement as to what they wanted.

"To this purpose, there will be things we will need to do as we move forward." Kestrel continued, "We must find others who will be willing to join the cause and offer them the same power that now flows through your veins. We must create an army of Weres. Soldiers for you to command in the fight."

"What do we do when the others come for us, eh?"

This came from the new guy. Surprisingly, he had an Australian accent which was unmistakable. She had never met anyone from Australia.

Kestrel turned to regard the newcomer.

"I mean. We already got into a bit of a row with one group of them. And you told me there were others who he," he jabbed a thumb towards Blain, "mucked up a chance at taking out."

Blain let out a growl and shifted, in seconds Blain went from being a hulking, menacing looking man to a horrific monster. Shae had witnessed this transformation up close once already and it still terrified her, even from a distance and she wasn't Blain's target for his animosity.

What happened next almost stopped her heart, though. The newcomer responded by shifting himself. His body immediately bulked up. Arms and legs became corded with thick, meaty muscles. Gone was the tanned skin, and instead, quickly replaced by dark, olive-green scales which flowed over his body to cover every inch. Bones snapped and cracked as his head flattened and his mouth jutted forward to form a large, elongated snout filled with sharp, knife-like teeth. He grew in height and weight and now stood as a massive crocodile on two legs with long sharp claws.

Shae stood in awe. This monster was undoubtedly a match for Blain in height and muscle mass. Where Blain sported two nasty looking tusks, this other creature had a large gaping maw that would have little trouble taking a sizable chunk of Blain's hide.

The sides of the croc's mouth slid back to reveal more teeth in what Shae could only assume was its attempt at a smile.

Kestrel strode between them.

What had almost been an epic battle between two powerful foes was halted by a woman. Her mere presence, enough to, if not calm tensions, to at least put them in check. She glared from Blain to the newcomer, and as quickly as they had shifted to horrible beasts, they were back to their human forms, with looks of murder passing between them.

"I said no violence between us, Blain, Gordon." Gordon. That was the man's name Shae realized.

"As to your question, Gordon. We made two attempts to end this war before it got started. Two attempts to catch our adversaries by surprise." Kestrel's lips turned down and she gazed off to the side. "We failed."

She walked back over to stand next to Samuel who stopped staring towards Sarah, who had patently ignored him.

"We will not confront them again. That is not how we will win this war." Her voice was hard. "I lost the last one because some of us arrogantly thought we could fight personal wars. We will not do it again.

"This war will be won by raising armies to attack the leaders around the world and taking control of their lands."

"If the wolf and his friends come for us? Are you saying you don't want me to destroy that piece of shit?" Blain snarled.

Sarah made a sound that, to Shae, seemed like a growl, but the woman made no other move.

Blain smiled a cruel smile toward Sarah but didn't pursue the torture.

"For now, Blain. For now. We no longer hold the advantage of surprise. Sylvanis will be the one pursuing us. While she is doing that, she can't work toward creating an opposing army to try and fight our goals. It is best if we string them along as long as possible. Also, as long as they are out there, the powers that be will be looking to deal with them just as they will be looking to deal with us."

That bit of news seemed to hit them all with a reality that, for some reason, had been lost before Kestrel uttered it. If they were indeed going to try and raise an army to go to war with the world of men, how long before the world of men decided to stop them?

"For now, I need you to avoid confrontation with Sylvanis and her Weres. If you fail to do this," she stared hard at Blain, "there will be consequences." She waited patiently, never taking her eyes from Blain until he at long last nodded.

She returned the nod and looked around at the rest of them.

"Blain. Gather up Sarah and Taylor and go to room 8013. I have arranged the room for you."

"This is our room . . ." Blain began, and Kestrel turned a cold stare at him. He met her gaze for a long time and the room held a collective breath as they waited for what might happen next between these two. In time, Blain let out a half grunt, half growl and turned from Kestrel.

"Taylor. Sarah. Come with me."

Taylor stood, and Sarah followed suit, if with great reluctance.

"I will come to you later to tell you what I have planned for you, Blain."

Looking over his shoulder as he began exciting the room, he asked, "And Joseph?"

"I have other plans for him. Don't worry. I will return him to you soon enough."

"You can keep him," Blain grumbled as he shut the door behind him.

Kestrel turned to the remaining three men.

"Samuel, can you please escort Gordon and Joseph to the other room we leased?"

Samuel nodded and beckoned to the other two men to follow him as they left the room, leaving Kestrel alone with Shae.

Kestrel turned to Shae, her eyes holding an appraising look. She smiled and walked, no, flowed over to Shae. The woman lost her authoritative attitude she had moments ago and instead looked warm and friendly as she sat down next to Shae.

Shae sat in silence for a time, uncomfortable being this close to such a beautiful and obviously powerful woman.

Kestrel seemed content to allow the silence to linger, and in the end, it was Shae that broke it.

"I don't want to fight in your war!" She hadn't intended to blurt it out as vehemently as she did. She had seen what outright defiance got you with this woman.

Kestrel smiled. Shae's mouth dropped open and her eyes widened. She expected the woman to lash out at her, or at the least demand obedience. Instead, Kestrel merely smiled at her.

"I know Shae." Kestrel told her. "I have no intention of having you fight for me, though there may be times you might be required to protect yourself, but I won't ask you to go to war for me."

Surprisingly, Shae felt a little angry about this. Did Kestrel not think her capable of fighting? She had killed already. Freed herself from captivity and fought her way out. Did Kestrel think her afraid?

It seemed her anger showed upon her face, for Kestrel held up a placating hand.

"No, Shae. It isn't because I think you are incapable. It's just I have other plans I need your help for. Probably the most important plans of them all."

"What are those?" Shae studied her, intrigued.

Kestrel laid a hand on Shae's leg and patted it lightly. It was such a simple gesture, something Anne had done to reassure her when Shae first came to live with her. Before George. A gesture of affection of caring. To Shae's surprise, she didn't flinch from it.

"I will tell you more of it at a later time. For now. I would like to hear your story. What happened to bring you to us?" Kestrel reached up and touched the edge of her shorn hair. It had only started to grow back and was still bristly to touch. Shae felt her face grow flush with embarrassment at what she did to her hair. Especially next to Kestrel's long, beautiful tresses.

She pulled away from Kestrel's touch and hung her head.

Kestrel let her hand drop back in her lap.

"It is obvious you have been through much, Shae. None of it good, I imagine?" She leaned forward and craned her neck to try and look into Shae's eyes.

"You have been hurt?"

Shae nodded. A slight sniffle escaped as she thought of her time in that prison.

"Abandoned?"

Shae nodded again. Tears flowed freely now as memories flooded her mind, of her birth parents leaving her, then Anne giving her away.

"Used?" Kestrel asked, almost a whisper as she leaned in closer to Shae. Shae nodded one last time before burying her head against Kestrel's shoulder. Thoughts of George. Of Daniel.

Kestrel hugged her close. "Tell me child. Let us meet these pains together so you needn't bear them all alone."

So, Shae told her. She told her of her childhood, of being abandoned. She told her of Anne and the brief happiness they shared before George came. With shame, she shared what George did to her and what she did to herself in response. When she told Kestrel of what happened to her in that prison, the woman grew visibly angry, her pale skin reddened, and her teeth clenched. Shae told her what she did to the man who hurt her so often in that prison.

That she sliced his throat open. Kestrel nodded her approval and her anger subsided some.

Shae left out what happened between her and Daniel afterward. That Daniel survived and was now a Were like her. Why she kept this from Kestrel, she didn't know. Perhaps it was because Daniel was hers, and she didn't want Kestrel to take him from her like she did with Joseph and Blain.

Regardless, she kept that part to herself. She told Kestrel about what she did to George and Anne. Again, there was no recrimination from Kestrel. In fact, there was outright approval.

"In the end, I heard about what happened here and came as quickly as I could in hopes of meeting others like me who might be able to explain what was happening."

Kestrel nodded at that.

"I don't want you to be upset about what you did to those people, Shae." Kestrel held her out at arms-length, studying her through long, beautiful lashes as she tilted her head to better look the shorter Shae eye to eye.

"Those evil people had it coming to them. They deserved what they got. No one will ever treat you that way again, Shae." Kestrel told her. "Not if I have any say in the matter."

Shae saw enough of this world to understand it was likely Kestrel wouldn't have a say in the matter. But the fact Kestrel wanted to keep her safe, to try and make sure no one every abused her again brought her a sense of calm she thought lost to her.

"Thank you, Kestrel. I mean, My Lady."

Kestrel tsked. "It's Kestrel to you, Shae. I only make the others use 'My Lady' so they understand who is in charge." She winked at Shae. "Men tend to forget those things easily."

Kestrel laughed. A warm, throaty laugh which brought a smile to Shae at first, then as she wiped the last tears from her eyes, a laugh. It was her first laugh in over three years, and it felt good.

Neither of them had any idea Officer Ben Charles watched them the whole time.

# *Chapter Seven*

Kestrel left the room where Shae slept. They had spent a few hours talking and Kestrel got a sense of the girl. She always had a knack for reading people which made it easy to manipulate them. A slight tugging at the corner of her mouth was the only indication she gave of her satisfaction at her interactions with Shae. She would need to tread lightly with the girl. She was vulnerable and had a serious lack of trust for people who were being kind to her.

A short trip down the hallway led her to the other room she rented for Samuel and Gordon. That she would need to keep Gordon and Blain separate for the time being had been an easy decision. Those two had egos which would war with each other until they came to an understanding. She, however, didn't feel like dealing with it.

With a quick insert of her keycard, she was through the door. Samuel sat at the kitchen table, his laptop illuminating his face, which leaned in toward the screen, forehead furrowed as his eyes darted back and forth as he read. Gordon lounged on the lone chair, a cozy, maroon recliner he hadn't bothered to recline. He sat with one hand resting in his lap, the other, propped up on the armrest, two fingers pressed against the side of his head as he watched a game of American football on the television. Joseph was nowhere to be seen.

Neither one bothered to stand when she entered. This didn't bother her as the way she dealt with these two was vastly different than Blain and his group. That group needed to be kept in check. Samuel had proved his loyalty and she valued him, not as an equal, but as a close confidant. Someone she could trust and seek advice from.

Gordon took to following her with alacrity. She doubted his belief in her cause, but she didn't doubt his loyalty. He saw her as a means to live the life he now desired. She would not curb his appetites, in fact, she encouraged them. As long as he left enough alive to build her army.

He was invested in her now. He was one of the few Weres who had been identified by the authorities. When they came, and they would come, they would come because of Gordon. It was only a matter of time before they knew he fled Australia and came here. And while they were trying to keep a low profile, Samuel assured her they would be found.

She hoped to have her plans fully in motion at that point and so be safeguarded if it came to that. She would not like to have to send Gordon away, to offer him up as a sacrificial lamb to the authorities in order to buy herself more time. She would if she had too, though.

Striding across the room she moved to stand behind Samuel to see what he read. As she moved behind him, he gave no recognition she was there, but she knew better. Little escaped Samuel's notice.

The screen on the laptop showed an article spotlighting Zach Van Stanley, the leader and founder of E.A.R.t.H. Kestrel recognized the article as she had already read everything published about the man and by the man. He was an interesting individual. At the age of sixteen, he organized protests outside coal plants and logging companies. After being arrested dozens of times for trespassing and vandalism, he eventually stepped up his game to destruction of property.

After blowing up several miles of newly constructed pipelines which had been built to transport oil, an accidental death landed him in jail for ten years. He had been released six years ago, and instead of going right back to what he had been doing, he instead founded, E.A.R.t.H or Earth, Anger,

Retaliate to Heal and created a large organization with extremely loyal followers. They were the largest, what they referred to as an eco-terrorist group in the United States, and had followers in many other countries as well.

Members of E.A.R.t.H continued to launch attacks against companies which raped and pillaged the Earth, but they did so, as far as the authorities could determine, autonomously. Over several dozen attacks and bombings had occurred, and yet, each time the perpetrators had been caught they denied any involvement from their leader, Zach. This kept him free to continue to be the face of the group.

Oh, he would backhandedly denounce his members' actions. He would claim they were unsanctioned, but in the same breath would promise more would come if the governments of the world didn't punish these companies for what they were doing to Mother Earth.

Samuel scrolled down the article, obviously entranced with the exposé. The reporter, though unwilling to condone the man's actions, seemed to hold a grudging respect for his beliefs and his willingness to go to the extreme to enact change.

Kestrel also respected the man. In fact, he was the person she was looking for. Someone with the desire to set things right. Someone willing to do what needed to be done to end the blight of civilization. She needed him, and whether he knew it or not, he needed her. With her magic, her Weres, and his people, they could take the necessary steps in bringing this world back from the damage men had done.

Samuel finished reading the exposé and turned to look at her. His face held a quiet smile and she nodded to him in silent understanding. He understood why she told him to read the article. He knew what she intended.

The smile faded from Samuel's face and the sides of his lips drooped down and worry lines formed upon his brow.

"What is it, Samuel?"

Samuel's eyes darted towards Gordon and he leaned forward to speak softly to her.

"I'm worried."

Kestrel arched an eyebrow.

"This world is dangerous. More dangerous than the world you . . . parted from. There are powerful forces out there, and soon, sooner than I would like, we will be exposed, and they will be coming for us."

"You think I don't know this?" She tried to keep the offense from coloring her tone, but the way in which Samuel flinched, she apparently failed.

"Of course not," he assured her. "I just worry for you. You have your magic of course, but it won't help you from a sniper's bullet, or an airstrike. I don't want a knife in the heart to take you like it did all those years ago."

Of all the people who followed her, or had followed her over the years, Samuel had always been the most faithful. Well, except when he abandoned her at the end of the war, but she forgave him. In the end, it had been the right move.

A slow, wicked smile crept on to her face. Her full red lips curled, and a devilish sparkle appeared in her eyes.

"Oh Samuel, this will not be like last time. I have a plan to ensure it."

As she told him of her plan, his expression moved from uncertainty, to shock, then gradually, his smile matched hers.

Detective Ben Charles stumbled out of the room he used to spy on the girl and her new 'friends'. That he managed not to get noticed when he practically fainted when the one of the newcomers turned into a walking crocodile and refrained from yelping was a testament to how much other weird shit he had already seen this day.

He needed to get some air, and he needed to think. With his head feeling like it was stuffed full of cotton, he managed to make his way to the lobby. By the time he stepped out of the elevator, his mind was clear, and he had a plan. Well, somewhat of a plan.

Night had snuck up on him and there were few people in the lobby. The hotel was a luxurious looking place, with marbled flooring, and fluted pillars flanking the main concourse leading to the front doors. There was a security guard posted at the front door. Ben had seen his fair share of security guards in his day and was surprised to see one so alert and not bored. These posts often left one with hours of doing nothing but idly people watch.

Crossing the lobby, he made his way to the officer. Given the man's posture and alertness, Ben figured him for an off-duty cop who wanted to make some extra money on the side. As he approached the man, the officer must have noticed his determined stride and he turned to face Ben as he approached, his hand nonchalantly falling to his side piece. Ben was thankful he already retrieved his badge from his back pocket, so he didn't have to try and make a grab for it now. Given the wariness of this fellow, he likely might have taken a bullet before he could properly identify himself.

The guard was a tall man, young, perhaps a few years out of the academy, with sandy blond hair and hard cut facial features; his face was a little too blunt to be called attractive. The man took care of himself though. The muscles in his arms barely fit within the sleeves of this uniform shirt.

Ben checked the man's name tag and it read, 'Paskins'. Flashing the officer his badge he moved in close to the man, so he could speak privately.

"Officer Paskins?" The man nodded slightly; his lips turned down slightly upon seeing an unfamiliar badge. Ben flashed it quickly so the man

72

wouldn't get he was an out-of-town officer, who most definitely had no jurisdiction here.

"Are you familiar with the man who lives in apartment 1010?"

For a moment, it looked as if Officer Paskins might pursue the matter of the badge, but something in Ben's tone must have convinced him this was more important. The officer took out a tablet and after several pokes and swipes on the screen, he turned the tablet towards Ben. It held the picture of the man whose apartment he commandeered.

"This the man?" Officer Paskins' voice was far reedier than Ben would have ever imagined given the strong masculine features of the man's face.

"Yes. That is him." Ben nodded. "Earlier this evening I commandeered his apartment due to an ongoing investigation." The man's earlier frown reappeared and deepened. Ben couldn't blame him. Here was a police officer from another city investigating a crime where he clearly shouldn't have been doing so. Worse, he was now involving an off-duty police officer instead of following the proper channels.

Ben held up his hands apologetically. "I know, I know. This is a shit sandwich you didn't ask to be given, but circumstances have left me no other choice but to hand it off to you." Ben crooked a smile. "And believe me, this is worse than you are even thinking it might be."

The officer's brows lowered as he stared hard at Ben. Ben could tell the man waged a war inside. On one hand, duty told him he should cease listening to this man and call it in immediately. On the other, he was quietly intrigued about where this was going and given Ben's urgent demeanor understood something was going down and it was important. Ben decided to take the man's silence as permission to keep talking.

"At some point, this man will return and wish to return to his apartment." Ben paused to emphasize his next point. "He must not be allowed to return."

"Am I supposed to arrest him?" A look of uncertainty crossed the man's face about this course of action. But Ben shook his head.

"No, no, no. He is not the issue. It's for his safety." Ben hesitated to tell the man the next part because he worried, if he did, the officer would, in fact, call it in and if the police showed up this would turn into a bloodbath.

"There are criminals in the room adjacent to apartment 1010 that I used to stake them out. It is possible at some point they might discover the means of which I used to observe them and if that were to happen . . ." Ben shrugged and left the result unspoken.

"Are the guests here in danger?"

This was the question Ben feared the officer would ask. To be truthful, Ben didn't know. He didn't believe so. From what he could determine from the conversations he overheard; these people wanted to keep a low profile. But he also knew it could change in a heartbeat. From what he saw, they were violent and dangerous.

"I believe the guests are safe . . . for now." Again, the frown returned. "As long as the criminals are left alone, I believe they will not cause harm to anyone." He tilted his head and peered at the officer sidelong, his eyebrow raised, as if to say, 'I'm talking about you.'

Slowly, the officer bobbed his head to acknowledge the unspoken warning.

Officer Paskins blew out a breath through tight lips. "So. What are we going to do?"

"We aren't going to do anything. You are going to stay here and stop the guy from 1010 from returning to his room."

"He isn't going to like that," Paskins interjected.

He was right. The guy hadn't wanted to leave his room in the first place. Ben scanned the room while he thought about what to do. He came to a decision.

"Send him over to the James Hotel and tell him to mention, Ben Charles, and they will have a room for him." Ben dug into his back pocket and pulled out his tired old wallet. Pulling out two twenties, he handed them to Paskins. "Give this to him for the cab ride over."

Paskins nodded. "That might work."

Ben gave the officer a flat stare. "Make it work."

He received a stiff nod in response.

"And you?"

Ben once again scanned the lobby before answering. "I have to meet some people, but I will be returning as soon as I can with reinforcements."

That answer seemed to satisfy Paskins and Ben left.

Ben knew where he was going but had no idea if what he hoped to find would be there. It was a hope and a prayer. He worried what he might have to do if he couldn't find whom he was looking for.

Night had completely fallen on Chicago, not that you could tell. Stores and restaurants lit the night with their bright signs and illuminated store fronts. Ben weaved his way through the milling crowds of people still thick at this hour. His pace was brisk as he quickly made his way to his usual corner, the one he waited at day in and day out while trying to find the one who was responsible for the death of that man in Sacramento. The tiger. Instead, he found more than he bargained for.

By the time he reached his corner, the crowds had thinned somewhat. The Magnificent Mile was still vibrant with life. The soft thrumming of music could be heard from a nearby establishment. Its muted sound barely reached Ben as he began scanning the people who were passing by or paused in front of various buildings.

His gaze whipped from one face to the other, frantic to find those he sought. The problem, of course, he had no idea whom he searched for. The tiger or the wolf could be standing right next to him and he would never realize unless they changed.

A sharp yelp brought his head around as he saw a woman trying to duck around a man and get to the side, away from a dark alleyway they passed. The look of confusion on the man's face told Ben, whatever spooked the woman, the man had not noticed. The woman's eyes were wide, the whites looked enormous even from where Ben stood. Whatever she saw or heard coming from the alleyway clearly frightened her.

Ben felt elated. One of *them* was there. He knew it!

Darting across the street, Ben approached the alley. A lone light sat high upon one of the walls in the alley. Its warm yellowish light gave scant illumination in the alley. Barely a car's width wide, the alley was empty except for a lone dumpster on the right and a metalwork staircase which switch-backed up the side of the building on the left. Peering into the gloom of the alley, Ben saw nothing to have caused any fright.

Or so he thought at first. A shadow detached itself from beside the dumpster.

Yellow orbs stared at him, caught him, and held him as if by some magical will. Try as he might, he couldn't look away. A deep growl rolled out from the alley, chilling Ben to the bone. The only word Ben could think of to describe the sound was . . . menacing.

Shaking his head to clear it and regain some control over his body, Ben began to back away from the alley. The shadow matched his speed and began to take shape. Ben had seen it before. He had seen it in a shaky, hand-held video of a witness to the battle which took place here not too long ago. The bright yellow eyes were set deep within the canine-shaped head. Two, swept-backed ears rose to either side of the head; deep brown fur coated them and came to a sharp tuft at their crest.

The creature loomed in the alley, its bulk apparent and its muscles sharp and defined. Strangely, as it approached Ben, it would lower itself to use its clawed hands to propel it forward before standing up slightly, only to repeat the process after a step or two bipedally.

This was the wolf. Supposedly one of the good guys, but Ben wasn't getting a good guy vibe from him now. In fact, Ben got an altogether different vibe.

Ben continued to back away. The wolf loped out of the alley and was now fully visible and a sight to behold. This beast was powerful and scary. Yellowish-tinged fangs showed, their sharp points visible as the wolf kept its mouth parted slightly, as if always ready to take a bite.

There were gasps and shouts from bystanders, even a cheer. Ben wondered if they were seeing this thing as he saw it. Not the hero who saved that woman from the boar, but an animal. A hungry animal currently stalked its prey. And its prey was Ben.

Ben knew, at any moment, this beast would pounce on him, and there was quite literally nothing he could do about it. He never felt so helpless in his life. He kept watch on the wolf, waiting for some sign it would attack. His best bet would be to do his best to avoid the initial lunge and to try to get away as quickly as he could. It was a lousy plan, and Ben knew it, but what else could he do?

Looking left and right, he desperately sought a way out as this creature — this beast came closer and closer. It seemed the crowd who gathered around came to the same conclusion as he, and were now, if not outright fleeing, moving away briskly.

The wolf came to a halt, and Ben froze as well. Then, as if in slow motion, the creature's knees bent slightly, and it lunged. Ben belatedly thought to reach for his gun, knowing it was too late. The wolf's maw stretched wide to tear into him and Ben flinched back as death flew at him.

77

# *Chapter Eight*

Ben could do little as the beast descended on him, when out of the darkness, a missile of orange and black slammed into it.

Ben watched as the wolf's body tumbled and bounced a dozen feet or so before coming to a stop. Another figure rolled after it but bounded back up to land on its feet. Easily a head taller than Ben, stood a creature, sleek of body, yet powerful. Its arms and legs were corded with muscles and covered in fur of orange and black. It faced away from Ben, but he knew from the videos its belly was covered with white fur. He didn't need to see it from the front. He knew this was the tiger he searched for. But why did she fight the wolf?

Kat left the hotel they were staying at with her duffle bag thrown over her shoulder. As quickly as she could, she made her way downtown to the Magnificent Mile, the place of her earlier fight with the Boar. Night rolled in and darkness tried desperately to overcome the bright lights of the city.

Kat walked in her own darkness.

Regret and guilt darkened her mood as she moved fluidly, seemingly unaware of the crowds of people. Despite knowing, rationally, she wasn't at fault, she still could not shake the feeling she should have done something else that night in the hospital. She had abandoned Sarah to that . . . monster. Yes, she did so because Sarah pleaded with her to get Clint out of there. And yes, if they stayed, they likely would have died at the hands of the Boar and his friends. But knowing this, it still didn't make her feel any less horrible for leaving. Especially after Sylvanis told them Sarah now had to do everything the boar told her to do.

Kat interacted enough with that creature to guess what the sick fuck would do to Sarah. She left her to that fate. Maybe she would have died trying to fight the Boar that night, but maybe she could have ended him and freed Sarah. Now, they would never know. All they did know is the Boar would take full advantage of the control over Sarah.

Kat's face contorted as anger flowed through her at the thought. After a moment. A long moment. She unclenched her fists and ceased grinding her teeth and took a deep breath. This recrimination would not help Clint. Clint was the key. She needed to find him and save him. Saving him would, in some small part, redeem her from failing to save Sarah.

*Sarah isn't dead,* she reminded herself. They would save her. They would free her from the Boar. Kat would rip that monster's heart out to make sure.

Before she knew it, she was downtown and standing on a corner of Chicago's famous Magnificent Mile. It was night, but people were still prevalent, walking up and down the main drag, laughing and talking loudly. Kat envied them. There was a war coming and they were oblivious to it. With ignorance came peace. She no longer had that luxury. She was now a soldier in a war to save the lives these people took for granted.

Kat stood for a time on the corner and watched people as they passed. Occasionally she sniffed the air for some sign of the smell that came from someone with lycanthropy. There was a hint. A whisper of a scent. Something of an echo of their presence here, or perhaps others; then it passed, and it was no longer here.

Kat's lips went straight and all but disappeared as she pondered what to do next. She needed a new perspective. A different view.

Turning, she spotted an alley not far off and made for it. There were two iron stairs on either side of the alley leading to the tops of the buildings. Trash and loose papers lay strewn upon the cobbled stone roadway here, though there were several dumpsters sporadically placed up and down the alley. A light hung above a doorway halfway down and Kat made for it. The door, a dark black metal thing, sat back from the outside wall creating a little alcove big enough for her to fit in.

Kat ducked into it and peered out, looking left and right. There was no one in the alley and as far as she could tell, no one saw her enter this doorway. Satisfied, Kat disrobed and put her clothes into her duffle. Within seconds, Kat shifted to her tiger form, tossed the duffle back over her shoulder and quickly mounted the stairs to the roof of one of the buildings.

Stepping over to the edge, Kat scanned the street below. People flowed beneath her, like tiny paper boats down a stream. Using her ability to see in the dark, she searched other alleys she could see from here.

Nothing.

She believed Clint would come here. It was the last place they saw the Boar and so, the best place to start to look for him. It was a long shot, but Clint wasn't thinking straight.

Kat hoped she could get through to him. She had seen him the night Sylvanis told him about Sarah and the Boar. She had seen his anger. His rage. It had been feral. Untamed. Uncontrollable. She wasn't sure she could get past that to help him see reason.

She didn't have a choice. Kat needed to make this right.

Darting to the far side of the building, she leaped. Flying through the air, she easily made it to the next roof over. Not allowing herself to slow she took the next jump and the next one in rapid succession. Before the fourth jump she paused before leaping, needing to not only jump some distance, but also, to gain altitude as the next building sat slightly higher than the one she was on.

Backing up to the far side, she dropped into her runner's stance and took a slow breath in before pushing off with her bent leg, propelling herself forward. Like a bullet she shot across the rooftop. There was a slight lip on the edge, and she planted her foot on its top before catapulting herself across to the next building. Soaring across the distance she realized she wasn't going to make it.

"Oh, fuck!"

The building rapidly approached, and she tucked into a ball pitching her downward. It was enough. She crashed through a window amid screams and cries of alarm. Kat kept herself wrapped in a ball as she rolled across the floor of a bedroom in an apartment complex. Slamming into the far wall, her momentum slowed as her body punched through the wall and into another wall on the opposite side of the hallway.

Scrambling and crying came from the room she rolled through, but Kat didn't bother to try and figure out what they were about as she scrambled up and darted down the hall. Thankfully, the hall led to an open floor plan room. A kitchen, dining area and family room were all visible, but more importantly, so was the front door.

Crossing the room quickly, Kat threw open the door and entered the hall. A short distance away sat the stairs for the complex, which should, Kat hoped, lead her back onto the roof. A gasp behind her alerted her she was not alone in the hall. Turning she caught sight of a mother, clutching her little girl to her. Fear was evident upon the woman's face and a mix of fear and wonderment was shown upon the girl's.

Kat stared at them, and they stared at her. Kat knew she was a frightening sight, and frankly, there was little she could do that would not inadvertently frighten them more, so she turned and fled down the hall toward the stairs. With any luck, since she didn't attack them, they would understand she was not a threat.

She could hope, anyway.

Making her way back to the rooftops, she continued to get some distance from the Magnificent Mile. Though now, she stopped trying to make jumps she didn't think she could make. Her plan was to move away from the Mile and create a search radius moving closer and closer. Hopefully, if Clint was here, she would leave him no way to avoid her detection.

Hours passed as she spiraled her way back toward the Mile. Pausing occasionally, Kat would sniff the air, hoping to catch a scent which would lead to Clint, but still, nothing.

It neared midnight when she again approached the Mile. Her dark mood which had fled after she took to the rooftops, returned. She had been unsuccessful in locating any indication of Clint. Because of this, she hadn't noticed anything going on the streets below her until she heard a scream.

At the mouth of an alley, she saw a crowd gathering, all looking toward what now exited. Clint! His powerful Were-form emerged from the darkened alley. Deliberately, he approached a man in black slacks and a light blue jacket. He was a middling looking man, with short, brown hair, a slight bald spot peeking out at the back. She couldn't make out any of his features from atop the building, but she could imagine they showed a great deal of fear.

Clint in no way appeared to be approaching this man in a friendly manner. If Kat had to guess, this man was mere moments away from getting killed.

Kat acted.

Leaping from the roof of the building, she flew toward a building on the opposite side of the alley. The moment she hit the wall, she bunched her legs and thrust out, launching herself back toward the building she had left. She continued this maneuver, in a downward trajectory. When at last she felt she could make a landing safely, she allowed herself to drop straight down.

Landing with an audible thud, the pavement buckled, and sent spiderweb-like cracks away from the point of impact. Kat took no notice as she was on the move the moment she hit. Darting out of the alley she had landed in, she sped across the distance to where Clint and the man faced off. The people who had been gathered around earlier were quickly dispersing as they realized this was not the wolf hero from the other day. This was a killer.

Kat willed herself to go faster and was rewarded by a sudden burst of extra speed. As she closed the distance, she saw Clint's knees bend. She reached them as he attacked. Launching herself on an intercept course, she slammed into him and they both went tumbling away.

Clint, who had been completely caught off guard by her attack bounced and rolled farther than Kat, who had quickly regained her feet and rolled into a crouch. She would fight him, if necessary, but she hoped to reason with him if she could.

She wondered at her chances fighting him. Clint was physically stronger than her, but she, faster and had years of practice fighting, not to mention the training she had done in her hybrid form. For Clint, all of this was still relatively new. He had only changed, on purpose, for the first time, a short while ago.

Kat liked her chances in a fight, but she hoped it wouldn't come to that.

A low growl, deep and reverberating rolled out from Clint, and she began to wonder if talking would be an option.

The Wolf rose to his full height and turned toward her. With his arms slightly held out and his clawed hands splayed, their sharp tips visible in the streetlights, Kat didn't recognize Clint at all.

"Oh shit," she muttered, readying herself for a fight.

The Wolf came at her.

"CLINT!" Kat shouted at him as she worked vigorously to block his onslaught. Using her arms, she caught each of his attacks at his wrists, keeping those sharp claws away from her flesh.

He gave no sign he registered her calling his name as his attacks didn't slow. Fortunately, he attacked her with wild abandon, and she could, without difficulty, parry or avoid them as necessary. Unexpectedly, he slashed at her with both of his claws, sweeping them in at her from opposite sides. Stepping in slightly so she could effectively take the hit on her forearms, she realized her mistake a little too late.

The wolf whipped his head forward and sank his teeth into her shoulder. Kat cried out. He swung his head with such force she was thrown from him, his fangs shredding her flesh. She could feel her pectoral and trapezius muscles tear and her right clavicle snap.

By the time she landed and regained her feet though, the damage had been repaired. Growling she stared at the Wolf.

"O.K." she grunted. "No more Mr. Nice Guy."

Kat charged the Wolf. Up until now, she had been on the defensive. Hoping against hope the longer she was in proximity with him, Clint would somehow resurface, but it wasn't working. So, now she would try and incapacitate him, or at least, beat some sense into him.

The Wolf hunkered down, waiting for her to clash with him, but that wasn't how Kat did things. As soon as she saw him brace for her impact, she launched herself high, using her strong leg muscles to send her soaring over him. Landing behind him, she had learned her lesson from fighting the boar, and crouched the moment she hit the ground. She was rewarded by her quick thinking as she sensed, rather than saw, the wolf's backhand sail over her head.

Spinning around in her crouch, she sprung forward past his legs, catching his ankle as she passed. Her momentum yanked the wolf off his feet, but that wasn't why she had done it. Savagely, she took her free hand and buried her claws into the back of the wolf's leg and with all the strength she could muster, she grabbed and yanked, tearing his quad muscle out, all the way down to his Achilles tendon which she proceeded to tear away from his bone.

A pained howl erupted from the Wolf and it tore at Kat's heart. She hadn't wished to cause Clint any pain, but he had left her no other choice. As quick as a cat, Kat pounced. She pummeled him repeatedly; her strong powerful blows rocked his head back to slam against the pavement. Caught between trying to clutch his destroyed hamstring and blocking her punches, the Wolf could do neither effectively.

Kat rained down punches upon the Wolf's face. She could see bones break in his face and could hear the breaking sound of his skull upon the pavement, but she wouldn't let up. She needed him to lose consciousness, if that was possible. She wasn't sure, but she remained relentless in her attacks.

Blow after blow slammed into the wolf and Kat wondered how much more he could take. She had her answer shortly. With a sudden burst of strength, the wolf grabbed her about the waist and launched her off him.

Kat flew but managed to twist herself and land on her feet, then she immediately went back after him. As she closed the distance, she saw him unsteadily gain his feet. He shook his head, as if to clear the fogginess that must be overcoming him after so many repeated hits to the head.

He had yet to see her coming. Or so she thought. Leaping at him, she had intended to knock him off his feet once again. Instead, he turned toward her and brought a claw skyward, burying it in her chest. The power of the impact, her velocity meeting his ferocity, snapped her sternum. Clawed fingers sliced through lungs until at last it reached her spinal cord which broke as she slammed against him, buckling around his arm, which was now buried up to the middle of his forearm.

Blood poured out of her body, staining the white fur on her chest and darkening the fur on the wolf as she hung there, limp, unable to move. Kat could not feel the lower half of her body, the nerves controlling those functions had been sliced. Blood gurgled up through her maw as her shredded lungs filled with the thick, red fluid.

That her body would repair all of this was scant comfort to Kat who felt a sense of panic take hold. She had never felt this helpless in her life. The Wolf moved slightly, and her head lolled to one side and she searched his canine-like face. He stared down at her with zero recognition in his eyes.

With one claw, the wolf pushed her off his arm and she thudded to the ground. Pain coursed through her body, but after going through the shift as many times as she had, this was next to nothing. Though it did make it hard to concentrate. And concentrate she must. Her body would heal. But it would heal quicker if she could direct it . . . will it to heal.

Slowly, the Wolf crouched down over her and tilted its head in a canine-like manner, to study her. The wolf grabbed one of her arms, lifted it, and let it go. It dropped unceremoniously onto the pavement, and the Wolf cocked its head the other way.

Kat didn't understand what it was doing, or what it would do next, so she desperately concentrated on repairing her body. She worked first on her lungs, mending the tears and reabsorbing or breaking down the blood as best as she could to clear them out. She felt her ability to breathe return to her. As she began work on healing the damage to her spine, she realized it was too late.

The wolf bent down toward her, its maw opening wide. She had run out of time.

# *Chapter Nine*

Bang! Bang! Bang!

Shots rang out and she watched as a bullet struck the wolf's forehead. Blood and skull fragments exploded away from the impact. Another bullet took the Wolf in the shoulder as it rocked backward from the first hit. A third bullet took it in its chest, knocking it farther back. The Wolf collapsed and rolled away from her and she closed her eyes, setting all her thoughts into repairing her spine.

As feeling incrementally returned to her body, she rolled her head to look at where the shots had originated and spied the man from earlier. The one the Wolf had been stalking. Kat could see him fully now. He was a scruffy looking man who appeared to be in his late forties. A salt and pepper blanket of hair thinly covered his chin and cheeks. Thin to the point of gaunt, his face was slack; pouches could be visibly seen under the man's eyes. This was a man to whom sleep was a stranger, Kat surmised.

The man held a gun with a steady hand, pointing it past her to where the Wolf was now gaining its feet. Without hesitation, the gunman aimed the SIG again and fired off nine more shots in rapid succession. The sound echoed off the surrounding buildings, falling silent moments after the last of the bullets left the chamber.

Kat knew they would have little effect and so continued to heal her body. There was a lot of damage and the severity of it to her spinal cord made healing a more intricate exercise than she was used to.

"Fuck!" the man cursed, and the clip of his gun dropped out and onto the ground as he released it bouncing with a clatter. Frantically he searched his jacket pockets and pulled out another clip to reload the weapon.

Fur covered legs flowed past her as the wolf leaped over her body to charge the man with the gun. Kat was desperate. She needed to stop this.

"CLINT!" she managed to shout again. "What about Sarah?!"

The Wolf stumbled and rounded on her.

Kat managed to prop herself up, never taking her eyes from him.

"What would Sarah think of what you are doing, Clint?" She saw confusion in his eyes as they narrowed, peering at her.

Sluggishly, she got her legs under her, facing him.

"It's Kat, Clint. Remember?" He continued to stare at her. The gunman had stopped trying to load his gun and was staring at them both.

"Please, Clint," she pleaded, "let me help you. Together we will get her back."

The Wolf shook his head, like trying to jar something loose inside. It peered at her once again, and then away.

Kat took a step forward, raising one hand toward him.

"Come with me, Clint. Sylvanis is here. She can help you. Help us, find Sarah."

The Wolf turned toward her once again. She thought she could see recognition there, but perhaps it was only her wish.

With a final shake of his head, the Wolf turned and loped away, quickly disappearing.

Kat stood there; her arm raised out toward his retreating form. A moment passed, and she let it drop. She stared off after him. Her body was still repairing the damage caused by the fight, and it was almost healed. She should have gone after him. Gone after him and try to reason with him some more.

No.

She could not force him back. He had built walls that refused to allow the Wolf to take complete control. He was there, still. She had to be patient. Had to help him regain control of himself.

Lost in her own thoughts, Kat realized the man still stood there. She turned her head to look at him staring at her. She gave him a nod in gratitude for helping her before turning to go.

"You're her? Aren't you?" His voice, a deep timbre, was rough around the edges, like the rest of him.

She wasn't sure what he meant. Perhaps he meant the same Tiger from the fight which took place here days ago.

"Yep," she continued to move away, "I'm her."

His next question stopped her in her tracks.

"The one from Sacramento?"

She had done her best to keep her actions in her hometown anonymous, but still there had been rumors of a giant cat-woman going around, so it wasn't completely out of the realm of possibility someone could have put two and two together and figured out they were one and the same. But something about the way the man asked the question had her believing it was more.

She didn't answer him.

"You know the rapist you cut? He died."

Kat squeezed her eyes shut. She had been dreading this possibility ever since Sylvanis had explained how it was transmitted. From what Hank and Sim had said, if she had transmitted it to that guy, and he had lived, she should have been able to sense him. She hadn't. Had refused to think about it. Too afraid to face the possibilities. Now she knew.

90

She remained silent, frozen in place.

"Did you know?" His voice was low, hesitant.

"Know what?" The words breathed out of her. She felt exhausted, too weary to talk.

"When you cut him?" Desperation tinted his questions, as if he was looking for an answer, and he desperately needed to hear the right one. "Did you know he would die?"

She sighed. There it was. He wanted to know if she was a killer.

"No." She tried to put conviction back into her voice, but it sounded hollow, at least to her. "I only learned recently about what might happen to someone who I cut."

Silence came from behind her.

"Did you come here to arrest me?" She was making a guess. She had no idea if he was a cop. But it made sense. He knew about the rapist. He knew about Sacramento. He had come here —for her.

"If you are. I'm afraid I'm not gonna let you do that today." She still had her back to him and for all she knew he was pointing his gun at her. Though, given what he had witnessed, he should know better.

"It's why I came," he admitted. "But no. No, I don't think I am going to try and arrest you." He barked a laugh. "To be honest. I don't even have the authority to do it even if I wanted to.

"Regardless, I don't want to arrest you." A firmness came into his voice. "I've seen the others. The bad ones. I know where they are."

Kat whipped around.

"What?"

"The Boar. I know where he is. Though he is not alone. There are . . .", his voice cracked a little and his throat bobbed as he gulped, "others."

Kat nodded at this. She moved over to him and unconsciously, he flinched back.

"I won't hurt you," she reassured him.

He nodded. "I know. It's just. You are . . . scary."

Kat's lips peeled back in a grin she realized didn't do much to alleviate the man's fear. "I'm Kat."

The man snorted. "You're kidding?"

Kat let out a soft growl.

The man held out his hands in calm her. "O.K. O.K. Sorry. I'm Ben. Officer Ben Charles."

"You need to come with me. I have friends. Others, like me," she told him. "You need to tell them — everything."

He stared in a mixture of fear and awe at her but nodded.

It was at that moment a scent reached her nose and she raised her head and sniffed, testing the air to try and get a better sense of the smell.

"What is it?" Ben peered around warily.

Kat didn't answer immediately as she took a strong inhalation and scanned about.

Ben waited patiently.

"There is a smell. It smells like . . . like someone with lycanthropy, but strange." She struggled to find the words to describe the scent. "Something about it isn't quite right."

The idea she could smell others like her didn't faze the man.

"Well. Could it be your Wolf friend? Something isn't quite right with him, correct?"

Kat pondered this notion. The man had a point.

"Perhaps you're right." She searched the buildings and alleyways around them, hoping to catch a glimpse of Clint, but nothing.

"We should go," Kat told him. "We have no time to lose."

Crossing the street, Kat led him over to the alley next to the building which held her clothes on its roof. She quickly retrieved them. Moving over to the doorway where she had changed before, she told Ben to wait at the mouth of the alley. She stood there for a time and stared at his back as he kept watch.

She was about to trust him with something few people outside of the group knew. Her real identity. However, she couldn't walk down the streets of Chicago as a Weretiger, so this was out of necessity. It left her feeling vulnerable though. She wasn't sure she could trust this man, though he had risked his life to save hers. Maybe he still planned on arresting her and hoped he could trap her in her human form. He wouldn't realize she could simply change back.

She shook her head. She was being stupid. This was necessary, and she was wasting time. Stepping back into the alcove, she shifted. It happened so quickly and effortlessly now it amazed her. She donned her clothes and stepped out into the alley and approached Ben.

He turned at her approach and his eyes widened.

"Not what you expected?" she teased him.

He shook his head. "I didn't expect you to be so . . ."

"What?"

"Pretty," he admitted.

Kat chuckled. "Why is that?"

Ben's shoulders rose and fell. "Don't know. I guess with how well you fought, I thought you would be more . . ." He shrugged again and cocked his head apologetically, "mannish?"

Kat laughed again, shook her head and patted him on the chest as she moved past him.

"Come on. We're losing time."

She led him off toward the hotel where Sylvanis, Hank, Sim and she were staying. Neither one of them saw the dark, looming shape of a Werewolf pad off after them.

93

None of them saw the other figure detach itself from the shadows of a nearby building to follow them as well.

"Are you sure of what you saw?" The worry in Sylvanis' voice was palpable.

"Yes. There was eight of them there. I saw three of them turn into, into . . ." Ben stumbled over the words.

"Weres?" Kat interjected.

"Yeah. The boar from the video. A rat and a crocodile, or alligator. I can never remember which is which."

Sylvanis was pacing and she corrected him absently, "Crocodile."

"Oh," Ben murmured. "Yeah. So. Anyway. The crocodile was some guy from Australia as far as I could tell. The rat. Well. She is a young girl. Maybe fifteen."

Sylvanis looked at Hank. They had all gathered in Sylvanis' room when Kat brought Ben back here to relay the news of what he saw. "Kestrel has gathered them all. This puts us at a great disadvantage."

Kat agreed. But she didn't care. Ben had told them Sarah was there. If Sarah was there, they had to go and get her. Kat owed her that much. She owed Clint that much. Not to mention it might be the only way to bring Clint back from what he had become.

"That isn't going to stop us though, is it?" Kat tried to keep the desperation out of her voice but failed.

Sylvanis turned toward her for the first time since Kat had told her what had happened between her and Clint. Sylvanis' green eyes locked with hers and she stared at her for a long moment. Studying her. Whatever she saw helped her make a decision, and she nodded to Kat.

"No. That isn't going to stop us. We will need to strike hard and fast. There is no way we will be able to win this fight in a head-on match. They have

94

the number advantage." Sylvanis brought her finger to her pursed lips and tapped them. "We need to try and take out the Boar, or at the least, get Sarah away from them."

"And then?" Hank asked. He had been silent almost the whole time. Though he had grown visibly distressed when Kat told them of the fight.

Sylvanis turned to Hank. "We will have to flee. We cannot win this fight and I will not risk losing any of you to a battle that will lose us this war."

"Then why go at all?" Sim piped in. "I mean. I know this Sarah is important and what is happening to her is horrible, but is she really worth the risk?"

"Sim." Hank's word held a bit of caution. He seemed to have read the situation when it came to Kat's feelings about this.

Sim turned to his father. "What? It is a reasonable question, Dad. We are talking about the end of civilization here if Kestrel gets her way, right? Don't you think it might be more important than just one woman?"

Kat growled. Even though she wasn't in her hybrid form, her growl still sounded feral.

Sim turned towards her. His face held a hint of fear, which satisfied her immensely.

"That woman," Kat bit the words out, "is the key to getting Clint back. And if we are going to win this war," she threw that back at him, "then we are going to need him."

Hank stepped forward and rested his hand on Sim's shoulder as if to say, 'It's O.K. son, you just didn't think this through.' Sim considered her for a time and nodded.

"Kat's right," Sylvanis agreed. "That is why we need to do this."

She looked to each of them, searching their eyes for something only she knew. They all stayed quiet but returned Sylvanis' regard. Even Ben.

Hank shuffled his feet a little and Sylvanis raised an eyebrow toward him, indicating if he had something on his mind, he should go ahead and say it now. There wouldn't be a later.

"This will be a full reveal of ourselves to the world, Sylvanis." Hank's tone held a fair amount of uncertainty, which was uncharacteristic of him as far as Kat had seen. "We can't enter that hotel as hybrids. We will have to enter in as we are and when we engage Kestrel and the others, then, and only then will we shift."

The idea hit Kat like a ton of bricks. Earlier she had been hesitant to let Ben see who she was. This could result in the whole world knowing who she was, or rather, what, she was.

"Shit," Sim muttered, echoing Kat's thoughts and summing them up into one word. *Shit, is right.*

"It was going to have to happen eventually. There was no way we could have stayed in the shadows forever," Sylvanis replied, though to Kat, she seemed as upset over the idea as the rest of them were. Sylvanis was no lycan, but a druidess, and if Kestrel was there to fight, Sylvanis would have to unveil her power as well.

The only comfort was, Kestrel and her group would be outed as well. A small comfort.

Ben spoke up. "I don't mean to rush anybody. But I got the impression now that they were all there, the one you call Kestrel had plans for them and they would be leaving soon."

He didn't mention anything about the off-duty cop at the hotel, Kat noticed. Ben had filled her in on everything which had happened to him since he had arrived in Chicago. Up to, and including, covering for himself with the off-duty cop so the owner of the hotel room didn't re-enter his room. Kat guessed it didn't matter. Ben had told her he had warned the other man away from the room, and so, as long as the other group didn't decide to leave already, they should find them, in their room, unmolested.

Sylvanis was through explaining and was about to get them ready to go, but Kat wasn't done with Sylvanis yet.

"What about Clint?" she demanded.

The look that passed between Sylvanis and Hank said volumes to Kat.

"What?" She glanced at them both. "You going to take him out, Hank?" Kat could feel her face grow hot as anger built like a well of lava about to overflow.

Hank didn't back down from her fire. "If I have to, Kat." His voice was low and almost drowned out by the thrumming of blood in her ears.

"You of all people should know what he is now capable of." He shook his head in obvious confusion of her lack of understanding as to why this might be necessary. "You saw the reports as well as I."

"Those hunters could have been attacked by anything!" she yelled at him, though the fire cooled inside. She knew it wasn't true.

Hank peered at her with sympathetic eyes and tilted his head as he watched her. He had reached her. She was reasoned enough to understand the way of things. Taking out Clint might be necessary. *God help her, it just might.*

"Let us hope it doesn't come to that." Sylvanis spoke in a rush, seemingly unaware of Kat's change in demeanor. She glanced at Kat, and Kat saw something she hadn't thought she would see from Sylvanis. Shame.

*She is trying so hard to be an effective leader, to make the hard calls, but it's killing her inside.* Kat nodded to her to try and alleviate some of the hurt the woman felt about making a difficult choice.

"He just needs Sarah. He needs her free," Kat insisted. "You'll see. Sarah will reach him, just as mentioning her tonight reached him."

Sylvanis' lips turned down. "I do hope you're right, Kat. There were few who never came back from turning wild. Let us hope Clint is stronger than most."

Something occurred to Kat. Something she had failed to mention when telling them about the fight earlier.

"Sylvanis?"

"Yes, Kat?" She had been about to turn away but turned her full attention back to Kat.

"Something else happened tonight. Something that . . . I don't know what it might mean."

"What happened?" Sim asked, curiosity evident in his voice.

"After fighting Clint. I caught a scent." She cocked her head thinking of how best to explain it. "It smelled . . . like a Were, only . . . different . . . strange." Different and strange didn't feel like the right words either, but she couldn't figure out anything better.

Sylvanis' eyebrows drew down, lines creased her forehead, her blonde hair hanging loose and framing her pretty face. She was a beautiful girl. Kat had to keep reminding herself this girl was not technically a year old. Not even a year old, and yet, over two millennia old. Thinking about this crap always gave Kat headaches.

"What do you think it was?" Sylvanis watched her, expectant.

"I don't know, Sylvanis. Ben here," she thumbed towards him, "thought I might be Clint. You know? Since he isn't quite himself."

Sylvanis mused over it for a time and gave a slight nod of her head. "Seems like a reasonable explanation," she said firmly, "though, I've never heard of anything like that."

Kat frowned. If it wasn't Clint, then what the hell was it?

Sylvanis sensed her disappointment in her answer and so added, "Though, to be honest. It wasn't talked about much. It was an . . . uncomfortable topic among the Weres."

"I'll bet." Sim stood up from the edge of the bed he had been sitting on for most of the conversation. "Well, if we are going to enter this shit storm, we might as well get going."

"Son, just because I haven't cuffed you yet for saying shit, don't think I won't if you keep using it every five seconds." It was all seriousness from Hank, but Kat couldn't help but snort out a laugh.

Sim smiled broadly at his father. Hank's frown grew deeper.

Kat out and out laughed. After a moment, Sylvanis giggled as well, clamping a hand over her mouth to stifle it. Next, Sim started to laugh, then Ben chuckled trying to cover it up with a cough when Hank's gaze fell on him. The rest of them were unmoved by Hank's glare. Kat loved Hank and Sim's relationship. It reminded her of her and her dad.

Hank sighed and shook his head. "I thought we needed to get going?"

The sobriety of what they were about to head into shut the laughter down immediately. Each of them had been forced to fight already. Each of them had the moment they realized this wasn't a game. This wasn't a competition to see who would win the trophy. This was life and death. Kat had learned tonight how quickly you could go from feeling invulnerable, given these strengths and abilities, to feeling powerless and realizing you could die any second.

Everyone looked at her now, as if sensing she was the one who truly understood the stakes here, and if she was ready, they would be as well.

She met their gazes. "Let's go."

# *Chapter Ten*

Shae dreamed. The dreams, elusive in their nature, still left her feeling a sense of peace. Peace was a concept she knew little about. Yet, she felt it while she dreamed. Something encroached on that peace though. First, along the edges it began wounding the tranquility of her dreams, like someone grabbing two sides of a piece of paper and deliberately moving their hands away from each other. A tearing, causing ragged edges on the periphery.

Peace clung on. Cushioning her. Protecting her from the impending arrival of unease and tension. Exponentially, the feeling of peace dwindled. Dread and worry approached till it stood on the doorstep of her soul. It was going to enter.

Shae awoke with a gasp.

Darkness blanketed the room. Muted shapes of furniture sat in quiet regard of her as she propped herself up to search the room for what woke her. Quick, ragged breaths forced themselves out of her chest as she tried to compose herself, but the feeling of approaching unease would not leave her. It took her a moment to realize why.

*Daniel?*

Swinging her legs over the side of the bed, Shae quickly crossed the room and flung open the door. Standing in the doorway was Daniel. The days she had been away had apparently not treated him well. His customarily close-cut beard had grown longer and creeped past his normal, well-manicured lines. Exhaustion was visible on his face. He had not been sleeping well.

Shae stuck her head outside the door and look furtively down the hall in both directions before grabbing Daniel's arm and yanking him inside.

"You should not be here!" Her voice came out in an angry hiss, barely audible as she feared others of her type may have the ability to hear with their acute hearing. Though she only shared the room with Kestrel, who appeared to still be meeting with Samuel, the others' room was adjacent to hers.

Daniel's pitched his voice to match hers. "You didn't come back!"

Shae all but dragged Daniel over to the far side of the room, away from the doorway.

"I wasn't planning on it!"

Daniel stared at her in the dark. She was surprised to see a look of hurt in his eyes. She figured he would be happy she was gone.

"What? Why?" She wasn't mistaken, because the hurt was evident in his voice.

Shae sighed and sat on the edge of the bed.

"Daniel." She glanced away from him. "We are not good for each other. This . . . this . . . thing . . ." Shae turned back and motioned to him and to herself. "It is poison. You are better off without me and I am better off without you."

"I don't understand, Shae." His voice was soft with a hint of uncertainty to it. "We are linked. There is no me without you, or you without me." He sat down on the other corner of the bed, close to her, but not too close.

Shae peered down at her hands and shifted between entwining her fingers and pulling them apart. "Yes. We will always be linked, but that doesn't mean we have to be together."

Daniel remained quiet for a long while, and Shae felt no desire to break the silence.

After a bit, Daniel spoke. "Who are these people?"

Though he didn't specify, Shae knew who he meant.

"Friends. Well. Sort of. They are like me. Like us." She stumbled over her explanation, uncertain as to how to explain who these people were. Mostly because she was uncertain as to who they were herself.

"I sensed fear from you earlier." She met his gaze fully and he continued. "Did they hurt you? Did they force you to go with them?"

Shae snorted. "You mean, like what you did?"

Daniel winced.

The edges of her lips curled down as she thought of Blain. "There are those, within the group, who I do not like." She thought of Sarah, and Kestrel and the way she treated Shae with kindness. A soft smile crept upon her lips.

"There are others though I like and who are nice to me." She looked up at Daniel, her face awash with a sense of optimism. "Do you know what that is like for me, Daniel? To have people be nice to me?" Again, he flinched, but it didn't stop her. "Do you know how long it has been since I was treated like a human being? To have someone who truly seems like they care about me and how I am feeling?"

As much as she tried to stop herself, tears pooled in the corner of her eyes before tumbling down her cheeks to land on the bed sheets.

Daniel regarded her, his expression soft, the muscles in his face slack and his eyes held a shimmer of their own. Whatever had happened between them had at least in some way, brought his humanity back. What she felt for him was a broiling sea of confusion, a tumbled mass of emotions, cascading in a turbulent froth. Anger. Hate. Need. Revulsion. Pain. Obsession. She wanted him dead, but she would die without him.

"You need to go," she told him. "I haven't told them about you, and I won't. I don't want you to get caught up in what is happening here. Go home, Daniel." She reached out and laid a hand on his arm. "You know you don't need to change if you choose not to. Live your life. Forget about me. Forget about all of this."

Daniel shook his head. "I can't, Shae."

"Yes, you can," she insisted. "In fact," she poured her will into her next statement, "Go. Leave, Daniel, and don't come back here."

Daniel went stiff. Slowly he stood; his eyes never left hers as he backed away from her to the door. His movements were rigid, like he was fighting every movement, and Shae imagined he was. Daniel didn't want to leave her, but she left him no choice. She had enacted her will upon him, and whether he liked it or not, he had to obey.

"Don't make me do this, Shae," Daniel pleaded as he opened the door to leave.

Shae hardened her resolve. This was for the best. For both of them.

"It's already done, Daniel."

He shut the door as he left.

# *Chapter Eleven*

"So," Mike began, drawing out the word, "you want us, to become like you?"

Mike sat on the armrest of the sofa in his apartment, one leg resting on the ground, the other propped up, folded at the knee on the sofa cushion. Beside him sat Beth. They were both looking at Stephanie with a fair amount of skepticism at her proposal.

"Look," Jason sat forward in the chair he had dragged over from the kitchen table, as she rested in the other cushioned chair in the room. There were modest sitting arrangements here, but that was the simple life of college students. "I know this must seem like an outlandish suggestion."

"I'll say," Mike interjected, but Jason pressed on. "But if you understand what we face. I think. Well, I think you will want to join us."

"What do we face?" Beth, Stephanie had noticed, sat next to Mike on the sofa. Not just next to Mike. But, *next* to Mike. There was barely three inches in between the two of them on a sofa which sat four. Something had happened while Jason and she were gone from school. Something she was going to get Beth to tell her about later.

They had arrived that afternoon and Jason had called Mike to tell him they were coming over and they needed to talk to him. She had done the same with Beth, suggesting they meet at Mike's and Jason's old apartment. When they had arrived, Beth was already there ahead of them. Stephanie began to suspect Beth had already been there. She chose to table that thought for the moment as they had more pressing concerns.

"This is going to sound really out there." She gave them an apologetic look, as if to say, sorry for being about to sell you on some wacky shit.

"You mean like you being a Werefox? Or you infecting your boyfriend and making him into a Werefox too? Or you almost killed him in the process?" Beth listed off these in a flat tone.

"Well . . ." Stephanie realized Beth had a point, but still, what she was about to tell them was more bizarre than that.

"When Jason and I left, we did so because we felt a, for lack of a better word, summons."

"A what?" Mike's face scrunched up in incomprehension.

"A summons," Jason repeated. "Like a . . . pulling. We both felt it. So, we went to where it pulled us to." Jason turned toward her, and she nodded to him to continue.

"When we got there, we stumbled onto a fight."

Both Beth and Mike straightened at this. It wasn't as if they weren't paying attention before, but now, they were both fully focused on what Jason said.

Jason looked at them and then off to the side; his mouth opened and closed several times as he seemed to be trying to find a way to explain what happened next. Stephanie decided to intervene.

"The long and short of it is, there were other Weres there and not like us. There was a Were . . . er . . . snake, a Werecrocodile and two Werebears. There was also two women, who as it turns out are Druids from ancient Celt, who have been resurrected, or reborn, or whatever, and are now waging war against each other and we are their warriors.

"That is why I became a Werefox. My ancestor was one and fought alongside one of the Druidesses and so when she came back, the power came

back. Same as the others. Though some are on the side of the other Druidess."
All of it came out in a rush. Her rapid-fire assault of words rocked Mike and
Beth back and by the end, Mike had slid down beside Beth on the couch and
they were both, pressed against the back of the couch as if some weight held
them there. Their eyes were wide, their mouths open, and speechless.

Beth recovered first.

"Umm . . . O.K. So that was a lot to process."

Beth rested a hand on Mike's leg and quickly moved it off, but
Stephanie caught it and raised eyebrows at her. It was hard to tell with Beth's
dark skin tone, but Stephanie believed she blushed. Beth shrugged, and a slight
smile crept upon her lips.

"The point is," Jason began, "One of the Druidesses wishes to destroy
civilization and she is prepared to use Weres to do so. She will use the ones she
has on her side to spread lycanthropy to as many people as she can in order to
create an army." He let out a sigh. "So, we need to do this as well." A soft smile
lifted the edges of his mouth. "We immediately thought of you two as possible
recruits."

Mike and Beth were silent for a long time, neither looking at them or
each other, but looking elsewhere, as if searching for the right words to say.

"Why?" Mike said finally.

Stephanie eyed him and cocked her head. "Why what?"

Mike glowered, an expression he seemed to use, often.

"Why would you think of us? I mean, I have never given you the notion
that I'm a fighter, or that I would like to fight." He gave an exasperated grunt.
"I'm in college, dammit. I have my whole life in front of me and you want me to
abandon that, to physically change who I am, for what? Someone else's war?"
He stood and began pacing. "I'm sorry, I know that you guys are in this now;
your lives have already been changed by what you have become, and maybe,
for you, this all makes sense, but not for me."

"They will come for everyone, eventually," Stephanie replied calmly.

Mike wheeled on her. "We have armies for this!"

Stephanie was silent for a time, then stood and went to the kitchen.

Mike glanced to Beth as she left and raised his hands in a questioning shrug. Beth responded with her own shrug.

Stephanie returned from the kitchen with a sizable knife and approached Mike. When she came within a few feet of him, she took the knife and dragged it across her upper forearm, slicing skin, muscle and fascia. Blood flooded the area around the cut.

"Jesus!" Mike exclaimed and began looking around for something to stop the bleeding.

"Mike!" Stephanie demanded, "Look." Reluctantly, Mike turned back to her.

Stephanie thrust out her arm and everyone watched as the wound quickly repaired itself from the inside out. Muscle reformed and reknitted, arteries and blood vessels sent tendrils out to grasp at the strands of their severed pieces to reconnect and the skin regrew and closed, leaving not a scar.

Mike had been told about their healing of course, but she knew hearing about something was not the same as seeing it. Mike needed to see what this all meant.

"Now tell me, Mike. What will our armies do to people like me?" She motioned to Jason, who still sat where she had left him. He hadn't moved when she had cut herself, for he understood what she had been up to. "Jason here took a shot to the chest at almost point blank range from a shotgun and has no residual scars from it. I saw a column of stone, which almost certainly weighed a ton, land on the back of a Werebear and he shrugged it off."

Stephanie shook her head. "We are not like soldiers on the battlefield that once you shoot us, we are down. No. We get back up. They can't stop us;

107

they don't have the power. We are the only ones between them and the destruction of the world, Mike. It is what we were made for."

"We understand if you don't wish to involve yourselves," Jason told them. "It's just, well, you are our closest friends and we wanted you to be a part of this."

"We know it is asking a lot," Stephanie added. "We just know that this world is on the verge of something it is not ready for, and by the time they are, it may be too late."

Jason frowned and put his hands on his hips but didn't immediately respond.

Stephanie realized Beth had been quiet this whole time, allowing Mike to do all the talking, which frankly, was uncharacteristic of her.

"Beth?"

Her friend looked up. She had been lost in thought it seemed. Beth shifted uncomfortably as everyone turned to her. She cast a furtive glance at Mike before returning Stephanie's gaze.

"I will join you, lil sis."

"What!?" This clearly wasn't the response he had been expecting from her.

She sighed and turned in her seat to face Mike squarely. "Look, you've said your peace and now I'm going to say mine."

Mike's mouth closed with a snap.

Beth nodded in approval before starting again. "I trust Stephanie and if she believes that this world is in for a fight, then I believe her. I don't want to run the risk of being attacked by one of these bad Weres, only to then turn into one of them and lose control of myself." She grimaced at the thought. "I would rather choose the way I'm going to fight and which side I will fight on."

Beth held out her hand to Mike and after a moment, he lowered his head, moved to her and took her hand.

Out of the corner of her eye, she saw Jason's eyes bulge and his mouth open slightly. Obviously, the earlier clues of Mike's and Beth's relationship had been lost on him.

"I understand if you don't want to do this, Mike. I do, and I won't care for you any less. But, for me, I want to do this."

She reached out and stroked his arm with her other hand and offered him a sad smile.

Mike stared at her long and hard, as if searching for some way to chip away at her resolve, to turn her from this course of action. He apparently couldn't find any.

"Fine. What do you need for us to do?" Mike capitulated.

Stephanie glanced at Jason to see he was as surprised as she at Mike's reversal.

Beth on the other hand, positively glowed with an enormous smile.

Jason gave a mischievous smile, "Oh, this next part you're going to love. We have to scratch you with our claws."

"Then," Stephanie continued with an equally mischievous smile, "you are going to almost die."

Mike groaned.

Stephanie stepped into the bathroom and leaned against the doorframe as Beth fixed her makeup.

"So?"

Beth pretended innocence. "So, what?"

"Oh please! You. Mike! Come on big sis, dish!"

Still pretending innocence Beth finished up her makeup without responding. The moment she finished though, she spun around, a big smile on her face.

"I know! Right? I didn't see it happening until it happened!"

"Well, tell me! Everything," Stephanie pleaded with glee.

"Well. When you and Jason spirited off with almost no    information . . ."

Stephanie rolled her eyes at the attempt to make her feel guilty, then rolled her hand to indicate Beth should move on.

Beth smiled teasingly. "When that happened, me and Mike started communicating more often as we kept checking to see if either of us had heard anything. Then one night he invited me over for a drink so we could talk about what had happened to you guys, and well, we talked about more than that. We laughed and joked with each other, and well . . . One drink led to another, and then one thing led to another." Beth's smile turned to a naughty smirk.

"Ah, so one of those drunken hook-ups you were always warning me not to fall into . . .?"

It was Beth's turn to roll her eyes and Stephanie gave her a sweet smile back.

"Yeah, well, it's just that I knew you would never forgive yourself for doing so." Beth lifted her head imperiously. "I, on the other hand, wouldn't be bothered by it."

"Hmm hmm," Stephanie murmured knowingly.

Beth's eyes became slits as she peered quizzically at Stephanie's response.

"Anyway . . .?" Stephanie prompted.

"Right." Beth's eyes widened again in excitement. "So, after that night," she smiled again naughtily, "which was fun, by the way. We just sorta fell into this . . . thing. We hang out, we make out, we . . . do other things …"

"Ugh. I get it. You like fucking him!"

"Lil Sis! Language!"

Stephanie attempted to convey as much of a "give me a break" expression as she could into her look and stance.

110

After a minute of feigned indignation, Beth relented. "Yeah. I like fucking him."

They stared at each other for a moment and broke out laughing.

When the laughter subsided, Beth turned serious.

"I really like him, lil sis. I didn't think I would, but I do."

Stephanie moved to her 'big sis' and gave her a long hug.

"I'm happy for you. I really am. Mike seems like a good guy, if a little dour. And he clearly likes you, otherwise he wouldn't have agreed to do this thing."

Beth lips dropped at the corners. "I know. I feel bad about it. He clearly doesn't want to do this but is only doing it because I want to do it.

"I'm just afraid to tell him not to, because I don't want to do this alone."

This admission shocked Stephanie. Beth was one of the most fearless people she knew. If it scared Beth this much, perhaps she should reconsider asking her to do this.

"Look, Beth . . ."

Beth held up her hands to forestall anything Stephanie was about to say.

"I still want to do this, lil sis. I understand what is at stake here. But I would be lying if I didn't say it scared the crap out of me. Not only the having to die first, but also the life being changed for, like, ever."

Stephanie offered up a small smile. "Not forever big sis. You will be free as soon as I am dead."

"Why would you say something like that!?" Beth's tone was a mixture of fear and anger.

Stephanie shrugged. "I'm not a fighter, Beth. What we face. The things we face. This isn't a game. This is life and death." Stephanie felt a chill steal into her as she contemplated her own demise. "We faced only two of these monstrosities. Two and Kestrel. I have no doubt in my mind if Hank and Sim hadn't shown up . . . we wouldn't be having this conversation."

Beth gave her a flat stare. "As reassuring talks go, this one sucks ass."

Stephanie couldn't help herself and snorted out a laugh. Beth chuckled along. "Sorry. I just don't want you to be under any illusions about what we face out there."

Beth nodded. "I get it, lil sis. I get it. But the way I see it, if we let them have a free hand and don't check them now . . . well, instead of facing a half dozen of them, we will be facing hundreds, maybe thousands."

Stephanie couldn't argue the point and truth be told, it shored up her own misgivings about entering this war.

"Well, I'm glad I will be having my big sis along for the ride."

Beth hugged her. "I wouldn't have it any other way, lil sis."

The plan was simple. Stephanie would shift and would create a small cut into each of them in order to pass the lycanthropy on. Mike initially protested, but when Stephanie explained that if Jason cut him, he would be less powerful than Beth, who would have gotten her lycanthropy from a True. She would be a Pure and he would be just a Were. Or at least, that was how Sylvanis explained it.

Mike wasn't about to let his new girlfriend be more powerful than him. It wasn't, as he explained it, he couldn't handle her being a strong person, only how would he 'protect' her if he was weaker?

To Stephanie's surprise, Beth merely smiled and kissed him, instead of berating him for his use of classical gender roles. Stephanie could do naught but shake her head. *It is amazing what love does to a person's identity.*

After she had given them lycanthropy, Jason and she would drive them to the hospital separately. Mike and Beth had not been too keen on this idea, but after Jason reasoned with them that two people showing up at the hospital together, going into cardiac arrest at nearly the same time would draw too much suspicion. They were already risking enough by going to the same hospital. The same hospital Jason had gone to where he had an unexplained heart attack as well.

They decided to wait until the next day, talking long into the night. Superficial words which shied away from the heavy topic that hung like a dense fog which made it impossible to see anything else. Exhaustion took each of them in turn and they fell asleep.

Light stole into Mike's and Jason's apartment, a soft light, dawn's timid approach upon the sleeping group. Stephanie rose first, as these days she needed little sleep. Jason was quickly up beside her and they made their way noiselessly to the kitchen to make them all breakfast.

The sound of sizzling bacon and the scrape of a turner on a pan as eggs were flipped and scrambled were enough to wake the other two. Sleepy and bleary eyed, the couple walked like a pair of zombies into the kitchen to briefly say good morning before stumbling over to the couch and snuggling together, their eyes closed in either an attempt to sleep, or outright sleep.

After a moment, a soft snoring could be heard from the couch. As to whom it was, Stephanie couldn't guess, but she offered Jason a beaming smile at the pair. She felt good about the two of them. She knew she was being a little selfish, as with Beth and Mike paired up, Jason and she would not feel awkward showing affection around them.

Stephanie sidled up next to Jason, who turned the heat off on the eggs and started transferring them to a plate. She wrapped her arm around his waist and pressed herself against the side of him, prompting him to look down at her.

She pouted her lips and he answered with a pleasant, soft kiss before disentangling himself and getting the eggs taken care of before they burned.

Stephanie let him go, but not before harrumphing, to let him appreciate she hadn't wanted him to go. Jason gave her an apologetic smile as he turned and moved to the kitchen table to distribute the scrambled eggs to the four plates Stephanie had placed on the table earlier.

As Stephanie watched him go, a warm full feeling enveloped her. She felt close to bursting with how much she loved him. This whole thing still seemed like a dream to her. She knew it was the same for him as well. They had longed for each other in shy solitude for so long. When they breached the wall that they had individually and unnecessarily put between each other, it was like two worlds had been spinning in opposite directions only to stop in the one spot where everything lined up perfectly.

She let out a soft sigh, and Jason glanced at her quizzically and she grabbed the bacon and moved to join him, giving him a quick kiss on the cheek.

"Whatcha thinking?" he asked.

"Oh, you know." She sat down.

"I love you, too." Jason sat next to her and side-eyed her.

Stephanie didn't look at him but gave a knowing smile.

They ate quietly so as not to wake the others. As they were finishing up their breakfast. Beth rose and joined them.

"Will I be as wakeful as you in the morning after this?"

"Yep," Stephanie told her. "One of the perks."

Beth grunted. "Is it?" She unceremoniously began to devour her eggs.

Mike fared a little better, pouring himself, and Beth a cup of coffee as he made his way over. Sitting down heavily, he grabbed a piece of bacon and chomped down on the end, chewed, swallowed and chased it down with a healthy gulp of hot coffee.

"Morning."

"Morning, Mike."

"Morning."

Beth leaned into him a moment and back in a silent 'good morning'.

Finished, Stephanie and Jason sipped at their own coffee while they waited for Beth and Mike to eat and wake completely.

When at last everyone was done, they sat in silence for a time. Now it had come time to do what they were going to do, no one wanted to be the one to initiate it. In the end, it was Mike who stepped up to the plate.

"Well. Might as well get on with it." Mike stood and faced Stephanie.

She gave him a nod and stood, moving to the middle of the main room to allow her space to shift. Even after all this time and shifting several times in front of both of them, she still felt self-conscious. Steeling herself, she pictured herself in Werefox form and felt the tell-tale snap of bones and burning sensation which came with her body's rapid transformation into her hybrid form.

The pain, distant now, felt as if it happened to someone else and they were describing it to her. Her discomfort now came more from never having wanted this power to begin with.

Though it had been Mike who had moved them to proceed, it was Beth who strode over to Stephanie now. Standing before her, Beth stared up at her with a mix of fear and awe on her wide-eyed face. It was more fear than awe as Stephanie could see Beth visibly shaking. Stephanie, once again, was about to call the whole thing off. She couldn't bear the frightened look Beth gave her at this moment.

At that moment, a hard resolve came over Beth and she thrust out her arm, the agreed area Stephanie would cut. Stephanie looked hard at Beth, waiting for her resolve to crumble, but Beth thrust out her arm again as if knowing what Stephanie waited for. Stephanie sighed, reached out and made a quick drag of a clawed finger across part of Beth's arm. She was precise so it wouldn't damage anything more than needing some stitches.

Beth gasped and clamped her hand over the cut. Jason cut Mike off as he moved over with a sterile pad and gauze, sitting her down and quickly tended to the cut. Tears leaked out of the corner of Beth's eyes as Jason wrapped her arm up, but she made no further sounds. Mike hovered over her like a hen protecting her chick from the fox, which Stephanie supposed, was an apt simile.

When Jason finished, he stood and moved away from Beth and Mike took his place, squatting down in front of Beth.

"Are you O.K.?"

Beth wiped the tears from her cheeks. "I'll be fine. It just hurt like a bitch, that's all." She smiled. "Your turn."

Mike grimaced but stood and moved over to stand in front of Stephanie. If someone could be less pleased about their situation than Mike, Stephanie didn't see how. Mike seemed to be in a perpetual dour state. Too serious most times, but the expression upon his face now was like someone on death row.

"You don't need to do this, Mike," she growled.

Mike glanced back at Beth then back at her.

"Yeah, I do." He held out his arm for her to cut.

Stephanie felt more and more like this whole idea of hers and Jason's to recruit these two to the cause was the wrong thing to do, but she didn't think she could back out now, not after already giving lycanthropy to Beth.

Once again, she reached out with a sharp clawed finger and cut Mike's arm. A slice of skin. It was a moment before blood started to well out of it. Mike sucked in a breath between clenched teeth as Jason stepped over and clamped a pad onto his arm and wrapped it in gauze.

116

After Jason finished with Mike, Beth pushed him aside to move in and give Mike a long, deep hug. Their bodies seemed to fit so nicely together with little space to be found between them. With Stephanie's acute hearing she caught Beth whispering to Mike. "Thank you. I love you." Her voice trembled and Stephanie was sure she cried a little.

Mike held her for a long moment and Stephanie shifted back and stepped over to Jason. "We need to take them to the hospital. I am unsure of how long it will be before their bodies try to reject the lycanthropy."

Jason nodded and audibly picked up Mike's car keys. Beth disentangled herself from Mike and moved past him, not looking at Jason or Stephanie. She dragged the uninjured arm across her eyes and turned, offering a somewhat reassuring smile.

They spent the rest of the day wasting time and doing nothing but spending time together. It would be some time before they would need to go to the hospital in order to ensure they would be there when the rejection set in. Stephanie waited till dusk before suggesting they should head to the hospital. Beth hopped up, eager to get going.

"Right. Let's get going." She moved over to Stephanie and handed her the keys to her vehicle. It would be better if neither Mike nor her drove as they might go into cardiac arrest on the way to the hospital.

Beth gave Mike one last long hug before joining Stephanie as Mike joined Jason and they left the apartment to drive separately to the hospital.

They were silent on the car ride over. There was nothing more to say. The weight of what would happen next lay like an oppressive blanket over them, stifling any conversation.

The next few hours were spent sitting in the ER, filling out insurance paperwork and medical histories. Stephanie and Beth busied themselves texting Jason and Mike accordingly. A nurse came in after what seemed like an eternity and stapled up Beth's arm, explaining all the while how she had cut herself long enough to warrant stitches, an inch or so less and they would have simply changed bandages and sent her on her way.

Beth smiled tritely at the nurse, knowing full well it had been their intent all along to need stitches to maximize the longevity of the time they would be in the hospital, so when the attack came, they would still be there.

A short while later there came a bustle outside their little emergency waiting room, as nurses and doctors ran by. Beth's eyes were wide with worry and she gripped the sheets of her hospital bed so hard her knuckles were a soft pink. Mike was dying.

# *Chapter Twelve*

Stephanie grabbed her phone and immediately texted Jason, but he didn't respond. Beth also attempted to text Mike to no avail. This was it. They both knew it. Mike had gone into cardiac arrest and now it was only a matter of time before he came through, or Stephanie gave no more thought to that outcome.

Whatever happened in a different part of the ER wing, they would find out when Jason or Mike replied to them, and they could do nothing but wait.

"How are you feeling?" Stephanie glanced at Beth.

"How am I feeling? How do you think I'm feeling? My boyfriend, the man I love may be dead, or dying . . . somewhere in this hospital, and I can only sit here, waiting for it to happen to me next!"

Stephanie examined her feet and shuffled them. "I told you that you didn't need to do this."

"Well, you didn't make it seem like I had much of a choice!"

Stephanie knew the words were said out of a place of fear. A place where she might lose her new love, or worse, lose her own life, but they stung just the same. She had pitched this whole idea and had sold it as their only real option to survive what came next. She had used fear tactics and pressure to win them over to the idea. Mike had seen through it, but in the end had chosen to do what Beth had decided, out of love.

Now there was no turning back.

A feeling came closer and closer and it took her a moment to recognize it as Jason's presence. He came their way. Stephanie sat up and Beth responded immediately by getting out of the bed and heading toward the drape which covered the entrance to their room. When she got to it, Jason ducked in and came up short as Beth was right there. She grabbed both his arms and the look on her face, one of such pleading it almost broke Stephanie's heart.

Jason smiled. "He's fine. They were able to immediately revive him, and he is resting comfortably." His lips straightened. "Well as comfortable as he can be considering that the same will be happening to you soon."

Beth wasn't listening though, she had stumbled away from Jason almost immediately, tears of relief streamed down her face.

Stephanie couldn't keep the tears of relief from her own eyes. So much had been riding on this and now they were halfway there. Moving over to Jason she placed a hand on his chest and peered up at him. He covered her hand with his own and offered a soft smile down at her. She could see the relief plain on his face.

Mike was his closest and best friend and while Jason had agreed with this whole idea of recruiting the two of them, he had his reservations. He had voiced them once, on the way back to college. He had agreed with the necessity of recruiting people but had worried at what this would do to the two people they both cared for.

If he had further reservations coming in to today, he kept them to himself, which was for the best. Any further questioning of the plan from him and Stephanie would have abandoned it without looking back.

The sound of equipment slamming into other equipment brought their heads around as Beth had collapsed upon the floor. Stephanie quickly crossed the room and lifted Beth effortlessly onto the bed as Jason ducked out and called for help.

Nurses ran into the room and they quickly ushered Stephanie and Jason out as nurses, from a freshly disturbed anthill, swarmed over the area. A doctor arrived shortly afterward, so Jason moved her farther down the hallway to keep out of everyone's way. The cacophony of noise coming from the room, the sound of machines beeping, the whine of defibrillator as it charged and the back and forth between nurses and the doctor made determining what was happening impossible. Even for someone with as good as hearing as Stephanie.

The sounds died down within the room. Words were spoken and though Stephanie heard them, they failed to take root in her brain. The doctor, a middle-aged Pakistani stepped out from the curtained room and stood unmoving for a long minute, before turning and searching her out.

Stephanie watched as he made his way down the hall toward her. He was a short, wiry man, whose black hair was ghosted with gray. His brown skin, heavy with wrinkles for someone his age, was devoid of all emotion as he came to stand before her.

"Ms. Boles?" His accent, while Pakistani, wasn't as thick as she had imagined it would be when she had first saw him.

He already knew she was Ms. Boles, so didn't wait for confirmation before continuing. "There is never an easy way to say this . . ."

He didn't get any further. Whatever muscles kept her standing ceased functioning, and she collapsed to the floor.

"Nooooo!" she cried out. "Noooooo!" Her heart, usually so full of hope and love, emptied. It was hollow. A numbness overcame her. Tears fell, and sobs wracked her, but she registered none of it. Her body responded to what had happened, but her brain had shut itself down. All she could focus on was the hallway leading back to Beth's room. Her view narrowed, hazy around the edges, so only a tunnel remained. A tunnel leading right to Beth. Her big sis. Who was now dead, and it was her fault.

121

She sensed his presence before he arrived. Her newly formed connection to a man who must hate her now. Now she had taken the woman he loved from him. He moved to stand before her, blocking her tunneled vision of the hallway to Beth's room, his back to her.

Distantly, she was aware of Jason moving to Mike's side.

"Mike . . ." Mike turned to him and Jason's words trailed off.

Mike moved away from them and to the curtained room which held Beth and he stopped. He stood looking in the room for a long time. At long last, he glared back at them, before turning and walking out of the hospital. She would be aware of where he went of course, but she buried the connection deep down. She would hide her presence from him. How she did it, she didn't understand, but she knew he would be unable to have a sense of her because of it. It was the least she could do for him.

How long she sat on the floor crying she wasn't sure. Jason squatted down beside her, saying something. Comforting words, she imagined. Useless words. Sylvanis had said the connection between who transmitted and who received lycanthropy was important to the survival of the one who received it. She had said, if the connection was strong, they would survive. There was only one other connection stronger in her life than Beth and hers. Sylvanis had lied. Or she had simply been wrong. It didn't matter. It wouldn't bring Beth back.

Stephanie collected herself and stood. She headed down the hallway to the one place in this world she wished she didn't have to go. What she wished didn't matter anymore. She needed to see. She needed to make this concrete. Her mind needed to accept this if she had any hope of moving past this. She understood this if only at a subconscious level.

With Jason by her side, she moved to the entrance of the room. The curtain was open enough for her to see Beth lying on the bed. She lay there so peacefully. Long, black, slightly wavy hair framed her face. Her cheeks, typically so round and full, were slack. A slight tinge of blue was evident upon her lips and in the shading of the skin on her fingers.

Jason stood at the entrance as she moved into the room and next to Beth. Gingerly, she took Beth's hand into hers, as if afraid to wake her, though she knew she wasn't asleep. Her hand felt cold and slightly stiff.

"Oh, big sis. I am so sorry." A sob broke free and she choked it back. "This was never supposed to happen. You were the strong one. The fighter."

Tears fell like a hard rain, full and torrential, to bathe her face, arm and shirt with their salty wetness. She ran her arm across her nose to deal with the mucus dripping from it. Her other hand never left Beth's.

Stephanie felt Jason's hand upon her arm, and she knew it time to go. Bending over, she kissed Beth's forehead. Felt the coldness of her skin. The life now gone from inside this amazing woman. Her friend. Her big sis. Stephanie's part in this war was as over as Beth's. The war was already lost to her and she felt no reason to continue in its fight.

# *Chapter Thirteen*

When they arrived at the hotel, it truly was a shit storm. Police had cordoned off the front of the hotel and there were barricades set up to prevent people from approaching. The red and blue of cop car lights danced around the adjacent buildings.

"What the hell?" Ben said to no one in particular as they pushed their way up against the barricade to see better.

Kat sidled up next to him. "I thought you said the off-duty cop was going to sit tight and wait for you to get back?"

Ben continued to stare at the commotion of cops running from one point inside the cordon to another. Others, stationed around the perimeter, were keeping people out, forcefully if necessary. "Something else must have happened. Or, I took too long in returning and he called it in."

Sylvanis approached on Ben's right. "What should we do?" It didn't surprise Kat, Sylvanis would ask this of Ben. Sylvanis, in truth, knew little of the world. Kat imagined, when it came to matters of police, she knew even less. If Kat was being honest with herself, she didn't know much as well.

Ben continued to search the area till he seemed to find what he searched for. Kat saw the man now. He was a tall, youthful man, with sandy blond hair, his face all straight lines and flat. Clearly the man worked out as Kat could see clear muscle definition beneath the man's uniform. She liked what she saw.

"PASKINS!" Ben shouted, trying to be heard over the din of the crowd.

"PASKINS!" The man started to look around and Ben frantically waved his hands to get the man's attention. At long last, Paskins saw Ben and hurried over.

The moment he got there; Ben lit into him. "What in God's name did you do, Paskins?"

For a moment, Paskins visibly reeled back under Ben's verbal onslaught, but quickly recovered.

"My job." He practically growled out the words, but softened his tone and leaned in. "Regardless, it wasn't me. The precinct got a call about a hostage situation. Something about a young girl being held against her will. Descriptions of the hostage takers matched the descriptions of some of the people you told me about."

Ben shook his head. None of this made sense. "You don't know what you are dealing with here, officer. This is not what it might seem like. A lot of people could die because of this."

Paskins narrowed his eyes at Ben. "What do you mean? How dangerous are these people? Do they have weapons? A bomb? Dammit man! Tell me something!"

Ben turned to them, ignoring Paskins' questions. He seemed completely at a loss for what to do and helplessly held out his hands. "I don't know what we can do to avert a bloodbath now."

Sylvanis took a step towards him and took his hands in hers. He focused on her face. "You must get us into that building, Ben. You are the only one who can."

Ben studied her for a long moment. He seemed more tired now than he had when Kat first met him. Slowly, resolve entered his features and he rounded back on Paskins. "Take us to your captain, Paskins."

Paskins gaped from Ben, to the rest of them.

"I can take you." Making a point of singling Ben out with his comment.

"You can take all of us," Ben cut in, leaving no room for argument.

It looked like Paskins might give him one anyway, but in the end, he moved the barricade out of the way and motioned them in.

Paskins led them around the outside perimeter. The police had set up an area where they had positioned some cruisers to offer cover in case of a shootout, and Paskins led them behind it so as not to come between the officers standing there and the front of the building. Though it took them a little longer to make it to their destination, the fact they followed without complaint or deviation, went a long way in convincing Paskins of their integrity, she imagined.

Near the back corner of the cordoned area sat a black, mobile command center. To Kat, it looked like an armored motorhome with all the trimmings. Two satellite dishes kept their post on opposite ends of the camper, while a sizable, collapsible antenna sprouted from the middle. What windows it did have were tinted so dark as to be completely opaque. At least from this side, Kat imagined.

Paskins marched them right up to the door of the vehicle and opened it. Without preamble, he stepped right up and into the command center. Ben glanced back at the four of them, turned and climbed up the little metal folding staircase extending from the bottom of the vehicle.

Sylvanis came next. Kat followed her, and Sim and his father came right after her. The vehicle was cramped, especially with the addition of the five of them. Paskins and two others occupied the interior. Kat was impressed with the setup. On both sides there were several computer stations with swivel chairs which were fastened under the counter, so they gave the appearance of floating if you eyed them a certain way. One corner of the center held a bank of small monitors, like security camera screens. At the other end, sat a caged off section which held an extensive variety of weaponry – shotguns, gas grenade launchers, tactical rifles and several sniper rifles.

Of the two others, only one looked like he could be the captain. Dressed in a suit and tie, he had black hair, shot with gray, combed back from his forehead, giving it plenty of volume. It carried a slight sheen which Kat realized was some form of hair gel the man used to keep his hair so perfectly coiffed. His skin was reddish brown, like bleeded leather. Kat wasn't sure if he was of Mexican descent, but he was clearly Latino.

The captain leaned over the shoulder of the other man there. They were both staring at one of the monitors. The captain held one half of a headphone up to his left ear. The other man was beefy looking, so hefty in fact, he dwarfed the chair he was sitting on like he was sitting at some grade school child's desk. He had dark, brown hair squeezed against his head by a set of headphones. A mic on a flexible stand jutted up from the countertop in front of them.

"Captain?" Paskins spoke tentatively.

"What is it, Paskins? As you can see, we're a little busy." The captain didn't bother looking up from the monitors.

"I think you are going to want to hear what this officer has to say. He has intimate knowledge of what is going on in the hotel."

The captain glanced their way. When he saw all of them standing there, he stood up straight, disapproval on his face.

"What is the meaning of this, Paskins? Why are there civilians in our command center?"

Paskins eyed them, pleading to them with a glance, as if to say, 'My ass is on the line here, so please have something to make my captain happy. Or at least, angry at you so he will forget about being angry at me'.

"Captain." Ben took a step forward. "I'm officer Ben Charles of the Sacramento PD. If you have men within the hotel, I suggest you have them retreat immediately."

The captain turned his frown on Ben.

127

"And why the hell would I do that, Officer? An officer, I might add, who isn't supposed to be doing police work inside my city, without my knowledge or permission."

Ben shifted uncomfortably under the man's gaze. Hell, even Kat felt uncomfortable, *this man can really glower.*

"Well. Ahem. Unless you want what happened on these streets a week or so ago to happen again." Some resolve entered Ben's voice. "Unless you want to lose officers again to the same monster who ripped through them before, I suggest you get them out of there. Now."

It was hard to say with the man's ruddy brown skin if he paled any, but it sure seemed like he did. He knew what Ben talked about. He knew all too well.

"That . . . monster. . . is in there?" The captain's voice had lost all the authority it had so clearly wielded only moments before and was now a quiet thing.

"Worse."

The captain stared at Ben for a long moment before turning to the other man at the console. "Get them back," he told him. "Get them all back, now!"

The other officer quickly relayed the captain's order and had to confirm it a second time to a confused SWAT team.

When the captain was certain his team was on its way out, he turned back to them. His voice had located its authority again.

"Explain how it could be worse, and while you are at it, explain who the rest of these people are."

Ben offered an apologetic smile. "This might take some time and it isn't going to be what you are going to want to hear."

It was indeed a tale the captain had not wanted to hear, considering how often he shook his head during the telling. He did, however, not interrupt

128

or question anything Ben told him. In the end, it was Sylvanis who convinced him to allow them to handle this situation. Which was astonishing, considering she looked barely old enough to drive.

"Captain, I know all that you have heard here tonight might seem fantastical to you, but I assure you, it is real. The danger is real." Her lips turned down slightly in a frown. "Your officers can't fight this enemy. They will die if you let them try. You know this, as they faced only one of these creatures." Kat watched how mesmerized by Sylvanis the captain was. No matter the age she appeared to be, Sylvanis was older than all of them. She had led armies. She had dealt with men like this captain long before Kat's great, great, great, great, great grandmother had been born.

"All I can tell you, Captain, is that we are on your side. That these people you see before you, including myself, can and will face this threat for you." She took some steps toward the man. She was such a diminutive figure. The captain, who wasn't a tall man by any standards, still seemed to loom over her.

"I ask that you trust us. To let your men know we are not the enemy here. No matter what they might see."

This seemed to register with the captain, and he glanced up at them with a look of understanding . . . and fear.

He glanced back down at Sylvanis. "Are you the tiger?"

She offered him a smile. "No, Captain. But she is here."

The captain gazed back up at them and Kat gave him a little wave. She saw his Adam's apple bob as he swallowed hard. Regardless of what Sylvanis had told him of them not being the enemy, Kat could tell the captain wasn't entirely convinced.

The captain stared hard at them for a long while, visibly weighing his options.

Whatever decision he had been going to make was interrupted by the other officer in the command center.

"Captain? Something is happening at the front of the hotel."

The captain wheeled around and bent over the monitor. After a moment, reluctantly, he motioned for Sylvanis to join him.

Gracefully, she moved to the monitor and bent to see what they had been looking at. On the monitor, Kestrel, three men, a woman and a young girl had stepped out of the hotel facing the police cordon. Sylvanis didn't see Syndor, or Samuel as he called himself these days, anywhere, but that didn't mean anything. He could still be inside, or he might have left already. The woman she recognized from Kat's description as Sarah, Clint's girlfriend. The three men were identified from Ben's encounter. The big, brute of a man was the True Boar. The handsome man, the True Croc. Next to the True Boar was a taller man, timid looking, who was almost certainly one of the Pures of the Boar. That left the young girl, whom from Ben's description was the True Rat. All were here except Samuel and one of the Pure Boars as far as she could tell. Studying them for a moment she glanced back at the rest of them.

"It's them," was all she said.

Kat grimaced. Show time.

# *Chapter Fourteen*

Kestrel woke her with some urgency.

"Shae. Something has happened. It's time to go."

The tone of Kestrel's voice woke her instantly and she sat up and got out of the bed in seconds.

"What is it?"

Kestrel frowned. "Trouble. There are police outside." She paused and gave a faint smile. "Nothing we can't handle."

Shae was a little uncomfortable with what that statement implied. Yes, she had killed people, and apart from that family, those she had killed had all deserved it. Killing police was an entirely different matter altogether.

Her hesitation must have been noticed as Kestrel moved up to her and rested her hands on her shoulders. "It's alright my dear. As I said, I will not make you do anything you don't want to do." Her smile was kind and her eyes caring. "You leave them to the rest of us. We were planning on leaving this morning anyway. Just the two of us."

Shae cocked her head. "Where are we going?"

"Remember? I said I had an important task for you, probably the most important of all?"

Shae nodded. She remembered.

"We are leaving to do that task. We just need to make it out of here in one piece."

Shae smiled. "I'm not worried. There is little they can do to me."

Kestrel nodded sadly. "True. But I am not like you. If I get shot. I will die."

That was the last thing Shae wanted to happen. "Stick with me. I will protect you."

Kestrel smiled at her but did not respond.

Motioning her out of the room, they joined Blain, Sarah, Gordon and Taylor.

She scanned around. "Where is Samuel and Joseph?"

"That's what I wanted to know," Blain demanded, his face flush with anger. This had apparently been discussed before she had arrived and not to Blain's satisfaction.

"They are taking care of something for me," was all Kestrel would say.

She turned to face all of them. "This . . . intervention by the police, steps up our timetable a bit. Blain, you know what you and Taylor need to do. Sarah will go with you, but you must deliver her to me where I told you and when. Gordon, you will accompany them."

Both men groaned at the prospect.

She rounded on them. "You will learn to work together. Enough of this," she stuttered over the words, trying to find the right ones, "dick measuring." Her uncomfortable use of the slang word was almost comical to Shae.

"No point in measurin'." Blain made an obscene gesture implying his length.

Kestrel sneered at him but turned to Gordon. She stepped close and put her hand on his chest. "I know this is unpalatable for you." Her voice, a bare whisper, was clear enough to Shae, and she could imagine the rest of them with their hearing. "You must go along with Blain," she continued. "Keep him in line and on point, but he is in charge."

Gordon made to say something, but Kestrel put a finger to his lips. "You know why this must be the way." A bit of steel entered her voice. "Don't make me explain it again."

Gordon searched her face for a moment before nodding.

Blain snickered. "That's right. I'm in charge."

Gordon ignored him.

Kestrel stepped away from Gordon and faced them all, once again.

"Right now, however, we need to make it out of the hotel. Most importantly, me and Shae must be allowed to escape relatively unnoticed."

Blain appeared about to ask a question, but the cold, hard stare Kestrel gave him, shut him up.

"When we get downstairs, Blain, Gordon, Taylor and of course, Sarah, I will need you to create as much mayhem as possible. Remember, if you must attack someone, make sure it is lethal. Eventually, they will learn to use those you turn to track you with the bond. It is best if we don't give them that opportunity just yet."

Shae got the impression this last bit seemed a little rehearsed and it seemed like everyone had heard it all before. But why she would repeat her instructions, Shae didn't understand. Reluctantly, the men nodded.

Sarah ignored them all.

Shae felt conflicted about Sarah. Of all the people here, except Kestrel and maybe Taylor, Sarah was the only one to be kind to her. It was clear Sarah was only here because of the bond to Blain and clearly didn't want to be here. Shae couldn't imagine the horror of being at Blain's beck and call, and if there was something Shae could have done to free Sarah, she would have. There wasn't. At least, not anything Shae could figure out anyway.

As they made their way through the hotel, it was clear the police had done their best to remove as many people from the hotel as they could. Occasionally, sounds could be heard coming from inside one of the suites, but for the most part, it was eerily silent. When the elevator reached the lobby, it was devoid of people. Blue, red, and bright white flittered across the bank of windows at the front of the lobby, informing them the police were entrenched outside.

She turned to Kestrel, "Why don't we just sneak out the back?"

Blain answered. "Because Rat, the police will have the back door covered as well. If we are to have any hope of covering yours and the Lady's escape, we need to hit them here and hit them hard."

Kestrel eyed Blain as if seeing him truly for the first time. She nodded, and Shae took it as acknowledgement Blain was right. Shae frowned. She would have rather Blain been wrong, so Kestrel could have shut him up again. She decided to take a stab at him instead.

"Thanks . . . pig."

He turned to her; his upper lip curled upward in a leering smile. Shae growled under her breath; angry her barb hadn't cut the way she had hoped.

Kestrel ignored the exchange and instead, straightened her back, swept her long raven color tresses back, the pieces of crystal she had woven into them clacking together. Once ready, she strode forward as regal as a queen. It was time for the world to meet Kestrel.

The world wasn't ready.

Flanked by Gordon and Blain and followed closely by Taylor, Sarah and herself, Kestrel reached the outside door and strode through it. It was a few hours before dawn and night still held its grip on the city. Not that you could tell from the multitude of lights illuminating the hotel.

Police cars were placed strategically behind the barriers and where police had once stood idly about waiting for something to happen, they were now lined up behind the cars, handguns pulled and pointed at their group.

Crowds of people lined the barricades watching what happened. Cellphones were raised above heads, snapping photos and taking videos of something they had no idea they were about to witness. All they knew was the police were here and something was going to happen. Never mind they might be caught in the crossfire. Social media needed their posts.

Kestrel had pulled up and now stood facing the police like they were her subjects. Shae watched her expectantly, as she had no idea what to expect. Kestrel opened her mouth to speak, but then clapped it shut, teeth snapping together audibly, and Shae saw something had caught Kestrel's attention, something which had her jaw clenched hard and put fire in her eyes.

Shae searched the scene for what had caused Kestrel's anger. After a moment, she thought she figured out what. A woman, no, a teenager, maybe four or five years older than she; hair like bleached wheat, long and flowing framed a soft oval face. She was pretty. She was young. And yet, she moved with a poise she had only seen from Kestrel.

This was Sylvanis, Shae realized. The sworn enemy of Kestrel.

There were others with her. A large, burly man, broad of chest and with thick arms. He had brown hair and bushy eyebrows. His face was blocky, and he had an oft broken nose. Beside him was a teenaged boy, tall and lanky, though he was building some bulk. It seemed to not fit him yet, as if he had yet to grow accustomed to it.

On Sylvanis' other side was a young woman. She was slight of build, with just enough curves. She had light tawny colored hair cropped short. Feminine lethality was the best way to describe her. Whereas the older man looked like brute force, she looked like calculated harm.

Next to her, but a step or two back, was a middle-aged man. He seemed somewhat familiar to her, as if she had seen him recently, though she couldn't figure out where. It seemed unlikely as she hadn't been anywhere in a few days.

135

The group moved forward, and the police moved the barricades, so they could step through. It wasn't difficult to figure out who the people next to Sylvanis must be. They were Sylvanis' Weres.

"Oh, shit." She knew what must happen next. Even though she had told Kestrel she wouldn't fight in her war, it seemed like she wasn't going to have a choice.

From some unseen cue, Blain, Taylor and Gordon shifted as one. One second three men stood there, the next, three monsters.

Terror ripped through the crowd.

Screams and shouts filled the night air as the throng of people got more than they had bargained for. Some fled, but more, gripped with panic, stayed to see what would happen next. Of course, most of them had seen the footage of what had happened in these streets not long ago. Some of them most likely hadn't believed what they had seen. They did now.

Sarah hadn't changed, and neither had Shae. She wasn't supposed to be a part of this. Kestrel and she would flee. That was the plan. Though, now Sylvanis was here, who knew what would happen? She watched as Sylvanis turned to one of the men behind her, the one Shae somehow recognized, and said something.

The man reached into his coat, pulled out a gun and aimed it at Kestrel, and fired.

# *Chapter Fifteen*

Simon stood next to his father and though he had power beyond anything these cops could handle, he still was afraid. A shiver had started at his upper arms and had migrated into his chest and to his lower jaw. It was all he could do to keep his teeth from clacking together and letting everyone realize how frightened of this scenario he was.

It had been one thing to arrive on the scene at Sylvanis' house and wade into the fight. That had happened with no planning and little thought to what would happen. He had plenty of time to think about what was about to happen here.

The Werecroc had shifted and Simon was all too familiar with that visage. He and Jason had fought that monster and while they had been able to deal with it, at least enough for it to retreat from them, he didn't look forward to facing off with it again.

The Wereboars were a new element, but he had seen the video as well. He had seen how merciless the True had been to Kat, Sarah and Clint. What he had subsequently done to those police officers had been . . . disturbing, to say the least. He hoped his father capable of dealing with him, because he didn't think any of the rest of them were.

The woman, Kestrel, had noticed them and she did not look happy. The scene sat frozen. There was two Wereboars and a Werecroc on the steps of the hotel. Kestrel, in all her beautiful fury, seemed uncertain as to what to do next.

The woman, Sarah and the girl, who seemed a few years younger than he, had yet to change. Both appeared unhappy about being there.

Now, there were three Weres that had made it clear they were in this fight. *Three of them for the three of us.* Of course, they had Sylvanis, but she would be negated by Kestrel, he imagined. There were two dozen Chicago police officers arrayed behind them who, hopefully, would only shoot at the enemy and not at just any Were.

They stood there, as if waiting for some signal as to what should happen next. Sylvanis turned slightly and spoke back to Ben.

"Ben, could you please take out your gun, and shoot that woman?" Her voice was devoid of feeling, as if she had merely asked him to hang up his coat after stepping in out of the rain.

The shiver returned, but this time it wasn't out of fear. Simon was reminded, though Sylvanis looked young – she wasn't. She had already lived a life. Had commanded armies, sent soldiers to die, had sent soldiers to kill.

Ben Charles reached into his coat and pulled out his gun, quickly pointed it at Kestrel, and fired.

It seemed to be the signal everyone had been waiting for.

The moment Ben's gun went off, the world went from being frozen to flooring the gas after dousing the engine with nitrous oxide.

As the bullet left the gun, the girl who had been standing next to Kestrel flew into motion. Throwing herself in front of Kestrel, her body shifted as she flew. Brownish fur covered her body, nose and mouth extruded forward to make her face pointy, rat-like. A pink, ringed tail flowed instantly from the girl's backside.

The bullet entered her left shoulder and blood spurted from the wound. The impact pitched her slightly, but she righted herself instantly. She now stood equal in height to Kestrel and blocked her completely. Which was good news for Kestrel, as the rest of the cops opened fire as well.

Still, Simon and the rest of them didn't shift or move.

As the Weres were riddled with bullets, they all staggered back as bullet after bullet entered their bodies. Kestrel, as vulnerable as she was, wisely kept herself behind the rat girl. Sarah was bent, down on one knee. Her arm held out before her bowed head. Bullets had torn the arm apart. Chunks of flesh were hanging loose, held on by a strip of skin here, a band of muscle there.

Blood rained down from the limb, but she had managed to protect her head, at least somewhat. Still, Simon could see pale white patches where bullets had careened off her skull, exposing the bone. In other places there were dark patches where the bullet had shattered the skull plate and entered the brain.

The others didn't fare any better as the sheer volume of ammunition being used, perforated their bodies. Holes sprouted everywhere over the creatures, puncturing abdomens, cheekbones, legs, and shattering kneecaps. If they had been anyone else, they would have died long ago. But Simon could already see signs of healing. The Boar seemed adapt at manipulating his healing, as bullet holes were closing almost as fast as they opened.

Sylvanis, mumbled something in some language Simon had never heard before. As she spoke, the ground beneath his feet began writhing.

Roots!

A webbing of roots spread out in a layer around the ground in which they stood. Twisted, gnarled things, like grotesque, misshapen snakes, spread out from Sylvanis. Simon had no idea what she was doing. Moments later, it became clear.

"*Talamh bris a-mach!*" A shout from Kestrel.

The ground bolted upwards all around them. People were launched skyward with chunks of pavement and concrete, a twisted geyser of flesh, rocks and debris. Vehicles were thrown into the air as well. Over three thousand-pound missiles lifted from the ground as if they weighed nothing. As Simon watched, people, vehicles and other items which had been unfortunate enough to have been in the vicinity of the spell – fell. Then sickening thuds of bodies collided with concrete, most of whom had been knocked unconscious from either the force of the upheaval, blunt force trauma from pieces of the road, or from the pain of having their bodies shredded from flying debris.

They were followed closely by a rain of vehicles and shattered pieces of concrete, crushing many of them. Bile rose in Simon's stomach as bodies were summarily demolished by falling metal. A police car landed trunk down and it hung motionless vertically for what seemed like an eternity before canting and landing on its roof. It rocked for a moment before settling.

Cracks spiderwebbed underneath them, and Simon braced himself for fear he would also be thrown upward, as the ground underneath their group attempted the same upheaval. The network of roots, which Simon had not understood before, revealed their purpose as they held to the concrete and pavement preventing it from shooting into the night sky. Sylvanis had thwarted Kestrel's spell. Simon glanced at her in time to see a sly smile play across her lips. She knew Kestrel all too well, it would seem.

Unfortunately, the roots had spread too slowly. Cops had been thrown into the air along with police vehicles. Simon glanced back to where Kestrel stood with her Weres. The momentary respite from the barrage of bullets had given them time to recover. Wounds closed in seconds. Dozens of bullets clinked to the ground as they were pushed from reconstructed muscle and skin. As quickly as the flesh had been destroyed, it healed.

The Boars and the Croc were on the move. But not at them.

The crowd who still lingered around the barricades had flinched back from the earlier eruption and were only now giving thanks it had missed them. Their words of thanks quickly turned to screams of terror as the monsters bore down on them. The two Boars went right, and the Croc went left.

"This is it guys," Kat stated. "After this, everyone will know who we are. There is no going back."

His father rolled his shoulders and the move was accentuated by him shifting to his bear form. "People are about to die, Kat."

Kat gave Hank a sidelong glance and smiled. "Just wanted to make sure everyone was on the same page." She shifted. Simon followed suit.

"Hank?" Kat started to stalk forward.

"Yeah?" He turned his head to regard her.

She met his eyes for a moment before turning back towards the awaiting fight. "Fuck that Boar up for me, please."

Hank growled his accent, shifting. "I got the big one. Sim, can you handle the smaller one?" Hank studied his son questioningly.

Anticipating how things were going to go down, Simon already moved to intercept the slightly smaller of the Boars, allowing his actions to answer his father's question.

"I'll take the Croc," Kat said confidently. "I hope," Simon heard her mutter less self-assuredly as she moved off to deal with the enormous lizard.

The corner of Blain's maw curled up in a semblance of a smile as he barreled towards the crowd of onlookers. This was what he enjoyed. Spreading terror and fear. He caught Taylor out of the corner of his eye charging a different part of the crowd. Reluctant as Taylor might be, he still did what needed to be done. He *would* do what needed to be done, because he feared what Blain would do to him if he didn't. As close to indestructible as they may be, they still could feel pain.

Thoughts of Taylor vanished as he came upon his first victims, a couple. The man looked to be in his early twenties, with a brown curly mop of a hair which sprouted from his head like some kind of mushroom. *What a tosser.* The man had a doe-eyed expression as he turned and ran past his girlfriend, a black girl oddly asymmetrical with a narrow upper body and wide hips. She gave a look of surprise, mixed with outrage as her boyfriend moved past her, leaving her to face this nightmare alone.

That look vanished quickly.

Blain swerved to move past her as well, but as he did, he slammed his hand into her throat. An audible snap. Her head lolled listlessly. He continued the motion with his hand, lifting her as he passed. He came to an abrupt halt and with all his might, flung her at her fleeing boyfriend. The human missile struck him in the back with such force, it shattered his spine and they both collapsed into a heap.

Swinging around, Blain surveyed the scene around him. People were fleeing from him in all directions. A boy, about ten, huddled down against a car. He cried, his hands to either side of his face, his fingers, splayed on top of his head as if, by hunkering down, he could weather the storm that was Blain.

He was wrong.

Striding to the boy, he reached down and wrapped his clawed hand over the boy's head, lifting him with ease. The boy wailed now, clawing at Blain's hand. Blain almost laughed at the idea this boy thought he could hurt him. He heard a scream.

"NOOOOOOO!!!! Please!? Don't hurt him!"

He saw her now. A woman, presumably the boy's mother. He had her look. Blain sneered. Mothers were all weak. If this one wanted to save her son, she should be throwing herself at him. As Blain rounded on her, he caught sight of something which truly brought a smile to his tusked mouth. Running towards him from beyond the woman was a monstrous Bear. *Now, the true test begins.*

As the Bear started to pass the woman, Blain raised the struggling boy up and out before him. The mother and the Bear could only watch in horror as Blain collapsed his fist, crushing the boy's skull with an audible crunch.

The woman screamed again, the sound ripe with the grief and agony of loss.

The Bear roared!

Blain tossed the boy's lifeless body aside and readied himself to meet the Bear.

$$\text{꩜}$$

Kat sprinted across the road littered with debris, bodies and overturned cars. The Croc had already reached the crowd. With massive claws, he ripped through bodies like a scythe through wheat. Blood sprayed everywhere. The heavy scent of copper and emptied bowels permeated the air, especially to Kat's keen senses.

As she watched, he drove his claws deep into the back of woman who had been running heedless of where she went. Her panic had been so overwhelming, she ran within striking distance of the Croc, who, with clawed hand buried up to his thick wrist in her back, swung his hand back so quickly, it tore through her body and exited out her side. Her left lung, stomach, intestines were sliced clean through. She died before she hit the ground.

Kat angled herself so she could cut him off before he could get to his next victim. Urging her body to give her a boost of speed, she felt it respond and the ground became a blur beneath her feet.

Leaping she stepped lightly onto an overturned car and used it to launch herself the rest of the distance. Flying out in a high arc, she had timed herself perfectly. Straightening her body, she tightened her muscles to increase the strength of the impact when she collided with the Croc.

The beast loomed over another woman. She had collapsed on the ground, feet desperately trying to gain purchase as she backpedaled away from him. One of her hands, outthrust, held a taser, its blue lightning sparking across the front of the pathetically small weapon.

Kat's feet caught him right below his left armpit. The impact jarred her bones, but sent the Croc flying away from the poor woman. Using the forceful stop in her momentum and the momentary solidness against her feet to push backwards, she threw her legs over to do a back flip, landing on her feet, hands pressed to the street, tiger tail whipping this way and that.

The Croc, unsuspecting of the aerial attack was knocked off his feet and momentarily airborne; his bulk, however brought him down quickly and he skidded and rolled to a stop a short distance away.

This was the first time Kat got a decent look at the Croc as it righted itself. It topped her by a few feet. Not to mention it outweighed her by at least a hundred pounds. Dark scales covered the bulk of its body. Bumpy and ridged it had the look of the pebbled floor of a dark river. Its underbelly, checkerboarded in appearance, like wall tile in an old home, was olive green and smooth.

The most frightening aspect was its maw. It was slightly agape, with rows of horribly sharp teeth, some exceeding four inches in length. Dark beady eyes stared at her across the distance with malevolence.

"Oh, Sweetie," the Croc began in an Australian accent. "Your flesh is going to taste sweet. I just know it."

Kat rolled her eyes. "Why you assholes think you need to say stupid shit like this before fighting I will never understand." She moved into a fighting stance, a mixture of the Filipino fighting style Kali and Muay Thai –knees slightly bent, arms out and loose. "I'm not here to chitchat. I'm here to put an end to you. So, bring it."

She waited for him to come at her. She didn't have to wait long. Like a striking snake, he crossed the distance to her. Leaning forward as he came, he thrust his long snout out before him. He was quicker than she had expected.

144

She was faster. Squatting slightly, she launched herself upward, knee up and bent before her to collide with the underside of his jaw. His mouth, which had been opened slightly, slammed shut with an audible clack and his head, thrown back.

Kat didn't wait for him to recover. The moment she landed she moved. Zig zagging at her hip, she slashed first with her right claws, then with her left, before bouncing back to the right. Scales separated under her sharp talons and she felt the muscles which lined his underside, part as well.

He roared and swiped for her, but she had already moved past his reach and was behind him. With another leap, she was on his back and raking at his eyes. She could feel his right eye pop and sink in as one of her claws punctured it. The Croc thrashed about. His tail swung around and slammed into a parked car, smashing in the door and shattering the window.

Bucking, he desperately tried to dislodge her, but she held on. As she attempted to blind his left eye, he managed to reach around and grab her wrist in his meaty claw and with all his might, he threw her. Her back claws raked along the Croc's back as they dragged across it when she was thrown.

They say cats always land on their feet. That is assuming, Kat realized, if you didn't hit anything before you landed. She struck the electrical pole hard across her upper back and felt her left shoulder blade shatter. The damage would have been worse if the pole had withstood the impact of her body, but it also broke, slipped apart and dropped down before tipping over. Electrical lines landed across several car tops, sparking and popping loudly before falling silent.

Kat landed on her side with a thud and a groan. The shoulder blade mended itself, and she willed it along quicker, doing the same with several lacerations she had received.

Not waiting for everything to finish healing, she bounded to her feet in time to get knocked sideways by a viscous swipe from the Croc, who looked no worse for wear from her earlier attacks. His right eye had already recovered, and his abdomen, was now unscathed.

Again, Kat was airborne. And again, not by her choice. *This is not going well*. This time, however, she controlled her descent a little better and twisted herself to land on her feet. Turning around she saw the Croc had followed her flight and was right on top of her. Another swipe, but this one she batted away as she jumped slightly back. The other claw came in, and again was batted away.

Memories of fighting Jeff, her old martial arts teacher, entered her thoughts. He was bigger and stronger than her, just like this Croc. That's where the similarities ended though. This wasn't a match in the gym at her home. This was a fight to the death, and she couldn't play possum and do a hip throw to subdue him. She needed to do as much damage as she could to the point where she could hurt him quicker than he could heal.

She couldn't do this alone. The realization of this shook her. None of them could win these battles alone. If it remained one on one, like now, the best they could hope for was a stalemate.

A slash and a bite, but she kept out of his reach, knocking aside each attack as they came, giving her time to think. She needed help, but she knew the others would be equally matched in their fights.

"Sylvanis! I need help here!" she shouted, hoping the Druid could spare a moment from her confrontation with Kestrel to give her a tactical advantage.

"Busy!" Was the only response she got.

The corners of the Croc's mouth peeled back in a frightening smile.

"It looks like the only one who is going to be ended here, is you."

"Shut the fuck up." Kat attacked.

Moving in quickly, she lacerated his incoming arm. Tendons and ligaments were sliced clean through, causing it to flop down uselessly. At least for the moment. Spinning around inside his reach, she slammed an elbow into what would typically be his sternum. What it would be on this creature, she had no idea.

He grunted though. Good sign. Spinning back around she slammed the heal of her palm into his throat, crushing his esophagus. The enormous beast staggered back from her, but she did not relent. Following right after him, she straightened her fingers into a spear hand attack and jabbed into the soft underpart of his left arm. Her claws acted like the sharpened head of a knife and cut in deep. She could feel the ball of muscles, the rotator cuff which encompassed the shoulder joint tear away from her hand as they rolled up after being severed from their connected bone.

The Croc howled. She repeated the process, jabbing deeper this time till her fingers struck the joint with enough force to pop it out. Methodically she stabbed and angled her hand to quickly work at severing the entire arm.

As concentrated as she was on this goal, she hadn't realized he had healed from the other damage she had done. At least until she saw peripherally his snout arc down, jaws open to crunch down between her shoulder and neck. Dagger-like teeth pierced her skin and she sucked in a breath. The position of his mouth made further attacks on his armpit impossible and she knew it would heal again. She had missed her chance to incapacitate him, if only momentarily.

Now, she realized with dread as he reared back his head, lifting her up off her feet, it was his turn.

Sylvanis was indeed busy. As much as she wished to help Kat with that monster, the Werecroc, she was needed to fend off attacks from Kestrel. Standing as she was, Kestrel still managed to appear regal in her bearing, while hiding behind the Were-Rat.

"Goid Blàths!" Kestrel sang out. her voice like the sound of a church bell, cold, crisp and melodic. Immediately, the air around them had the heat drained from it. Sylvanis' breath ghosted in front of her, the warm moisture in her lungs haunted her as it fled. Her inhalation brought pain as the icy cold air created by Kestrel's spell filled her chest.

Bang! Bang! Bang! Ben fired his gun beside her, and she could see bullets sending chips of stone into the air as the shots went wide. Ben, shivering from the tundra-like temperature couldn't hold his gun still.

Through chattering teeth, Sylvanis moved to counter Kestrel's spell. "Thoir Blàths." Heat returned and Sylvanis fired back.

"Uisge Tuit." Sylvanis' spell pulled moisture out of the air and it coalesced above and behind Kestrel. The Druidess frantically scanned about, searching for where the attack would come from. When the huge ball of water fell, it struck the ground behind Kestrel and the Wererat. A surge of water, an impromptu wave, slammed into the back of Kestrel, and the Wererat, knocking them from their feet, causing them to tumble about in a twisted mass of brown fur and expensive silks.

"Shoot her!" Sylvanis yelled at Ben once again and the cop, now warm, his shivering ended, took aim again and fired. Blood sprayed as the bullet struck Kestrel in the thigh, rolling her over from the impact.

Click! Click! Ben scrambled to pull a spare clip from his pocket and reload his weapon, but it was already too late. The Rat was back up and hovering over Kestrel who had clamped both hands on a darkened stain on her dress, the color expanding out to mar the fine garment.

Sylvanis thought to end this, but Kestrel was quicker.

Crying out, her voice terse with pain, Kestrel cast her spell.

"TEINE TARBH-THONN!"

A massive story-high wave of fire began rolling toward her, Ben and the cops who had recovered from the initial attack. The heat felt like holding your hands mere inches from a hearth. It seared skin and caused smoke tendrils to rise from clothes, seconds from catching fire themselves. Oxygen sucked into the fire, leaving them all breathless and gave the wave urgency as it inflated as it barreled down on them.

Blacktop melted and coagulated, like chocolate syrup. Smoke billowed in great clouds, dark gray and aggressive. The fire. The smoke. Everything burning made it hard for Sylvanis to act, let alone think. She knew little moisture remained in the air, as her earlier spell had pulled as much as it could. She would not have the ability to attack this fire with water.

But perhaps.

"*Deigh balla,*" Sylvanis managed to croak out, her throat dry and sore from the heat. The wave, only a few feet away from them, hit a wall of ice, the color of iced coffee as it sprung up between them and it. Sylvanis had used the dust and debris from Kestrel's earlier attack to lend structure to the wall.

The fire wave struck the wall and a high-pitched hiss filled the air; dark smoke from the fire was quickly overwhelmed by a mountain of white steam, making vision impossible. The cloud of steam struck them and Sylvanis could feel her protective spells flare up to protect her from the heat. The others weren't as lucky. Ben screamed out next to her and collapsed into a heap.

Police officers, some of whom had yet to recover from the eruption writhed about the ground in pain, their skin reddened and blistered as the air boiled about them.

"*Fionnar gaoth!*" A wind blew out from Sylvanis. Whipping around, it gathered up the steam and pushed it away, cooling as it went. The damage was done though. Sylvanis quickly moved to Ben and examined him. Wherever his skin showed, pus-filled blisters rose like sheets of bubble wrap. Some had deflated, oozing with a yellowish-clear liquid mixing with the weeping from the rest of the skin.

"*Craiceann càirich leighis.*" As she took Ben's head in her hands, she sent her magic into him. The sharp intakes of breaths he had been taking slowed and steadied. She saw the color of his skin return to normal, the blisters flattening and turning to loose skin above newly healed flesh. They would slough off in time, Sylvanis knew. Until then though, he would not be a handsome man.

The other officers needed her attention as well, but she had more pressing matters to deal with. Standing, she wheeled back to face Kestrel. Who was . . . gone?

Swiveling her head this way and that, Sylvanis quested for Kestrel, but she was nowhere to be seen. Neither was the Rat.

Shae led the way as she and Kestrel darted back through the hotel and made their way to the rear exit. Kestrel had done what she had been able to do to heal her wound, but she still hobbled lightly. Her left leg made a swinging movement with each step, as she was unable to bend the leg at the hip.

Kestrel muttered a steady stream of curses, or at least, Shae believed they were curses, since they were in a language she did not understand but came to recognize as the same language she used to cast spells.

Shae glanced behind Kestrel and saw through the enormous front windows, to see white clouds, obscuring everything, had replaced the wave of fire. Sylvanis had found a way to douse the fire, as Kestrel assumed she would when she had clawed her way to her feet. She yelled at Shae, her voice sounding distant beneath the roar of the flames, to get them out of there.

Shae did just that. Looking to the sides, she still saw the others, now engaged in combat with the Sylvanis' Weres. They would need to make their own way out, she knew. For now, getting Kestrel out of here was her job. Running back toward the hotel, she opened the door and ushered Kestrel through it before taking the lead again.

She dreaded what would happen next. When they reached the back exit, there would be police stationed there and she would be forced to deal with them. *It is me or them. I will not be captured again!* That didn't mean she was looking forward to killing people. She didn't have a choice now.

She put some distance between her and Kestrel, not wanting to step outside and have Kestrel gunned down by the waiting cops. She would have to remove the threat before Kestrel got there.

With a burst of speed, she slammed into the exit door at the back of the hotel and flew outside. Landing in a crouch, she quickly scanned the scene. Six or seven bodies lay strewn upon the ground, some with torn off limbs, blood creating significant pools under the ripped flesh. The scent of copper and fear lingered in the air.

This had just happened.

Movement from the around a stone wall caught her attention and Daniel stepped into view. He wasn't in his Were form, but he clearly had been. Sounds from behind alerted her to Kestrel's impending arrival. With a hiss of frustration, Shae leaped at Daniel.

Slamming into him hard, she knocked him flat and landed on top of him, her pink rat tail swishing back and forth behind her in agitation.

"I told you to leave, Daniel," her voice a harsh whisper. She didn't know how long she had before Kestrel arrived on the scene.

"I did. I left the hotel, and I haven't gone back in since." There was a calm in his voice and little bit of smugness for having outthought her command. "I wasn't going to leave you with those monsters though. I had to do . . . something."

It hit her . . . the police. There had been no reason for the police to have come there to find them. They had all been circumspect in their comings and goings and, for the most part, their true identities had not been known. So why did they come to the hotel to get them?

151

"You fool! Now the world knows who I am! They will never stop hunting me. Worse, when they find me, they will lock me up again, just as you did!"

He blanched at her verbal assault. Clearly, he hadn't realized the ramifications of what he had done. By bringing the police here, he had brought an end to her ever being free.

"I didn't . . . I mean . . . I . . .," he stammered, as if trying to find some way to excuse his actions. There wasn't any.

The sound of pained breathing reached Shae's ears as Kestrel stumbled out of the doorway. Without hesitation, and not without a bit of satisfaction, Shae reached back with both arms and stabbed them downward into Daniel's chest.

He grunted as they snapped ribs and sliced organs. She leaned down close to whisper in his ear. When she replied, she poured in all her will, so there would be no mistaking her intent. No loopholes.

"You will stop following me. LEAVE. ME. ALONE."

Righting herself, she turned toward Kestrel who finished surveying the dead cops and returned her gaze to Shae. There was a look of measured regard and new appreciation directed her way.

"Let's go," Shae told her, swinging her leg up and over Daniel's bleeding body. He had the good sense to lie still and pretend being dead. If he hadn't, he would have ended up that way for real. Despite how angry she was at Daniel now; she did not want him tangled up in this mess. He was better off forgetting all about her and trying to live some semblance of a life. Away from her.

Kestrel hobbled her way, the hip still hurting her. She offered Shae a soft smile.

"Thank you, Shae. I know this is not what you wished to be doing." She motioned around at the fallen cops. "But I am glad that you are here for me. I don't know what would have happened if I couldn't have counted on you."

152

Shae was thankful for her brown fur so Kestrel couldn't see her blush. She had never been relied upon before. No one had trusted her before like Kestrel trusted her. She had helped Kestrel stay alive and the woman was grateful to her. Of course, in truth, it had been Daniel who had killed those police, not her, but Kestrel didn't know that, and Shae certainly wasn't going to correct her.

Shae's lips pulled back in an attempt at a smile. Kestrel seemed to understand the expression though as her smile broadened.

"You are right. We should go."

Together, they fled the scene. Shae didn't need to look back to know Daniel's eyes followed them as they went.

Sim ran toward the smaller of the two Wereboars as the beast waded into the crowd of onlookers. Men and women ran in all directions. Some headed in his direction first before noticing him. Then they fled in a different direction screaming. Sim couldn't blame them. Even though he was there to save them, he must have looked scary as a huge bear-man bearing down on them. *Ha! Bearing down on them.* He shook his head at his own joke.

The closer he got to the Boar, the more he realized it wasn't truly attacking any of the people. Oh sure, he swiped his immense claws toward them, but, at least to Sim, he was missing on purpose. *It's like he has no desire to kill anyone.* Before the implications of this could register, Sim was on him.

Thrusting out with both hands, he pushed the Boar hard, sending him sliding backward several feet before he managed to slow himself down by grabbing a light post. Sim followed right after, punching him hard in the jaw, snapping his head backward, and the Boar reeled. Sim did not relent and moved in to swing again. The Boar ducked under his swing, and up thrusted into his chest. Tusks pierced him, their sharp points burying into his skin and muscles or sliding between his ribs.

Pain lanced into him as the Boar continued his thrust upward, lifting Sim up. Up off the ground he went, but he felt his ribs tear away from his sternum and the tusks ripped back out of his chest, dropping him back down.

Landing hard, he stumbled back from the Boar and righted himself. He could feel his ribs reconnecting to his sternum and the puncture wounds begin to close.

A low growl reverberated through his chest and he opened his maw wide in open challenge to the Boar. A forceful huff escaped the Boar's nostrils in answer to his challenge, causing them to flare briefly before contracting.

Facing off against each other, they circled around. Sim searched for some kind of advantage, and he assumed the Boar did too. Circling around, neither he nor the Boar made any moves to attack. It hit Sim then. *He doesn't want to be here. He doesn't want to be doing this.* His True controlled him and he had no choice

Sim relaxed his stance, a release of tension in his muscles and he lowered his arms down. A puzzled look overcame the Boar.

"This isn't who you are, is it?" Sim asked him, his voice deep and rumbling, like a rockslide.

The Boar glanced to the side and Sim looked the way he had glanced to see his father locked in combat with the other Boar. The True.

"I don't have a choice, Bear. He will destroy me if I don't do what he wants."

Sim nodded. It was what he had surmised.

"But you don't want to do these things, do you?"

A cautious shake of the head.

154

Sim felt conflicted. This Boar. This man was not a bad man. He was a victim, like Sarah. Trapped by circumstance and by a magic he could not control, nor escape. Sadly, though, it didn't change the fact Sim could not let him hurt anyone.

"I have to stop you, you know?" Sim asked him.

There was a slight downturn of the Boar's lips, somewhat comical in appearance. The Boar nodded and lowered himself down in a charging stance.

Sim sighed. He would do what he could to stop this Boar, as he must, but he would understand in his heart he'd hurt an innocent, a pawn, and it would weigh on him. He realized now it wouldn't end with this Boar. There would be others in the war. Others he would be forced to fight and possibly kill. He considered the alternative though. He would do what he needed to do, he decided.

He started forward and the Boar charged him as before, only this time, Sim halted and waited. As the Boar reached him, Sim sidestepped and brought his fist down hard against the side of the Boar's head. He felt his fist meet with some resistance and felt that resistance give way as the Boar's skull collapsed from the impact.

Leaning forward, as the Boar had been for his charge, he didn't have far to go for his face to slam into the pavement. His forward momentum causing him to slide some distance before coming to a rest away from Sim. He wasn't moving. The damage Sim had caused the Boar's brain must have been enough to render him helpless, for the moment.

Sim was about to search out his father when a roar which deafened all other sounds came from behind him. A searing heat washed over him, and he threw himself forward as light and pain flowed past him. Rolling, he tucked himself into a ball and came out of it sprawled across the pavement, his eyes wide as he took in the monstrous fire wave, a cascading inferno baring down on Sylvanis and Ben.

Sylvanis, miraculously seemed to be weathering the onslaught, though her clothes smoked, and her skin reddened. Sim saw her say something and motion as a mottled wall of paper-thin ice sprung up between her and the wave. The tide of fire struck the ice wall, melting it instantly, but in doing so, caused it to be buried in a shower of water.

White steam blossomed from the confrontation, everything awash in scorching hot moisture. As the cloud rolled over them, the wave's momentum slowed slightly, and Sim could make out screams of agony from police officers who were in defensive positions behind vehicles, as if modern metal could protect them from this ancient sorcery.

The opaque cloud left Sim uncertain to Sylvanis' fate, or that of Officer Ben Charles. They were, however, not his concern at the moment. Spinning around, he sought out his father and the confrontation he was having with the Wereboar.

The white-hot rage overcame Hank at seeing that monster crush the head of the little boy, like some over-sized grape. It threatened to burn him from the inside. It was as if someone had set fire to his senses. His skin burned. His vision narrowed to the point only the Wereboar occupied it. Only one thing drove Hank at this moment, the destruction of this *creature* before him, waiting with avid patience to engage him.

And engage him he would.

How he had traversed the distance from where he had been and where he was now, right on top of the Wereboar, Hank could not remember.

Hank was a brawler. Always had been. He had never been opposed to getting his point across by throwing a fist, or two. His size and strength had

156

most people agreeing with his point by the end. In this Wereboar, however, he'd met his match. The man who had become this hellish looking boar had clearly been a brawler as well because he met Hank blow for blow.

Each swing he made with his meaty paw was answered by one from the Boar. Before long, Hank lashed out wildly, the moments between each punch, a pain-filled blur as the Boar would strike him in the head, the face, or the stomach.

Bones broke, organs were crushed or punctured. His head rang with each subsequent blow and the only thought which managed to gain traction in his pummeled brain was the hope he gave better than he got.

It seemed he did, because he pressed the Boar backward, moving forward, bit by bit. The Boar retreated before his attacks and that inspired a renewed ferociousness to Hank as he pushed his foe back.

It was this mindless attacking and his renewed assault that was his undoing. He, like so many others, had seen the Boar as an animal; Incapable of proper thought, let alone strategy. And because of this, he had allowed the Boar to lead him into a trap.

As Hank landed fist after fist, he knew where the Boar stood because he continued to hit something solid.

Until he didn't.

Swinging hard, his fist flying toward what should had been the Boar's snout, it met nothing but air.

Not meeting any resistance, Hank's swing carried him around, spinning him so his back was toward where the Boar had been. The Boar came right back in and planted a hoofed foot into Hank's lower back.

There was a noisy snap as his vertebrae broke under the impact. Hank felt himself flying, pitched forward. He slammed into the side of a car. Smashing into the door, his upper body slammed through the window, crushing the door panel to the point where his body became wedged halfway in the car and halfway out.

Desperately, he tried to extradite himself so he could face what would undoubtably be another attack from the Boar, but the lower half of his body would not respond. He could feel his body enacting repairs on his broken back, but he feared it wouldn't be soon enough. He couldn't have been more right as an immense weight landed on top of him. The screech of metal on metal and the angry sound of it being twisted and bent, filled his ears until he blacked out.

Sim watched as his dad went toe to toe with the Wereboar. The impacts of each punch they delivered made sickening crunches. Sim couldn't help but wince every time the Boar's fist slammed into his father. These two titans were battling with such ferociousness you could hear bones snap.

His father looked unhinged. His fists flying, it seemed, of their own accord. Some blows struck upper arms and hips but achieved little to no damage. The Boar, however, retreated. Slowly, but surely, his father pushed the beast back.

But why? If anything, the Boar scored better hits upon his father. Knocking him senseless, it would seem. As the Boar gave ground, they moved between two vehicles and suddenly everything made sense to Sim. His father lashed out wildly at the Boar making a desperate swing at the Boar's head, but the Boar took a step back, moving himself out of harm's way.

Not striking his intended target, his father's swing spun him around, his back to the Boar. Sim watched in horror as the Boar raised his leg up and punched out with his hoof, striking his father in the middle of the lower back.

Unbalanced and unprepared for this attack, his father flew forward into one of the vehicles, his body ripping through the glass of the window and wedging between the metal frame.

Sim watched on, urging his father to free himself. For some reason, his father seemed unable to move. What happened next Sim could hardly believe. Turning around, the Boar faced the other vehicle, a small coupe. Its surface had been streaked with cuts and scratches from the explosion of concrete earlier.

Bending at the knees, the Boar gripped the undercarriage of the car and strained. A load guttural growl rumbled from him as he righted himself, impossibly lifting the small car before pivoting and letting it drop back down upon the car holding his father.

"NOOOO!!!!" Sim screamed and charged. The car landed with a crunch, its chassis caving in the roof of the other vehicle. His father's body was obscured by the car as it rocked slightly upon the other vehicle before coming to rest. Nothing moved.

A few feet away and Sim leapt at the Boar. Body outstretched, his claws reaching, he flew toward his father's attacker, only to be met with an upper hook. The Boar's mammoth fist connected with underside of his jaw. He felt some of his teeth snap as they were slammed together from the impact.

The Boar had the forethought to understand he wouldn't be capable of stopping his momentum, even with his powerful punch, so sidestepped as he punched, allowing Sim to be carried past to end up crashing upon the ground several feet away to land near the mouth of an alleyway.

Shaking his head to clear it of the fog after the pummeling it had taken, he leveraged himself up onto his hands and knees and gazed toward the Boar, who was now making his way over to Sim, a broad sneer on his face. *I tried, Dad.* Sim stood to meet his doom.

# *Chapter Sixteen*

Kat felt the ligaments and muscles tear along her scapula and chest as the Croc swung her up and over and with a flick of his maw, sending her flying – once again. Unfortunately, the upper half of her shoulder, skin, muscle and fascia stayed inside the Croc's mouth.

Tilting its head back, it jostled its snout, causing Kat's torn flesh to tumble into its gullet. "Mmmm . . . you do taste sweet."

Kat landed hard and tumbled a bit, but pounced back up, gingerly touching her shoulder, her finger resting against the bones of her joint, coming away wet with blood. She rolled her eyes at his comment.

"Look," she began, willing the wound to close at her shoulder and feeling the skin and muscle begin to regrow. "You might scare some girls down under with that crap. But to me, you just sound like over-the-top B movie dialog . . . and that's being generous."

She readied herself for the attack she knew would be coming. This Aussie didn't take insults well. As she crouched, claws splayed, a strange odor reached her, one she had only smelled once before. The smell of a lycan, but one that smelled strange. She knew that smell. She knew, and she smiled. *CLINT!*

Sarah had not moved the entire fight. Well, except for earlier when the police had opened fire. She had tried to protect herself, crouching down, covering her face and head. It hadn't helped much. The pain from the hail of bullets, like acid rain, boring holes into her skin wherever they fell, would stay with her for some time. Though her wounds closed shortly after the pain started, the pain hadn't gone away. As a doctor, she understood it was trauma that made her feel those wounds hit her body, again and again.

Knowing this, didn't stop the pain.

She had stayed where she was though, because Blain had not told her to do anything else. Whether on purpose, or an oversight on his part, she did not know but was thankful for it. Though she wasn't acquainted with the Bears, she had spent some time with Kat, fleeting as it was, and she had no desire to attack any of them.

And so, she wouldn't. Unless Blain made her, of course.

Sylvanis and the others were not doing well. The giant Bear had gone down, buried beneath a ton of car. Kat was in a terrible battle with Gordon, who had thrown the Tiger, after taking a sizable chunk out of her shoulder.

The only thing going in their favor is that Shae and Kestrel had fled. Of course, it had been the plan from the start. Sarah couldn't help but wonder where she went and why she took Shae. It was unlike Kestrel, from what she had seen of the woman so far, to turn her back on a confrontation. The bitch wasn't stupid though. She clearly had a long play in mind. Sarah simply didn't grasp what it might be.

The more compelling question here was, where was Clint? When she had seen Kat step out with what had to have been Sylvanis and some other Weres she searched for Clint. But he was not among them. It seemed impossible Clint wouldn't be there to come and try and rescue her. Yet, he was nowhere to be seen. During this entire fight, he had not shown himself. She began to wonder if something might have happened to him, but from everything Blain had implied, Clint was still out there. They expected him to come for her. And now, here they were, but not Clint. Why? Where was he?

She missed him so much. She needed him. She had barely had a chance to truly love him before that monster, Blain, took her away from him. If he knew what she had been through, what Blain had done to her —made her do.

Tears glistened down her cheeks. She seldom had a moment to cry alone as Blain always kept her close and she would be damned if she would cry in front of that asshole ever again.

It was almost funny that being surrounded by so many people, while a brutal combat swirled around her, she now felt safe to shed tears.

Reaching up, she dragged the back of her hand across her nose and sniffled. Allowing one finger to sweep up and clear the tears from her cheeks, she continued to watch the fight unfold. It became clear to her now this fight would not go in her favor.

A roar tore through the dark night causing everyone's head to snap around, questing for the source of the roar. It had come from up the street and Sarah stared that way as well. Her heart was in her throat. She thought she recognized the sound.

And then, he came.

Loping between two cars, came Clint, shifted in his wolf form. He seemed different from what she remembered, but still monstrously big, with bulging musculature and deep chocolate brown fur covering his body. The fur, however, was matted and tangled in places. The fur which covered his feet were dirty, with pale gray clumps of dried mud woven in it.

His long-fingered claws were dark, almost black, like dirt, as if he had been digging in the dirt, or, as shock hit Sarah, someone's blood. The most

162

startling change she could see in him was his eyes. They reminded her of that first night she had seen him change. Those eyes had been — animalistic. Rabid. Scary. They looked that way now. Sarah was thankful they seemed to see only one thing. Blain.

She watched as Clint, in a mix of two-legged running and four-legged loping, made a straight line for that horrid beast. Sarah felt elation and a little fear. Something was not right with Clint. He seemed more animal, than man.

Comprehension seemed to blossom in Blain's expression as he realized the situation had changed. Sarah's elation turned to dread, as she heard Blain call her name.

"Sarah," he bellowed. "Come and defend me!"

She could feel his will engulf her, stealing her own and supplanting it with his. She fought with everything she could, but she was no match for this ancient magic which gave Blain command over her. As Clint barreled towards Blain, he began to back up and Sarah moved. Blain's demand forced Sarah to use all she could to intercept Clint and she barely made it there in time.

Coming to an abrupt halt in front of Blain, she turned on Clint.

He didn't stop.

It was as if he wasn't seeing her at all. Or worse, didn't care she was there.

"CLINT!" She held up a hand before her as if that could stop this enormous beast speeding towards her like an avalanche of muscle and fur. But like what happened a few short weeks ago, her voice, saying his name, seemed to reach him and he stumbled to a halt in front of her — his chest heaving, jaws agape and eyes burning. They stared down at her and she felt the same fear she had felt that first night all over again. This monster was going to eat her.

"Clint. It's me. It's Sarah. I love you." Tears began to stream down her face, leaving wet tracks in their wake. "Please!" Her voice cracked from the ache she felt. She saw the fire in those eyes gradually recede.

"Aww. Did you hear that, pup?" That awful voice came from behind her and Sarah closed her eyes. Gods did she hate him. "She loves you."

At the sound of Blain's voice, Clint ceased seeing her and his eyes fixed on Blain. The fire returned with a vengeance.

She could feel Blain's breath on the back of her head as he leaned down over her.

"Now shift and fight him. Stick around long enough for me to get away then go to our meet up point."

Sarah shook. She could feel herself beginning the shift and yet she hung on. Not wanting to give in.

"Go on lass. Fight your little bitch of a boyfriend."

Bones broke within her, but they snapped and refused to reform. Brown hair began to push their way out of her skin, causing her whole body to itch. She would fight this. She would not do what Blain wanted her to do.

"DO IT! NOW!"

Her will broke. Bones mended and grew. Her face shattered and reformed. Muscle grew. Tusks burst from her jaw as it protruded outward. Sharp claws burrowed out from her fingers as they elongated. She gasped as pain racked her. Then it was done.

Now, Clint could not help but look at her as she neared his height and filled his view. Blain ran away behind her. Clint tried to move past her to follow and reluctantly she blocked his path.

A low growl, deep within Clint's chest let Sarah understand she pushed his patience.

Well. She would push it more.

She launched herself at him, slashing with her right claw and her left. He brought his arms up to block her attacks and her talons ripped through the flesh, scoring bone.

164

Clint backed away from her and she followed in close, continuing to swipe at him.

"Clint. Please. Understand. I don't have a choice." Slash. Skin flayed off his arm. "Help me. Please." Cut. Tibia snapped. "Whatever is going on with you. Come back to me. Save me." Stab. Blood spurted.

Something happened. A light of understanding seemed to blossom in Clint's eyes. Understanding flowed to recognition and then — horror. Clint stumbled back from her and fell, his head whipping from left to right as if seeing where he was for the first time.

Sarah couldn't relent though. She had to give Blain some more time. So, she came for him.

"SIM! NO!" A scream of anguish froze her. It was followed by the scrape and twisting of metal as the car Blain had dropped upon the Bear lurched upward.

Sim had stood facing toward the Boar when a loud roar echoed from down the street and both he and the Boar turned to see what caused it. A Werewolf appeared and charged the Boar. *CLINT!* Sim didn't know what would happen next but was happy Clint had drawn the Boar's attention away from him.

When he heard the Boar command Sarah to come and protect him Sim's heart broke. Those two have been through so much; this must be like salt on the wound.

Sarah moved to block Clint, then Blain spoke to her again and fled. Sim let him go. He couldn't take that beast, and there was no way he would get involved in what was happening between Clint and Sarah.

Looking around, he saw the other Boar he had fought was gone; he fled like his master. Sylvanis had begun to move to those police officers who had suffered the worse from Kestrel's spells, so his gaze slid past her and searched

165

for Kat. He found her. Her eyes were locked on Clint and Sarah as she moved little by little toward them. The Croc was nowhere to be seen.

A sound came from behind him, in the alleyway, and he turned to see what it was. White hot pain slammed into his chest. Fire burned from within and he stared down in shock as a man stood before him.

He was Latino, his skin, brown, like the color of leather. Dark brown hair, slightly curled, framed a narrow, long face. The man was heavily muscled, and one arm held something he had buried into Sim's chest.

With detached fascination, Sim watched as the man pulled a knife from his chest. It was a strange weapon, as the blade looked to be dark green in color, jagged and oddly shaped. The man withdrew it from him, turned and fled down the alley.

Sim dropped to his knees. He could feel his bones breaking and his body altering as he began to shift back to his human form — through no choice of his. The fire continued to rage in his body, and he was struck with a sudden realization. The wound in his chest was not healing.

Remotely, he felt himself fall to the side, his head striking pavement, bouncing off the concrete, but next to the fire, that pain was nothing. His vision began to dim, and he realized, unexpectedly, he was dying.

Desperately he arched his back and moved his head to try and find his father. To see him one more time. To tell him he loved him and to not let his death ruin him like it did when Sim's mom died. To not let the darkness take him again because Sim would not be there to bring him out of it.

Searching, he couldn't find Hank anywhere. He wouldn't be able to tell him. To thank him for being such a great father. For teaching him to be the man he had become. Oddly, he could feel his heart slowing. The blood oozing from the wound in his chest was a bare trickle now.

He had reverted completely to his human form and lay sprawled upon the pavement at the mouth of the alley. A clouding misted his vision and he felt himself growing cold. Again, he searched for his father, but the car still rested upon where he had seen him go down. A great sadness overwhelmed him. He so desperately wanted to look upon his father one last time.

*Dad. I love you. Be strong. Please.*

Darkness closed in and he was gone.

"SIM! NO!" He had felt it. Hank had felt the severing of the connection to Sim and he had known. Gods, he had known. There could be only one answer to the sudden loss of Sim from his consciousness. He was gone.

With a roar, using all his strength, he sent the car the Boar had dropped on him off to the side and ripped his way out of the other car. Torn metal lacerated his skin, tearing it apart like a zipper, a little at first but as it dragged, pulling it apart. He ignored it. Absently, he noticed the Boar had left and now a smaller, decidedly female one faced off against Clint.

None of that mattered to Hank though as he rushed to where he saw Sim lying awkwardly, back arched and twisted so his body was up on its side, with his head tilted back. Looking back toward Hank.

Hank crashed down beside him in an instant, shifting as he fell, but he already knew what he would find. Sim's eyes, open and still. His mouth parted slightly as if he had died trying to utter something. A plea for help? A call for his father? Hank did not know. Hank would never know.

Hank gathered up his son. Not the son of his blood, but his only true son of his heart. "No, no, no, no, no," he murmured over and over. Grief took him hard and swift. Everything he had ever cared for had been taken from him. First Jennifer and their unborn son, and now, now Jennifer's son, his stepson was gone. *What have I done to deserve this? I have tried to be a good man.*

167

Hank gazed to the sky, tears drowning his face as sobs took him. All he could do was shake his head in denial of what had happened.

They weren't supposed to be capable of being killed, not like this. What had taken his boy?

Through blurry eyes, Hank eyes quested over his son, looking for some clue as to what happened. It didn't take long. A slightly vertical gash was visible upon his chest. The skin torn and covered with dark red blood. *It hadn't healed. It had struck him in the heart and hadn't healed.*

Someone squatted down opposite him and he glanced up. He could feel his chin quiver as he, with as much willpower as he could manage, held back the onslaught of pain and tears.

It was Sylvanis. She examined Sim. Tears flowed down her cheeks and Hank could see the anguish in her expression, the pain in her eyes. Gently, she reached out a hand and pressed it to the wound in Sim's chest and closed her eyes, head bowed.

A moment passed, and she did not move.

"What happened Sylvanis? What took," a sob racked him again, "what took my boy?"

It was another moment before Sylvanis answered.

Taking her hand away from Sim's chest, she raised her eyes to look at him followed by a slight shake of the head. "I don't know, Hank. Not really, anyway." Her lips turned down at the corners and her eyes narrowed. "It was magic, but not Druidic. No. It feels old. Primal." She shook her head again. "I don't think it was of Kestrel and her group. This was . . . was . . . something . . . different."

Even as she spoke the words, Hank realized he didn't care. It didn't matter. Sim was gone, and nothing would bring him back. Hank was alone. Nothing mattered anymore. A well of darkness loomed before him and Hank, without a second thought, threw himself into it, to fall and let it take him.

Kat stood off to the side. She felt numb inside. The Croc, when Clint came to attack the Boar, had run and Kat had felt no desire to give chase. This fight had been brutal, and she had felt unprepared for it. After years of preparing herself to fight this war it was nothing like what she had thought it would be.

With the emergence of Hank from those cars and the realization Sim had been killed, sometime during the chaos, Sarah had also fled. Clint, she could see, had shifted back to his human form then sat, head bowed, arms curled up around his knees and weeping openly.

He had returned to himself, but at what cost? He must have some memory of what he had done. To her. To those hunters. He had crossed a line and now, he would have to drag himself back across it.

*Oh, Sim.* She grieved for the loss of his youthful energy. His frankness and honesty. She grieved for Hank's pain, for she knew it was something he might not recover from. *He's been through so much already.* Sim had told her of his mother. One of these nights they had been talking about their lives before all of this and Sim had talked about his mom. About how her death had devastated them both. That they had helped each other climb out of their despair. *Oh, Hank. How will you get through this without Sim?*

They had won this battle. The enemy had fled. Kestrel. The two Boars. The Rat and the Croc. All fled. *Then why does it feel like we lost?*

# *Chapter Seventeen*

Hector fled to the far end of the alley and glanced back. The Werebear he had stabbed had shifted back to human form. *He is just a kid. Not more than fifteen or sixteen.*

He had done what his grandfather had sent him here to do. He had killed a Were. But now he didn't believe he had done the right thing.

A roar of anguish tore through the night and Hector could see the other Bear run to the boy. Whatever they were to each other, it was clear to Hector there was a deep love there. Father and son? Hector did not know. He fled the alley altogether.

*They had fought to save the onlookers.* Hector had been there for the start of the fight. He had seen what had happened. The lines had been drawn. He'd watched a battle between two sides of Weres. One side had attacked innocent people and the other side — they had not only fought those ones but had defended the innocent people.

These monsters had tried to save lives. Hector shook his head as he hurried away from the battle site. These monsters *had* saved lives, and now, Hector had taken one. This was not how it was supposed to be. Weres were evil. Sent by the rival gods to kill us.

Sirens wailed into the night as if to join the chorus of grief coming from the other Werebear. The sound pulled at his heart. There would be a lot of loss felt tonight. The magical attacks and the brutal slaughter perpetrated by the one — witch? Sorceress? Hector didn't know what she was, but she and her Weres had left many officers and onlookers dead.

*They had fought for them.* Hector felt a sharp pang in his chest. An ache. *What have I done?* A loud wail and flashing lights preceded a cop car as it flew past him. He had no reason to worry about any suspicion. There were many people on the street, and all seemed to be trying to get as far away from what had happened as he was, though for different reasons.

Hector had arrived in Chicago a few days ago and had quickly made his way to the site of the earlier fight, the one he had seen on the internet. The day had been overcast and brisk, not unlike how Boston gets in late autumn, so it wasn't anything he wasn't used to.

The wind however, the way it barreled down at you from between the high-rises, had left his cheeks numb and his lips chapped. He had been forced to hunker down in his coat, head lowered and only occasionally lifting to see where he went.

Even though the battle had taken place over a week ago, there were still people who were obviously only there to check out, 'the site'. They stood near the corner of the building the Wereboar had buried the manhole cover into and took selfies. A street vendor sold Werewolf masks.

For a few days ago Hector came and went from this stretch of road and nothing had caught his attention. He started to return at night. After all, when else would these monsters return? They wouldn't come back during the light of day. Of that, Hector was sure. The light was no place for these creatures. He would hunt them at night. Hunt them and kill them. He was ready for this fight. Needed it.

On the flight over from Mexico, Hector had gone through his grandfather's notes. There had been more to this knife than his grandfather had told him. For one, the knife had done something to him.

It hadn't been apparent at first, but the longer he had been in possession of the knife, the more he has started to notice changes in himself. These changes had frightened him at first, but he had come to understand why they needed to happen. Now he didn't fear them, he relished them.

His grandfather had trained him to be a superb fighter. Combined with his training, he had grown strong and agile, making him a deadly combatant.

He had been nothing compared to what he had now become. The knife had granted him superior reflexes and unfathomable strength. He also found his senses were more acute. All in all, it made him dangerous indeed.

He understood he would need these abilities if he had to battle these Werecreatures. Did his grandfather have those same abilities?

His thoughts went to how he had found his grandfather that morning. He was looking old and frail, as if something vital had been taken from him. Hector's mind quickly recoiled from that line of thought as the answer held the painful sting of blame.

But, no. His Grandfather had given Hector the blade. Had known what it would do. Or so Hector told himself to forestall any real self-recrimination.

The only way for him to push away this cloud of guilt was to accomplish everything his grandfather had asked him to do. He would kill these lycans, these Were-creatures. He would end the threat of these creatures onto the world of men. When he did that . . . well. *Your faith in me and your sacrifice, Grandfather, will have been justified.*

On the second night, Hector found what he had been searching for. Keeping to the shadows as he was wont to do, he caught a glimpse of movement from an alleyway. Something hulking emerged from an alleyway across from him. A woman screamed. Men began to shout.

A lone man seemed to have placed himself in the path of the Werewolf on purpose. He had erected himself like a barrier between the lycan and those casual onlookers who were now fleeing this ferocious beast.

When the Wolf was only seconds from attack, Hector caught movement out of the corner of his eye and by the time he had adjusted his view to see what it was, the Tiger was already there and slamming into the Wolf, knocking it to the ground.

The battle which ensued was the most brutal thing Hector had ever witnessed. When the two combatants care little for the actual damage done to them, it can get bloody.

The conclusion of the battle had not been what Hector had thought it would be. The Tiger, who in Hector's opinion was the better fighter of the two, had been defeated. Only the intervention of the lone man who had earlier stood in the lycan's way brandishing a gun, then shooting the Werewolf, had prevented the Tiger from being killed. If such a thing was possible. At least without his knife.

There had been an exchange at the end. Words were said, at this distance, he had been unable to hear, but whatever had been said, caused the huge Wolf to hesitate, turn and flee.

Hector let him go.

Instead, he waited to see what would happen with these other two, this Weretiger and the man with the gun. Again, he was in no position to overhear the conversation which passed between them. No matter. Whatever was discussed ended with them leaving together.

As Hector moved to follow, movement made him hesitate. He caught sight of the Werewolf as it left the shadow of a neighboring building. The monstrous beast loped after the pair. Hector smiled. This had become an advantageous night. Not only did he have a lead, but he had also gained some measure of these two's fighting style.

When the Wolf was almost out of sight. Hector detached himself from the shadows, just another dark form in this hard night. Stealthily, Hector followed as close as he dared.

$$\text{☙}$$

In the chaos following, Hector had mostly been a bystander. He had lost track of the Wolf when the Tiger, who was no longer a Tiger, but a pretty, young woman and the man with the gun had entered a hotel. Was the man with a gun a cop? Hector wasn't sure. Either way, they had entered the hotel with some urgency and Hector had deposited himself in a lush red velvet chair in the lobby — and waited.

Fortunately, he hadn't had to wait long. The woman, the Tiger, returned to the lobby with others in tow, the man she had come with and three others. Somehow, Hector knew the two other men, well man and a teenager, were other Weres. The other one though — the girl. She was . . . something different.

Of all of them, the girl frightened Hector the most. That admission hit Hector hard. After all, this girl looked barely old enough to drive. She was a slight woman with straw-colored blonde hair, which lay flat against her scalp. Parted, it framed her soft, pretty face.

At first glance, she looked so . . . innocent, to Hector, the moment he saw her eyes though. At that moment, Hector knew she was something more. Something powerful.

Casually he watched them as they quickly exited the building and Hector pursued them out into the street.

The night was dark and cold here in Chicago, but the ones he followed seemed either unaware of the chill air, or uncaring. They walked at a brisk pace

Hector found barely manageable. There was a nervous air about them that other people walking this fair city tonight seemed to instinctually feel, because they gave them a wide berth.

They didn't seem to notice they had a tail and Hector chalked it up to their preoccupation with where they were going. He followed them for at least a dozen blocks where they arrived at a disturbing scene.

Cops were everywhere. They had cordoned off the entrance to a hotel. Blue, red and white lights flashed in dueling pockets from police cars. People, perhaps forty of them, pressed against the barriers, trying to see what would happen and what could conceivably involve so many police.

Hector watched his prey, and surprisingly saw them pass the police barriers with an escort and enter the police command center. Hector didn't think he would be capable of doing what he came here to do. But he wasn't ready to leave yet.

An alley, next to the hotel, would suit Hector as a place to watch whatever happened next, but remain unobserved. Skirting the whole scene, Hector made his way circumspectly around and into the alley where he waited. For what, he didn't know. At least, until it happened.

The battle he witnessed was epic and devastating. It was not anything he had been prepared for and it put all his grandfather's warnings into perspective. *What if there were armies of these creatures? How would we survive that?* Hector couldn't allow it to come to that.

When the fighting had moved closer, Hector had almost fled. In truth, he wasn't anything more than an assassin. He would have to be. He could not face any of these creatures. *Not now. Not while they are all together.* He would need to keep watch for an opportunity to strike and after that, slip away into the darkness so to be ready to strike again.

The notes his grandfather had left spoke of how the knife worked for the Ko Yumi, or lord, as it was translated, which referred to the original Were.

They were so closely bound to their totem animal that a piercing of the *cavity*, which his grandfather believed to be the torso, would cause 'a breach of the body, a piercing of not only the dermis, but the muscle layer as well,' his grandfather had written in his notes. It was all that was needed to sever the link between the Ko Yumi and their totem, and by doing so, kill them.

For the Tzhsi, or child, the one who changes because it has been made so by the Ko Yumi, it had to be something more. Because the Tzhsi were not as tightly linked to the totem animal, as they were forced to choose the animal by the Ko Yumi, the piercing must be to the heart. 'A breach of the body would not be enough. The knife will sever the connection but will only suffice if it will prevent the Were from being granted the powers of swift healing. Because of this, a killing blow must be used. A stab to the heart, a slice across the throat, or a severing of the head.'.

His grandfather, it seemed, had a penchant for writing clinically. To discuss the murder of another human being in such a sterile way, Hector believed, was his grandfather's way of removing the humanity from the act. It hadn't helped.

Reading what his grandfather had written about what Hector must do, had once again made Hector question this madness. He was not a killer. He could not take a life. He went to college, not murdered people. And yet, now that he saw the devastation and the horror of what these monsters could, and would do, if they were left alive, the more he realized someone would have to do something to stop them. And that someone, unfortunately, would have to be him.

The how of it, however, eluded him. Given his new strength and agility and his heightened senses, he would still get ripped to shreds by these beasts.

He had been lost in thought when the smaller of the two Bears landed only a few paces from his hiding spot. He looked shaken from the blow he had received. Hector watched as the Bear climbed shakily to his feet. Past the Bear, Hector could see the Boar storming toward them.

When the roar sounded, and the Boar halted its advance to turn and face a new threat. Hector realized an opportunity when he saw one, and he acted. The Bear's sole focus had been on the Boar, but now the Boar wasn't paying them any attention. Hector could attack and flee.

Quietly, he stalked closer to the Bear. A sudden tenseness to the Bear's stance, and Hector realized he had been sensed. Lightning quick, he closed the distance as the Bear whirled around. Hector swung; his arm raised high in a downward stab. The Bear turned into the swing, his knife sliding into its chest and piercing the heart.

The Bear gaped down at Hector with a look of surprise, followed by a look of fear and one of deep sadness. As Hector drew out the knife, he could already see the shift happening. Bones moving under the fur-coated skin, cracking noises of bones breaking, like the sound of a frozen river as the afternoon sun warms it to the point of melting, could be heard.

Hector stood transfixed momentarily, watching the battling emotions on an all too human looking bear face as it shifted to more and more human. When he heard the anguished, growling scream coming from the direction of the battle, Hector could wait no longer, and fled.

In a fog of recrimination, Hector returned to his hotel. *What have I done?* That question had chased him all the way back here. *What have I done?* Entering his room, Hector immediately went to the bathroom and started the shower. He had hidden the knife in his coat and had kept his blood-soaked sleeve hidden in its deep pockets.

Now, he slid the knife from under his coat; its jagged jade blade was mottled with dark patches of dried blood, making it look like some sordid emerald jewel of sacrifices. The blood had dripped down onto the pictographs circling the hilt of the knife, filling in the depressions of the symbols lining it. Hector ran a finger across the glyphs, digging in the caked blood with his fingernail. With perverse satisfaction, he watched as the blood curled up in front of his nail, making a tiny, in-turned spiral, before snapping off to fall to the ground.

With some shock, Hector realized his hand which had wielded the blade also had blood dried upon it. The reddish-brown coagulation clung to his skin, like another layer of dermis holding all his guilt.

He moved to the sink to try and scrub it clean.

# *Chapter Eighteen*

"Did you get that? Please tell me you got that?"

The beaming smile and eyes almost glowing with excitement told Clarrisa Yotes that her cameraman, Malcom, had managed to film the battle they had witnessed.

She still couldn't believe what they had seen. The excitement she felt was like an electrical charge coursing through her body. It felt like the way your leg does after you had been resting on it for so long it had grown numb, but now that you moved, all the feeling comes rushing back in.

She returned Malcom's smile and wiped away the sweat still clinging to her hair line. A strand of her sandy brown hair had come loose, and she moved it back in line. *That . . . fire*, had been so intense, so hot. Even from where they had been standing it had sweat-soaked them both.

What she had witnessed, no, reported on, would change her life.

When the police scanner in the live truck started issuing commands for all units to converge on the Windy City Luxury Apartments, they had been on their way back to the station after filming a story about the local SEIU meeting to discuss their proposed walkout if their demands weren't met. This had been the second such meeting and a consensus had yet to be reached.

It had been a long, and frankly, boring meeting and Clarrisa had wanted to leave five minutes after they had arrived, but she had a job to do.

That didn't matter now. None of it mattered now. Everything had changed, and she had been there to report on it.

Smoke rolled over them, so thick it obscured Malcom for a moment as he stood facing her. His short stocky frame with broad shoulders made him perfect for a cameraman as the camera unit sat perched on their expanse. He had dark, tight curly hair which was like a second skin because it held tightly to his head.

He had a wide face, a wide nose and broad full lips, which were always quick with a smile and a sharp joke. It was what she liked about him. In many ways, though, she was his opposite. Not only physically, as she was tall, at least a head and a half taller than he, with long straight hair. She had a slight build and fair skin, compared to his dark shade. But in personality as well.

Malcom had a quick, biting and sometimes dark humor. Clarrisa, was not known for her humor. It wasn't she didn't have a sense of humor; it simply wasn't as flippant as most peoples were. She got jokes. Laughed at them, when they were funny. She merely didn't offer any herself.

He provided the humor and she was the 'straight man' as it were.

That call out on the police scanner had come as they had left the meeting and since it hadn't been far away, they scrambled to get there first. They had arrived right as things were about to go from a normal standoff to the outright bizarre and otherworldly.

After arriving on the scene, they had desperately tried to reach the station. Strangely, both her and Malcom's phone had lost their signal. They had tried to send a transmission from the live van as well, to no avail. Clarrisa thought it must be some type of jamming the police were doing, which would be new to her. As far as she knew, the police didn't have that kind of technology, nor could they legally use it if they did.

That was a completely different story though, and one Clarrisa would address once she finished reporting on whatever was happening here. Though they had no means to transmit to the station now they filmed it and when they returned to the station, they would report it. As far as Clarrisa could tell, they were the only news channel on the scene and so the exclusive would be theirs.

The police were arrayed in front of the apartments and a group of eclectic individuals had emerged from the front door. They had the look of, Clarrisa hadn't been sure, like some weird group of fighters from a superhero comic or something. It included a woman, beautiful and regal, who was dressed in a glamorous, revealing gown. A large, brutish looking man, broad of shoulders and had a face which looked like it hadn't been hit with the ugly stick but had headbutted it instead.

In contrast, they were accompanied by a handsome man, with almost flawless features, dressed like a professional — a lawyer, or a doctor. There was another man, tall and gangly, with long arms and a hesitant look, and a young teenage girl, wearing a long duster coat with a caged expression on her face.

Nothing was said, but clearly the police were here for them, and what seemed ridiculous, or at least it had at that moment, they didn't appear to care. It was like they saw the multitude of police, armed to the teeth, ready to gun them down at the slightest provocation and they all collectively shrugged.

The tension which had been so thick in the air, abruptly got a lot thicker. *What had happened?* She noticed another group of individuals had detached themselves from the line of policemen, to face off against this other group.

When she had, it had once again brought the idea back of a superhero comic or movie. Here we had another eclectic group of individuals. A young female, blonde hair, slight, like some life-like angel. Flanking her stood a handsome looking man. Tall and wide, undoubtedly a match for his counterpart across the way. Except he had a rugged handsomeness about him. *Like a hot lumberjack or something.*

On the other side, stood a young woman. When Clarrisa took a good look at this one she had gasped slightly. She had short, ruddy brown hair and slightly upturned eyes. She was strikingly pretty, but she radiated— violence. That was the only way Clarrisa could think to describe her. It was the way she held herself, as if ready to strike at a moment's notice, like a hunter and Clarrisa shuddered in fear for whomever her prey was.

There were two others with them. One was a teenage boy who looked to be barely past puberty. Tall and broad of shoulders. The other, an older gentleman, was slightly balding with a flat face. He had the look of a man who had seen too much, and yet, still surprised by what he had seen.

She had instructed Malcom to pan over to this new group when screams swelled like a symphony of terror back from the direction of the apartment complex. Clarrisa swung her gaze back in time to see a nightmare turned flesh, no, several nightmares turned flesh.

Monsters. Huge, horrible monsters now stood where some of the men had stood in front of the hotel mere seconds ago. There were two grotesque, boarish looking creatures and one reptilian — like a walking crocodile. She barely had time to register what had happened when gun shots rang out from behind her. As she turned toward the group with the young blonde in the lead, the older gentleman, who had been standing back a little, had his gun raised with a hint of smoke curling from the end.

The rest of the group split up, each heading toward a different monster, and if she hadn't witnessed it herself, she wouldn't believe it, before shifting into monsters themselves. Only two remained back. The young blonde woman and the man with the gun.

When the earth exploded around them, Clarrisa lost all sense of what happened. She spent the next dozen minutes or so flinching from one unbelievable event to the next.

Before she realized it, the battle appeared to be over. All that remained was the group led by the slight blonde who now knelt over the teenage boy who lay motionless on the ground, his upper body wrapped in the huge embrace of the older man, *the lumberjack,* who rocked back and forth, wailing with so much pain it broke Clarrisa's heart.

The police were in shambles. Bodies lay everywhere. Some were mangled and broken, their arms and legs sprawled in perverted angles, as if someone attached them with no semblance of how they were supposed to go. There were few still mobile. Others appeared to be unhurt but appeared to be sleeping.

The police who were still standing seemed unsure of what to do with the remaining group of monsters, well former monsters, as all of them, except the Tiger, the fierce female from the group, had changed back to being human. There was a newcomer. A male who sat hunched over himself, weeping. She couldn't get a decent look at him, but he had brown, disheveled hair and was muscular.

For a moment it seemed as if the police might make a move to arrest these people, but somehow, sensing the danger, the Tiger whirled on them and bared her fangs. A low growl emanated from deep within her. They shrank back.

"We fought. For you." She growled, pointing at the cops. "But make no mistake. You try and take us; we will cut through you so savagely you will have wished you had died when the rest of your friends did."

The police instead turned to help their fallen comrades, not wanting any more of this fight, and Clarrisa couldn't blame them. It was true. From what she had seen, this group had done their best to save the police and the innocent bystanders who had been standing here watching.

*They may not be our allies, but they are most definitely not our enemies. At least, until we make them.* Clarrisa believed it would ultimately happen. *These people. These monsters are not like us.* They were deadly. They were a threat. They couldn't be allowed to walk free, and it would only be a matter of time before someone in charge decided to try and make it happen. *Gods, what a disaster that will be.*

Then there was the, what would you call it? Sorcery? Magic? The ground erupting, waves of fire, walls of ice, all appearing out of nowhere. She had seen no weapons which would have been able to produce such effects — if such weapons existed in the first place. No. Each time they had been proceeded by some strange language emitted from either the tall, dark haired woman by the apartments, or the slight, blonde teen with the other group.

Witches?

If they were, they weren't like any witches existing today. Those were merely worshippers of natural forces. A religion. They were not practitioners of any actual magic.

Clarrisa shook her head. *What in the world was happening? There were monsters in this world. Women wielding magic. Where had they come from? Had they always been here? Are they just revealing themselves for the first time? Or did something happen to . . . make them? A government experiment?* Her reporter senses were reeling.

It was pointless to wonder, she realized. There was no logical explanation — for any of this. However, the implications of what all this meant in the grander scheme of things, sent her reeling. It left her shaken.

"We need to get this back to the station." Malcom words snapped her out of her thoughts, and she smiled at him, sheepishly, as he had apparently been standing there staring at her for some time, waiting.

"Right. You still have no signal on your phone?"

Digging her phone out she checked it as well. *Still no bars*. She didn't need to see Malcom's head shake to know he didn't have any as well. Something jammed their signal. Worse, they hadn't been able to transmit the feed right to the station, which went by satellite.

Clarrisa took one last look at the scene to make sure nothing momentous was about to happen. But all she could see of the group was the Tiger who had moved to the new one and squatted down next to him. Her orange and black striped arm wrapped around his shoulders, comforting him, while the big lumberjack man still held the young man in his arms. His earlier wails had now moved to gasping sobs. *Yes, these people were monsters, but they were people as well.* She would make sure to spin that angle when she reported on this. She would do what she could to delay what she thought was inevitable. The turning of the powers that be on these six, well five, now one lay dead, individuals.

Malcom had already lowered his camera and made his way back to the van. Since it appeared, for the moment, nothing new would happen, and as much as she would love to approach someone from the remaining group, she, quite honestly, was scared to death of them.

She would find out who they were, though. She would pursue this and in due course she would talk with one of them. Or all of them! An exclusive interview with this group would almost guarantee she would get the news anchor position she had always wanted.

Malcom disappeared into the back of the van to secure the camera and lower the satellite tower. Moving to the passenger side of the van, she grabbed the door handle when she thought she heard voices coming from the back. She leaned back slightly, in a futile attempt to see what might be happening at the back of the van. When nothing more seemed to occur, she called out.

"Malcom?"

No answer.

*This better not be one of his pranks.* After all they had seen tonight, the last thing she needed was one of Malcom's pranks.

"Malcom?"

Still nothing.

Securing the door, she made her way cautiously to the rear of the van. The doors were still open, and she peered inside. Along one side of the interior of the van lay a bank of consoles they used for on-the-site editing and monitoring live feeds as well as broadcasting a signal. Two swivel chairs were attached to the underside of the desk which lined the van in front of the consoles. On one of these chairs sat Malcom. He was leaning over the desk, head nestled into the crook of one arm, like he was either catching a nap, or hiding the fact he was crying.

Frowning slightly, she crossed her arms under her breasts.

"Malcom. Whatever joke you are planning on pulling on me right now, forget about it. This story is too important, and we don't have time for your games."

Malcom didn't move.

"Malcom!"

Still nothing.

Clarrisa's frown deepened. With a sigh, she climbed up into the van. Any minute now, Malcom would spring his little joke and she would be laying into him about the appropriate time and place for such antics.

He still made no move.

*Ah, so I am to get closer, I see.* Moving to him, she tapped him on the shoulder. He still didn't move. She moved to give him a playful shove when the van dipped slightly, and she wheeled around to see a man step up into the van. The door closed behind him.

Clarrisa tried not to panic.

The man made no move toward her. Instead, he squatted down at the back and seemed to be examining her, so she took the opportunity to do the same.

He was a nondescript looking man. If she had seen him in a crowd, her eyes would have passed right over him and not given him a second thought. He

186

wasn't an attractive man, nor in any way ugly. His brown, almost black hair was cut short, but it was full and came to a point in the middle of his forehead. He had a fleshy face, slightly sagging as if he had lost a considerable amount of weight recently. He dressed in a relaxed outfit— jeans and a black coat, neither expensive nor cheap looking. He wore black gloves long enough to disappear under his coat sleeves.

He smiled at her humorlessly.

"Miss Yotes. I wish to apologize for this intrusion, but in light of recent events, I'm afraid I have no other choice." His voice was soft, yet firm, like a loud whisper.

Without taking her eyes of this man, she reached back and shoved against Malcom. He gave no indication she had touched him. In fact, there had been no resistance to her nudge either.

A lump formed in the pit of her stomach.

"Who are you?"

"Ah," he watched her attempts to get Malcom's attention with a bemused expression.

"Normally, this is probably the moment where I would tell you all about myself and who I work for, while you look for some means to escape out of this van."

Clarrisa heard a soft 'phhhtt' sound and felt a sharp pain in her chest. Sometime during the exchange, the man had moved one of his hands to his coat pocket.

'Phhtt.' And again, a sharp pain in her chest. She opened her mouth and yet no words formed. He had shot her. Twice. She had been shot and now she would die.

Collapsing back against Malcom, she absently noted he fell out of the chair and landed on the floor, unmoving.

Dead. He had already been killed — by this man, and she had no idea who he was. The only thing she knew was he would be one of those people that will make the Tiger, and her friends, our enemy. *I hate being right,* was the last thought she had before darkness took her.

Eric Moran leaned over the corpse of the reporter and her cameraman.

"Alas, I have no time for such subtle cat and mouse games."

The door to the back of the van opened and Chad stood there looking in, awaiting orders.

"Clean it. All evidence of what happened here, I want gone. The footage I will want. Everything else — gone."

"Of course."

Eric turned himself about in the low ceiling van, bent at the waist, then made his way to the back and out of the van. He stood up right next to Chad. The man was a head taller than Eric and wider by almost double.

He didn't intimidate Eric in the slightest. Chad understood that Eric knew every facet of his personal life and had contingency plans set if anyone he knew harmed or killed him; everyone that person loved, or ever loved would meet an untimely death. It was the only way to ensure loyalty, as far as Eric was concerned.

"Did you initiate the wipe?"

Chad nodded. Now all the phones in a half mile radius had a virus uploaded onto them which would delete all photos and video files on the phone. Eric had already instructed the home team to monitor social media and remove any comments or pictures relating to tonight's events.

While they had already blocked all cellphone signals and satellite feeds, they had arrived shortly after everything had started and there was a chance someone had gotten outside their range of influence and uploaded something.

An effort which would ultimately fail. There was nothing he could do to keep this all away from public knowledge. He could, however, slow it down. No need for the public to panic — yet.

He had done his best to let those in charge recognize the threat now existing on their shores. Making sure the Director of Homeland Security got those files and the video of the earlier Chicago incident and patient 12 had been a necessary step, though it put his organization at risk.

Chad motioned to the two other agents who were ghosting the operation on either side to ensure no one approached and they closed in on the van. Chad hopped up inside and the other two moved around to the front and got into the cab.

In short order, the satellite tower lowered, and the van sped off, never to be seen again. All traces of the van and the two dead people inside would cease to exist.

Eric surveyed the scene in front of the apartments. It looked like a war zone. Fires burned, vehicles were overturned, and the street had been ripped asunder.

Ambulances started to arrive and EMTs were running about everywhere trying to deal with the injured and dying. People were stumbling about. Most of the onlookers had already fled earlier during the attacks by the Were-creatures. Yes. That is truly what they were.

After observing patient 12's metamorphosis, and the man, Clint's change to a Werewolf, no other conclusion could one come to. Sometimes, the obvious answer, no matter how out there it seemed to be, must be the answer.

They were all gone now. He had missed a great opportunity here to somehow track them. But he had been so concerned with containing this and keeping it from the rest of the population, he hadn't had the manpower to do what needed to be done.

After all, this hadn't been what he had expected to find when he and his team came here. In fact, generally, all of this, unpleasantness, would be beneath his paygrade. But he had been here searching for patient 12, and Daniel Mathis, whom he surmised travelled with the girl.

She had been there. He had seen her flee with the other woman. The other woman who could somehow call down fire and cause the earth to heave. He would love to get ahold of that one.

Eric smiled. *Oh yes. That one. Or the other female. The blonde teen.* She also seemed to have the same powers as the woman who fled with patient 12.

He searched the area in front of the alley next to the apartments. He had learned something new today, though. They could be killed. One of them, the younger Bear had died. Eric had no idea how it had happened. Whatever had happened to the boy, it had happened when he hadn't been watching.

The corners of Eric's lips turned down. A shame he had to destroy all the video and photos taken by all the cellphones here. Perhaps one of them had managed to film what had happened.

Glancing around, he searched for any CCTVs in the immediate vicinity that might have had a bead on the alley, but he didn't see any. The death, it would seem, would remain a mystery. For now.

He wasn't sure they could be killed.

With a quick nod to the evidence extraction team, he pointed to the site where the young Werebear died, and to where the main battle between the Weretiger and the Were . . . croc? *I guess that's what we are going to call it,* happened.

His team quickly moved into those locations. The police were not in any state to deal with what they were doing and if any of the police had taken the time to investigate . . . well, there would have to be a few more casualties from tonight's attack.

With luck, they would get blood samples and other DNA from the scenes. They needed to better understand these . . . creatures. To find a way to find them, or to use them.

A sardonic smile crossed Eric's lips, a slight upturn at the corner of his mouth. To think, they had one of these creatures in their control, and had lost her. Sure, they had no idea what she had been. But they had known she was something.

There was much to do. Too much. Eric wondered, not for the hundredth time, what the endgame was here. What was this fight truly about? One side had clearly meant these people harm. The other side? Well, he didn't know if they had moved to protect these people, or to engage their rivals. Like some kind of supernatural gang war.

Was it time for a face to face meeting with the Director of Homeland Security? Did he bring his organization out into the open? No. Too early. He needed to continue working within the shadows. To act with impunity. Red tape he could do without and entering 'the game' of politics and subjecting his group to oversight would only bring it.

His agents, well-trained, concise and efficient, returned quickly with all the available samples from the scene. They briefly checked in before melting out into the city. They would, as they had been trained, scatter and ghost anyone who might have caught wind they were up to something nefarious. They would ghost them or remove them if ghosting wasn't an option.

They were never there. They did not exist. For now. Until this country needed them and then they would step into the spotlight with all the help they could offer. When that happened, the how and why would no longer be relevant. They would be heroes, and their means would be justified by their ends.

# *Chapter Nineteen*

Ian Kaft stepped out of the cab in front of Samuel's home, a massive structure of three stories, surrounded by sprawling green hills. The verdant color of the grass was so vibrant it hurt Ian's eyes.

The house itself was a medieval looking — a stone edifice, with towers and crenulations. *For God's sake. Crenulations? Who does that?* The house seemed in contrast to what he knew of Samuel. He had always been a refined individual, with rich tastes, not eccentric.

Ian paid the cab and sent him on his way. He had never met Cirrus before, but the man whom Samuel had left to steward the boy would not turn him away. He had a signed letter from Samuel with explicit instructions for the man to house and feed Ian for as long as Ian felt it necessary.

As he began the walk up to the front door, he shook his head slightly, still surprised Samuel had approached him with this. Ian hadn't known Samuel had a son. Not that their relationship had ever been one of mutual revelations about their own personal histories. Which was why it had been a shock when Samuel had approached him shortly after landing in Topeka.

"I need you to do something for me, Ian." There had been a hesitation in Samuel's voice Ian had never heard before and so he gave over his full attention.

"Of course. What do you need?"

Samuel had stared at him for a long moment. So long, in fact, Ian had started to get nervous. Shifting weight from foot to foot, he kept his gaze directed at Samuel.

The moment passed, and Samuel stepped past him, reaching out to catch his arm and drag him along as Samuel walked. Ian strode beside him, waiting for the man to speak his peace.

They walked a short distance from the dark-haired woman and the arrogant doctor they had arrived there with, before Samuel continued.

"I have a son."

Ian faltered a step and caught a slight upturn of Samuel's lips. Ian recovered quickly.

"You never mentioned . . ."

"I didn't. Nor would I have ever mentioned it if not for my . . . concern as to how he is."

Ian didn't miss the unease Samuel had with expressing the notion of 'concern', as if the meaning of the word was something he was unfamiliar with. Perhaps he was.

"Why don't you just call him?"

Samuel glanced at him sideways and Ian immediately felt stupid for suggesting it. Samuel was no idiot. If calling had been an option, or if it had been something already tried, they wouldn't be having this conversation.

Samuel decided to not make a point of what he thought of Ian's suggestion and instead sighed and came to a halt.

Ian stepped past and turned to face Samuel.

"My relationship with my son is . . . complicated. For the moment, it is best for me to not interact with him. I hired a gentleman to be a steward over the boy and my estate.

"I feel that maybe something bad has happened to him. When I last spoke to the steward . . . something didn't seem right."

194

Samuel glanced back toward Kestrel and Gordon, before returning his gaze to Ian.

"Given everything that is going on. I don't have time to go and check on him. So," he paused, "I'm asking you to go in my stead."

"What is the boy's name?"

"Cirrus. He is almost eighteen and will be reaching the age of maturity and will receive his trust."

"And what would you have me tell him?"

There was no need for Ian to elaborate on what he implied.

Samuel glanced away for a moment then back.

"Nothing." He gave Ian an envelope. "Give this to the steward. His name is Christian. It will explain who you are and what you are doing there. He will let you stay at the home for as long as you feel is necessary.

"Evaluate the situation. Make sure that Cirrus is fine. Collect any information about him and what he has been doing and what he intends to do and then contact me."

Ian nodded. It seemed like a simple enough task. More importantly, it would get him the hell away from whatever Samuel and those other two were intending to do. The farther away he could get from what he had overheard them talking about on the plane, the better.

"I will leave tonight."

Samuel nodded, turned and walked away, leaving Ian to stare after him.

When he reached the door, he knocked, and waited.

He knocked again, harder and waited some more.

Sticking his hands back into his long black coat, he hugged it closer around him. The sun remained absent. Dark gray and dirty white clouds blanketed the sky. The lack of sun made the day chillier than it had a right to be and it cut through regardless of his coat.

After what seemed like an eternity, the door opened, and a middle-aged man answered the door. He peered out, not fully opening the door so Ian could only see the man's face. It was a wide, comely face, with a narrow broomlike mustache and a sharp, axe-like nose.

As the man peered at him, he scrunched his forehead, which made lateral lines high up his face as he was bald down the middle of his head.

"Who are you?" the man questioned.

"Christian Haptil?"

The man hesitated before nodding.

"Samuel sent me, can I come . . ."

The door shut in his face.

Ian stood staring in surprise at the door for a moment, then knocked again.

No one answered.

Ian pounded on the door.

Still Christian didn't open it.

Ian raised his voice, shouting. "Mr. Haptil! I am only going to explain this once. I am sure you are aware of our mutual employer's temper and what it would mean for him to become angry at you. So, I am going to give you one more chance to open the door before I call him."

He couldn't know for certain how Samuel had interacted with the man, but something in the way Samuel acted — it held an implied threat, a warning. Ian did not doubt this man would have sensed it and was not astonished when the door opened again.

"It wasn't my fault."

Ian stared at the man. He had no idea what the man was talking about. What wasn't his fault?

"Can I come in?"

The man nodded and stepped aside to allow Ian entrance.

The inside of the house appeared more like what Ian had expected. The stone walls, so evident on the outside, were absent inside. Warm colors, light blues, yellows and shades of white covered various walls of the various rooms which were visible from the doorway.

A great room could be seen with a cobblestoned fireplace. The rock framing the hearth travelled up the wall to the ceiling. There were two green sofas and a black recliner arrayed in front of the fireplace. Red embers could be seen in the hearth; their red glow pulsed and throbbed eerily.

Christian closed the door behind them, and Ian turned to face him. Now he could see the man fully, he quickly took in the expensive clothes the man wore, the $500 dollar watch and fine shoes. The man had expensive tastes. Christian's eyes darted around nervously, and Ian could tell the man was frightened.

"Could you please elaborate on what isn't your fault?"

The tension evaporated from Christian's face. The tightness around the eyes, the clenched jaw. The skin off his face slacked and his shoulders slumped.

"Oh, thank God!" It came out like a sob. "I thought he knew. I thought you were . . ." He paused, uncertain about voicing his suspicions.

"You thought I was here to kill you?" Ian finished for him.

The man nodded hesitantly.

"I'm not. But you must tell me. Where is Cirrus?"

The apprehension returned as again the man's eyes darted around, as if he believed Samuel lurked somewhere close by and if he spoke, the man would attack. *Of course, nothing Samuel could do would surprise me these days.*

"Out with it."

The man sighed. "He's gone."

When Christian failed to elaborate, Ian put the pressure back on.

"Look. I don't have time for this, and if you keep wasting my time, you will have Samuel to deal with and not me. That is not something you want to happen."

"O.K., O.K. He left months ago. He gave me no indication he was leaving. I went out for groceries and when I returned, Cirrus was gone.

"I didn't think anything of it at first. He would leave sometimes and camp out in the woods for a couple days. Living off the land or some shit. I don't know. He didn't tell me, and I didn't ask."

He frowned. "Perhaps I should have been more cognizant of where he went and what he did, but he was always so independent, and Samuel had told me to expect it."

The man paused again.

"Go on."

"Well, after a few days went by I started to worry. When it got to a week, I went in search for him. I knew of the places he usually went, and I checked all of them.

"It was then that I checked all of his accounts and found them all cleaned out. Most of his clothes and his, umm, gear? Was gone."

"Gear?" Ian had no idea what the man would be referring to.

"The boy had a large assortment of weapons, tools, explosives and the like. All things he had gotten from Samuel."

Ian's eyebrows raised.

"He never used any of them. Or at least if he did, he didn't use them *on* anybody."

Ian took in the man's clothes again and a suspicion started to creep in. "Why didn't you inform Samuel?"

A bead of sweat trickled down the man's temple and his furtive eyes told Ian all he needed to know as to why the man hadn't come clean about losing track of Cirrus.

"Well . . . I . . . it's just . . ."

"You decided to stay quiet and keep collecting the checks," Ian pointed out matter-of-factly.

Christian dropped to his knees, clutching Ian's coat as he groveled. Tears held at bay until now spilled forth as the man began to plead for his life.

"You can't tell him! You can't! He'll kill me! I know he will!"

Ian pried the man's hands off his coat and stepped back before the man could bury his tear-smeared, snot runny face all over his expensive coat.

In a way, he sympathized with this man. He understood he was one mistake away from being afraid of the same thing. Ian held no illusions about what Samuel would do if he believed Ian had betrayed him in some way. If he had any illusions before, they had been dashed by the conversation he had heard on the plane.

"Do you have any of the money left?"

The man nodded between sobs.

"Take it." Ian had no desire to be the cause of this man's demise. He was most likely dead already. The only thing he could hope for was Samuel would be too busy with what Kestrel had in store for them to come after him. Christian stared up at him through tear-filled eyes.

"Take it and go. Flee as far as you can and hide."

The man's eyes widened in surprise. Still, he didn't move as if waiting for the punchline of a joke that would see him dead.

Ian sighed.

"At some point, I *will* have to report this to Samuel. The longer you linger here, the easier it will be for him to catch up to you."

199

He didn't have to say anything else. The man jumped to his feet in an instant and scurried upstairs.

Ian made his way to the kitchen to see what remained in the fridge. He was, after his long trip, hungry.

He could catch noises from upstairs. Loud bangs and scrapes as Ian imagined Christian quickly packing everything he owned.

In what seemed like record time for one person to pack, Christian came back down the stairs and shot out the door before Ian had made himself a sandwich. He wasn't used to making himself sandwiches anymore. Oh, he certainly made plenty before he fell in with Samuel, though.

That earlier life seemed so far away now. He certainly didn't think of himself as 'above' making sandwiches for himself. He didn't need to do it anymore. Didn't have sandwiches much at all. *What a shame.*

Ian frowned and stared absently at the gray and tan granite countertop of the kitchen island he made his sandwich on. The glossy surface seemed to give an extra depth to the swirls and patterns of the rock. All those designs reminded Ian of tree rings. Not so much the configuration, for these were not rings, but how they showed the passage of time, like the footprints of ages past.

Grabbing his sandwich, he made his way to the great room and sat in front of the fireplace and contemplated what he should do next. Samuel would be wanting his report about what happened with his son and Ian did not think it would benefit him to delay in giving that report.

He would give Christian some time though. He could make excuses about arriving late and choosing to rest before heading out. That would give Christian at least a day head start. He didn't think he could offer him anymore.

It occurred to Ian the man might tell Samuel, Ian had let him go. He tsked at himself for not thinking of it sooner. He glanced toward the door. Should he go after the man?

*And do what, Ian? Kill him?*

Ian sighed audibly and shook his head at his foolishness. Samuel knew he was no killer. So, what could he expect Ian to have done when confronted with the truth of Cirrus' situation?

*I could have beggared him. Taken all the money he had been siphoning off from Samuel these past months.* He could have done that. Ian shrugged to himself. But he didn't. There wasn't much he could do about it now.

Ian finished his sandwich and sat for a time, staring at the dying embers in the fireplace, lulled into a hypnotic-like state as the light from the coals wavered and danced in his vision.

Shaking himself, he realized he had started to doze off. Fire had a way of doing that. Standing up, Ian stretched. Well, if he was going to give the man a day or so, he might as well take a nap. It wouldn't be too much of a lie to say he had been exhausted.

Striding to the open staircase, he mounted them and climbed to the second floor. After opening several doors, he found a bedroom which appeared to have not been slept in recently and undressed. When he had stripped down to his boxers, he slid beneath the covers. The sheets were blessedly cool and gave his body a satisfying comfort.

His body exuded its warmth, held in by the thick comforter; he was brought to a pleasurable temperature and he fell quickly asleep.

# *Chapter Twenty*

After they had fled the scene at the hotel, Kestrel had spouted what Shae had assumed were curses, spoken in the same language she used to cast her spells. Leaving Daniel lying on the pavement, Kestrel and she fled down a series of side streets.

Shae had reverted to her human form, thankful, as usual, for the long duster she wore which covered up her mangled clothing underneath. They made their way out of an alley and onto a main road Shae had never traversed before. Kestrel flagged down a cab and they made their way to the O'Hare airport.

They wasted no more time in Chicago and were in the air in under two hours. Shae understood their flight. They were known now. People had seen them. She believed images of them would appear all over social media, not to mention the news, in short order. The quicker they were gone from the scene of battle, the better.

"Where are we going?" she had asked Kestrel in the cab.

"Texas," had been Kestrel's curt reply.

Shae hadn't pressed for more information. Clearly, though Kestrel had healed herself from the gunshot wound, there was still residual pain. Shae could tell from her clenched jaw and the way she shifted how she sat in a futile quest to find a more comfortable position.

As they flew over the plain states, Kestrel covered her lower half with one of the blankets the plane provided and quietly did her magic to do whatever she needed to do to heal herself properly. Afterward, she had slept, and Shae kept watch.

They hadn't run into any trouble buying the tickets and boarding the plane. The assumption being, the news hadn't gotten out yet. But if it did, and they discovered they were on this plane, it was still possible for an Air Marshal to attempt an arrest.

*Foolish. Hopefully, their passage went unnoticed and unreported.*

Shae would like to avoid bloodshed if she could.

She couldn't help but wonder what was in Texas for them. Perhaps the job Kestrel had alluded she had for Shae? Fighting Kestrel's war was not part of the bargain. Kestrel had said she had something else in mind for Shae.

Shae glanced at Kestrel's sleeping face. The woman was uncannily beautiful, like a goddess. She had pale skin, high cheekbones, and black satiny hair. The woman had a curvaceous form as well. Shae knew little about what men found attractive in a woman, but Shae had to imagine if she thought the woman beautiful, and she wasn't attracted to women, men must find her more so.

It certainly seemed likely from the looks Shae had seen her receive from men.

Shae shook her head. She was confused. This woman was beautiful and powerful. What could she want with Shae? It would be understandable if she wanted to use her as a weapon, a way to help her win this war against Sylvanis. But she had told Shae she wouldn't do that.

Again, she wondered at what they were doing, and more importantly, what Kestrel's plans were for her.

Zach Van Stanley sat alone in his organization's headquarters staring at nothing out the floor to ceiling glass windows which lined the west side of his office. It had been a long day leading up to the rally, as they usually were. There were so many things to organize and do at the last minute to make sure the event went smoothly.

He sighed, loosened his tie and pulled it up and over his head to toss it on his desk. Rubbing his eyes, he powered up his laptop to check his emails and send some as well. There were plans.

As leader and spokesperson for Earth, Anger, Retaliate, to Heal, or E.A.R.t.H., he stayed constantly busy. He had been the leader of the organization since his last stint in jail. Since then, he had used all his available resources and charm to consolidate hundreds of autonomous eco-terrorist groups into one significant group under the E.A.R.t.H umbrella.

Some of the groups had only a half dozen activists, while others had hundreds of members. After meeting with Zach, usually only once, they came to understand his mission and the need for coordinated efforts.

They had agreed he should be the face of the organization. He had the cred, having spent many years in jail after blowing up a pipeline. Plus, he had the look and charm to sway people to their side.

A handsome man, tall and solidly built, he prided himself on his exercise regimen to keep himself fit and full of energy and it showed in his trim muscular frame. His face was warm and inviting, and yet, at the same time, masculine with a well-defined jawline and cheekbones. His dark brown hair was combed and sculpted. Bright blue eyes, which women enjoyed staring into, shined and twinkled or brooded, depending on what the occasion called for.

He was a subtle mixture of characteristics which made working a room almost natural for him. He could be endearing when he needed to be, or somber depending on which group he entertained. Warm and inviting, or hard

204

and uncompromising. All he needed was to understand who he dealt with. Which he always found out long before he would meet with them.

A soft knock on the door outside the office caused Zach to frown. There should be no reason anyone would be here. He had sent all of the activists home after the rally.

Standing up from his desk, he moved to the office door. He should let whoever it was believe there was no one there and let them leave, but curiosity motivated him.

Possibilities ran through his mind. A fellow activist? The cops? They were always stopping by to ask questions about one of the organization's members who had took it upon themselves to set fire to the office of a logging company or some other form of industrial sabotage. He would explain he had no idea why they would do such a thing; their organization did not condone such actions.

They would try to blame him for what the activist did, and he would of course ask, 'Did they name me as a co-conspirator?' To which they would hang their heads and admit they hadn't. That, in fact, they had no evidence linking him to the crime.

He would tell them he appreciated they had apprehended the criminal and he would once again, remind his organization's members violence was not allowed. They would always look at him with suspicion, but he had long ago learned to push aside their doubt. They had no evidence. And they never would. He was too clever.

What he saw when he opened the door a crack to peer out, was not what he thought he would see. Not one of Dallas' finest. No unwashed, unkempt hipster with pledges of loyalty to the cause.

No.

What stood out in the foyer to his office was a woman of surpassing beauty. She had pale, almost white skin framed by raven locks which held colored beads threaded within it. Her long face had high cheekbones and beautiful dark eyes. She wore a long flowing satin green dress which plunged deep at the front, revealing a full and ample cleavage, bordering on showing too much. Her breasts were the color of milk and as inviting as a cold glass of the liquid.

The rest of her body was as shapely as any model and her dress clung to each curve, each plane. As much as he would have liked to show some restraint in his reaction to this beauty, he found he had little control over his eyes as they avidly roamed the woman's body.

When his gaze managed to return to her eyes, he found a knowing smile on her full red lips making his heart beat faster, if only to transfer more blood to a lower portion of his body.

"Ahem." A voice from the woman's side dragged his gaze from the eyes looking at him with lurid promise and he found the woman's companion. She changed the hue of the redness of his face to a brighter shade of embarrassment.

The girl who stood next to the woman couldn't have been more than fifteen. She had short, ruddy brown hair growing back from some poorly performed hatchet job, uneven in places and not well cared for. The girl was pale, but not like the woman. She was paler, wan even, with a smattering of freckles about her cheeks.

She was slight of build, or at least, he believed her to be so. It was hard to tell since she wore a long coat which, given the heat in Texas, was an odd thing to wear.

The look she gave him made it clear she had not missed the eye-roaming, nor did it leave any question as to her understanding of where his thoughts had been.

"Ahhh," was about all he could get out. He had no idea who these two were. Nor did he have any clue as to why they were here at this time of night. They clearly weren't cops, and they did not have the look of activists.

"Can we come in?" the woman spoke, her voice full, rich, and carried an exotic accent. *Almost a crime to have such a voice to accompany such a body.* Her accent was difficult to identify though. Zach believed it might be Irish.

Absently, he nodded they could enter. *Dammit, Zach. Get ahold of yourself.* He cleared his throat.

"Of course. Please, come in. How rude of me." He swung the door wide and motioned with his hand for them to step inside. To his surprise, the girl ducked in first and quickly surveyed the room, before turning back to the woman and nodding.

A slight frown crept up on Zach's face and his brows furrowed at what had happened, and he gazed back at the woman. Her lips were pressed into a thin line and she rolled her eyes as if that was all the explanation she need give. When Zach realized this, he shrugged and again motioned for her to enter.

As the woman entered his office, she strode forward as if entering her own personal kingdom and anyone who was currently in that kingdom better make sure they treat her as such.

Zach closed the door and moved around his desk to sit down. The woman took the chair opposite him, but the girl remained standing and moved to the wall of windows and began peering this way and that in a somewhat distracting show of surveillance.

He dismissed her. She obviously wasn't the important one here.

"You'll have to excuse my bluntness here, but it's late and been a long day." He paused. "Who are you people?"

This clearly wasn't a social call. They were here on some sort of business. This woman had a proposal to make. What it was, and what it meant

207

for him, he had no idea, but they were clearly part of some group, or organization who had reason to come to him.

The clandestine nature of this meeting, the lateness of the hour, he being the only one at the office at the time, led Zach to believe, regardless of outward appearances, these two were dangerous. Or at least, representatives of dangerous people.

The woman smiled at him in a sultry way, but he had a hold of himself now. He understood the use of charms to try and sway people. He had been doing it for years. This woman was beautiful, and she understood its effect on people. Mainly men. She tried to use it to keep him off-balance. To keep his mind on her tits and less on the subtle nuances of her words.

It wouldn't work. At least, he kept telling himself that.

"Things are happening in this world, Mr. Van Stanley."

"Zach. Please. Van Stanley always makes me feel like an elitist."

She smiled again and tilted her head in acquiescence.

"As I was saying . . . Zach. Things are happening in this world. Things that will change the face of it for all time."

He frowned at her. This had the sound of a sales pitch, but as to what she was selling he had no idea. At his frown, she had paused, and he smoothed his face and motioned for her to continue.

"When you turn on the news in the upcoming days, you will discover of what I speak. There is a new power in this land, and it is vengeful and angry towards what has been done to Mother Earth.

"You and me. We share the same goals. To put an end to the waste and destruction of the most precious gift that is nature. The difference is, I have the power to enact that change."

Zach stared at her dumbfounded, unsure of what she meant.

Whatever this woman spoke about was foreign to him. What new power? Some new political party who had somehow come to power while he

208

had slept last night? Or, had some new eco-terrorist group chosen to step up their actions? They must realize all it would get them was prison time at best or killed at worse. The only true way to wage this war was from the shadows, with calculated, sporadic attacks which harmed no one.

"I'm sorry . . . miss?"

"Kestrel."

"Miss Kestrel."

"No. Just Kestrel. I don't use those archaic labels of gender"

*Oh. She is one of those.*

"Fine. Kestrel. I'm sorry, but to be honest, I really have no idea as to what you are talking about. What new power? What is happening in the world that I don't know about? Are you with some new environmental group? If so, I'm sure we can work together to pool our resources and move toward a world that is free of $CO_2$, poachers, loggers and unregulated commercialism."

She shook her head. "We are not part of some environmental group. I am a sworn protector of the Earth. I am a druidess; whose task was to keep nature safe from civilization. Long ago, I failed." It was clear by the way she said those two words that they stung her. As if failure was not something she could stomach.

"A druidess?" He recognized the word, of course. They were some ancient sect of priest in England, weren't they? They worshipped Stonehenge or some such thing? Stonehenge. The menhirs of Stonehenge had all recently fallen. Could that have something to do with why they had come here?

"Well. A druidess. It is as you have said. We want the same things. However, you have alluded to the notion that you are prepared to take things further than I have. Not that I have done anything but hold rallies and made speeches, of course."

"Of course," she replied with a tone which implied she knew how inaccurate the assertion was.

209

They shared a smile.

"That being said," he began, spreading his hands wide, "I would be willing to hear your proposal." He leaned forward. "You do have a proposal, I assume. That is why you came here. You need something from me. So. What is it?"

She offered him a sincere smile, which now he saw it, he realized how insincere all her other smiles had been. *Oh, she is good.*

"I like you, Zach," she stated and glanced toward the girl. He started. He had totally forgotten she had been there as she had made no sound or drawn his attention to her in any way.

The girl offered Kestrel a sour frown and Kestrel snorted, and the girl's frown fell away and was replaced with a cold look.

Kestrel dismissed it. "Oh, calm yourself, Shae. I meant no insult. I just know you lack trust in anyone you just met, especially a man. I laughed at myself for looking to you for an opinion, knowing precisely what I would get."

She turned back to him.

"You are correct. I do need something from you. I need your organization. Its resources. Mainly . . . your members."

She held up a hand to forestall his protest.

"If they, and you, truly believe in what you are fighting for. I offer a chance to actually win that fight."

Zach stared at her. She must be insane. It was one thing to fight for things to change. But none of them, even the most die-hard believers, deep down, truly believed they would ever *win* this fight. Oh, they could win a few battles here and there. Win some new regulations. Close some bad companies and put their CEOs in jail. But to actually win the fight? *What would that even look like?*

"Win the fight? What do you mean?"

"Show him."

"My Lady?" the girl protested.

"Shae." The woman's voice brokered no argument.

Zach stared from one to the other. Not sure what he was supposed to see.

And then it happened.

The girl changed right before his eyes. Pops and cracks sounded as the changes started to take place. *It's her bones!* Bile rose in his stomach as her body seemed to tear its way out of itself. Brown hair, or fur sprouted over almost every inch of her. Her face jutted outward, elongating and forming a long snout. A long, pinkish scaled-like tail erupted from her tailbone.

When the changes were done, she looked much like a humanoid rat.

"Holy shit!" Zach scrambled up, falling out of his chair, scrambling to his feet, and stumbled back against the wall.

"What the fuck is that!"

"That. That is the weapon that will win this war."

And like that, the girl returned to her human form, the change no less sickening to Zach.

He gulped and was rewarded with a little acid rising into his throat.

"I don't . . . . I don't . . . what?" His mind couldn't focus on anything. All he could see, all he could feel, was the horror of that monster which had stood where now a young teenage girl stood. He couldn't take his eyes from her though.

"There are more of her kind. More Weres. They carry the power of Lycanthropy within them. You know this word?"

Zach gathered his thoughts. Lycanthropy? Yes. He knew the word. What was it again? "Werewolves?"

Kestrel sneered. "The most common translation. Yes. It did, however, have more colonized meaning. It referenced humans who could take the shape of animals. Not only wolves.

211

"The thing about lycanthropy is that it can be gifted to others."

His head whipped around.

"What do you mean by . . . 'can be gifted'?"

"The power can be transmitted through the blood. By a cut, or bite."

"Why would anyone choose to be that . . . that . . ." he motioned disgustingly at the girl, "monstrosity."

The girl narrowed her eyes at him and emitted a soft growl.

"No offense," he assured her and tried his best to recover his charm and smiled at her. "I'm sure whatever was done to you had not been your choice."

Her look softened. "No. It wasn't." She glanced toward Kestrel who seemed disinclined to halt her from speaking her mind. "It just . . . happened. A product of my heredity, apparently." She took a step toward him and he involuntarily flinched.

"I didn't choose this, but it has made me strong. Now, no one will ever control me. No one will ever abuse me. And no one . . . *no one*, will ever imprison me. Ever again."

She trembled with anger as those words spilled out.

"No. I didn't choose this. But if I had the choice, I would choose this freedom."

Zach found he viewed this girl in a new light. She had clearly been through something traumatic. Something bad had happened to her, had left her feeling without control over her life. And it had been at someone else's whim. And now? With what she had become, she could ensure something like that never happened again. He found he couldn't blame her.

Zach turned back to Kestrel. "What does this have to do with me?"

She leaned forward in her chair. "An opportunity. I would offer this gift to you, but I see, you, for the time being, are uninterested in becoming more powerful than you could imagine."

212

The way she worded things. She was as capable as he in manipulating people to her side.

"However, those of your organization might feel differently."

"Why do you believe so?"

She cocked her head. "It is as I said. If your members truly believe, they will embrace this ability to enact true change. I am going to war. They will need to decide whether they want to win the war or continue to allow humanity to destroy this beautiful world."

She smiled again, not sincere, but calculated. "And, I believe, if you and I present this right, we will have no shortage of volunteers."

Zach sat back down at his desk and considered what Kestrel proposed. He had the numbers. His organization was worldwide, with most members living here, in the States. Altogether, he could rally several hundred thousand members. If, only half of his members were willing to accept this . . . *gift*, well, they would be a formidable army.

A spark of hope came to life inside of him. For the first time after he was released from prison, he started to believe they might make some real, lasting change.

When he was young and wild-eyed, he thought he could change the world. He had done some good, and had made some progress, but it usually only lasted until the next administration changed policies again. Then they were back to square one.

Deep down he had always known it would take an actual uprising. The government, and most of the people were too entrenched in their ways of thinking. They were too attached to their cars, their electronics, their luxuries that only ripping apart the Earth could get. Poisoning the water and the air to produce them. Raping the world of its resources to manufacture.

Environmentalism was noble in words, but not in action. Action meant sacrifice, and there were few people in this world willing to choose sacrifice.

213

No. They wouldn't choose it. They needed to be forced. They needed to be given no choice in the matter. And who would do that? Not our government for sure. Maybe one of the European governments. Never at the level it needed to be done, though.

With Kestrel and her were-creatures, they could create an army to force change. To wrest control from those who lived in the back pocket of companies and give it back to the people who cared for the Earth and didn't wish to see it exploited.

He returned her smile, as calculated as hers.

"Yes. I believe we can help each other."

Zach informed them it would take a few days, perhaps a week or so to 'rally the troops' as he called it. It seemed to Shae, Kestrel had already anticipated this and reacted nonplussed about the whole thing. They had left him there, in his office, already making phone calls and sending e-mails. The call would go out to all the activist groups E.A.R.t.H was tied to. They would come and together, Zach and Kestrel, would work to sway them to join the war.

Since they had some days to kill, Kestrel surprised her the following day with an unexpected question.

"How would you like to go shopping?"

Shae eyed Kestrel quizzically.

"Shopping?"

"Yes. Shopping. That is what females do together in this age, isn't?"

Shae frowned. "I wouldn't know." Which wasn't entirely true. She did know. Or at least, if Hollywood and TV's portrayal was accurate, she guessed it was what they did.

"I mean," she gave an exaggerated shrug, "maybe?"

Kestrel pursed her lips and clicked her tongue.

"Forgive me. I forgot. You never truly got a chance to do the things girls your age should be doing."

She stepped close to Shae, reached out with both hands and took hold of her arms, drawing them forward, sliding her hands down as she did to take Shae's hands in hers.

"I also wasn't given much chance to do what girls my age were doing around the same age as you."

Shae cocked her head. "Why is that?" She continued to hold Kestrel's hands. The kindness and closeness of the gesture warmed Shae. Because of how George behaved at home, she had never brought anyone over. Had avoided getting close to anyone in order to avoid the inevitable self-invite over to her house.

When it had only been her and Anne, it hadn't mattered. Anne had been fun and crazy and, in some ways, much like the twelve-year-old Shae was at the time. They did everything together. Anne had been her one and only friend. At least, until George came into the picture. Unexpectedly, Shae had found herself bereft of a friend. Worse, she had gone from a safe home environment, to one filled with violence at any given moment.

She had been a lonely girl.

Then, she had been raped. Kidnapped. Tortured. Mutilated. And finally, transformed into a humanoid rat. All in all, her life had been shit for quite some time. Now, for the first time in a long while, she had someone who genuinely seemed to care for her.

"Well," Kestrel began, still holding Shae's hands as she led her to the edge of the bed in their hotel room and sat them both down, angled toward each other. "When I was young. I began to show talent."

"Talent?"

"Magic," Kestrel responded.

Shae's mouth rounded in a silent, 'that should have been obvious', "Oh."

Kestrel smiled at her. "When it became obvious that I had an affinity toward nature, my parents apprenticed me to the local Druid."

Kestrel turned from her and stared off to the side, her mind leaving this room and travelling back to a time two millennia ago.

"His name was Olt, and he was a harsh Master. I had little time for anything besides learning the ways of the Druids."

She turned back to Shae. Returned to this room.

"He would wake me long before the dawn, for there were creatures who lived for the time between night and day. Animals whose entire day encompassed those early hours, before retreating at the fullness of the sun's light.

He would teach me about Druidic magic, natural law, the cycle of life and survivalism, long past dusk. I would usually collapse on my pallet and it always seemed I had barely closed my eyes before Olt woke me all over again.

"I learned fast, though, under his tutelage. In time, he felt he could do no more for me and sent me away to the Calendar, where the Druids went to study."

"Umm . . ." Shae interjected. "What is the Calendar?"

"Ah, yes. The Calendar is what they refer to now as Stonehenge."

That made sense to Shae. She remembered hearing something about how archeologists had believed Stonehenge was used to track the seasons, or the passage of time.

One of the corners of Kestrel's lips pulled back as she examined Shae's face.

"Anyway. It was a long time ago." She patted Shae's leg. "It doesn't matter anymore. Needless to say, I spent most of my teenage years training hard to become a Druidess, which very few people got the privilege to do.

"But it did mean I didn't get a chance to really be 'a young girl'."

Shae picked up on Kestrel's reluctance to go into further details about that time, but perhaps . . .

"I would love to hear more about your earlier life," Shae began hesitantly. "If you want, some time?"

Kestrel gave her a quaint smile. "Perhaps. Some day."

Kestrel stood and peered down at Shae.

"So? Are we going to go shopping?"

Shae offered up a warm smile. "Please?"

Kestrel laughed softly and smiled back.

For the first time in what seemed like forever, Shae went out without her long coat. Instead she wore jeans and a light blouse. It felt strange to not wear clothes which carried her knives or cover herself in case of a shift. A shift was still a possibility. They had lost their anonymity. Though Kestrel had been surprised, and a little alarmed as no footage of the battle made the news. Not the news. Nor any social media.

There had been mention of a firefight between the police and some unknown assailants. Speculation of a terrorist attack and the use of explosives. Video of the aftermath was making the 24-hour news cycle. Mention of Were-creatures though? Monsters? Nothing. It was definitely disturbing. But Shae had been held captive by an unknown government agency. Experimented on, and yet, no one knew anything about it. So, the cover-up didn't surprise her much.

She assumed the authorities knew their identities though. So, it was only a matter of time before they were recognized, and Shae would be forced to protect Kestrel all over again. Perhaps hurt or kill someone. She didn't want to hurt police, but if she got the slightest hint the members of that government organization who had held her was coming for her, she would kill them all.

Kestrel insisted they go out anyway. There was nothing they could do about being hunted. Well, nothing but hide, and Kestrel wasn't the hiding sort.

"Perhaps," she had said, "if more attempts to capture or kill us end like the last time, they will stop trying."

Kestrel still didn't understand what kind of world she had awoken in. They wouldn't give up, Shae knew, they would bring bigger guns.

Shae decided to take Kestrel's attitude, at least for today, and take advantage of a chance to do something normal, before everything went to shit. So, off to the mall they had gone.

Kestrel, of course, had gone dressed to the nines. A long, flowing black dress this time, made from sort of material which seemed to stretch, and yet cling to her every curve.

Needless to say, they drew a lot of stares.

Shae took this opportunity to get Kestrel into clothes more appropriate for, well, life. It took some doing, but in the end, she managed to get the woman into some jeans and a t-shirt.

As much as she tried not to, Shae couldn't help but find herself laughing at Kestrel's awkwardness when it came to trying on normal clothes.

The first time Shae had laughed when Kestrel's face took on a look of childlike glee after putting on her first pair of sneakers; she had stifled it immediately. She had been afraid to have offended the volatile woman, but instead, Kestrel had broken into a huge smile, laughed, and strutted around for a moment in a skin-tight black dress and tennis shoes.

It had gone on like that for much of the day. They had tried on hundreds of clothes. Jeans, skirts, blouses, sundresses and short shorts. Everything Kestrel tried on, she had looked amazing in. Shae couldn't help but feel jealous.

The only thing which made seeing the woman shine in every outfit she tried on from stinging too much, was her awe at wearing all these new clothes. The genuine pleasure the woman experienced, and shared with Shae was infectious, and Shae found she truly enjoyed herself.

"I never had a sister, or even," Kestrel shrugged, "a daughter before."

They sat in the mall's food court. Shae had opted for chicken nuggets, which Kestrel had frowned at, but said nothing. Kestrel ate a salad. *Of course, she did.*

"Most of my life has been in pursuit of one thing or another. First, the mastery of my druidess skills, and then, trying to stop the devastation of civilization on nature.

"My parents sent me away when I was very young." Kestrel's face went slack, all visual signs of emotion, gone. Shae had come to recognize this as her look of sadness. Regret, even. "If my parents had more children, I never knew."

She tapped her plastic fork on the container for her salad, causing a strange sounding clicking noise.

"By the time I reached childbearing age. Well," she proffered a sad smile, "I was in a middle of a war, and not much longer for that world."

Her smile brightened. "The point is. With you, Shae, I feel I have found something I had been missing but had never realized it had been absent.

She cocked her head. "Does that make sense?"

"It does," Shae replied. And it did. Shae felt much the same way. She had been close to Anne, at least before the coming of George, and this felt like

219

that. But different. She felt a kinship to Kestrel she had never felt toward Anne. Perhaps it was an age thing? Kestrel, despite her apparent maturity, had 'only seen twenty-two season changes' as she liked to call years.

They shared a smile.

Shae's lips made a straight line as she drew them in together. "Are you planning on fucking him?"

Kestrel's eyes widened and she glanced around to see if anyone had heard. Some of this time's propriety was starting to rub off on her it seemed.

"Who?" she answered coyly, bring her cup of ice water to her lips, drinking it while peering over the cup at Shae.

Shae tilted her head and gave Kestrel a withering look.

"Oh please. You know who!"

Kestrel lowered her cup and eyed Shae. She appeared to be assessing Shae. Weighing her and her response.

Whatever she had seen, decided her and she shrugged.

"I am not sure yet. I don't believe I will need to."

That statement shocked Shae. *Need to?* For Kestrel, it wasn't about whether she wanted to or not. It was a question of necessity. Kestrel used sex to manipulate people. To get what she wanted. Shae wondered if she had ever been in love.

Kestrel appeared to have noticed her distress.

"Shae. You must understand something. The war I will be waging is more important than anything. It is about saving this planet. It is about saving the creatures on this planet, and by doing so, saving mankind from itself. If we do not set things right, and soon, the world will spiral further and further into unsustainability.

"In the face of that, I must use everything I have. All my abilities, my body if necessary, to succeed. There is nothing I won't do to save this world."

Kestrel's eyebrows rose, and her forehead furrowed. "Do you understand?"

Shae wasn't sure she did. She had never cared about anything so passionately to be willing to do anything for it. She examined her food and frowned. That wasn't entirely true. She would do anything to remain free. To never be trapped again. Captured. She would use her body, if she had to, as long as she could remain free.

She peered up and met Kestrel's eyes and nodded. Kestrel held her gaze for a long moment, seemed satisfied Shae did truly understand and gave her a curt nod.

Shae decided to change the subject.

"What happens now? What do you intend for me?"

For a while Kestrel didn't answer. Instead, she took several bites of her salad, and Shae waited, eating some chicken nuggets. She would be patient. She would. Kestrel would tell her when she was ready. Shae knew she would.

Kestrel grabbed a napkin and dabbed her lips to mop up any dressing which might have escaped her mouth, though Shae knew she never would allow that. She was too perfect of an eater.

"What happens now? Many things. As we speak, Blain, Gordon, and Taylor are on their way here. Though," she offered a devious smile, "they will be making a few detours on the way down."

Shae waited for Kestrel to elaborate, but she didn't.

"We will meet again with Zach and organize a meeting with his followers, where, if all goes well, we will have thousands of volunteers to join our cause, and our army."

"Do you really believe you will get that many?"

Kestrel stared off to her right and tapped a finger to her pursed lips several times before looking back at Shae.

"Yes. I believe we will. Zach is all but worshipped by his followers. They view him as their hero." She shook her head ruefully. "With his help, and my hopefully persuasive speech, we will have many volunteers."

Shae wasn't so confident. What Kestrel would be asking of people was essentially for them to give up everything they were. To give it all up and become a monster. A powerful monster, to be sure, but a monster. Their families, their loved ones, their jobs . . . all of it would be lost. It was a lot to ask. Too much, if you asked Shae. She didn't voice her doubts to Kestrel though. She was pretty sure she didn't need to.

"And me?"

Kestrel smiled warmly.

"For now, I would just like the pleasure of your company. Do you believe that is a task you are capable of?"

Shae eyed Kestrel for some sign this truly wasn't, too good to be true. Could she truly have found someone to be *friends* with? After everything she had endured? After everyone she had ever loved abandoned her? What she saw in Kestrel's eyes was true kindness, though. Genuine warmth and an earnestness.

"Nothing would make me happier," Shae responded, and she found, she truly believed it.

# *Chapter Twenty-One*

Elias Tepper had started this day like any other day. He woke to the soothing sounds of a rainforest leisurely escalating in volume in order to draw him gently out of sleep at 5:03 A.M. He had left the alarm at 5:03, mainly because he didn't wish to click past the fifty-seven other numbers in order to set it for 5 precisely. Sure, he could hold the button down so the numbers would fly by more quickly, but that was precisely what had created this problem to start with.

So, at 5:03 A.M. Elias climbed out of bed and into the shower. His morning routine had differed only slightly for the past decade or so. He occasionally watched the news a bit in bed before getting into the shower or checking his e-mails from his laptop in bed, but not much alteration beyond that. Wake up. Shower. Get dressed. Eat breakfast while watching the news or checking his e-mails, and then off to work.

Elias worked at Yulchik Petroleum, a Russian-owned oil company with a growing bottom line and goals to make it grow more. They had opened this refinery in northeastern Texas a little over ten years ago and had hired Elias right out of college with a chemical engineering degree and a mountain of debt.

The first thing Yulchik did, and why Elias would almost certainly work for them until he died, was pay off his school loan. Sure, he had to sign a contract to work for them for the next five years and considering how much they were willing to pay and the benefits, it was a no-brainer.

He had signed the contract and hadn't looked back. Now over a decade later he lived his best life. He had been promoted to chief engineer three years ago and had over a dozen employees beneath him.

Two days a week, he worked from home via a satellite program allowing him to monitor different projects which were being implemented at any given time. Usually, today would be one of those days he would work from home, but the company's president from Russia was in town, and it was 'all hands on deck'. They needed to make a decent impression.

Elias put on his best suit and took the long drive out to the refinery. Placed a good distance from any major metropolitan area, the refinery was a bit of a drive for him, but the traffic was non-existent. It was much better than trying to fight the morning rush hour trying to get to work downtown, in his opinion.

The morning was warm, not hot . . . yet. It would get hot, in a few hours, but blessedly, Elias would be ensconced in his air-conditioned office. The tech area was kept cool, but down by the CDU and the other processing equipment, the heat would be unbearable.

When he pulled up to the security gate, Ryan who manned the booth, stepped out to great Elias.

"Good morning, Elias. Aren't you supposed to be off today?"

Elias grimaced.

"Yeah, but the president of the company is supposed to be here today —"

"He already is."

"What? Shit. I hoped to be in the office already to make sure everything looked good for his walkthrough."

Ryan nodded in understanding.

"Yeah, you aren't the first one to utter a few curses upon hearing he was already here. He and his entourage came in at 4 A.M. You know, time differences and what not."

Elias grimaced.

"Well, I better hurry in. Salvage the situation as best as I can. I keep a pretty tight ship, so everything should be in order already. Just wanted to make sure."

"Well, hope it all turns out fine for you, Elias. Have a good day."

Ryan stepped back, reached into the guard booth and opened the gate.

"You too, Ryan."

Elias drove through the gate and parked.

Walking fast, as he was decidedly *not* running — he wasn't! He quickly entered the building housing the offices of management and engineering, the first building inside the sprawling complex of the refinery which covered over ten acres of land.

By the time he reached his actual office he had been relieved to hear from most of the others the president had been in meetings all morning with upper management and as of yet, had not made any rounds through the offices.

His first order of business when he got to his office was to make sure his personal office was in order. Taking a few moments to address the memos in his inbox, he would straighten his desk and do his best to declutter it.

He liked his little office. It sat on the east side of the building on the third floor. He had a large expanse of windows overlooking the parking lot, which meant he got the full exposure of the sun for most of his workday and could check to see if the boss' cars were there or if they had gone for the day. The sun was harsh, but he had shade blinds which tempered the brightness. He enjoyed the sunlight though. It made him feel a little like he worked outside.

There were quite a few offices with no windows or those on the west side of the building which only got the sun's blessing as they were leaving to go home.

Elias was about to check on his employees when he heard loud popping noises from outside. It had sounded a little like fireworks, which was strange. *Why would someone be shooting off fireworks in the morning? Especially this close to a refinery. They wouldn't be. So, what was it?*

Getting up from his desk he crossed to the windows and gazed out. Nothing immediately caught his attention, but he continued to scan the parking lot. A vehicle had cleared the gate and pulled into the parking lot. Nothing odd about that, though. The gate remained open, though, which was odd.

Elias moved to the far corner of his windows in some vain attempt to see if he could see into the guard booth, though given the distance and the angle, he wasn't able to. There was a window on this side, but Elias saw no movement inside.

He squinted at the window, waiting to see some movement from Ryan. Something on the window made a peculiar pattern near the bottom left corner. It reminded Elias of how children sometimes draw the sun. They make a wedge-shaped semi-circle before drawing rays of light, little streaks of yellow crayon or marker radiating outward from the sun.

The problem was. This sun wasn't yellow, but dark red, almost black. As Elias watched, the rays of the sun began to trickle downward, like a red melting popsicle. Elias frowned. No. Not like a melting popsicle. Could it be? No. Impossible. Again, Elias scanned for Ryan. He was nowhere to be seen and the gate remained open.

Elias backed away from the window and went to his phone. Dialing the gate, he waited as the phone connected and rang. It continued to ring, and Elias waited. No one answered. Stretching the phone cord, he went back to the window. No answer. No movement. A sense of dread landed like a brick in Elias' stomach.

When his door opened, he jumped and dropped the phone. It was Reva, the short, pretty, blonde engineer who was part of his team. Her face held a look of concern.

"Do you know what is going on?"

The question caught Elias by surprise.

"Going on with what?"

"With the president of the company?"

"How do you mean?"

She frowned at him, as if anybody should be aware of what went on, it should be him. Which, he supposed, was true.

"Like, three buff-ass Russian bodyguard looking guys came and went into the meeting room and bustled him out." Her concerned look came back. "They looked . . . worried."

The sense of dread came back, and Elias again glanced out the window toward the guard booth. *Still no sign of Ryan.* Those red sun rays were leaving long streaks down the glass. *If I'm wrong, I'm going to look a fool.*

He picked up the phone, pushed the hang up button and looked to Reva. "Reva. Keep calm and quickly gather the team. I believe we have an active shooter situation and we need to follow protocol."

He dialed 911.

Reva stared at him; her face drained of all color.

"Active shooter?" It came out as barely a whisper.

"Reva. Please. You need to get the team together and start to follow protocol."

"Police department." The voice over the phone was female.

"Yes. Hi. I am at Yulchik Petroleum. I believe we have an active shooter situation."

227

Reva still stood at the door, staring at him.

*REVA!* He mouthed to her and shooed her out. She fled.

*I wish it had been Susan. That woman could stay calm during a sharknado.*

"How many assailants are there, sir?"

"I'm sorry?"

"Assailants, sir. How many?"

"I'm not sure. I heard gun fire. I think. And the guard who is supposed to be guarding the gate is gone. I think there is blood. The gate is still up. The president of the company was rushed out of here with bodyguards." He realized he rambled, and he felt stupid. Everything he said was circumstantial. He hadn't seen anyone with a gun. He wasn't sure if he had heard gunshots, or something else. Ryan was missing, and the gate was up. Which was suspicious, to say the least, but there could be other explanations. The blood . . . He went to the window again and viewed the guard booth. Was it blood?

He realized the dispatcher had been asking him something.

"I'm sorry, what?"

"Has there been any other gun shots, sir?"

"More gun shots? Um . . . No. I don't think so."

A pause.

"So, you heard what you believe were gun shots, but you haven't heard them again and haven't seen any of the shooters. Am I understanding the situation correctly, sir?" The dispatcher's doubt was so palpable, he felt his face grow flush.

"Look. I know how it sounds, but I'm trying to prevent something worse from happening."

"Can I get your name, sir?"

He sighed.

"Elias. Elias Tepper. Look, could you just send over someone? Please?"

Commotion came from outside his office and he stared fixedly at the door trying to ascertain what was going on.

He could hear loud noises. They were muffled with the door shut, but some were short, deep bursts of sound, others were higher and longer. His brows furrowed. He could hear the dispatch talking, but he couldn't focus on their voice. The sounds outside his office were the focus of his every sense as he tried to comprehend what they were.

He picked up the phone cradle and moved around his desk to his door. Pausing in front of it, he hesitated. Then opened it.

Into chaos.

The sounds he had heard were people screaming. Screaming and running. There were countless men and women running about the cubicled central space. They tried to open office doors; some were still unlocked and those they disappeared in, but others were locked and refused entrance to those screaming and pounding on the outside.

"Sir? . . . Sir? . . . Sir? . . ." The voice on the line was insistent. Apparently, where he hadn't been convincing before, the sound of screaming in panic and fear had been convincing enough.

He stood in the doorway to his office, staring out at the maelstrom of panic right outside.

"Send someone," he told the dispatcher. "Now."

He let the phone drop and stepped out into the storm.

# *Chapter Twenty-Two*

Elias was relieved to know his team would have already taken cover in one of the offices. He began motioning to those scrambling through the cubicles and the hallways. "Over here!"

Men and women peeled away from the rush to barrel past him into his office. After the fourth person ran by, he reached out and grabbed a young tech as he tried to enter his office.

"What is going on?!"

The young man turned to him and Elias could see the horror in his face. His eyes were wide, his pupils dilated. The man shook in Elias' grip.

"A monster!" He wrenched his arm, breaking Elias' hold and ducked into Elias' office.

*A monster? What the hell was he talking about?*

At that precise moment, the door leading to the outer hallway slammed open so hard, the knob punched through the drywall holding the door fast, and in walked a monster.

Ducking under the outer doorframe and turning its body slightly to fit, the beast towered into the office. With its ridged back it almost brushed the ceiling tiles. A wide, boarish face, large yellow tinged tusks thrusting up from its lower jaw, and beady eyes under a sloped brow, stared at him from down the hall. Blood-soaked clawed hands, clenched and unclenched, causing the bulging muscles in the creature's arms to swell and flatten, like the roll of the tide.

Elias ducked back into the office, shut and locked the door. For all the good it would do them. They were all going to die.


Blain, Taylor and Gordon arrived at the Yulchik Petroleum refinery right after 7 A.M. They drove up to the gate and the security guard had stepped out of the guard booth.

Blain attempted a smile.

"Hello. Can I ask what your business is?" The security guard examined Blain, then glanced at Taylor in the backseat and peered across at Gordon.

Gordon stepped out of the car and started to move around it toward the guard booth.

The security guard straightened from leaning over to look at Blain and eyed Gordon.

"Sir. I'm going to have to ask you to remain in the vehicle."

Gordon didn't slow.

"Sir." The guard rested his hand on the pummel of his gun. "Please return to the car."

Gordon began to shift.

"What the . . .?" The guard managed to get out his gun and fire off three shots before Gordon was on him.

Reaching out with one of his massive claws he grabbed the guard's weapon hand and squeezed. Bones snapped and popped inside as Gordon crushed fingers and palm. The guard cried out in pain and arched his back, lifting on his toes. His hand, trapped between the crushing force and unyielding metal of the gun, was too much. Like a fleshy sack of marbles, they had lost all their cohesion.

In a wide arc, Gordon's other clawed hand swept down, slicing the man's chest from clavicle to groin, leaving deep tears in the flesh and cloth, like a freshly tilled field. Bright red blood welled up from those wounds and the man staggered back.

Surprisingly, he had the audacity to attempt to taser Gordon, which only angered the man. Roaring as the electricity from the little handheld weapon burned the side of his torso, right below the ribs, Gordon lashed out with a vicious backswing. The guards head snapped sideways, and blood sprayed out from his torn face, decorating the window of the guard shack, as Gordon's scaled hide on the back of his claw tore through skin, muscle and tendons. Following a popping noise, the guard fell back into the shack, his head flopped at an awkward angle.

Gordon stared down at the guard for a moment and moved to get back in the car, shifting back as he went.

Once back in the car, Blain turned to him.

"You do remember she didn't want us to kill any of the workers, right?"

"Fuck off, Blain."

Blain chuckled. They had managed not to come to blows yet, remarkable, considering how much Blain pushed the man. He had wanted to get a rise out of the pompous ass, but Gordon was nothing, if not calm and collected. No matter what Blain threw at the man, he would not take the bait. It didn't stop Blain from trying though.

Blain drove the car forward and brought it around in front of the main entrance to the refinery offices. According to Kestrel's info, the president of the company was here, in town from Russia, and expected to be touring the facility today.

Their task was two-fold. Kestrel wanted this refinery essentially rendered inoperable and they needed to increase their numbers. To do this, they were to sweep through and injure as many workers as possible, creating potential Pures, or Weres in Taylor's case.

They were not to kill any of the workers, if they could avoid it, but as for the president of the company, the CEO and all the other higher ups within the company, she wanted them slaughtered.

They exited the car. Blain moved around the car to join Gordon and Taylor in examining the building. Blain turned to the other two.

"Gordon. Go around to the back. My guess is when the shit starts to hit the fan, the president is going to try and make a run for it. He's all yours."

He sneered at Taylor. "You. You can cover the side entrance." He pointed to the left of the building. "There should be a few who will try and make it out from that direction. I get you don't really have the stomach for all the fun stuff, Taylor, but you will injure as many as you can who try and get past you."

Taylor ignored him and instead began making his way toward the side of the building.

Gordon crooked an eyebrow at him. Blain shrugged. "I need to put him somewhere and I want the front. He will do what needs to be done." Blain returned his focus to the front of the building. "He doesn't have a choice."

Gordon nodded. "See you on the other side."

"Try not to stop for a snack."

Gordon gave him an unreadable look and Blain flashed what was left of his teeth. Gordon turned and began to make his way to back of the building.

*Well, you do like to eat them. Just saying.* He watched Gordon go for a moment before heading toward the front door. As he approached it, he decided to start the panic immediately. Jogging toward the front door, he shifted as he approached, gaining momentum.

When he hit the front door, it was at a devastating charge. The glass door shattered into a thousand pieces. Shards of glass flew inward, followed by twisted pieces of metal from the door frame.

There were four people in the lobby when he struck. A woman had been approaching the front door and took the brunt of the shrapnel. Streaks of red seemed to appear out of nowhere on her face and bare arms. Long thin cuts tore paths through thousands of puncture wounds as pieces of glass hit her with enough force to bury themselves deep within her skin. Like a night sky filled with stars of blood, her body shimmered as it flowed to the surface, glistening.

Screaming, she clutched at her eyes, their tiny orbs perforated, their viscous fluids mixing with tears and blood to leak from beneath hard-pressed palms.

The secretary had managed to dive behind the welcome desk by instinct and had yet to rise as Blain took in the rest of the scene. Of the two others in the lobby, one, an older man, had taken a sizable piece of bent metal in the throat and was now dying a slow and painful death as he bled out onto the tiled floor of the lobby. His gurgling breaths could barely be heard over the other woman's screaming.

The other man had taken a wound to his leg, or so Blain surmised, as he tried to drag himself across the floor and get around a corner into an adjacent hallway.

Blain strode in. With a casual flick of his hand, he dragged his claws across the huddled back of the woman clutching her destroyed eyes, gouging her flesh before passing right by as she screamed again, sprawling onto the ground.

With a measured pace, he moved toward the welcome desk. His cloven feet clicking on the tile as he moved. He knew she could hear him approach. Her fear, almost palatable. Manic whimpering whined from behind the desk.

As tall as he was, when he reached it, he could see her huddled down behind it. Reaching down he grabbed a fistful of hair and yanked her upward.

234

Screaming in pain and fear, she clutched at his wrist to take the weight off her scalp. Kicking her legs wildly in the air, all she managed to do was to set herself on a slight rotation, spinning her face away from him.

He waited.

When she rotated back around to come face to face with him, he smiled. The corners of his lips peeled back, revealing protruding canines and his yellowed tusks.

She screamed again.

He punched her. Hard. Not so hard as to kill her, but he could hear the crack of broken ribs. He had made sure to clip her with a claw as he hit her. The force of the impact flew her backward. Her hair ripped away from her scalp leaving him with a pelt of hair attached to a bloodied slab of flesh. With a solid impact against the far wall, she slumped.

Tossing the mangled, hairy piece of scalp at her motionless body, he didn't give her another thought.

The man who had been dragging himself away to hide was no longer visible, but the streaks of blood left an easy trail to follow and he made his way to the hallway. He found the man, his back against a wall talking on his cellphone, sobbing.

"Honey, if you get this. Just know that I love you. Tell Rachel that I love her too, and that daddy will always be with her."

He caught sight of Blain.

"No. No. No. Please. Don't."

Blain moved closer. The reek of piss in the air reached him and there was a dark stain at the man's groin.

Blain growled.

"Oh, for fuck's sake, pussy. Stand up and face this like a man instead of lying there, pissin' yourself and blubbering like a woman."

Blain reached down and grabbed the man by the collar, hauling him to his feet, lifting him up higher into the air till they were face to face.

The man whimpered. Blain sneered at him in disgust. Moving closer so his snout was almost touching the man, he angled his tusk and forced it into the man's mouth. Try as the man did, there was little he could do to avoid his mouth being penetrated by the daggerlike protrusion. Once inside the man's mouth, Blain jerked his head to the side, tearing his tusk out through the man's cheek. The man wailed and grasped at his ruined face.

Blain tossed him aside, not caring how or where the man fell.

There was a loud, 'ding' and Blain whirled around in time to see an elevator open. There was a clutch of people inside. Upon seeing him, standing there, claws and tusk stained and dripping blood, they screamed and backed up in the elevator as if it would give them some sanctuary.

Inwardly, Blain smiled and crowded into the elevator. Turning once he was inside, he dragged his claw up the row of floor numbers, lighting each floor before pressing the 'close door' button. He could feel the press of bodies behind him, scrambling over each other in an attempt to get as far away as the confines of the elevator would allow.

As the doors closed, Blain turned around. "Going up?"

Then the horror began.

Taylor wanted nothing to do with this madness. He hated killing. He hated what it did to him. How it made him feel. The disgust. The thrill! It didn't matter though. He had no choice. Blain's will enveloped him, choking to death any resistance Taylor might try to bring forth. *Right. When have I resisted anything in my life?*

As Taylor waited in front of the side door to the office complex, he thought back to that fateful day when his life went to shit. *Ha! Which time?* Well, the last time, he guessed. He had entered that hotel with thoughts of being a hero, and instead left a villain.

It wasn't fair. It wasn't right. He had spent all his life a nobody. And now he was somebody. Somebody he didn't want to be. Someone he wished to never have been. He thought to leave. To walk away. He had tried to leave once and felt Blain's force of will slam him back into place. He was a prisoner. A prisoner within his own body with no hope of escape. His captor was all but immortal. He wondered when the real resistance would come. When would they get serious about stopping them? Perhaps then he might find his freedom?

These bodies could only survive so much, couldn't they? At some point, they would be put to the test. It won't be merely handguns and assault rifles. No. There will be grenades, smart bombs, hell, maybe tactical nukes when they realize the other stuff wasn't working.

He started to hear screams from inside the building. They were headed his way. With a shake, he shifted. Body expanding. Bones breaking and reshaping. In moments he stood before the door in all his dreadfulness.

The door flew open and the man who came through was looking back over his shoulder, so he didn't see Taylor. He slammed into Taylor's body, and bounced off falling to the ground. The door, which had closed again, tore open and took the man full on the side of the head as he tried to scramble away from Taylor.

A wet thud, and the man's head was knocked to the side, where he collapsed. The door, stained red near the base, started to close again. Another man came through it, but this one, with his eyes open wide, saw Taylor clearly and tried to veer away from him. Taylor reached out with one hand and shredded the side of his face. The man screamed and went down.

237

When the door opened for the third time, a stream of people poured out, like a dam bursting, only to be met with a larger, more imposing dam. The ones in front were brought up short as they took in the scene. In front of them on the ground lay an unmoving man, the side of his head bleeding from a long straight gash. Another man writhed on the ground, clutching the side of his face, screaming.

Unfortunately for the ones in the front who wanted to stop, the tide of people behind them hadn't seen what had halted them and pushed them forward.

Right into Taylor.

Taylor began to lash out indiscriminately. Tearing flesh here. Goring another there. A score of people went down before panic and terror forced those who were still standing to scramble back into the building.

When the last person had disappeared back through the door, Taylor walked around and took stock of those who were still here. Roughly twenty or so people lay about in a tangled mess. Many were sprawled out on top of others as they had attempted to flee Taylor's attacks.

None had made it past.

Only one looked like she had been wounded beyond recovery. He had done his best to only wound, not kill, as he had been instructed. Dragging the people off to one side, he took up position in front of the door and waited.

There would be more. Gods, there would be more.

# *Chapter Twenty-Three*

When Gordon arrived at the back of the building, he dashed to the back exit and waited. He didn't have to wait long. Out from the door came a burly looking man — broad of chest and tall. He looked like a professional wrestler, only in a fine suit.

He was followed by another man, this one an older gentleman. His black hair was peppered with gray, though still thick and full. He was a solidly built man, not as solid as the man leading, but he appeared like he had been a fighter in his youth, maybe not only in his youth.

Two more fierce looking men came out behind the older man and flanked him. *Ah. He is the one I'm looking for.* Gordon moved to block their path. They stopped. The one in the lead brushed back his coat and put his hand on the hilt of his holstered gun at his hip.

In a thick Russian accent, the man said, "Get lost."

All four of them were watching him suspiciously, which didn't surprise Gordon. Afterall, he looked a wreck. He had already shifted once, and despite the bulkiness of his clothes, they still never handled the transformation completely intact.

He smiled his winning smile. "I'm afraid I can't do that. You see, I'm here for him." He pointed at the president.

All three of the bodyguards drew their weapons and trained them on him, and the one in the lead spoke again. "Afraid that won't happen. If you don't want to get shot, leave."

Gordon kept his smile.

"Counter-offer. If you don't wish to be torn to pieces," he shifted before growling out, "then walk away."

He knew their response and readied himself for what would come his way. There were dozens of loud bangs, and he was perforated with bullets. He had put one clawed foot to the back in order to brunt the impacts and stand his ground, turning his head to the side, closing his eyes.

When at last, the weapons were empty, he opened his eyes and turned back.

"*Ty che, blyad!*" one of the other bodyguards exclaimed.

Gordon parted his jaws slightly, his maw of sharp teeth revealed in the sunlight.

"Oh well, I wasn't going to let you live anyways."

He waded into them. Moving startling fast, he closed the distance to the front guard and his head snapped out, closing his maw on the man's head. Twisting his body away from the group, he pulled the man off his feet in a swinging motion. When he had turned around completely, he stopped his momentum. The head, trapped in Gordon's mouth, came away with a sickening ripping noise, and the now motionless body fell to the ground.

His spinning motion had brought his long crocodile tail around, taking another bodyguard at the hip. Gordon, with his acute hearing, could hear the hip bones shatter, and the bodyguard, who had been attempting to reload was thrown a short distance away, screaming in pain.

Spitting out the head of the other guard, Gordon spun around again to face the remaining two men. The president had turned and ran toward the side of the building and the last bodyguard finished reloading his gun and was running after him.

Gordon snarled, taking off after them.

The guard, running as he was, his body angled back toward Gordon, started to shoot at him. Gordon ignored the occasional burning sensation as a bullet pierced his scaled hide. The dozen or so wounds he had received from the first barrage had already healed themselves, and these would be no different.

By the time he reached the guard, he was out of bullets. Punching forward with one huge clawed fist, he sent the guard sailing backward. The president was only a few yards in front of the guard and was almost hit by the man's body.

With a burst of speed, Gordon took several strides, then planted his clawed foot on the back of the fallen man. As his full body weight bore down on the man, Gordon could feel his ribcage collapse and his torso flatten with a disgusting mix of snapping and squishing sounds.

Launching himself forward and upward, Gordon sailed through the air. The president turned his head, searching for Gordon, only to find him descending on him. The man threw himself forward, and Gordon landed with a heavy thud, shattering concrete.

The moment he landed; Gordon used his momentum to hurl himself forward. Stretching his body out, he lunged at the president as he flew, snapping his jaws as he did, taking the man between the legs, his mouth closing, encasing the man's groin and lower torso.

They both landed with a crash.

The president screamed as Gordon's fangs pierced his flesh, muscle and in the case of his torso, vital organs.

With an impressive show of strength, Gordon lifted himself up, with the man still entrapped within his jaws. Standing up fully, the man dangled from his mouth, the weight pulling his snout downward. The president struggled, his hands pounding against Gordon's nose and the side of his mouth.

Bracing himself, feet splayed apart, he raised his head, bringing the body of the president arcing upward. The man, neck bent to stare, first upward at Gordon, and now downward at him in a mask of fear. His eyes were wide and his mouth open in an 'O'.

When Gordon had the man near vertical, he brought his head back down in a swift movement. The speed and force of the action was so hard, when the man's head struck the pavement it collapsed from the impact. Skull and brain matter flattened out to either side. Blood sprayed outward, like a watermelon dropped from a roof. Red blood mixed with pinkish-gray brain matter and pieces of hair-covered skull fragments littered the ground.

Gordon released his grip and the man's body slumped down. A whimper came from behind him and Gordon glanced back over his scaled shoulder to see a clump of people by the back door, frozen in place. Dozens of eyes, wide in horror, stared at him. Which one had made the sound, he couldn't guess.

He turned to face them, his teeth now dripping blood, and attempted a grin.

"We can do this the hard way. Or the less hard way," he told them.

They scattered.

Gordon rattled out a sigh. "Hard way it is."

He took off after the nearest one.

Blain stalked the cubicles of the upper floor, knocking their chintzy walls over. He could hear shouts of fear occasionally from the side offices. After flattening the middle of the office floor to make sure no one hid in the warren of half walls and poorly built desks and eliminating any cover, he moved to the first office door.

Lifting one hoofed foot, he slammed it against the wooden portal near the handle and it broke around the lock but didn't open. He had seen how the door had pulled away at the top, but the bottom of the door held fast. He realized they must have some sort of locking mechanism near the base of the door to prevent someone from busting the door open.

But he wasn't just, someone.

Backing up a dozen paces, he lowered his head and bolted at the door. Driving his forehead into the door, it shattered around him and he barreled through to shouts of alarm and terror.

Bang! Bang! Bang!

Someone had a gun and shot him. Once. Twice. Three times.

Blain turned toward the shots. A woman stood there in front of seven others, a handgun held out in front of her. She shook so much; he was surprised she had managed to hit him. He approached her, and she turned her head away, clamped her eyes shut and shot again, striking him in the throat.

He felt blood, momentarily, flow into his esophagus and windpipe, gagging him. The bullet hole healed quickly, but the blood was still there. Hawking it back up, he spat it at her. A huge globule of blood and mucus splatted against the side of her face.

He growled. She had pissed him off.

She sobbed now. The gun had fallen from her hands to the ground and she desperately tried to wipe the sticky, disgusting mass from her face when he reached her.

Picking her up with his hands, he turned and threw her through the window. Glass shattered outward as her body sailed through, out and down. She screamed as she plummeted. Thud. Then silence.

Blain remembered back, not to long ago, when he had thrown a whore through a window in much the same way. *My calling card.* He snorted. Turning to the rest of the huddled workers he closed on them, lashing out, cutting and tearing. Not so much as to kill any of them, but he left them in a sorry shape.

He left the office to a chorus of screams from his left. A group of workers had tried to flee after he had entered the first office, but he had torn away the handle and the locking mechanism after locking both. The door was inoperable.

Turning, he began stalking toward them. Many of them dashed back into the office they had come from. After the fifth person had made it inside, someone had prematurely closed the door and locked it. Leaving three unlucky individuals outside.

They evaded him for a time, but he ultimately caught them and injured them enough to pass along the lycanthropy. He went back to the office they had come from. *What a bunch of wankers. Locking other people out to die.* With a short burst of speed and power he shouldered his way in, the door snapping off its hinges and falling inside the office. *They would have lived if they hadn't done that.*

Blain left no one alive in the room.

Dripping gore, blood and viscera, Blain marched from the room and back into the central office. There was a dozen more rooms, but Blain had a more specific target. He would return for the rest later. Striding deeper inside, he made his way to the back hallway and located the CEO's office and burst his way inside.

Four people were here, pressed into the back corner.

*Good. They are all in the same place.*

The upper level management was all here. Three men and one woman. All marked for death by Kestrel. These ones, in Kestrel's eyes, were the purveyors of what had been raped and pillaged from this earth.

*Who the fuck cares?*

Blain certainly didn't, but it pleased him enough to do her bidding in this. He loved killing in this form. The feel of power, the feeling of invulnerability.

They pleaded with him. Offered him money as he unhurriedly made his way over to them. Mostly they cried, called for help — pissed themselves. It availed them nothing. He tore them to pieces. That was one of the things Kestrel had asked of him.

"When you kill them. Make it bloody. Make it frightening! I want this to be the first message of many. No longer will we tolerate those who oversee the killing of this planet and its wonders," she had told him.

If he got to kill and spread mayhem, whatever her reasoning, it didn't matter to him. He wanted to kill. She gave him focus for killing, so it served them both. For now.

After he killed the CEO and the rest. He moved back into the office. It seems he had been gone long enough a group had once again gathered before the outer hall door and were beating on it, trying to get it open.

They had set a lookout and she screamed the moment he rounded the corner. The group turned. Frightened faces stared at him as he approached. Women were sobbing and crying. Hell, men were sobbing and crying. *Pathetic.*

Blain cocked his head. Decided on a different tact.

He shifted back.

Stunned, most of the crying and sobbing ceased. Most.

"People," he glared at those still crying and made shushing gestures with his hands. After a few moments, the last crying subsided.

"I have a proposal for you," he began. He saw some of them look at others in the group as if to say, 'What the fuck?'

He went on. "I am not here to kill you. Though some of you had to die." He jerked his thumb back the way he had come to indicate the CEO's office.

"That doesn't mean the rest of you need to join their fate. So, I'm going to make an offer. I can make you into someone like me. You will have power! You will have strength! No one will be able to hurt you. You will be unstoppable!" He roared, eyes blazing as he glared from one person to the next.

They were murmuring amongst themselves. He could hear the skepticism in their voice.

"But," he cut in, stopping all discussion. "You must come to me willingly. I will need to draw blood from you, to give you what I have. Just one little cut." Oh, there was more. Some of them would die when their body tried to fend off the lycanthropy, but no need to let them know that now.

He smiled wickedly at them, and he saw a few of them pale, which made him smile broader. "For those who don't volunteer. Know I will still cut you, but it won't be a little.

"You have a minute to decide."

Many of them turned to the person or persons next to them and began to talk in a mad rush, sounding out what they should do. There were those in the crowd who didn't talk to anyone. They simply stared at Blain. He stared back.

Those were the first to approach him. They didn't say anything, only came forward, one at a time and offered up their arm. Blain shifted back to his hybrid form and carefully, almost gently, ran a claw across their skin, cutting them.

These he marked as those he knew would follow him. Would wish to join him. They were the dark ones. The ones who had been mistreated all their lives. Hurt by others and now, when offered a measure of power to fight back, to hurt back, jumped at the chance.

When the first few who had come willingly to him had gone, gradually, the rest, after seeing how he had treated those others, one by one, came to him.

He didn't treat them as gently.

When they were all done, he moved to the next office and made the same offer to the groups in there, bringing forth one of the volunteers to make his case for him, to convince them. After he had to burst through the door of the first office and taken them all by force, the rest complied.

After he had seen to all the rest, he left them there. The three who had volunteered followed him out and he did nothing to dissuade them.

When he had made it to the lobby, Gordon and Taylor were waiting for him there, returned to their human form.

Gordon turned to him as he exited the elevator.

"We got company."

Blain could tell. Out the front of the building, through the bank of windows, cop cars were arrayed in a blockade a dozen meters back from the front door. He could see several ambulances beyond them, and he smiled. Good. Though they were going to need a few more of those.

"Taylor?"

"Yeah?"

"Can you see if you can figure out if they have an intercom on the secretary's phone there?"

Taylor shrugged and made his way around the desk, pausing a moment when the secretary's body came into view. He quickly glanced away.

*Gods, he is such a pussy,* Blain thought.

After a moment of examining the phone system Taylor turned to him.

"It doesn't have an intercom which reaches all the floors, only one which can address each floor individually."

Blain nodded. It would have to do. Moving over to the desk opposite Taylor he motioned with his hand for Taylor to hand him the phone. Once Taylor gave him the headset, he turned to him.

"First floor."

Taylor peered down, pressed something, looked back up, and nodded towards Blain.

"Listen up!" His voice poured out of speakers set into the ceiling. "Police and ambulances are out front. So, get the fuck out."

He nodded to Taylor who again pressed something below before pressing something else, indicating he had accessed second floor, anticipating correctly Blain's need.

"Hey, the coppers and ambulances are here. So, get out while you can."

Again, he nodded to Taylor and they repeated the process for the last two floors. As they were finishing up with the final floor, the elevators began to open, and the wounded began to filter out. Some had been injured badly and were being carried by their fellow workers, others had only received minor injuries and walked out on their own.

Every single one of them eyed the trio of them, and their three new recruits with fear and trepidation, as if wondering when they would change back into their monster forms and attack them.

As soon as they exited the building, they ran toward the police, many raising their hands in fear of being thought of as the bad guys and get shot themselves. Police officers were moving forward and waving the injured onward, eyes still locked on the entrance of the building. Of course, the police still had no idea what they were up against. As they began to interview those who made it out, at first there would be disbelief, doubt, maybe some anger at being lied to.

But as more and more of them heard the same stories, their doubt would begin to fade. The unbelievability of what they were being told would begin to move toward reality as they could no longer question what was being said by so many different people. The same stories. The same words. Monsters had attacked them. Horrible creatures who also could become human and turn back again into monsters.

Blain wondered how long it would take for them to decide to call someone who might grasp what the fuck they should do.

Glancing over, he took a moment to look at the ones who had willingly joined him. There were three of them, all men. One a Chinese, Japanese or whatever the fuck Asian country the man was from. Blain could never tell, nor did he actually care. He was a short, squat, roundish little man. He had pale skin with straight jet-black hair, falling straight down from the center of his scalp in clumps, like the fronds of a coconut tree.

He stood there in pale blue button-down shirt and black slacks. One sleeve of his shirt was rolled up to reveal a slight gash in his arm where Blain had cut him. He noticed Blain's regard and shuffled his feet, met his gaze for a moment before looking down.

The second man was tall and lanky, awkward in the way he stood. he slumped over as if he constantly had to bend over for fear of hitting his head. He wasn't that tall, though. No. If Blain had to guess it was a physical reaction to having been beat down all his life. It wasn't slumping, it was shying away. Flinching.

These two had been harassed and picked on all their lives. Blain knew it. Their abuse had turned their minds to hate. To anger. Though they had never had the means to retaliate. Blain had given them an opportunity and they had leapt at the chance.

The third man was a younger man, barely into his twenties. He was broad of shoulders, tall and good looking. He had the look of a rugby team captain or something. Blain doubted he had ever been mocked in his life.

Blain studied him, and the man studied him back, unflinching. Blain gave him one of his smiles, the kind he usually gave people he was about to beat the shit out of. The man paled. *That's better.*

Whatever had brought this one forward to his side, Blain didn't know. Some people were merely born angry, Blain surmised.

249

"You three. Go with the crowd." He motioned to the still fleeing mob of people.

"Get out of here. Go to the hospital."

They were looking at him with confusion.

"There will come a point when your body will try to fight off what is happening to it, and you will need medical help.

"So, go. Stay at the hospital until that happens. You will know it when it does. Trust me."

"What do we do then?" Rugby asked him.

"Don't worry about it. I will find you. Or you will find me. But, go for now, and hurry. You aren't ready for what is about to happen."

They nodded and jogged off after the crowd and filed outside with the rest of them. When they had all left, Blain turned to the Gordon and Taylor.

"You guys ready?"

Gordon smiled, and Taylor contemplated his feet and didn't respond.

Blain shifted. Gordon followed suit and reluctantly, so did Taylor.

Blain moved past them and began heading toward the exit. The other two followed.

When they exited through the smashed front doorway, the police didn't hesitate. They opened fire. Who wouldn't? If three enormous monsters came barreling out of a building where they had killed and injured close to a hundred people, who wouldn't fire everything they had at them?

Which is precisely what they did.

Blain, who was out front, took the bulk of the initial barrage. He barreled toward the closest cop, but the bullets did little to stop his attack. Still, dozens of bullets struck him all over his body. He could feel their searing entrance into his chest, abdomen, around his face and legs.

The police had their cars between them and the building and the closest car to Blain had three coppers lined up behind it. Blain slammed into it with such force it slid two meters back. One of the policemen was thrown backward to slam against the hood of another car. His back struck it and bent. He slid down to the pavement, unmoving.

The other two were knocked down and the car slid over on top of them, ripping clothes and skin as the undercarriage dragged across their midsections, effectively pinning them underneath.

Gordon had been following directly behind Blain and had launched himself forward in a high sailing jump. Tucking his legs to clear Blain, he stretched them outward and came down hard on top of the car Blain had shoved forward. When he landed on its roof it caved. Windows shattered and tires blew, and the car sank downward from his weight.

The two policemen who had been trapped underneath were crushed instantly, their screams of pain cut off as the full weight of a Werecroc and a police car came down on them.

Taylor had veered to the right at another vehicle, lifting it up on its side. Immediately grasping the underside, bending his knees and thrusting upward, he tossed the vehicle, causing it to roll over on top of the two police officers who had been using it as a shield.

Just like that, they were on the other side of the car barricade and were cutting through police right and left. They left none of them standing.

The cops unloaded everything they had into the three of them. When it became apparent, they would be unable to stop them, the police lined up in front of the ambulances who were doing their best to load as many survivors as they could inside and were fleeing as quickly as they could.

The police couldn't have known those people were not at any risk. They hadn't been killed for a reason. As soon as the reason was discovered, it would be too late.

As the police made their final stand, Blain, Taylor and Gordon stalked toward them. Using their arms to shield their eyes from gun shots, they approached the last cops, slowly, deliberately.

Three of the cops had already used all their ammunition and stood there with batons waiting to do battle, knowing full well they were dead men. *Fucking idiots.* Blain wasn't a coward, but he wasn't an idiot either.

There was nothing to be gained by standing there waiting to die like these guys were. None of those people were worth protecting. Certainly not with your life. Blain would have driven away already, let someone else deal with this problem.

As Blain approached the last cops who had used all their bullets and pulled their batons, Blain snarled at them. One of the cops, with a yell, came at him, swinging his baton in an overhand strike.

Blain caught his wrist.

Yanking the man off the ground, he hung the man in front of him, letting him dangle. The man grabbed the baton with this other hand and began striking Blain's wrist with it.

Another man ran at him to help his comrade and Blain swung the man he carried in a high arc so fast the other man couldn't respond quick enough as the body of his fellow police officer slammed onto the top of his head. Blain could hear the man's neck snap from the impact and his body crumpled. The man he had swung grunted once when he hit the other guy, and a second time when he hit the ground. That impact dislocated the man's shoulder.

Blain wasn't done.

With a jerk, he lifted the man off the ground, his arm loose, and as his body spun slightly, the man to shrieked in pain. As the man rose skyward, Blain let go of his wrist. When he fell, he flailed his arms and legs in an attempt at some control.

When the man's body was level with Blain's face, Blain swung downward with his hands, clasped together in a hammer of claws and slammed against the cop, increasing his downward momentum. The cop gave out an oof, before he hit the pavement with a sickening splat.

Gordon and Taylor had engaged the other four officers, ripping and tearing them to pieces as the last of the ambulances left the grounds.

Blain moved off to examine all the policemen to ensure none of them lived. That was one of the other instructions Kestrel had given them. To kill any and all law enforcement who got in their way. They didn't want to risk injuring one as it would give the police a way to track them.

It would happen sooner or later. They would find a way to capture one of the people they had infected and use their connection to find them, but Kestrel wanted to avoid it for as long as possible.

They moved off into the rest of the complex. It appeared a sizable portion of the workers who worked in the actual refinery had fled when the cops had shown up. They found some stragglers who, for whatever reason, had stuck around or had been working in areas where they had no idea of the carnage taking place in the other parts of the refinery.

They hurt them all and sent them running. They would all die in the end or become part of Kestrel's army. Blain had no idea how many they had infected, or how many would survive, but he knew Kestrel would be happy with the results. They had effectively closed Yulchik Petroleum. They had killed the company's president, the CEO and all the rest of the upper management. They had done so in a way to send a clear message as to what would happen to companies like this. And they weren't done.

There were two other businesses they would hit as they made their way down to meet Kestrel — one more refinery and a logging company. In each one, they would kill those who ran the company and try to infect as many workers as they could.

As Blain, Gordon and Taylor drove out through the open gate, they left a building filled with blood and gore unlike anything this country had ever seen before. It wouldn't be the last.

# *Chapter Twenty-Four*

Jason hit 'end call' and the phone dropped in his lap. His face dropped into his hands and a muffled sob escaped him. *Tragedy and tragedy.* Sitting back up, he wiped the tears from his eyes. First Beth and now Sim.

*Damn.* He had not known Sim long, but he had saved Jason's life, and besides, Jason liked him. From what Kat had told him, Sim had been killed by some unknown weapon. Something Sylvanis didn't know anything about.

They had fought the bad Weres. Their first true battle. It had been horrific. Police and bystanders were dead; the streets of Chicago looked like a battlefield, torn asunder and strewn all over the place.

Jason had said they had seen nothing about it on the news. Kat shared his surprise. They hadn't seen anything about it either. They were assuming the government had somehow been able to cover it up.

He then told her about the disaster with Beth, and Stephanie's refusal to return to Sylvanis.

"She is hurting, Kat. She sees this as not only her fault, but Sylvanis'. Sylvanis had pretty much guaranteed if there was a personal connection to the person, they would survive the transfer."

"That's not what she said."

"True, but she implied there was a far better chance of survival. Perhaps we should have been more reticent about involving our friends."

"No," Kat insisted. "You did what you thought best. You don't understand what we face out there, Jason. We didn't even face all of them.

Thankfully. It was all we could do to keep them contained and survive ourselves. If Clint hadn't shown up . . ."

"Wait. Clint is back?"

There was a pause.

"Sort of. He isn't . . . right. Not yet. Things happened when he . . . was gone. Bad things. Things he did, he needs to come to grips with."

Another pause.

"It will take time."

"Same on this end, Kat. I will work with Stephanie. Try to bring her around. This news about Sim isn't going to help though."

"I know."

"How is Hank?"

"How do you think?" came the sarcastic response.

"Right. Stupid question."

"Sorry," Kat apologized. "It has been a rough time here and I'm a little irritable. I'm not handling this well. Sim. Clint. Now Beth. I mean, I didn't know her, but I know the two of you, and well . . . I'm sorry."

Jason didn't respond. he couldn't respond without losing it all over again.

They were both quiet for a moment before Kat continued, "Just do what you must, Jason. No one will begrudge either of you for ending your involvement right here. Hell, I don't even know if Hank will stay on at this point."

Again, a pause.

"Maybe this is too much for us. Maybe we should just let the authorities handle this."

"Are you quitting?" Jason asked.

"No," Kat answered without hesitation. "This is what I trained for. This is what I have been preparing for all these years. I cannot. I will not step away from this fight."

Jason smiled, though he knew she couldn't see it. It was what he expected from her.

"Well, I can't leave Stephanie right now. But, when the time is right, I will come. With or without her." It was hard to say, but he meant it. This was too important. He didn't think he would give anyone lycanthropy. He couldn't deal with what Stephanie dealt with now, but he would fight. That he would do.

"That's good to hear. We could use you. These assholes are tough and mean."

"Yeah. I remember." He would never forget his fight with the Croc. He was not looking forward to a repeat of that confrontation.

"Take care, Jason," Kat told him. "Look after Stephanie and let her know we are thinking of her."

"I will, Kat. Thanks. You take care as well. Let Hank know the same, O.K.? Let him know . . . you know . . . that Sim was a great guy." It seemed like such a lame thing to say, but Jason didn't know what else to say.

"I'll tell him. Bye."

"Bye."

*Tragedy*. The word hung in his head. He was unable to see this in any other way.

It had been two days since Beth had passed. Two days and Stephanie had barely left her room. The only times she did was when Jason refused to bring food into the bedroom and forced her to come to the table to eat with him. Though he wondered why he even bothered.

The times she came to the table to eat she was mostly unresponsive. Monosyllabic responses or looks which spoke volumes was all he got from her. He didn't push, though. He cooked for her and ran errands. He held her when

257

she cried and listened when she yelled and screamed and railed against the unfairness of the world.

He did all he could for her. He would give her the time she needed, and he would be there for her as she got through this, but in the end, he would need to decide what he had to do.

The world truly was unfair. All this time pining for the woman he loved, only to now make a decision taking him away from her. He had meant what he said to Kat. He would go to them — with or without Stephanie. He hoped with, but she wasn't ready. She was still angry at Sylvanis.

Right or wrong. Stephanie blamed Sylvanis almost as much as she blamed herself for what happened to Beth. It was like Stephanie forgot everything Sylvanis had told her about the upcoming conflict. Not only that, but what Beth had said. She had known the risks but had understood the necessity.

There were forces in the world now. Forces who would destroy the world as they knew it and the only way they could be fought was with an equal force, both in power and number. That meant they needed as many Weres as they could get.

Beth had been brave. He and Stephanie had fallen into this mess. Stephanie had been born into it and Jason had been pulled in by accident. But, Beth. Beth had chosen to be a part of this. Yes, they had done their best to convince her to join, but in reality, it hadn't taken much convincing.

Beth was a fighter. She cared for people. Wanted to protect them, like how she had been protective of Stephanie. This was a way for her to do it for others and she had relished the chance.

Jason stood and put the phone back into his pocket and moved to the door to Stephanie's room and placed his hand on the doorknob but didn't go in.

He stood outside her door for a long time, trying to figure out a way to tell her about Sim. He didn't want to add to her pain. Didn't want to add to her anger. *I will tell her another day.* He took his hand off the knob.

258

"Jason?" Stephanie called from inside the bedroom.

He squeezed his eyes shut. *Damn.*

Reaching down he grabbed the knob, turned and stepped into her room.

It was midmorning, though it wasn't recognizable in Stephanie's room. The curtains were drawn tight and only a thin line of sunlight eked into the room, creating a long yellow strip dividing her bed in half.

Stephanie lay in bed propped up on her elbows, looking toward him, bleary eyed with sleep still clinging to her features like a veil.

"Who were you talking to?"

Jason sighed and walked farther into the room, then sat down on the bed close to her. He watched her for a moment. The light which always seemed to shine from her had dimmed. She was no longer the cheery, positive person he had known. She drowned in darkness. In depression.

He couldn't say he blamed her. In her mind, she had killed her best friend. How does one move on from that? And now he had to add to her misery.

"Kat. She called to let us know what happened." He studied his hand which rested on her bed, not wanting to look her in the eyes.

She sensed there was more. "What happened?"

He refused to look back up at her. "There was a battle. Lots of people died. We were able to fight them off, but . . ." His throat constricted, and he couldn't go on.

"Jason. What happened?" Her voice was insistent.

It was a long moment before he answered.

"Sim's dead."

She gasped, a hand going to her mouth and her eyes wide.

"No."

259

He nodded slightly. Tears dripped to her bedsheets with abandon as he had still not raised his head to look at her.

"Oh, Jason." Her tone broke him, and he sobbed. Leaning forward he rested his head on her shoulder and she wrapped him in her arms.

She held him for a while, and he knew she cried as well. Sim had been young, vibrant. A good kid. Someone who had stepped up to do what was right. Had fought, even knowing the danger.

They cried together for a time before she spoke again.

"I don't understand, though. How was he killed? It is next to impossible to kill one of us."

He removed himself from her arms and wiped his eyes, grabbed several tissues from the box next to her bed and handed her some. Using the rest, he wiped his nose before answering.

"They aren't sure. Something that Sylvanis didn't even recognize." He turned his gaze to her. "Whatever it was, it wasn't from Kestrel or a Were. Of that much, Sylvanis is certain."

Stephanie's forehead lined as she pondered what he told her. Then she frowned. "It doesn't matter. Just another victim in this stupid fight."

He didn't respond. She glared at him, hard.

"I'm glad we're done with it."

Jason nodded hesitantly and glanced away once more.

"Jason?"

"Yeah." He turned back.

"We are done with this, aren't we?"

"Stephanie . . ." Jason began, and her eyes narrowed on him at his tone.

"Look, the loss of Beth hit both of us hard. Not to mention the loss of Mike." They hadn't seen Mike since Beth's death. Stephanie knew where he was, or at least, *could* know where he was if she chose. As far as Jason knew though, Stephanie had been leaving Mike alone.

"I think we both need time to grieve and be at peace with what happened."

Stephanie still studied him with a penetrating look.

"You're planning on joining *her*?" There was quite a lot of venom attached to the word, her, when she spoke it.

"This isn't about her, Stephanie, and you know it."

"It's her fault!" Stephanie yelled at him, her face reddening with anger.

"Is it?" he replied calmly. "Is it really? Is it Sylvanis' fault Kestrel created a spell to come back and wage war on us? Can you really blame Sylvanis for doing what she thought was the best way to fight Kestrel, knowing we wouldn't be able to fight her and her minions without the power of lycanthropy?" He tilted his head and held her gaze.

"Kestrel is the one who is at fault here. She is the one that caused all of this to happen. It was through her actions that everything else followed. You want to be mad at someone? Be mad at her."

His tone had been firm, but he softened it as he continued.

"I know how you feel, Stephanie. Believe me. But this war is coming to us and we can either sit back and let innocents die, or we can rise to meet it."

He could see his words were reaching her, if only a little.

"Hundreds of people died in Chicago. How many more would have died if Sylvanis and the others hadn't been there?"

The heat had left Stephanie's face and she relaxed somewhat.

"I don't know, Jason. I just don't know."

He patted her arm and stood.

"You take all the time you need till you do, Stephanie."

He left her as she had turned and stared toward the thin strip of sunlight visible through her curtains. A tiny bit of light blooming into the darkness.

# *Chapter Twenty-Five*

The director of Homeland Security, Colonel Carl Simpson sat with the FBI and CIA director, along with the director of NSA and the CDC in a conference room at the DHS. It was a simple room, narrow and long. It held a conference table spacious enough to sit twenty people in comfortable brown leather office chairs.

The table itself was made from polished oak. It was thick and smooth; a clear resin had been poured over the wood to seal it, revealing the swirls and knots of the tree's life underneath. Several portraits lined the walls of varying past directors of Homeland Security.

Each one of the directors had a tablet in front of them with all the up to date information they had on the threat. The most recent reports had come in early that day from a Russian owned refinery in Texas. They had managed to obtain security footage of the attack.

From the colorless faces surrounding him at the conference table, Carl could see they had the same feeling he had when he had watched the footage for the first time.

"Now, you are saying there is no footage from the incident in Chicago? The recent one I mean?" That came from Lisa Pendrige, the Director of the FBI. She was a tall woman, and slender. She had almost no figure whatsoever, a stick of a woman.

She had blonde hair, which she kept in a ponytail which hung over her right shoulder. Bright blue eyes hid behind frameless glasses sitting upon a small, slightly upturned nose.

Carl nodded. "Nothing. Not a thing. All video and photo evidence have disappeared. Been wiped from everyone's phones and social media. Everyone we interviewed who had recorded something, or took pictures said the same thing. When they went to retrieve them, they were gone from their devices."

He surveyed the room of astonished faces. "Worse, many of them claimed to have posted them to their social media accounts or made posts about what they were seeing." He paused for emphasis of the importance of this next part. "All of those posts have disappeared as well."

He watched them for some sign of knowing. These were the only players he could think of who could do such a thing.

Nothing.

Either they were all terrific actors, or none of them had any knowledge of how this had been done.

"How is that possible?" Paul Rice, the Director of the NSA muttered to no one in particular. His long face scrunched up with a questioning look. "I mean. Some of that we could have accomplished, but not all of it. The shear scope . . ." He blew out a gust of air through his thin lips, causing his mustache to quiver and he shook his head. "What are we dealing with?"

"What I want to know," Lisa spoke again, "is which side did this? Was it," she waved a hand at her tablet, "them?" She scanned the room, "Or was it, us?"

Carl sat back and steepled his fingers in front of his face, tapping his lower lip. "I have to believe it is someone on our side, given the information I was given at the beginning of this."

"The experiments?" Lisa again.

Carl nodded. "That thumb drive was given to me by someone in our government. Someone who could have entered my office unseen, and unreported." Again, he studied the room for some indication if any of them were responsible. "Someone, who kidnapped, no purchased, imprisoned and . . . experimented," his face contorted in disgust at the memory of what had been done to the poor girl, "on a child."

Roland Espi, the CIA director chimed in. "We know that some of these, er . . . creatures, hail from overseas. At least the ones we have been able to identify seemed to have all come from either England or Australia. As to what their purpose in coming here is, we don't know."

Roland was part of the old school. At 71, he was the oldest participant at this meeting. His hair was gray, at least most of it was

"Their motives are unknown to us," Carl agreed. "What we have been able to ascertain, from both this recent fight in Chicago, and the last one is that some of them seem to be, for lack of a better description, 'good guys'."

"Several police officers who we interviewed said that a group of them came to their aid in fighting off another group. They were the reason the other group fled. It certainly wasn't because of the police."

"So, what is in these reports is . . . true?" Incredulity was written on Paul Rice's face, and Carl knew what he referred to.

"As far as we know, something akin to," Carl motioned uncertainly with his hands, "magic was used."

"Magic?" Roland guffawed. "Are you serious?"

Carl gave him a look. "Waves of fire from nothing, walls of ice . . . gallons of water falling from nowhere? What else would you call these things?" He scrutinized each of the directors in turn, challenging them to come up with a better term.

He leaned in and reached forward planting one finger in front of him, pointing downward at the table. "This is what we know. . .

"One, there are humans out there who can transform themselves into manlike beasts, and back again. Two, they seem almost impervious to conventional weapons and can heal themselves of almost any wounds. Third, some of them definitely are not good people, and fourth, they are here for a reason."

He sat back.

"We need to figure out what we are dealing with and why. And, how do we stop them when we can't even seem to hurt them."

Silence answered him.

"Ahem." Gina Valen cleared her throat. Her light brown skin flowed nicely with the brown leather of the chair. As director of CDC, she had largely been out of her element at this table and most likely wondered why she was there.

"I understand why all of you are here, but why am I?"

Carl had been waiting for this, and it was something he hadn't put in the debriefing he had uploaded to all their tablets.

He stood and moved behind his chair, gripping its sides.

"There was something I didn't put into your briefings."

He let it hang in the air for a moment, and like a boulder suspended above them, they waited for its weight to drop.

"Attached to the thumb drive was the report describing the girl's escape and what happened after."

They waited.

"When she escaped, she attacked the man who oversaw doing the experiments on her. She changed into that . . . creature, and with her claws she sliced the man's throat."

Gina's mouth parted is shock, but Carl noticed a satisfied look on Lisa's face which he empathized with.

"There had been a doctor nearby who managed to save the man's life. This is where it becomes important to you, Gina." He nodded to her. "While he recovered from his injuries, he suffered a heart attack. Which he survived. Miraculously, his wounds healed. After he left the hospital, he disappeared. He drained his bank accounts and dropped off the grid. He hasn't been seen since."

Gina was looking down at her tablet and flipping through pages of briefings before her finger stopped swiping and he could see her eyes dart back and forth as she scanned the page.

She turned to him.

He nodded at her.

"She . . . infected him?"

"That is my belief."

Roland nodded.

"That would correspond with the events which occurred in London."

Carl regarded him blandly as this was the first he had heard of this.

Roland shrugged apologetically.

"Honestly, this information came to us just recently and our best put this theory together a couple of days ago. Most of it seemed unrelated, until the rest of this started to come to light."

Carl accepted this. All of this was well outside their scope of understanding, putting the pieces of a puzzle together when you can't see the final picture was damn near impossible.

"Go on," he encouraged Roland.

"The night of the earthquake, there was an apparent attack on a hotel in London. It was a hotel known to be used by hookers and criminals, but the place looked like it had been attacked by a wild animal more than by people, or injuries sustained from an earthquake.

"Only two people survived and after being interviewed by the police separately, they both claimed the same thing."

266

"Let me guess. They were attacked by some giant monster?"

Roland nodded. "Yeah. The police dismissed it as drug-induced hallucinations or something. Even though their tox screen came back negative."

Lisa snorted. "They interviewed them separately, and they didn't have any drugs in their system, but they dismissed it?"

Paul eyed her before responding, "As opposed to accepting that they had actually been attacked by a large monster?"

Lisa considered this for a moment before inclining her head at his point. Roland continued.

"The two survivors proceeded to have heart attacks, mysteriously healed and fled the hospital. They disappeared as well. Off the grid."

Gina stood, then sat back down. She ran a coffee-colored hand through her dark black hair.

"So, let me get this straight. We have people who can transform into, as far as we can tell, unstoppable killing monsters and who can make more of them?"

"So, it would seem."

"Dear God," she responded, sinking lower in her seat.

"What are we planning on doing?"

Carl sat back down.

"I have dispatched agents to locate these groups and determine what they can find out about them and their motives. I have dispatched strike teams to be at the ready in Texas and the surrounding states to act if needed."

"What do you want us to do?" Paul asked.

"Information. We need to identify these people. Who they are, who they know, what kind of people they are? Plus, we need to find them, and find them fast."

"And me?" Gina asked.

"Study everything they gave us from those experiments. I know it isn't much, but it is about all we have. Get with Paul and see if you can get the medical records from those two who survived in London. Maybe there is a way to counteract this infection."

Gina nodded, as did the others.

"For the time being, we are going to be keeping this quiet. Whoever was responsible for the cover-up in Chicago had the right idea. We need to keep a lid on this for as long as we can."

He stood again, and they stood with him. "Fortunately, the ridiculousness of the possibility of this should keep it from going viral."

He looked around the room one more time.

"Dismissed."

As the directors filed out of the room Carl felt a sense of relief. He had been keeping this threat to himself for almost a week and it was nice to get it off his chest, to share the burden of knowledge. It had weighed on him and he had no one he could share the information with, apart from a select few agents whom he had already dispatched.

He hoped they were doing well.

# *Chapter Twenty-Six*

Kat ended the call, sighed and looked around the room. The battle had taken place the night before and it was almost noon. Sylvanis, Clint and Ben shared the room with her. Hank was in his own room and everyone was giving him his space.

"What happened?" Sylvanis questioned, her soft features pensive as Kat had failed to keep the despair from her facial features.

She set her phone down on the nightstand and rubbed her palms on her legs. She sat on one of the beds in her hotel room. Sylvanis and Ben had arrived an hour ago. Clint had slept in the other bed.

She glanced at Clint. He had slept fitfully throughout the night —tossing and turning, sometimes waking with a jerk, sometimes lying awake before crying himself to sleep.

Kat had hardly slept at all. She was worried about him, about what he had gone through. Where he had gone. What he had done. What it had done to him. She vowed to be there for him when he needed her, and if it meant staying up all night watching over him, so be it.

She glanced back at Sylvanis.

"That was Jason. Beth, Stephanie's friend didn't make it through. They were unable to revive her when her body rejected the lycanthropy."

Sylvanis closed her eyes and her head dropped. After a moment she let out a long sigh.

"She blames me?" The question was rhetorical, but Kat answered it anyways.

"Yes. They aren't coming. At least," she spread her hands in resignation. "At least for now. Jason will do what he can to convince her, but he isn't sure she will change her mind."

Kat shook her head. This wasn't going well.

"Jason says he will come regardless, but . . ." Kat trailed off.

Sylvanis nodded. She understood it was likely he would choose to stay with her if she didn't come.

There was silence for a long time, their thoughts their own, no one choosing to further burden anyone else for the moment. In the end, it was Ben who broke the truce.

"Are we going to talk about what happened to Simon?"

No one answered him. Kat didn't have any answers to give. The only one who had the slightest idea was Sylvanis, and she had made it clear she didn't understand either.

"I have been giving this a lot of thought since last night," Sylvanis began, frowning.

"I can't say I understand it more today than I did yesterday. All I know is that it wasn't Druidic, and it wasn't Were. Whatever killed Simon was something new to me but smelled . . . old." Her nose crinkled as if she had smelled something foul.

"Druidic magic and even Were have a certain sophistication about them. Druids were a learned people. We studied and for the most part we were civilized."

She stared off into a place none of them could see.

"The . . . thing that killed Simon. The *weapon* . . . it was raw. Uncultured. Primal."

She shook her head. "I don't know how else to describe it.

270

"Whatever it was, it was something I have had no experience with."

"But it was magic, though, right?" Ben stumbled over the word magic. Like Kat, he still had some difficulty with the idea of magic. She, at least, was a product of it, and so had no choice but to accept its existence and functionality. Ben . . . well, Ben was a man of evidence. Proof. And though he had seen plenty of it, his brain still told him he was mistaken.

"Yes. It was magic. Just not a magic I have ever encountered."

"And that should make us . . . very afraid," Kat concluded.

Sylvanis cocked her head in consideration and nodded.

"It most certainly should. Weres are as close to immortal as one can be. You are long lived, though someone like Syndor, er, Samuel, should still have died long ago, he would have lived for centuries. You can heal from almost any wound. Except decapitation. That is one thing you wouldn't recover from."

"So, a weapon that can kill one of them with what appears to be just one attack. That should be impossible?"

Sylvanis nodded again. "Should be."

No one had anything more to say. They were still left with no answers.

"Why did Kestrel flee?" Kat wondered aloud. It had been a question bothering her since that night. It was, at best, a stalemate at that point. Neither side seemed to be winning or losing, but Kestrel and the Rat-girl up and left. One moment, Kestrel and Sylvanis were exchanging spells and the next, she was gone.

Sylvanis sighed. "It is my belief that she had no intention of staying in the first place. They hadn't expected us to be there. Only the police. I believe she had meant for the Boars and Croc to be distractions. A delaying action, so that she and the Rat could leave without being noticed. Or chased."

Kat nodded to herself. It made sense. They knew Kestrel wanted to wage war on civilization. Engaging in street fights was not what she would want for herself. She needed to gather like-minded people to join her cause. Which

271

would mean she would need to be free to follow through with that. Her Weres weren't in any real danger, or at least they wouldn't have been if Sylvanis and the rest of them hadn't arrived, not that they put much of a dent in them.

Kat stared off at nothing, replaying the fight in her mind. She had gone toe to toe with that monster Croc, and while she gave it everything she had, she hadn't come close to winning. She didn't lose either. In the end, when Clint showed, the asshole ran.

"I need to get some air." Kat stood and headed for the door.

"Kat?" Sylvanis called to her as she reached the door.

"Yeah?"

"Be careful. This isn't like before. They know us now. Whoever covered up the fight will be looking for us, and anyone who has the kind of power to manipulate social media and the news should be taken seriously."

Kat smiled at her ruefully. "You forgot to mention the person who can kill us with a single blade attack."

"You are a fighter, Kat, not stupid." Sylvanis smiled ruefully back. "My guess is if someone approached you with a blade at this point, you would do your best to flee. An army, however, you might just stay and try and fight."

Kat snorted, turned and left. *Well, she's not wrong.*


Clint watched Kat leave the room, before returning to staring at his hands. He was not doing well. *Ha! None of them are.* Sarah had reached him. Pulled him back to his humanity. Again. With her calling his name, all the anger, all the savageness, left him. He returned to himself.

Then he lost her, again.

He took a shuddering breath and fought back the tears. He became aware of the silence in the room and looked up. At some point after Kat had left, Ben had also left. Now, only Sylvanis was left in the room with him, and she watched him with her soft green eyes.

Quickly he glanced away and wiped a tear which had barely formed at the corner of his eye.

"Do you wish to talk about it, Clint?"

He looked back at her. This girl, no, woman. He had to remind himself, despite her appearance, she was older than she appeared. She had lived long ago, when people had to grow up quickly. She had led an army. Fought a war. Had made decisions affecting the lives of thousands of people.

"No." He tried to keep the pain from his voice, but he could tell by the compassion in her expression, he had failed.

"You are not the first Were this has happened to, Clint. During the war, sometimes, men and women would go . . . feral." She made a face at the word. "Very few made it back. And even though they did, most were never the same."

He glanced away from her again. Her eyes seemed to delve into his soul. He had done awful things when he had gone . . . feral, *yes that is the right word.* He had killed. Worse, he had . . . fed. How does one come back from that?

"Clint." She stood and moved to squat down next to where he sat and rested a hand on his knee. It seemed like such a personal gesture for someone who hardly knew him, but somehow it felt, right. Natural.

"The man I knew, your ancestor, was the strongest, bravest and," she smiled, "stubbornest man I have ever known."

She reached up and grabbed his chin to make him look at her. He didn't resist and found himself staring down at this young, but old, woman with clear, beautiful green eyes holding so much understanding it made him want to cry all over again. But he held it back. Barely.

"I see some of him in you, Clint. The same stubbornness, the same bravery. I think if this had ever happened to him, he would find a way to rise above it. To not let it define him. He would understand that this hadn't happened by choice. What he did, even though it was he who did it, wasn't really his fault."

The corner of her mouth lifted slightly in a crooked smile as she watched his face and he realized something.

"You loved him? Didn't you?"

A sadness fell on her, like a dark curtain blocking out the light. The brightness of her eyes dimmed. There was a story there. A story of loss.

"Yes. Very much." She stood, now looking down at him. "As you love Sarah. Use that Clint. Let it be the light that brings you back from the deep."

"How can I? When she is being held by that monster?"

"And who will rescue her if you lose yourself completely, Clint?"

He stared at her, her eyes glistened, and he knew she was on the verge of crying herself.

She turned and left him.

'Who will rescue her if you lose yourself completely, Clint?' She had asked him. *Who indeed, Clint?*

Kat hadn't truly needed to get air. She was tired of being cooped up in the hotel room. She knew it was foolish to be out at this point. Sylvanis was right. It was dangerous out here now.

She had called her parents earlier to let them know the cat was out of the bag. Her mom and dad had chuckled at the pun but had understood what it would mean for them. It wouldn't be long before people within the government, law enforcement or the press, would come looking for answers. Her mom had assured her they would be alright. The moment Kat had left to find answers, they had started preparing for this eventuality. They had a safehouse to go to. Stocked and off the grid. They would hide out there for as long as Kat felt it was unsafe for them.

Kat had been afraid to tell them she didn't believe it would ever be safe for them. She knew they had been planning for her to take on this role since she was born, but now it was here, she wondered if they truly understood the impact it would have on all their lives.

In a way, she envied Stephanie and Jason. For now, they could walk away. Live their lives beyond this whole mess. True, if what Sylvanis believes Kestrel would do, it may be short lived, but they could avoid having their lives turned upside-down by being exposed.

She was tempted to call them and tell them to lay low. Forget about them and do their best to live the rest of their lives in peace. Her thoughts returned to the battle though, and how badly it all went. No. They needed Stephanie and Jason. And Mike if they could convince him to come as well. They needed all the help they could get.

Kat stepped out onto the streets of Chicago. Wind whipped around her, chilling her bare neck and she hiked up her hood, turned away from the wind and began walking. She had no destination in mind, she only wanted to get out.

The sun sat high in the sky, but the clouds were doing their best to interfere with the warmth giving light. The streets were crowded with people and there seemed to be an anxiousness in the air. Despite the coverup, it seemed the people of Chicago knew something horrible had happened in their hometown. Again.

There had been people on that street who had witnessed what had happened, and those people hadn't been quiet. Word would have travelled. Even in this day and age of less one-on-one social interaction, people would still talk.

Kat decided to make her way to the Magnificent Mile. To the place where it all began not too long ago for her and Clint. The place of the first battle. The place where she had returned to that night when she had met Ben and fought Clint.

She wondered what the word on the street was now. Surely people who had seen her fight Clint would have also talked. The news of the battle would have gotten out. They knew they had fought side by side against the Boar, but also had fought each other. Then, they fought again against the Boar.

She wondered if the people still thought of them as heroes after this last battle. Dozens had died. They had done their best to save as many people as possible, but in the end, they looked like the monsters who had killed. Would people be capable of holding their prejudices and see they were on their side?

She hoped so.

Without realizing how much ground she had covered, she found herself on a street corner looking out at the spot of their first fight. The destruction they had caused to the buildings in the area had been fixed. She caught a couple of females, perhaps in their twenties, taking a selfie next to the building which had been hit by the manhole cover. She shook her head.

She became instantly aware she was no longer alone and tensed.

"It's crazy, isn't? How something which should have been so impossible to ever have happened can suddenly be accepted as reality like it has always been that way?"

Kat glanced sidelong at the man who had spoken to her. He was tall, solid looking, with jet black hair which was close cropped with a little tuft in the front which stood straight up.

Despite the chill in the air, he only wore a t-shirt, which clung to his muscular frame like its life depended on it. Well-defined arms hung relaxed from his broad shoulders; his thumbs planted in his jean's pockets.

She could only see his profile; he wasn't an overly attractive man. He had a long scar, which ran from his lower jaw, across his cheek and ended right before his eye. It left a long white mark on otherwise black skin. He had been lucky whatever had caused that scar hadn't kept going, otherwise he would have lost the eye.

As if noticing her scrutinizing him, he turned to her. She realized she had been somewhat mistaken. While he wasn't overtly attractive, with a face flat, and his nose wide, his head was rather squarish, but he had beautiful blue eyes and a masculinity to his features and poise Kat found immediately attractive.

This man was a fighter. Like her. That made her more wary. She watched him, and he watched her as if patiently waiting for her to comment on his observation.

She turned back to study the street.

The man huffed at her rudeness but didn't leave.

She waited.

He waited.

At last, she turned back to him.

"Is there something I can do for you?"

He didn't look at her, but he pursed his lips and shook his head.

"No. But I think there might be something I can do for you?"

*Oh, for Christ sake. Is he hitting on me?* Of all the things she expected to happen today, this wasn't one of them. She was tempted to tell him he had no idea what he was getting himself into, but she feared she knew his type. A statement like that would only embolden him to try harder. And she didn't want that. Did she?

She sighed audibly.

"Look. I'm sure you're a nice guy, but . . ."

His laugh caught her off guard and she shut her mouth with an audible clack.

"I'm sorry. I just realized how I must be coming off. Approaching a pretty woman and making a statement like that." He shook his head, still chuckling slightly.

"Let me try this again." He turned to her fully and held out his hand. Now she could see all of him, including the tattoo of the eagle poised over a globe with an anchor through it. A marine tattoo. Now knowing he was a marine sent warning alarms off. Could this be the beginning of the government's involvement?

She didn't take his hand and after a moment he shrugged and let it drop. "My name is Jessie, and I know who you are."

She wanted to run, but something in the ease in which he presented himself made her choose to stay.

He had a friendly smile. A disarming one, and she guessed, one which charmed most people.

She wasn't most people.

"And?"

His smile faltered for a moment. "And . . . and as I said, I think there is something I can do for you."

Kat started to survey the crowd, ignoring Jessie for the moment. She wondered if there were other soldiers in the crowd. Waiting to make their move.

"I'm alone," Jessie told her.

She glanced back at him, not surprised he could read what she was thinking.

"Look, I don't know who you think I am, or what you think you could do for me, but I doubt you do or can, so if you aren't going to leave me at this corner in peace, then I will move on."

She began crossing the street and he moved in beside her. She closed her eyes for a moment and shook her head.

"Dude." She turned and grabbed his arm to turn him around to look at her and despite his muscular frame she did so with ease. His eyebrows shot up and he stared down at the hand holding his arm.

"Get lost. O.K.?" The fact she had stopped them in the middle of the street didn't bother her. When the light turned green, people would have to deal with it. "I don't want or need anything from you. Just leave me be."

His eyes raised to hers and his mouth parted slightly, as if wanting to say something but unable to get past how effortlessly she had moved him about.

"I . . . I . . ."

She scoffed at his uncertainty and let go of his arm and walked away. After a moment, he fell in beside her again.

This was getting annoying.

She stepped into a side alley, and he moved with her.

The moment they were clear of the crowds, she wheeled on him, planted her hand on his chest. Apparently, he had been waiting for it and grabbed her wrist and twisted it.

Or at least tried to. She decided she didn't want to have her wrist twisted and flexed her arm muscles. As his body moved to knock her off balance, which would have been the next move after twisting her wrist, he instead found an immovable object and his attempt to sidestep her attack had been thwarted.

She rolled her wrist around and grabbed his and squeezed. He gasped and halted his attempt to knock her down. She took her other hand and again planted it against his chest, forcing him backward to slam hard against the wall with an 'Oof'.

"You were asked nicely," she let a little bit of her tiger growl enter her voice, "to which you ignored. So, now I am going to ask, not so nicely."

279

She moved in real close to him, and although she wasn't as tall as him, she was close. She put her face inches from his and this time she did growl, low and deep. "Leave. Me. The Fuck. Alone. Got it?"

To his credit, if he was afraid, he didn't show it. He continued to look her in the eyes and didn't shy away.

"You need help," he told her. There was no fear in his voice. There was, however, a little bit of pain. She released the pressure on his wrist and eased up on pushing him against the wall.

She studied him for a long moment, wondering at his determination all things considered and arched her eyebrows at him.

"I was there. I saw. You all did your best, but in the end the only reason you won was because they weren't playing to win — only delay."

She let him go. He was right. They had been hard pressed. If they had Stephanie and Jason and if Clint had been with them from the beginning . . . maybe they would have won, but as it was, they won because the other side left.

"Go on," she told him.

He moved off the wall and straightened his shirt, massaging his wrist.

"If you are what I think you guys are, then you can . . .not sure what you would call it . . . transfer your ability? Or something like that, to others, right?"

She didn't answer, only stared at him expressionless. This guy not only managed to identify her, but follow her, and figure out she and the others were lycanthropes.

Jessie looked down at his feet and shuffled them, as if unsure as to what to say next now he had revealed what he knew.

He peered back up at her.

"I'd like to volunteer."

Her eyes went wide. This was not where she thought this conversation would go.

"You'd what?"

"Volunteer. Look, I saw, O.K. Not only did you fight those other . . . Were-creatures, but you did it to defend others. You fought for the police. You're the good guys! And I want to be a part of that."

"I don't think you understand what you are asking."

He stepped up to her. She was close to him in height, but he still topped her by a little as he stared down into her eyes. They were bright and full of energy.

"Something is coming. I know it. This isn't some random attack by this other group. This isn't like some gang war between two rival gangs." He spread his hands wide. "Tell me I'm wrong?"

She shook her head. "You aren't. But still . . ."

"Still, nothing. While this isn't the zombie apocalypse, there isn't much difference is there?" He raised his eyebrows in question. "It's like an infection, and it can be spread. And this other group . . . they want to spread it, right?"

Kat had to contain a snort. Zombie apocalypse. *He isn't that far off though, is he.* She had never considered it as something like that, but now that he mentioned it...

"Jessie, while I appreciate your desire to fight the good fight . . ."

"I'm not going to have a choice at some point, am I?"

She was getting tired of his continuing interruptions.

"Sorry," he apologized after noticing her expression. "It's just that I know your intention is to keep me safe, but if I'm right, no one will be safe, eventually."

It was much the same argument Sylvanis had given to them at the beginning and she couldn't fault him for his logic. He knew there was a fight coming and he wanted to be armed and on the right side.

She glanced away, off down the alley into the main street. Dozens of people passed right by the entrance to the alley and no one noticed them. This world was full of sitting ducks, waiting to either be slaughtered, or enslaved. Could she fault someone for wanting to fight instead?

Looking back at him, she nodded, and he seemed to relax, as if he had put everything into this moment and now, he accomplished his goal.

"O.K., but there is much you need to know before I let you agree to this."

"But . . ."

She held up a hand to shut him up.

"After. You will wait to make up your mind . . . after. You will listen to what I tell you. You will take the time to weigh what I tell you against your desire to join us. Then. And only then, if you still want to do this, I will agree."

He studied her as if looking for the meaning of her words in her eyes and after a moment he agreed.

"Tell me."

She gazed up and down the alley.

"Not here."

He smiled at her, and she had to admit, it was a nice smile. "Lead on."

When Sylvanis left Kat and Clint's room she didn't immediately return to her own. She had one more person to try and console.

She didn't feel up to the task.

Hank's loss, all their loss, seemed insurmountable.

Simon had been a breath of fresh air.

As much as she liked each and every one of her new Trues, Simon, who, besides Jason, had been the only other Pure, had been her favorite. Hank, Kat, Clint and to a lesser amount, Stephanie and Jason, had been fairly serious

282

people. Simon had been bright. Easy with a laugh and a joke, always provoking his father.

*Oh, Simon, you will be missed.*

Hank. Well, Hank was not doing well. Not well at all. Since the loss of Simon, he had barely said a word to any of them. Hadn't left his room. Sylvanis had brought him food, but when she had returned to retrieve the plates, they had appeared untouched.

Sylvanis was sure Hank wanted to die.

Only, he couldn't do it himself, and she surely wasn't going to help him.

When she reached his door, she knocked lightly, paused for any type of response. When none was forthcoming, she pushed the door open. It was unlocked. There was some hope for Hank. He wanted a way back. He wouldn't leave the door unlocked if he didn't want someone to rescue him.

"Hank?" she called lightly. The room was dark. The curtains were drawn tight and were close to opaque as most hotel curtains were. From the light bleeding in from the hallway, Hank's bulky form could be seen on the bed. His back was to her.

She turned the light on, and he made no move to show he noticed.

Nor did he answer her.

Crossing the room, she rested lightly on the side of the bed.

"Hank. I am probably one of the last people you wish to see right now. I am sure you blame me for Simon's death. I know, I do. Without me, the two of you would be living in peace in Canada. Away from all this violence."

Still no response. If it hadn't been for his uneven breathing, she would have thought him asleep.

"You most likely hate me. If I had given more thought to my response to Kestrel's spell . . . I don't know . . . maybe I would have found a better way. A way that wouldn't have dragged innocent people into this fight. People who wanted nothing to do with this war."

283

She hung her head and examined her hands. Her long delicate fingers moved around each other in a restless dance. She wasn't used to second guessing herself in this manner. The consequences of inhabiting a body meant for a little girl, she supposed.

"I . . ."

"It wasn't your fault, and I don't blame you."

Hank rolled around to look at her, and she met his eyes.

"You don't?"

"No. There are only two people at fault here. Kestrel, and whoever drove that knife in to my son's chest."

Sylvanis stared at this man in surprise and relief. He didn't blame her, even when she couldn't find blame for anyone else. And yet, what he said held wisdom. Wisdom she should have known if she had stopped letting self-pity rule her.

"I know why you are here, Sylvanis. I know because if I were someone else, I would be right where you were, trying to keep them alive."

Sylvanis looked away, color rising in her cheeks.

"No. Don't be embarrassed. You are right to worry. Or at least, you would have been right to worry before all of this happened to me and Sim."

He shifted down and swung his legs over the side of the bed to sit next to her.

"When this happened to us, it brought us so much closer than we had been before. Before this, I would have sunken back into the hole I had found myself in when Jennifer died. I almost did."

Hank sighed and shrugged. "Sim brought me out of that dark hole. Sim, being Sim. That connection to Jennifer that he brought into my life. It allowed me to hang on and climb back out."

He turned to her and she could see the tears welling in the corner of his eyes.

"I will not go back to that darkness. Sim would not want me to. I will not let him down." The fierceness in his tone gave Sylvanis chills. No matter what he said, he was on a precipice. One more loss and she believed he would break. She would have to make sure that loss would never come.

They stared into each other's eyes for a long time, before he turned from her.

"I just need some time to grieve. I know we need to decide what we will be do next. I understand it's importance. I just . . . can't. Not yet." He looked back to her, his eyes, rimmed with tears, implored her for patience. "I just need time."

She offered him a small smile of empathy. She reached out and took ahold of his hand dwarfing hers and gave it a soft squeeze. "Of course, Hank. Take all the time you need."

Releasing his hand, she stood, and walked to the door, turning as she reached it. What she saw there was not the broken man she had expected to find when she entered this room, but a man who had put all the pieces back already, except one. And with the help of the son he had lost, he would fit the last piece in.

And while he still seemed fragile now, she knew once that final piece fell into place, he would be stronger for it. Stronger and then the anger would come, and God help the one responsible for killing Simon.

# *Chapter Twenty-Seven*

Hector had left Chicago gladly. Had left shortly after the events in the streets that night. The night he had first drawn that horrible knife he had received word from one of his law enforcement contacts.

One of the many things which had been in his grandfather's notes were names and contacts of people throughout law enforcement and government, both in Mexico and the United States. There was even some contact information from Canada and European countries.

The breadth of secrecy regarding his grandfather still surprised Hector. He had yet to unravel the mystery of whom his grandfather had been. That he had been a man of wealth and influence was obvious. How he had managed to keep it from everyone in his family, and the why, was still something Hector couldn't figure out.

One of the first things he had done was contact a man his grandfather had listed among his most trusted informants within the United States government. Paul Betaan was the Associate Deputy Director of the FBI. When Hector had mentioned his grandfather, Paul had immediately offered him any assistance he required.

"Your grandfather was a good man; I was sorry to hear about his death. You have my condolences," Paul had told him over the phone. "Your grandfather told me a long time ago that if you ever contacted me, I should treat you like I treated him. So, whatever it is that you need . . .?"

Anger unexpectedly gripped Hector. His grandfather, it seemed, had planned so much of his life. Planned it and told him nothing about it. What other wheels had he set in motion for Hector?

He closed his eyes and calmed himself. No. His grandfather hadn't planned his life. Only prepared him. There was no way for his grandfather to realize that during his lifetime the Weres would return. The only thing he could do was make sure Hector was ready and to give him all the tools he needed to succeed.

"Hector?"

Hector opened his eyes. He needed information if he was to find those other Weres and to do what he needed to do. To try and fix what he had done, he would need to find those Weres who attacked the police and all those innocent people. Those were the ones he needed to hunt.

"I need to know what the government is planning to do about those monsters from Chicago. I need to know what you know and when you know it. I especially need to know where they are."

Silence answered him on the line, and it stretched for what seemed like minutes. Hector waited.

"Umm. Hector. There are very few people who even know what you are talking about. It is classified and we are doing our best to keep a lid on it for as long as possible. How is it that you even know about this?"

Hector thought about telling him he had been there. He had *witnessed* everything but decided it might get him entangled in what the government was doing about this and it was an entanglement Hector wanted no part of.

"It isn't important how I know. Only that I do. Will you get me that information?"

Paul didn't immediately answer him, which let Hector appreciate how important this information was and how important his grandfather had been. This man had not immediately refused to give Hector classified information.

Information, if given, might well see the Associate Deputy Director fired, or worse, arrested.

"What you are asking?"

"Is in the best interest of the government and the people of the United States, I assure you," Hector informed him.

"I don't see how that is possible."

"I wish I could explain, Paul. But I can't. But rest assured, no one will know you gave me this information. None of this will come back on you. Unless, someday, you might want to take credit for it."

Another long pause.

"Very well. I will get you the information. I will let you know if we receive any news about where they are and what, if anything, we are planning to do with that information."

"Thank you, Paul."

"I am doing this because your grandfather was a friend, and I owed him."

"I understand." Though Hector wasn't sure he truly did. There was obviously some history between the two men, but Hector had no idea what.

"I will contact you the moment I hear anything."

"Again, thank you." Hector ended the call.

It was a waiting game now.

He left Chicago and flew to New York City. Not for any particular reason other than he knew, when the time came, he might need to fly anywhere in the country and his best chance at getting a quick flight somewhere was in New York. Days had passed, and he had heard nothing. There had been no news about what had happened in Chicago. The government was indeed keeping a lid on things, it seemed. He knew, though, it was only a matter of time before this all came out.

He had been going through a series of *silat* moves, a Malayic knife fighting style when Paul called.

"We have located a group of them."

"Which group?"

He could hear Paul click his tongue in frustration. "You know way too much about this, Hector. I think you need to come in."

"Which. Group?"

Silence.

"The ones that attacked the police that night. Not the ones that were helping."

"Where?"

"If I tell you this, Hector, you have to give me something back."

Hector didn't immediately respond. He ran through options about what he could give Paul which might appease his curiosity, but also, not tell him anything important.

"Are you planning a raid?"

Paul didn't answer him, which was about all the confirmation Hector needed. "Well, don't. They will kill you all."

"That. That is what you are giving me?"

"Yes. Advice you should do well to heed."

Paul sighed. "Very well. They are in Texas. Houston to be precise. Some of them attacked several oil refineries on the way down. Injured hundreds of workers and killed all the executives. Or I should say, slaughtered all of the executives."

"Injured? Did you say there were injured?"

"Yes. Hundreds." He must have sensed the worry in Hector's voice. "Why?"

Hector wanted desperately to tell him they would be looking at hundreds more Weres if those people were allowed to live, but what could he say? Kill all the survivors? How could he even suggest it?

"Just surprised they left anyone alive."

Paul didn't respond. Hector wondered if he could hear the lie in Hector's voice.

"Where in Houston?"

"They have covertly occupied a small hospital in Stafford, a suburb. We have instructed local law enforcement to avoid the hospital and are making sure anyone who needs care is re-routed to a nearby hospital."

Hector nodded. They were decent ideas. They needed to keep people away, and since they knew how effortlessly this group had torn through regular law enforcement, they wouldn't want to send in the regulars. It would be time for more elites.

"When is the raid?"

"Hector. I can't tell you."

"Fine. Can you at least tell me if it will be within the next three days?"

Silence. Then, "Yes."

"Today?"

Paul sighed again. "No."

Well, that didn't leave many options. It would happen tomorrow or the next day. Plenty of time for him to get down there and ready himself. A raid would be the perfect opportunity for him to attempt a kill. The confusion would give him ample opportunity to position himself and choose his target.

"Thanks again, Paul."

"At some point, Hector, you will need to explain how you know so much about this."

"Goodbye, Paul." Hector ended the call.

He wasted no time. Grabbing his suitcase, he quickly packed and left in a matter of minutes. He caught a flight to Houston and was there long before sunrise the following day.

He would need careful planning and to be ready. Arriving at a hotel a short distance from the hospital, he promptly fell asleep. He had time, but not much. He couldn't be sure as to when they might raid the place, but he guessed it would not be midday. They would strike either early morning, or at dusk.

They almost certainly wouldn't attack at night. Hector couldn't be sure if the government would be aware of the Were's abilities, but he didn't think they would risk attacking monsters at night. They weren't stupid.

Hector slept only a few hours and as the sun made a blood-red line across the horizon announcing dawn, he was up. He had come prepared for this fight. He put on a vest of body armor. It wouldn't protect him from a killing blow from one of those things, but it would protect him from a swipe attack. Plus, there would be law enforcement with guns, so it would also protect him from friendly fire.

He opened his suitcase and removed the wooden box holding the knife and removed it. The dark translucent green blade seemed to suck in the light around it. He could feel the glyphs etched into the hilt against his palm. A lost story trying desperately to tell him through tactile touch.

He had held this blade every night since the first — memorizing its shape and feel. Familiarizing himself with it as one would do with a lover's body. He hated this blade, and yet, he craved it as well. He wished to be free of it, but it pulled at him, unable to let go. He needed the blade, and the blade needed him.

He hated it, though. With this blade he had ended a life. A good life, as far as he could determine. He killed a boy, well, not a boy, but not yet a man. A

b. who had a father, whose anguished cry had chased Hector down that alleyway that night. The cry haunted him still.

He couldn't take back what he had done. All he could do was try and make it right by ending the lives of those Weres who were evil. The ones who weren't trying to help people. That is what he could do.

He had made a mistake. He had killed out of ignorance. He had heard what his grandfather had told him and assumed it was everything he needed to know. He had been wrong.

These were not the Weres his ancestors had fought. These were . . . something different. The knife still worked on them, though. Whatever magic gave the blade its power didn't recognize the difference between these Weres and the ones from his people's past.

Cautiously, he ran his finger down the length of the blade, keeping to the side of the edge. The blade was jagged, cut from jade. Even keeping his finger away from the edge, there were still barbs that could cut.

Sliding the blade back into its sheath, he attached it to a harness he had made for the knife which strapped across it his chest, leaving the knife's handle jutting out right below his armpit. He put on a hoodie and checked to make sure the knife wasn't visible. Content it wasn't, he left the hotel.

The day was warm already and Hector felt conscientious about wearing a jacket, but he saw no other option. Most people wore t-shirts or light blouses. Most were wearing shorts. He wore jeans.

It took him several minutes to cross over to the hospital. The hospital was small compared to most. These days, most hospitals were sprawling complexes taking up entire city blocks. From the look of it, this hospital predated the current norm.

What had undoubtedly been a local hospital, to serve a smaller area, had never been shut down or repurposed. Instead, they had kept it open and made it into a cardiac specialty hospital.

It was a short, two story affair, with windows at what seemed like every ten foot interval. The parking lot held few cars and while he watched from a corner of a nearby building, he noticed not a single car passed by in front of the building.

*Shit! It was going down this morning.* He needed to get inside the hospital. But it had to be under surveillance. Now that he knew what was going to happen, he began to investigate the area.

Down several side streets he saw parked black vans with tinted windows, unoccupied as far as anyone could tell from looking at them. Hector knew better. There were almost certainly dozens of agents piled into the back of each of them.

Hector scanned the rooftops. It didn't take him long to spot two snipers — one on his side of the street and another on top of a building facing the left side of the hospital. He couldn't see them, but Hector didn't doubt two more could be found on the far side of the hospital and the right side.

He wondered what they were waiting for. He didn't have to wait long. A lone car came down the road and pulled into the parking lot of the hospital. Given the fact the police were rerouting any civilians away from this block, Hector had to assume this was an unfriendly.

Hector recognized the man who got out of the vehicle. He had been there that night. He was the one who had turned into a Werecrocodile, a fearsome beast who had given the Weretiger a good fight. She was a tough opponent.

He returned his attention to the man getting out of the car. He held a drink holder in one hand with four cups of coffee. The other hand had reached into his pocket and withdrawn a pair of sunglasses which he fitted onto his face.

Suddenly, it looked like some giant had flicked the side of the man's head with one large finger, and as it jolted sideways, the man was thrown from his feet; coffee cups flew into the air. That was when Hector heard the report

293

from the fired sniper rifle. Simultaneously, engines were started all around him and those black vans closed in on the hospital from all directions. The raid was on.

# *Chapter Twenty-Eight*

It had taken almost a week before Zach had rounded up many of his followers. They had rented out an indoor stadium for the rally. It had been necessary given what they were about to reveal to those who came.

Shae was still felt wary of Zach, but it had been hard given his obvious charm. She had decided the main reason she didn't like him was because he took Kestrel's time. Time she could be spending with Shae. Knowing it was a symptom of being selfish didn't ease Shae's mind.

During the days leading up to the rally, Shae and Kestrel had spent a great deal of time together. It had been surprisingly fun, which was something Shae had not known she would feel ever again after the night George had raped her.

In many ways, Kestrel was like a teenager herself. She had not experienced many of the things Shae hadn't experienced. Or at least, her experiences were completely different. But the excitement of firsts they got to share together had bonded them in a rather special way.

Kestrel's knowledge of makeup had been using pigments from crushed stones and kohl. Shae had little familiarity of cosmetics as well. Anne would occasionally 'doll' her up with them for fun, but Shae hadn't learned anything. So, together they would practice on each other—applying makeup and complimenting each other on how they looked.

Kestrel seemed to have a knack for how to properly accentuate her beauty. As if she needed any more. She helped Shae use foundation to cover up her freckles and blush to add color to her cheeks.

Now that her hair had grown back some, they had been using some nutrients to brighten up the red in it and to make it fuller and less stringy.

For what seemed to be the first time in her life, she felt healthy. It was true since the first time she had changed, she had been stronger and had felt more alive, but she had been kept in captivity for so long. Abused and treated like a lab rat. They had fed her, but the portions she had received were small and bland.

Since she had fled with Kestrel, however, she had been eating properly — full meals, morning, noon and night. She had gained weight, not only muscle mass like she had gained after her first shift, but healthy weight. She no longer felt like skin and bones.

All of this, she owed to Kestrel. Her generosity with Shae had warmed Shae's heart. For a long time after what happened between Anne, George and her, and perhaps further back, to when her actual mom deserted her, she felt she couldn't trust someone.

She had been sitting in one of those private VIP booths stadiums had, looking out over the preparations being made for tonight's rally, lost in thought. Hundreds of chairs had been unfolded and lined up in front of the stage. Along with the seating in the stands, there would be several thousands of people in the stadium tonight when Zach and Kestrel would make their play to fill the ranks of Weres.

Shae had already told Kestrel she didn't feel comfortable making anyone a Were. Shae hadn't wanted to say this to Kestrel, hadn't wanted to make the woman angry. She didn't want to lose her like she had lost everyone else. Kestrel had dismissed her worry with a wave of the hand.

"That part is not for you, Shae. As I have said, I have something special I will need from you and when the time comes, I know you won't let me down," Kestrel had told her.

Shae couldn't help but wonder what role Kestrel had for her. She would not let Kestrel down. She wouldn't. It was the least she could do. Kestrel had assured her she wouldn't have to fight in the war, and she wouldn't have to make any Weres for the war. Those were the only things Shae felt she couldn't be a part of, so whatever else Kestrel wanted from her, she felt she could help.

As if thinking about her summoned her, Kestrel flowed into the room.

"Good evening, Shae. How are you?"

Shae continued to watch the preparations. "I'm fine. You've been gone all day."

Kestrel sat down next to her, close enough to rub shoulders and glanced out over the workers as well and sighed audibly. "Yes. Well. Zach had me mingle with the guests. He felt it was best if they were to get to know me a little before I spoke to them at tonight's rally."

"Sounds boring."

Kestrel snorted which sounded strange coming from such an elegant woman. "You are most right, Shae. It was. But necessary. Zach does understand how to reach people, and that is precisely what we need." Kestrel tucked her hair behind her ears causing the beads in her hair to click and clack as they ran into each other.

"One of the main problems we ran into the first time I waged this war was that most of our . . ." She tottered her head a little as if going back and forth trying to decide on which word to use, "recruits were conscripted into our army, and so, when the fighting got tough, they fled because they did not believe in our cause.

"I won't make that mistake again. We will do our best to recruit as many willing participants as we can."

Shae was no fool. She understood what Kestrel avoided saying was they infected people and forced them to fight for them using their will. She was happy Kestrel would try a different way this time.

"Are you ready for your speech tonight?"

"Of course," Kestrel replied, her tone a little miffed as if there should not have been any doubt of her readiness.

"Is Zach?"

Kestrel chortled, again a weird sound coming from such a lady. "Zach was probably giving speeches as a babe."

*As a babe? Oh, right, a baby.* Shae shook her head in amusement at Kestrel's vocabulary.

"What?" Kestrel turned a quizzically look upon her.

"A babe is someone that you think is hot."

"Hot?" She scrunched her forehead. "Oh, right. Attractive. Ah, I see." She smiled mischievously. "Well then that too."

"Ugh," Shae groaned.

Kestrel laughed outright this time, and this had a musical quality to it more fitting for the woman.

"Oh please. You can't tell me you don't find the man attractive?"

Shae grimaced and rolled her eyes. "I guess," she conceded.

Kestrel reached over and patted her hand. "Don't worry, Shae. I won't leave you for him."

Shae felt the color rise in her cheeks in embarrassment. She hadn't known she had been so easy to read.

It looked as if Kestrel might laugh again but decided against it.

"I have to go and get ready. Would you like to come and help me put on makeup?" Kestrel nudged her with an elbow.

"Well, O.K., as long as you promise to put mine on for me?"

Kestrel offered her a warm smile. "Of course."

She stood and moved toward the door.

"Oh, I forgot to tell you. Gordon, Taylor, Blain and Sarah have arrived."

This time Shae groaned loudly.

"I wish we didn't need those assholes."

"I do too, Shae, but sometimes those are the types of people you need to get the job done. They are necessary for what I need to accomplish."

"Samuel and Joseph?"

Kestrel shook her head. "I expect them the day after tomorrow."

"Where were they again?"

Kestrel smiled at her. "Shall we go?"

Shae stared for a while at Kestrel but realized she would only get more info out of Kestrel, when and if she decided to. With resignation, she nodded.

Zach stood off to the side of the stage. In a few moments he would climb those stairs and give the speech of a lifetime. Everything was about to change. No longer would they be some fringe group everyone dismissed as crazed radicals. No. Now they would be a force to be reckoned with.

Kestrel had given him an opportunity he would not waste. What would happen tonight would reshape the world. It was fitting the warriors of this fight would take the forms of animals. That it would be nature's beasts who would exact revenge upon the world of man.

Men who had carelessly destroyed many of their brothers and sisters and continued to do so without abandon. Their continued destruction of habitats and hunting of endangered species would be answered!

Zach could feel his face heating and when he realized he'd clenched his fists, he forced himself to release them and calm himself. It had been a long time since he had felt this level of anger. Oh, it wasn't as if these things hadn't been happening all along, only he had been fighting this fight without making any headway for so long, his soul had become beleaguered.

He had been fighting the good fight, but these last few years he had been going through the motions. The passion. The anger. They had faded after all the years of not making any headway, and yet, he had continued to plod on because someone needed to try.

Now, though. Now, the passion returned. The anger. The reason he had founded E.A.R.t.H. in the first place. Anger and retaliation! Those were two parts of the acronym which had faded as time went by.

But they were back now. Kestrel had breathed new life into the cause. A new purpose. A new focus. And, the power to make it happen.

Everything depended on their speeches tonight. Everything depended on whether they could convince his followers to join their army.

Zach wondered again if he should allow one of Kestrel's followers to give him that same power. He had refused Kestrel's offer. She had nodded at his refusal, as if she had been expecting it all along. Perhaps she had. She was an uncanny woman. Brilliant, beautiful and dangerous.

He didn't trust her. He did, however, trust her motivations, and that is where their interest met. She would use him, obviously. Use him for his followers. But he would use her as well. She would give him the power and the strength to win this war he had been fighting for so long.

He glanced towards Kestrel's two followers. How different those two were. One, an obvious thug — a brute in every sense of the word. Broad of chest and waist, he was as bulky as a bus with greasy, slicked back hair which showed off a billboard sized forehead. An oft broken nose sat crooked above a thin-lipped, mouth missing more than a few teeth. Beady eyes scanned the crowd as if looking for someone to shake down and beat up. *Probably exactly what he was thinking.*

The other, was a well-groomed man with sandy brown hair, fine features and a winning smile. He dressed comfortably in a fine, if loose-fitting suit. He on the other hand wasn't watching the crowd. He sat leaning up against the side of the stage, staring unconcerned at the ceiling with the perfect air of boredom.

They were the two Kestrel would present as options. One was a Boar and the other, a Crocodile. Kestrel had them shift for him. Nobody had to tell him which one was going to be the Boar, and which one was going to be the Crocodile. It had been apparent to Zach from the get-go.

He wished it was only Gordon there and not Blain. Gordon was charming and attractive and would make a better case for becoming a Were than Blain ever could. Kestrel could have used one of the other two, Joseph or Taylor, but had insisted on Blain.

"Despite what your opinion of the man is, Zach," she had told him, "there are those in the crowd who Blain will appeal to, and those are the ones who will be the first to volunteer, I assure you."

He had tried to hide his skepticism but knew he had failed. It didn't matter. It was her show at this point. His speech would be done. His part in it, would be done. He would become a follower. Sure, a follower with a seat at the table, but still subservient to Kestrel. She had been clear about that point.

The appointed hour arrived, and Zach climbed the stage to thunderous applause. For a long while, he allowed the applause to wash over him. To lift him like a metaphysical buoy. He rode the tide of his followers' love and appreciation for him for what seemed like several minutes.

Zach rose a single hand and the room quieted.

"Many of you have come here today from not only across America, but from other countries as well. You have travelled here because in your hearts you know the Earth is under assault."

Angry shouts of agreement rose, quickly hushed back to silence.

Zach let his face grow blank, the muscles in his cheeks, to droop, as he allowed the graveness of what he said be mirrored by his expression.

"Oil companies. Gas companies. Coal companies!" More agreeing shouts. "Logging companies!" He pitched his voice louder, full of anger. "For too long these companies have been allowed to do whatever they wanted! To rape and pillage our lands. Pollute our skies, lakes, rivers and oceans! To kill nature's cherished children, some to the point of extinction!"

Chorus of angry shouts punctuated each and every sentence he uttered. His face was now tight and flush as he tensed the muscles in his jaw. His anger visible for everyone to see.

"And who is to blame?"

"Oil! Coal!" came the shouts from the audience. They were the loudest, but he heard some shout other names. A woman near the front had called out the name he had wanted to hear, and he pointed toward her.

"She knows! She understands!" The woman beamed from the recognition she received. Her neighbors in the crowd were clapping for her and some were leaning in close to find out what she had said. He didn't give her the chance to tell them.

"Government! That's right. Our government. Your governments!" No one shouted now, they were all eagerly awaiting what he would say next.

"Government for the people? Bah! They don't listen to us. They don't care about us! All they care about is the wad of bills they get stuffed into their pockets by these companies so they will turn a blind eye!

"Well. I've had enough!"

The shouts started up again. Angry and excited.

He pitched his voice quieter. Not so quiet those in the back couldn't hear him. But quiet enough so the crowd would strain to hear him, and when they did, they would feel his vulnerability. His sense of defeat.

302

"But what are we to do? The government is too big. Too powerful. Oh, I could stand up here and rally you to strike out as we have done in the past. Destroy vehicles, burn down their offices." He deliberately surveyed the crowd as he spoke. Meeting eyes, locking gazes and nodding in acknowledgment of their steadfastness. "We hold rallies. We hold marches. And still," he shook his head in exaggerated disgust, "nothing happens."

"The system is rotten to the core. We have been fighting a losing battle, but we have never given up!" he added, his voice, gradually raising in decibel. "We have never admitted defeat!" Higher still. "No! We have not given in to despair! We have not resigned ourselves as ineffectual! NO! We have fought on!"

Shouts and cheers sprung up around the stadium, and like wildfire it caught and spread with wild abandon. Soon, those who had been seated were on their feet, fist raised or clapping, some with hands cupped to their mouths hollering support.

Zach let it run its course. Let it quiet down on its own and even though he raised his hands and motioned for the crowd to quiet down, they had all but done so already.

"But I am afraid it is time to admit defeat." His somber expression returned as he frowned out over the crowd; he could hear murmurs of "no" and "never" but only softly for they did not want to drown him out as they knew, no, hoped for more. An answer for them. Not this surrender.

Grabbing the microphone, he rounded his podium and came to the edge of the stage.

"It is time to give up. Surrender."

Again, more and more murmurs of dissent, and he knew he had them.

He scanned the crowd again, finding those who truly looked lost and hurt by what he said and met their eyes, before continuing to the next one.

"Or at least, I thought it was."

He began walking across the front of the stage.

"I had given up. I had felt we had done everything we could do and there was still no change. No lasting change anyways. The world wasn't ready for our message and we lacked the strength to do it without them."

He stopped and turned towards them.

"Until now." He gave them a soft smile.

People were glancing to those next to them with quizzical expressions, shrugs and open hand gestures of bafflement. What did he mean until now? What had changed? How would they have the strength to make the world listen?

He let them stew before continuing. "The world has changed before our eyes and we didn't even realize it. Some of you may have heard the stories out of Chicago. Some of you may have heard rumors of the events in upstate Texas this past week. Some of you are still blissfully unaware."

He began to pace again. "Nature has given us the answer to our prayers. They have sent us arbiters of justice. More, they have granted them the power to recruit others to the cause. To join them in their war against the corruption and greed which prevents true change from happening."

He turned a smile on them and gave a half chuckle to diffuse the tension in the room which had been building. "I know. I am not explaining myself well and many of you have questions."

He nodded his understanding as if he was as lost and confused as they were, though he had brought them to this point.

"I could try to explain everything to you, but I think it best if I let our guests do the explaining. Allow me to present to you our guest of honor tonight, Kestrel El-Clare." He half turned toward the stair and began clapping and was soon joined by the thousands in the stands.

Kestrel, he knew, was all about the entrance. And enter she did. Sweeping up the stairs, she wore an emerald green gown that seemed to know her as well as any man could hope to know her. She had worn a similar gown before, but it had a plunging neckline. This one was modestly cut with barely a hint of cleavage.

She knew her target audience. She couldn't help her beauty or her body, and while she wore a gown accentuating her curves, it did not flaunt them overtly. It was enough to captivate the men, but not anger the women.

She was flanked by her two followers, Blain and Gordon. They followed her to the podium but stood back and to the sides. Sentinels guarding their matriarch.

He watched her though, and when she reached the podium, her steps faltered slightly, and she looked furtively between the crowd and the floor as if unsure as to why she was there and thinking of running.

Zach smiled. A nice added touch. If she came out looking like she did and been all full of confidence as well? It wouldn't matter if many of the women had already met Kestrel the night before. That they had talked, and she had ingratiated herself with them. If they still perceived her as a threat to enticing their men, she would be the enemy. Feigned trepidation should be enough to put the women at ease. At least, long enough for them to listen to what Kestrel had to say.

Listen, and hear.

"Hello."

Zach had been looking out at the crowd, checking to see if Kestrel's ruse was working when he heard her utter that word, and his head whipped back around to stare at her. She spoke it in flawless English. It held none of the accent he had grown familiar with this past week.

*Well, well, well. So, how long ago did you learn to lose your accent, I wonder? Had it all been a ploy to set him at ease when they met? The hapless foreigner?* Zach shook his head in admiration. He needed to remember whose sandbox he played in. Nothing should surprise him about her.

305

"My name is Kestrel. I could tell you my story, but it is long and would be fairly unbelievable for most of you, so I won't." She offered an apologetic smile as if to acknowledge some of them doubtless wished to hear it but wouldn't get the chance to.

"The important thing to know about me is I am a steward of this Earth. From a very early age I was raised to care and protect all things natural. As I grew older, I came to realize nature would never be safe while man could plunder her unchecked."

She spoke softly but succinctly. The melodic tone of her voice left everyone hanging on each word, eager for the next one. "Like you, I wondered what I could do to stop this. It made me angry. I wanted it to stop."

A sad smile.

"But I didn't know how."

A slow confidence built in her words.

"That was when I learned nature was also angry. The Earth was furious about what was being done to her. Because of this, she created people to fight for her."

There were nods in the crowd as people assumed, she talked about them, which had been the plan.

"I knew I must act, and so I sought out these people. I gathered them and I knew I must gather others as well. Those who would join us."

She motioned to the two men at her side and the crowd exchanged confused looks, realizing she hadn't been speaking about them after all.

"What I am about to show you will undoubtably surprise you. Scare you, even."

Murmurs of denial. After all, what could she conceivably show them that would scare them?

"These men next to me are not like us. They have been chosen by nature to give her justice. But they need our help."

She paused, eying the crowd.

Raising her voice, she continued, "Will you help them?"

Calls of 'yes' and other affirmations rose around her.

This was not the rousing speech like the one he had given. This had been a slow and steady climb. A building of layers. She had taken them on a journey with her, from uncertainty to righteousness and they had followed all the way, unknowing of where she might be leading them.

"I give you! Nature's crusaders!"

At the signal. Blain and Gordon moved slightly forward, still behind Kestrel, but closer to the crowd. They stepped forward . . . and shifted. No matter how many times Zach witnessed this it still left his stomach unsettled. How could someone not find the instantaneous reconstruction of a person's body repulsive?

It seemed like the entire crowd gasped. Their collective intake of air left the rest of them suffocated. Shouts and screams erupted.

That was Zach's cue.

Immediately he ran up onto the stage and approached the two beasts, looking out at the crowd as he did, motioning with calming gestures. The crowd, on the verge of stampeding from the stands, now watched as their leader approached these awful creatures.

Zach approached Gordon first. He strode confidently, though his stomach did its best to find an escape hatch. When he stood in front of Gordon, he stared up at him. Black beady eyes stared back, outer eyelids closing and disappearing under the orbital ridge.

The crowd fell so silent that if they had been behind a curtain, you would swear there was no one there.

Zach stuck out his hand and Gordon reached out with a massive clawed hand and took his. Though Gordon's hand engulfed Zach's, they still somehow managed and awkward handshake.

Then, Zach crossed to the other side and repeated the process with Blain, who managed to offer a sneer out of the side of his face pointing away from the crowd.

Zach went and stood next to Kestrel and offered her a broad smile, which she returned. In unison, they turned back to the crowd and Zach took her arm and walked her the short distance back to the podium and motioned her forward to speak again.

If members of the audience had left, it was impossible to tell. The stadium remained packed. Those who did leave would be followed and dealt with. Zach hid a grimace. He didn't like the idea, but he understood its necessity.

This gambit needed to play out until after their bodies accepted the lycanthropy. If word got out who they were trying to recruit through E.A.R.t.H, they would become targets before they were ready.

Kestrel stood before the podium again and cleared her throat.

"I understand your fear. But these are powerful creatures. Nature has chosen well."

She motioned with a hand back toward the two Weres.

"Don't you see? They bear the features of some of nature's most powerful animals. They have been chosen by nature to fight this fight for us!"

She gazed with recrimination out over the crowd.

"You called out your willingness to help them. Do you rescind your offer now? With these men and with your help, we can finally win!"

There was still uncertainty in the crowd.

Quietly, Kestrel turned to Zach.

"Show them."

This was the part Zach had not wanted to agree with. He had hoped the crowd would not need this demonstration. He had been wrong. Reaching into his jacket pocket, Zach drew out his handgun and pointed it at Gordon.

They had all agreed they would use Gordon for this demonstration, but that had mainly been because Blain had threatened to rip him to shreds and chew the fat off his bones if they tried to use him.

Gordon turned toward Zach, but otherwise made no moves.

The crowd had again grown silent the moment Zach had brandished his weapon.

Zach squeezed the trigger. One, two, three, four, five loud bangs echoing and booming across the stadium. Gordon rocked back slightly from each impact but managed to hold his ground.

Blood from dime-sized holes leaked out in five different places along his scaled underside. Red coating pale green in long streaks racing for the floor.

There was stunned silence from the crowd.

When the first bullet pushed out through Gordon's skin and fell to the floor with an audible clink, the crowd was a sea of wide eyes and open mouths.

One by one, the bullets fell to the ground and the wounds on Gordon's chest closed. Soon, all that remained were circular stains with tails, long and red.

"These men," Kestrel seized on the moment as people still stared dumfounded up at Gordon. "These. Men." Faces turned back to her. "These men are all but indestructible. Unkillable. Unstoppable.

"They have power like you could never imagine, yet there are only a few of them. They cannot win our war by themselves."

She motioned out to the crowd. "They need you. They need you to join them. You can *become* them."

Zach watched her as she scanned the crowd. What he read on her face left him at ease. She knew she had them. They were listening. They weren't running. His followers were intrigued by the prospect of becoming immortal or having the strength to truly fight this war.

309

Whatever the reason would be, they would show them this was the only way.

"We won't make you join this fight," Kestrel told them.

*At least, not yet,* Zach thought.

"But think long and hard about whether or not you truly believe in what you have been preaching all these years. Whether you truly care about this planet and wish to take care of her— or not?"

"If you choose to be a part of this great movement. This, army, that will wage war on those who wish harm upon this Earth . . ."

She paused for effect, for the next part would be critical for them to understand. "And, those who permit it to happen."

It was her turn to take the mic and move out in front of the stage.

"So, I implore you. The Earth implores you. Join us! Without you, the Earth will never be safe!"

Zach had to hand it to her. In one speech she managed to plead to them, shame them to action, and challenge them to do what was right. Even faced with what stood there, on stage, he could see her words had reached many, if not all.

The next part was imperative. It had to play right. He and Kestrel had already approached some in the organization Zach knew would be more than willing to take this upon themselves. They were the most zealous. The ones who had spent the most time being locked up for property damage and vandalism. Some had been in jail for manslaughter as their actions had led to deaths.

They had offered them first go at becoming part of this new army, and they had all willingly agreed.

"I ask now, for those who are willing, to come forward. To receive your reward for being true to the cause."

*Oh, now you are just pouring salt into the wound, Kestrel.* But he could see the words had the right affect. Some in the crowd were wincing at the recrimination of their thoughts of rejecting this.

There was movement within the crowd. Men and women, a half dozen or so, approached the stage.

Kestrel smiled warmly at them as they made their way to the steps on either side and climbed them to approach Kestrel. With each one, she closed the distance to them, took up their hands, her smile open and grateful.

She whispered words to each of them. Zach wasn't close enough to hear what she said, but he could guess it was some form of thanks or what have you. Kestrel was grateful, Zach knew.

She needed this to work. From here, it would cascade. With those who would come from what Blain, Taylor and Gordon had done, their ranks would swell. And from there, they could create more and more. They would spread like a swarm of ants over an offending trespasser on their hill.

There would be no stopping them.

Zach returned his attention to the proceedings. One by one, the volunteers approached either Gordon or Blain, though more approached Gordon than Blain. Which didn't surprise Zach. Though they both looked monstrous now, one could not forget the sharp looking man Gordon had been.

Both Gordon and Blain would carefully take a claw and gently make a small cut on their arms. Kestrel was there immediately, and she would bind their cuts and take a wipe and clean the blood of the claw so it would be sanitized for the next person.

He remembered the girl, Shae, asking Kestrel when they were going over the plan, why Kestrel didn't use her healing. Zach didn't comprehend what she had meant, but Kestrel had told Shae, her Druidic healing couldn't heal cuts created by Weres. That they would need to heal on their own. Most would heal the moment their body accepted the lycanthropy.

311

Before they had reached the last 'planted' volunteer, others had made their way on to the stage. Two long lines formed at the base of the stairs as members of the organization continued to form up.

Zach smiled. He knew if they could have people in the crowd who hadn't hesitated. Who had immediately volunteered, and once they had seen it only involved a small cut, which was being immediately treated, others would feel compelled to join.

At some point, the mentality of the crowd would overrule any hesitation and there would be a tipping point and once it passed, the rest would fall in line.

Of course, there would still be some who would refuse to join the army, and he understood their hesitation. After all, he had refused, hadn't he?

Those who refused to become Were, would be approached for other aspects of this fight. There would need to be people in charge of logistics and information gathering. They would be used.

And if they still refused? If they maybe threatened to go to the authorities with what they knew? Well, they would never make it. There was always collateral damage in war.

What seemed like hours passed by as more and more people stepped up to the two Weres to get their scratch. He had people usher them into smaller groups and put them in the various conference rooms scattered around the stadium grounds.

Kestrel had decided they shouldn't inform them of their possible impending death. That they would inform them they were going to be taking them to the hospital to be monitored while their body adjusted to the changes it would go through.

It would be at least a day before any of them went through the rejection process, or so Kestrel had assured him. For tonight, they had rented out the entire hotel attached to the stadium and there would be a catered feast, and drinks, of course.

They wanted the new additions to be relaxed when their moment came. It would be easier to handle. The bartenders had been instructed to cut anyone off who seemed to not be handling their alcohol well. The last thing they needed was an angry drunk going into cardiac arrest.

They were to make their move on the hospital tomorrow in preparation. He scanned the stage, remembering something else Kestrel had made plans for. Searching the stage, he found them. Off to the side stood a clump of individuals. These would be the health care advisors. Kestrel was separating the doctors and nurses from the other volunteers. She wouldn't allow them to become Weres. At least, not yet. For now, she needed them available to help Sarah as she dealt with the rejection process.

She had found five so far. Optimistically there would be more. If half of these people went into cardiac arrest at the same time . . . Well, I guess we let nature sort it out.

At long last, the parade of people finished, and Zach was glad for it. His feet hurt and he reeked of body odor. The stadium had AC, but with this many people in here, the air had become warm and uncomfortable and he was soaked in sweat.

The group Kestrel had set aside had reached over fifteen. *Well, it will have to do.*

Zach had to wonder; how many would survive? How many of these men and women he had talked to, waved to, shook hands with, would see Tuesday?

Kestrel had warned him they might lose a great many. Though she assumed the survival rate in this age would be far superior to her own. With the advances in medical sciences, there was an excellent probability they might only lose a third.

Still a staggering number, but in the end, the cost would be worth it. They would be in control of an unstoppable army. They needed time. The longer it took the world to react to this new threat, the better.

They would react, Zach knew, sooner or later. It would be incremental at first. They would underestimate. There would be losses. Terrible losses. Then they would step up their game. But still, Zach believed, they would trust their conventional weaponry, and their prowess to see them to victory.

By then, they would have a sizable force of powerful warriors ready to join the fight. The third time they came, would be the time they would come with serious intent. But it would be too late for them.

Zach smiled at the thought. They would show them true power. They would turn the war back on them.

Most of the people had filed out of the stadium. Gordon and Blain had returned to their human form and were in conference with Kestrel, so he approached.

The men eyed him as he joined them. Their faces expressed twin looks of contempt, though Zach was sure the reasoning behind the looks was different. The opinion remained the same. Zach didn't let it bother him. He was a player in this game as much as they were.

Kestrel was speaking. "We move into the hospital in the morning. I want it under our control as quickly as possible. We need to secure it and make it ready for when their bodies go into rejection."

Gordon nodded his agreement.

"They will move on us there." Blain told her, crossing his massive arms.

She studied him. "How soon?"

He shrugged. "I give it three days. Maybe four. It will be a time before they know we have taken it. A day to assess the situation and formulate a plan. Another day to lock down a perimeter to ensure there won't be any innocents in the way when they come."

Kestrel looked contemplative as she stared over at one of the doorways as some stragglers were making their way out. She sighed.

"It will have to do. We will be ready for them. It will be necessary to keep them from the recruits."

"Some of them will have already become Weres by that point." Blain observed.

"True. But they won't be ready to fight yet. Plus, I would rather not reveal our purpose or our full strength. Zach and I agree. This first attack will be a small one. They may take us seriously, and so they will come hard, but there will not be enough to cause you any trouble."

Blain studied him and Zach held his gaze for a moment before looking away. The man was hard to stand up to, so Zach didn't try. He knew he would be dead in an instant if Blain wanted it.

Blain returned his eyes to Kestrel.

"And what will you be doing during this time?"

She gave him a hard look. He always tested her. Pushing her buttons. Zach knew Blain resented Kestrel. Resented having to take orders from her, but he still did. "I will be busy. Hopefully, Samuel will have returned, and he knows what needs to be done."

"Speaking of which." Gordon said, his eyes fixed on one of the entrances. They all turned to see Samuel and Joseph coming toward them.

Zach had never met these two, but he had heard Kestrel often speak of Samuel. Though he had never gotten a description of the man, it wasn't hard to determine which one he was.

The taller of the two, he walked with assuredness and poise. He had an olive tinge to his skin which spoke to middle eastern descent, long limbed, but not gangly. His hair was dark and cropped short and while he dressed in casual attire, it seemed out of place on him, like he would be better suited in kingly garments. Or at least a fine suit.

The other man was portly and not at all pleasant to look at. He had fat fingers and his skin was pale. Strands of hair, which barely covered his scalp hung down like hundreds of rock-climbing ropes on the world's most pasty hill.

In short order they mounted the stage and approached while their party waited for them. Samuel immediately went to Kestrel, not bothering to acknowledge the others.

"My lady," he nodded his head.

"Samuel. How was your trip? I hadn't expected you back this early."

The question was loaded with all sorts of hidden meaning. One thing Zach had been able to gather, no one except Kestrel knew where Samuel and Joseph had gone. Their mission had been one of secrecy.

"The trip was well. So well, that we were able to return earlier than anticipated, My Lady."

"Excellent. Then we can move up the timeline, which is well as we expect an attack within days. We will speak more of this, Samuel. For now, why you don't both go and relax. Get something to eat. I will come to you shortly."

She turned toward Blain.

"Blain, I need you to scout the hospital. Determine how best we will be able to defend it and where and how the attacks might come."

Blain had been looking at Joseph the whole time, who had pointedly been ignoring him. Whatever was going on there, Zach remained clueless. At Kestrel's words though, he turned his head to her with a suspicious eye.

"I will see to it in the morning."

"I need it done now."

Blain looked to argue but changed his mind. "Very well, I will take Taylor and Joseph with me."

"You may take Taylor, but I need Joseph."

Blain's neck reddened and the muscles in his jaw clenched.

"Was there something you wished to say, Blain?" It was Samuel who cut in. He had moved closer to Kestrel and Zach saw Gordon had also moved closer to her.

Blain flashed a partially toothless grin as he never took his eyes from Kestrel.

"No. Of course not. What would I have to say?" The sarcasm, thick in his response.

"What, indeed?" Kestrel words were frosty.

Blain stood for a long moment regarding Kestrel. He ignored the hard looks from Gordon and Samuel though, as if their presence meant nothing to him. And perhaps it didn't. Blain was clearly the biggest of the three, though when shifted, Gordon matched him in size.

Blain was someone who needed watching. When he had uttered as much to Kestrel earlier, she had assured him Blain would do what he was asked to do. His desire for power and what Kestrel had promised him would keep him in line. Though, at some point, she conceded, he might need to be dealt with.

Blain turned and strode away, to look for Taylor he presumed. Kestrel moved to Samuel and whispered something in his ear. He never once took his eyes from Blain's departing form, though.

At last, Samuel spoke, "Joseph," he said, indicating the man should follow him. Joseph, who looked like the center knot in a tug-a-war rope, closed his eyes briefly before following Samuel out of the room, opposite to where Blain had left.

"Zach?" Kestrel called him over.

"Yes, My Lady?" It seemed odd to use the formality, but he had gotten tired of the icy stares she had given him when he didn't use it.

"Could you please go and find Shae and bring her to me?"

The corner of his lips dipped in a frown. "She doesn't like me."

She smiled, though it carried no warmth. "And?"

317

His frown deepened. *And I don't like her.*

"Very well." He left her in search of Shae.

There were too many working parts in this scheme for Zach's own piece of mind. Especially since he seemed only privy to about half of them. What Kestrel had planned was total world dominance, with her army of Weres to exact control.

Once accomplished, she would de-industrialize the world. It was the only true way to ensure the safety of the Earth. The war would be long and hard fought. Most people wouldn't accept this fate and would fight to keep the comforts they had.

They would lose.

No one could stand against the force they were amassing against them, and by the time they realize the scope of the danger, it would be too late.

But there was more to this than what Kestrel had told him. He knew of the opposing group of Weres controlled by another Druidess. And all this secrecy had something to do with dealing with that threat. But why Kestrel chose to keep it from all of them, Zach didn't know.

That she didn't trust all of them was a given. Gods knew she couldn't trust Blain. Samuel, from what he had gathered, had been with her the longest and so perhaps there was a measure of trust there, and while Gordon appeared to be her lap dog, could it all be for show? Could she know him well enough to trust him?

Then there was Zach himself. Did she distrust him? Undoubtedly. She knew him. Had studied him. She trusted his motivations, but could she truly trust he would align with her forever? He had refused to become a Were, after all.

The two oddities in all of this were Joseph and Shae. She had included Joseph in her plans at the risk of Blain discovering what they were. He didn't completely understand the dynamics of the Weres, but he did know, Joseph had been made into a Were by Blain and so, in a way, served him.

Was Kestrel simply using Joseph to keep Blain unbalanced? A way to remind Blain who is in charge? Perhaps. Zach didn't know. It would be interesting to see what would happen if Blain ever does manage to corner Joseph alone. From the looks Joseph gave, Zach was sure he would tell Blain everything.

Shae was another matter. He wasn't sure what, if anything, she knew of Kestrel's plans. She played a part in them, of that, Zach was sure, but how? And did Shae know?

Zach couldn't be sure and try as he might, he couldn't figure out what it could be. He arrived at the VIP suite he had spotted Shae in earlier and entered. She was there with another woman he had not met before.

The woman was pretty, long auburn colored hair, parted in the middle to cascade to either side of her attractive face. She was slim, but curvy. Her eyes, though. They looked dead to him. As if all the good in the world had been stolen away.

"Shae?"

The girl turned to him; her usual looks of loathing replaced with curiosity.

"What was all that about?"

For a second, Zach didn't understand the question, but he realized they had both been watching the drama unfold from up here. Zach noticed a flash of, something, cross the woman's face. But it disappeared as quickly as it came, and Zach wasn't sure what it had meant.

"I'm not sure. Something about what Samuel and Joseph had been about and Blain wasn't too happy about not being informed as to what it was."

Shae turned to the other woman.

"You went with them, Sarah. Where did they go? What did they do?"

319

That was news to Zach. He wasn't aware someone else went with Samuel and Joseph. There had been no mention of this woman, Sarah.

That look came over Sarah again before she stilled her face. *She knows something. She knows and it hurts her not to tell.*

Sarah shook her head. "They didn't tell me. They dropped me off at a hotel room and left me there." She smiled sadly. "I think Kestrel just wanted to keep me away from Blain."

Shae's cocked her head slightly as she considered, before nodding. "That seems like something she would do. She wouldn't want Blain abusing you anymore."

Zach went cold. "Excuse me?"

Shae turned to Zach, mouth opening.

"It's a figure of speech. Blain likes to antagonize me. Always pushing my buttons." Sarah interjected.

Shae's mouth closed with a click, and she turned a sharp eye on Sarah.

"What brings you here, Zach?" Sarah ignored Shae's look.

Zach couldn't miss the subject change. And while Sarah's explanation seemed plausible given Blain's tendency to rile people, he believed there was more to it. He wouldn't put it past Blain to be abusive, both emotionally and physically to this woman. But what could he feasibly do about it?

"Kestrel asked me to come find you, Shae, and ask you to go to her."

Shae smiled and hopped off her seat. The girl was such a paradox to Zach. He had seen darkness and malice from her, and yet, in many ways she still acted like a kid. He was glad her usual dislike for him was absent for now.

"I'll catch you later, Sarah."

Sarah smiled sadly at Shae again, and Zach wondered if she was capable of any other type of smile. "See you, Shae."

Shae ducked out around him and he eyed Sarah, and she eyed him skeptically.

He wanted to ask her what she knew. What she kept from Shae. He framed the questions in his mind, but the look she gave him, a look of utter despair and sadness, and he couldn't do it. He was afraid any question he asked her would only bring her more unhappiness, and he did not wish to be the cause of that.

In the end, he nodded to her and left.

He needed to make his way to the feast. He would be expected to make an appearance. Kestrel would want him to be there to ease fears and answer questions. Though, there was no going back for any of them, Kestrel had explained to him their acceptance of what was going to happen would increase their survival rate.

Doubts still plagued him as he entered the dining hall, but he hid them behind a sure smile and warm greetings.

# *Chapter Twenty-Nine*

Samuel had secreted Joseph away after they had dined and rested. Joseph, for his part, had no interest in interacting with Blain and so readily accepted being sequestered until they had to leave again.

Samuel didn't particularly care for Joseph. No, that wasn't true. He disliked Joseph. Immensely. A feeling he knew was shared by anyone who met the man. He would rather not have been saddled with the man, but Samuel knew better than to question Kestrel's motives.

Blain was a powder keg ready to blow at a moment's notice, and Joseph, an open flame who relished in dancing before him. Keeping them apart was smart for the group's cohesion. What there was of it.

This group was not unlike the group of old. They had constantly been at each other's throats. Bickering and snapping. It was amazing they had been able to accomplish what they had.

Samuel believed it had something to do with the temperament of their token animals. It played a role in their personality development.

He found Kestrel in her room. She had changed from her green gown to wearing blue jeans and a 'love pink' t-shirt. Seated at her desk, she penned something on a sheet of loose-leaf. A gauze bandage encircled her writing arm, which paused the moment he entered.

She turned in her seat and examined him.

He eyed her clothing, arching an eyebrow at her.

Standing, she did a little spin. "Do you like it? As much as I thought I would never wear a ridiculous outfit like this, I find it quite comfortable."

He had to admit. He did like it. Though the gowns she usually wore made her look gorgeous, there was something about her in plain jeans and a T which made her look even better. Perhaps it was the look of availability? Of approachability? She always seemed so aloof in the outfits she usually wore.

"I do, My Lady. They fit you nicely."

She smiled. "They do, don't they? Shae picked them out."

Her smile disappeared and she turned serious.

"All is ready?"

"It is, My Lady. And I see that your plans are already in motion." Nodding toward her arm.

Kestrel nodded. "We have little time. I need you back here as soon as possible. Take Joseph and Shae within the hour and return immediately."

"You have explained to Shae what we need from her?"

"In part. I will leave the rest of the explanation to you. I think it will make more sense to her when she sees what you have prepared for her."

He nodded. It made sense. It would work better that way.

"Where is she?"

"I sent her to pack. I explained that this is part of the special job I had for her, so she is eager to get to it."

He nodded in understanding. "I will gather up Shae and Joseph and we will leave immediately."

Samuel turned to go but Kestrel stopped him.

"Oh, and Samuel. It would be best if Joseph stayed away. I don't want him available to Blain."

Samuel turned his head slightly to look at her from his periphery. "Of course, My Lady." He tipped his head and left.

When Samuel came and got him, Joseph had been pacing. At the knock at the door, he froze, fearing it was Blain. Samuel had been explicit he would not tell Blain anything about what they had done or where they had gone.

Joseph didn't understand the secrecy. It had nothing to do with Blain. So why not tell him? Why put Joseph in the awkward position they had put him in?

Blain could make Joseph tell him everything. But Joseph knew he would resist. It was simply in his nature, and Blain would beat him, as he always did. Ultimately, Blain would use his will on Joseph, and he would have no choice but to tell. But that wouldn't be before Blain broke several bones in Joseph's body.

The pain was only temporary as was the damage. But it would hurt. At least for a while.

He wished they would simply tell Blain and leave him the hell out of it.

Cautiously, he approached the door and checked the viewer. It was Samuel and Shae. *So, it is time.*

He opened the door.

Samuel stood there with a travel bag, a look of practiced patience on his face as if he had endured a slew of questions he had avoided answering. Which was undoubtedly what had been occurring.

Shae had a miffed look to her, obviously unhappy with not being told what was going on. She wore her usual long coat, despite the warmth of the Texas air. He knew from experience she had a pair of wicked looking knives hidden there.

Her hair had grown since he had first met her. He remembered its choppy look when they had approached her on the streets of Chicago, as if someone had taken a dull pair of scissors to it. Now as it grew back, she looked more like a young woman and less like a sewer rat.

It was a shame.

324

Samuel stood in the doorway. "You ready?" He made no move to enter and Joseph made no move to invite them in.

"So soon?"

"You would rather stick around and hang out with Blain?" Samuel asked with a quirk of his mouth.

Joseph scowled at him.

"Fine. Let me grab my things. I haven't even had a chance to unpack."

Grabbing his go bag from his bed, he joined them at the doorway and motioned for them to proceed. Samuel turned and made his way down the hallway and Joseph fell in behind him.

Shae came up beside him. "Soooo, do you know where we are going?"

Samuel glanced back toward him as if he needed the look to remind him his place.

"Yeah. I do," he muttered, not looking at her.

She stayed silent for a bit as if waiting for him to elaborate. When it appeared he wouldn't, she followed up.

"Which is?"

"We are going somewhere that Kestrel needs you to be. If she hasn't told you, it isn't my place to do so."

He could sense her frown from beside him.

"That is almost exactly what Samuel said."

"And yet, you decided to ask someone else knowing the answer you would get," Samuel said from up ahead, not bothering to look back.

Shae growled.

"I just don't get why no one will tell me. If it is something I am supposed to be doing. If it is somewhere I am supposed to go — then why not tell me?"

Samuel halted and turned, bringing them up short so they didn't knock him over. Squatting down to bring himself more level with Shae, he gave her a serious look.

"Shae. Understand this. We are in a dangerous game right now. There are people out there who are desperate to find out what it is we are doing. What we are planning. By keeping things secret, we are trying to forestall them discovering what we are up to."

He reached up and gripped her upper arm gently. "What and where you are going is very important, and we can't let outsiders know. So, the less we talk about it, the less likely people we don't trust," he shot a glance at Joseph, "won't find out."

She had caught his look and Joseph knew she understood the implication had been about Blain and not him. Nobody trusted Blain. Frowning at Samuel, she eventually nodded.

"Good." Samuel stood, spun and continued down the hallway and they were forced to walk briskly to catch back up.

The trip took less than a day. Leaving Houston and its suburbs, they travelled north for a time and then east. Joseph, familiar with the route, napped for most of the way.

Shae had kept silent as they travelled. If she wanted to keep asking about where they were going, she kept her questions to herself. Instead, she gazed out the window.

Joseph knew little about her, but what he had picked up from conversations was she had been held captive by an agency of the government for more than a year. He imagined seeing all this, experiencing all this freedom, must be amazing to her.

He tried not to think about it.

Texas was so different from London. When he wasn't napping, he stared out the window, like Shae. London could be so gloomy, and yet, here, there was blue skies for miles. Clouds were like visitors here, not like the permanent residents in London.

In time, they left civilization behind and only the open road lay before them. Samuel drove like a professional driver. Unerringly straight. Never hugging the lines, always centered. The only deviation he did from being perfect was he drove one mile over the speed limit. Always. Never two. Never one under.

His perfection irritated Joseph. Anyone who Joseph viewed as better than him, he loathed. And he loathed Samuel. Though he undoubtedly shouldn't. After all, if what he heard was true, Samuel had over 2,000 years to become perfect.

At long last, they turned down a dirt drive. It had been unmarked and if Joseph hadn't known about it, he would never have spotted it. Shae perked up when they turned on it, as if knowing this would lead to their destination.

Which it would.

They travelled the dirt road for several miles until traffic from the highway was no longer visible. The ground became uneven, undulating in low hills. Their car sent a cloud of dust up behind them, obscuring the way they had come.

Passing between two hills they were abruptly in front of a steel-walled structure. The rounded roof sloped down to the ground on either side, making the building look like a semi-circle. A lone doorway sat facing them. Parked next to the building, was a small red coupe

A satellite dish rested on the crest of the roof and an antenna rose from behind the building. The building was an old bomb shelter Samuel had acquired. With some modifications they had been able to alter it for Kestrel's purposes.

"This is where we were going?" Doubt resonated in Shae's voice.

Samuel didn't answer, instead, grabbing his travel bag, he exited the car and walked to the front door.

Shae turned a questioning look on Joseph. He shrugged and got out as well. If Samuel wasn't going to explain anything to her, he sure as hell wasn't either.

Samuel had unlocked and opened the door by the time Joseph got there. They had to wait a moment while Shae exited the car and came over.

When she reached them, she stopped and crossed her arms under her breasts and scowled at Samuel. "I wish you would just explain what it is we are doing here."

"I will," he told her. "Once we are inside. You will understand better that way."

She huffed and strode past him into the building. Joseph gave him a plaintive look, but Samuel simply stared back, coldly, and followed Shae. Joseph shook his head and followed.

Before them was a small landing at the top of a long flight of stairs, leading down. Shae had already started down them and they followed. Once they reached the bottom it continued off into a long hallway which ended in a steel door.

Shae had stopped before the big door. There was a palm print scanner to the side, and she turned a quizzical eye to Samuel.

Her face lit up with surprise when he motioned for her to touch the scanner. Joseph watched as the girl placed her palm upon it. A blue light traveled up in a horizontal line from the bottom of the scanner to the top and back again. There was a beeping noise, followed by a click and a whoosh as the door began to open.

Behind the door lay a shorter hallway to another steel door with a palm scanner. Shae didn't hesitate this time. She moved quickly across the space and placed her hand on the scanner. Once again, it scanned her palm. Click. Whoosh, and the door opened.

This door led to a sizable room filled with shelves upon shelves of canned food. Although it wasn't apparent from where they were in the center of the storage space, Joseph knew from their previous visit this room also housed a washing machine and a dryer and several enormous freezer units packed with a variety of food stuffs.

The next door they came to didn't have any security measures and opened at a push. What greeted them was a considerable living space. There was a kitchen and dining area. In one section of the room sat a flat screen TV with a comfortable looking sofa in front of it. Two doors could be seen from this room which were open to reveal a bedroom and a bathroom.

At the far end of the room rested a bank of monitors, several computers as well as a couple of tablets. On the bank of monitors were news shows from various networks on mute.

Shae studied the room and the face she turned to them held a little bit of fear.

"What is this?"

Samuel offered a warm smile and moved to sit at the kitchen table and offered her a chair as well.

Hesitantly, Shae joined him and sat down.

"As you know Shae, you are very important to Kestrel. However, these next coming months will be full of conflict. Since you have expressed your desire to not participate in the fighting, Kestrel found a better way for you to help."

He gestured to the room they were in. "This was originally built as a bomb shelter during the cold war, but I repurposed it to make it a safe house for us and a monitoring station to keep track of what is going on in the world and what, if anything, the news is reporting about Kestrel and her activities. Or even Sylvanis and her Weres."

Joseph could see Samuel's words were easing the girl's anxiety some. Her curiosity and interest were overcoming her unease.

"That is where you come in. Because the rest of us will be fighting out there, we need someone we can trust here to let us know what we can expect from the rest of the world."

He shook his head. "We just won't have the time to do it ourselves.

"Kestrel has a lot of faith in you. And she cares about you, deeply. She wants to keep you safe, but she still needs your help. There was no one else she felt would be better for this job than you."

Joseph leaned his back against the wall and watched as Samuel charmed her down.

Shae bit her lower lip and side-eyed the room.

"I can leave when I want though, right?"

Samuel leaned back into his chair; his smile wide.

"Of course. Do you remember that little coupe outside?"

She nodded.

Samuel reached into his pocket and pulled out a set of car keys, placed them on the table and gave them a little push. They skidded across the tabletop to come to rest by Shae. Her eyes were wide in astonishment.

"All Kestrel asks is that you do this until she can be sure that the fighting has sufficiently turned in our favor. Then, she will come and get you herself."

Shae tentatively reached out and placed her hand on top of the car keys. A slow smile spread across her lips.

"O.K. I'll do it!"

Samuel offered her another smile.

"Kestrel said you would." He stood.

"As you might have noticed, there is plenty of food in the next room. A kitchen for you to make any food you wish. I think you will find the bed in the other room extremely comfortable. Kestrel made sure to put plenty of clothes for you to wear in the dressers."

Joseph knew it time to leave. Samuel was finishing up his explanation of the place. He would explain how to use the monitors. How to pull up different news feeds. None of it mattered.

"So, do you have any questions?" Samuel asked after explaining the last of equipment in the room.

Shae looked a little shell-shocked by all the information Samuel had unloaded onto her.

"I don't think so. But if I think of anything, I can just call, right?"

"Absolutely."

"I guess that is it then."

"Very good, Shae. We will leave you to get accustomed to your new surroundings."

Shae had already sat in front of the monitors and scanned between two news programs.

"Yeah. See ya," she said, giving them a backward wave.

Joseph followed Samuel out. They came to the first steel door and closed it, the second one and closed it as well. Samuel set down his travel bag and began rummaging through it.

Joseph turned back toward the steel door and the girl they had left behind.

"It just doesn't feel right?"

"What doesn't?" Samuel asked, his voice distracted.

331

"This. What we are doing."

"Well, it really isn't your concern anymore, is it?"

Joseph turned, "Why would you say . . ."

The sword punctured his side, slid between two ribs, then tore through his right lung. Joseph could feel momentary resistance as the blade reached his spinal cord before it eased and abruptly, he fell, all feeling to his legs gone. The blade Samuel held, slid out of his body as he fell, and the man lifted it quickly before bringing down in a wide arc.

Joseph willed his body to fix what was damaged, but the spinal cords and nerves that ran through it were complex and not easily fixed. As Samuel brought the sword down, he shifted and managed to attempt blocking the blade with his clawed hand.

The sword cut right through his fingers and slammed into his neck. Slowed, the blade only cut a quarter of the way into his neck. Panicked, Joseph put all his will into repairing his spinal cord. He would see to the severed artery in his neck after he could get to his feet.

Feeling returned to his lower extremities as Samuel raised the blade again and Joseph roared to his feet, swiping at Samuel.

In one swift motion, Samuel shifted, rolled over Joseph's swipe and a scaled tail slammed into the side of his face, knocking him back to the ground. In a slight daze, all he could do was watch Samuel dexterously land on his feet. He swung around, the sword, a blood-covered doom, curved down once again to strike him on the neck he had only begun to repair.

The pain was momentary, as was his vision, as it tipped, then, nothing.

Samuel stood over the headless corpse of Joseph, cleaning his sword. It had been a long time since he had used the thing. Centuries, in fact. He had always made sure it was sharp though. You never knew when you might have to draw it.

With Joseph gone, there would be no one to tell Blain about this place. Samuel wished things could be different, but this was how it must be, for now. He didn't regret killing Joseph. The man was vile and annoying. There would be some explaining to do though. Blain would undoubtedly sense the man's death.

Moving to the steel door, he brought up the menu and punched in his code. *There. What's done, is done.*

With one last look at the steel door, Samuel climbed the stairs, locked the outside door and drove away.

# *Chapter Thirty*

He knew what had happened the moment he felt it. A sudden... absence. That was the only way he could describe it. It is true, the longer you are linked with your Pures, the less you notice the connection. But it is still there. THEY are still there. And now, one of them was not.

This had to do with what Kestrel had been hiding from him and Blain was furious about it. True, he never cared for Joseph, but Joseph was his to do with as he saw fit, not Kestrel's.

Like a terrible storm front, Blain's fury rolled before him, sending anyone in his path scurrying for shelter as he stalked the halls of the hospital.

They had taken the hospital that morning. It had been easy. He, Gordon and Taylor had locked it down quickly enough. There had been no security and almost no resistance. There had been one civilian with a gun who had tried to be a hero. Gordon had let the man unload his clip in him before breaking his neck.

After that, everyone complied.

Once they had everyone rounded up. Kestrel, Zach, and those who had chosen to become Weres joined them. Kestrel had everyone taken to rooms. The hospital was seldom used, and a vast majority of rooms were unoccupied.

The members of E.A.R.t.H were confused and frightened by this move to the hospital and the fear was palatable in everyone he had dealt with since they had taken up residence. Blain hadn't cared.

He knew Sarah was here in the hospital, working with the other health care providers to begin monitoring everyone. He had confronted her about what had happened when she had gone with Samuel and Joseph. She claimed they had put her up in a hotel and had left her there. That the main reason she had been sent with them had been to keep her away from him.

He had gotten the feeling she was not telling him something, but as much as he had tried to force her with his will to tell him, her story never changed. The problem with making someone tell you the truth, you had to still ask the right questions.

So, he still had no idea about where they had gone, or what they had done and now, the one person who would have told him was . . . dead? That seemed to be the only possibility, but how could it have happened?

Blain knew they weren't *unkillable*, but they were damn close. Whatever happened to Joseph, there was one person who could answer him. Kestrel.

He found the office she had taken over and burst into the room, not bothering to knock.

Kestrel sat seated at a side desk, her head bowed slightly, the long tresses of her dark hair falling to cover her face. Her right hand rested on top of the office phone's receiver, as if she had just hung it up.

The moment he had opened the door, she glanced up at him and he could see she had been crying, for her eyes glistened and were red. More telling was the lone tear travelling down her cheek to fall upon the desk when she raised her head.

His breath came in forceful huffs. Anger and the exertion of his brisk walk to this office had him like a bull fighting a bullfighter.

His mouth opened to rail at Kestrel, to demand she explain herself, but she spoke first.

Tapping the top of the receiver, she turned her head back to it. "They were set upon by some members of the military, or police, Samuel didn't know. They threw everything at them, and Samuel barely escaped."

She turned back to him, "Joseph, and . . ." she swallowed, "and Shae . . ." Her head bowed, and he could tell she began to cry again, "and Shae, they didn't make it."

Blain knew Kestrel and Shae had gotten close, but he was still surprised by this show of emotion by Kestrel. It seemed so out of character. She was as cold hearted as they came, and Blain couldn't help but wonder if this was for his benefit and not because she cared if the girl died or not.

The idea, Joseph had been killed by ordinary men, let alone Shae, a fellow True, seemed absurd to Blain. Shae wasn't a fighter like he was, or Gordon, but Trues were harder to kill than a Pure, or a Were. It had to have been one hell of a fight.

Kestrel stood, wiping the tears, fake or no, from her cheeks with one delicate hand. When she spoke, there was steel back in her voice.

"They will be coming here next. We cannot be caught unaware. I will not lose another True!"

There was enough intensity in her voice that Blain didn't doubt her anger. But that could be a holdover from her loss from two millennia ago.

"What the fuck were they doing?" Blain wasn't going to let the news of the loss deter him from getting answers.

Kestrel stared him down for a long moment, before sighing. "I sent them to secure a base of operations. Somewhere formidable enough, if the need arose, we could hold out there for some time."

She shook her head. "Doesn't matter now. The place is compromised and no longer useful to us."

Seemed plausible. But he still had doubts. The answer had been surrendered too easily. After keeping it secret for so long, he was to believe,

336

with the deaths of Joseph and Shae, she would simply tell him? Why keep it a secret at all?

Blain watched Kestrel, as she in turn, watched him.

He wasn't going to get answers from her. He should have known better. She didn't trust him. Didn't like him. She needed him, yes, but it went nowhere beyond that.

He snarled, wheeled about and left her there.

Samuel would know, but the man is as slippery as the snake he became. He would not get his answers there. He would get his answers nowhere it seemed.

Well, it was a matter for another time. If at all. He hated not knowing. Hating not knowing all the variables. He hoped this little secret of hers wouldn't end up biting them all in the ass.

Blain had done all the preparations he could to prepare the hospital for the eventual attack. They had boarded up most of the lower windows and barricaded all but the front door.

Most of the members of E.A.R.t.H had been moved to the upper floor rooms to keep them out of harm's way. None of them had gone through the rejection stage yet, and so, were still vulnerable.

They had barricaded the parking lot and posted signs indicating the hospital was closed due to quarantine. Many people were still coming to the hospital, mainly relatives and loved ones of workers from the hospital itself. They were concerned about their loved ones and why they hadn't heard from them.

After they had turned several of them away, and as soon as Blain realized no one from news stations had arrived to investigate, he knew they were already under surveillance.

It was only a matter of time before they were attacked.

337

Samuel had arrived late the night before. Blain had tried to interrogate him about what had happened, and the man had given him a full account of what had occurred.

Or at least, what he had been instructed to say had occurred. The story seemed flawless and believable. But Blain knew it was bullshit. There was nothing he could do about it, so all he could do was prepare for the attack.

After doing a final inspection of the hospital defenses, he entered the lobby where Taylor and Samuel were. He had not seen Kestrel this morning, or Sarah, though he knew the latter was upstairs. Undoubtedly checking on the soon to be dying patients.

Morning sunlight barely lit the tiles on the floor of the lobby. The border of light and dark gradually crept its warmth farther in as the morning progressed.

Blain crossed his massive arms across his chest and was about to ask Samuel if there had been anything new, when a car pulled into the near empty lot. He recognized the car.

"What the fuck is Gordon doing?"

Samuel shrugged. "He wanted coffee. So, he went to get coffee."

Blain fumed. "Of all the motherfucking stupidest things . . ."

As they watched, Gordon exited his car, a cup holder with four cups of coffee precariously balanced in one hand as he shut the door with the other. He began to make his way across the parking lot toward the front door.

He only made it about halfway.

A red mist plumed from the side of Gordon's head. Knocked to one side, the man went down in a shower of coffee as the cups went flying into the air.

"Fuck!" Blain roared and shifted instantly. He sensed his companions doing the same.

"Here they come," Samuel said calmly next to him.

338

True to his word, a black van with tinted windows barreled toward the building down the street.

"To your positions!" Blain commanded and to his surprise Samuel and Taylor moved to comply.

"Where is Kestrel?" he questioned the Weresnake as he left. The man shrugged and exited the lobby, Taylor on his heels. Blain growled after the man. They could use the Druidess' help in this, but he hadn't seen her this morning.

Blain watched as the van, which had been approaching, zoomed into the parking lot as two others converged from either side, forming a half circle in front of the building. Blain could no longer see the body of Gordon in the parking lot as it was obscured by the vans.

Blain smiled a wicked smile. *Won't they be in for a surprise.*

Men dressed in black body armor and armed with assault rifles poured out of the back of the vans, spreading out before the building, weapons raised.

Blain offered them an obscene gesture and roared.

Six of the men held larger cannon like guns which they aimed at the building; a thumping came from them followed by smoke. Shooting caused their bodies to be pushed back slightly as their weapons fired pop can sized cannisters. Two crashed through the windows in the lobby, sending glass falling like rain as the panels shattered. Four more arched higher and were lost from Blain's sight.

The cannisters bounced into the lobby and Blain spun, dropping low and covering his eyes. Even with his eyes closed, the flash burned bright and the bang accompanying it was loud.

Simultaneous bangs reverberated from above as other flash grenades found their marks in upper floor windows which had been left uncovered for just this reason. They led into small offices which had been closed and isolated so any assault would be stunted.

339

A loud hiss, and gas started filling the room. Blain had seen enough. Not that he could see much now anyway. Like he walked from one room of his home to the next, Blain strolled out of the lobby and into the hallway where he would make his stand. He knew Samuel was in the opposite hallway leading off from the lobby doing the same.

The rapid popping of rifle fire rang out and Blain could hear more glass shattering. Clearly, they weren't going to take any chances. Or prisoners.

Which was fine.

Blain wasn't planning on it either.

Desks and doors were piled into his hallway to create a makeshift barrier. While bullets couldn't kill him, a decent amount of them would slow him down, his body needing to repair the damage they caused. So, as much as he hated hiding behind things, it was the best strategy to weather the initial onslaught of gunfire.

The crunch of glass under boots alerted Blain of the men's arrival into the lobby. Seconds passed before someone shouted, "Clear!" Echoed by two others.

*Any second now.*

Blain stared at the twin doors at the end of the hallway as one of them parted slightly. A silver snake-like object was pushed into the space and before it could tilt its head toward Blain, he ducked down behind the barricade.

*No need to let them know I'm here. Yet.*

His acute hearing heard the door click shut again after a moment. Their camera was drawn back. What assumptions they had made of the barricade, Blain would find out soon enough.

Another click and the door was opened again followed by rapid shuffling as bodies flooded into the hall.

Blain didn't give them time to form up. With a mighty thrust and rise of his body, he sent the barricade flying. Desks and doors were turned into projectiles and slammed into the mass of men at the end of the hall. The agents in the front took the brunt of the attack as one desk smashed into the man's chest, snapping his sternum and ribs.

A second desk cartwheeled as it flew, a corner coming down hard on the top of another agent, cracking tactical helmet and skull alike. A wooden door chased after the desks and knocked two others onto their asses.

Next there were shouts and curses as well as cries of pain, followed by the pop, pop, pop of gunfire.

Blain was ready. He had left one of the steel doors from radiology resting against the wall and lifted it now before him. Bullets peppered the door as the men panicked and unloaded their clips into it. The moment the attacks lessened; Blain struck.

He tossed the door forward; men screamed as it dropped into their ranks, crushing the first row. What followed it though, truly frightened them.

Barreling over the door, his weight upon it ensuring the deaths of those underneath, Blain charged. He was so close now only the men right in front got off any shots before Blain was among them.

Eight men were left in the hallway. With a swing of his right arm he sent one slamming against the wall, the drywall buckling from the impact and the man slumped to the ground. The man on the left sent a half dozen rounds of burning pain into Blain's side before he lashed out with his other arm with a blow so hard it snapped the man's neck, his helmet offering no protection from the side blow.

With impressive speed, Blain lowered his massive boar's head and burst forward and up, catching an agent under his body armor with a tusk, burying it in his gut. Thrusting upward, the man was lifted into the air, head punching through the florescent light fixture in the ceiling above. With a loud pop, the light went out, the bulb shattered, showering them with glass.

341

The man screamed in pain, as Blain's tusk gored him, his face now bleeding from shards of glass. Blows rained down upon Blain's head as the man he had gored began bashing his face with the butt of his rifle.

With a toss of his head, Blain threw the man off his tusk into one of the other men in the hallway, felling both. Again, there was the pop, pop, pop of the rifles as the four remaining men in the hallway opened fire. Pain blazed in his chest, neck and abdomen as bullets shredded his front.

Blain ignored it.

With a jab of his clawed hand, he punctured one of the men's throats, closing his fist on whatever he could get his hands on. Yanking it back out, he brought the man's esophagus and windpipe with him and the man dropped, silently screaming, while clutching at the gaping hole in his throat.

Blain tossed the mangled mess at another agent's face causing the man to back pedal, wiping at his face.

Pop! Pop! Pop! Two men were still firing at him and he roared his anger at them. One paused to switch out his clip and Blain charged him. Lowering his head, he rammed the man against the far wall. The man would have broken through but for the stud in the place where he struck. His body crunched as the armor offered little defense against the crushing weight of Blain's impact against the unyielding support.

The building shuddered from the impact and drywall dust filled the air. Blain moved, closing with the other agent. With one swipe of a claw he sent the man's rifle flying, with the other he sent the man's head flying.

Bullets struck him from behind and he spun. The man he had chucked pieces of throat at had recovered. His face was still streaked with blood and pieces of tissue. Somewhere, he had picked up another rifle and leveled both at Blain. With an almost inhumanly roar, he fired both at Blain.

The wounds were taking their toll on Blain. His skin, organs and muscles were ripped to shreds and he bled from almost everywhere.

Reaching down with both hands, he grabbed bodies at his feet and hauled them up in front of him. Dull thuds filled the air, as bullets now perforated the body armor of the men he held before him.

Concentrating his will, he began to heal himself. Bullets rained down from his body as his healing process pushed them out and onto the floor. As soon as the last of the bullets fell, he started healing his insides — repairing his lungs, his liver and stomach.

The man had tossed one of the rifles aside with a clatter but as two streams of bullets again struck the bodies before him, he had to assume the agent had retrieved another fallen rifle. After momentary pauses from one of the streams he could hear the man screaming into his radio for backup.

No one answered.

The moment his organs had been fully repaired; he tossed the bodies at the man. A shout, and the man went down in a wave of flesh. Blain stalked over to the pile of bodies.

The weight of two bodies and armor made it difficult for the man to free himself. He went still the moment Blain came into his view. The man started shaking his head, pleading words mouthed but not uttered as Blain raised his hoofed foot. With a sickening squish, Blain slammed it down upon the man's face, crumpling his skull and sending pieces of brain matter outward like a smashed cantaloupe.

With the last man dead on his side, he wondered how the others were doing.

Gordon lay prone upon the ground, unmoving. The bullet had passed cleanly through his skull and brain and his vision had gone dark and he remembered falling. As his body repaired his brain and skull, he became aware of vans descending upon the hospital.

Dozens of men poured from their backs and Gordon still didn't move. It wasn't until most of them burst into the hospital that Gordon pushed himself to his feet. Three vans were arrayed before him, blocking his view of the front of the hospital. Agents were still standing about, waiting to enter after the first assault secured a foothold in the hospital.

Gordon knew it wasn't going to happen.

Shifting, Gordon trotted to the nearest van. He could hear several people inside the van and on the opposite side of the van.

"Come again? Repeat?" A click and static came from the radio one used.

A frantic voice came back over the line.

"He's up! Dammit! That motherfucking monster is up!"

"What are you fucking talking about? Repeat."

Gordon didn't wait for them to give away his position. Grabbing the bottom of the van, he lifted with all his might. Muscles bunched in his scaly legs and arms as he roared, tipping the van.

Screams were heard from inside the van, and from the other side as well when the van toppled onto one agent and tossed those inside. Shouts of alarm rang out from around him and Gordon dashed around the side of the upturned van.

With a bunch of his legs, Gordon launched himself upon the side of the van and surveyed the scene of chaos below him. Twelve agents were backing away, guns raised toward him.

The hospital beyond them was still billowing smoke through shattered windows. Not fire smoke, Gordon realized, but most likely smoke grenades fired in prior to breaching.

His mass was buckling the door panel he was perched upon and he could still hear sounds of disorientation and confusion from inside the van. At long last, someone inside realized what was happening as the sound of muffled

344

gunfire reached his ears a split second before fiery hot pain lanced his lower legs and feet.

Before the group of agents arrayed before him reacted and fired, Gordon launched himself skyward. Gravity gripped his bulky form, bringing him back down, and he punched through the already buckling van door.

Shredded metal and glass rained down with him as he landed with a sickening crunch as the man who had been below him firing was smashed.

With a spin, his scale-armored tail slammed hard against another agent, his body folding around the impact before his momentum was halted unforgivingly by the wall of the van. Blood gushed out of the man's mouth as his insides flattened.

Gordon bit around the midsection of the third remaining man, clamping his dagger-like teeth within the man's body. In a macabre imitation of his totem animal, Gordon went into a death roll. Landing flat onto his belly, he rolled, tossing the man about like clothes in a bloody dryer. Bones snapped and limbs bent as flesh met unyielding metal.

With his monstrous body whipping around, not only did Gordon make short work of the man in his jaws, but further mutilated the other two bodies inside the van. Blood, gore and body waste painted the inside of the van and Gordon.

When at last he climbed from the interior, his dark green and lighter green underbelly were stained with ichor and blood. From the looks of the agents frozen to inaction by his disappearance and reappearance from the van, he must be truly frightening to see.

The corner of his maw peeled back, showing the full length of his deadly teeth, now dripping with pieces of torn flesh and blood.

"Who's next?"

To no one's surprise, nobody volunteered.

Assault rifle fire filled the air as a dozen guns were unloaded in Gordon's direction.

Gordon had been waiting. Leaping from the van, he hurdled the distance between him and the nearest man. Allowing his massive body to do the work, he tucked into a roll and collided with the man, knocking him prone before landing on and crushing him.

Bullets followed him, chipping pavement and narrowly missing him as he rolled over the man and got back to his feet in an instant. Whirling around he dashed to the next man, ignoring the shots hitting their mark and burning into his body.

Repairing the damage as he moved, he passed right by the next man, sweeping low with an outstretched claw, slicing through the man's thigh, gouging bone and tearing out his patella. With a painful scream the man fell.

Gordon ignored him and moved on.

Despite his monstrous size, he moved like lightning, his long-ridged tail stretched out behind him, swishing back and forth slightly as he ran. Not willing to stay in place long enough for anyone to get a bead on him, he waded into the rest of the group, keeping to the middle as much as possible to give pause to those unwilling to fire in fear of hitting a fellow agent.

One man didn't care and tracked his movement with his rifle, firing the whole time, riddling two of his fellow agents before realizing what he had done. Gordon disemboweled him.

One by one, the men went down as Gordon unleashed his claws, tail and jaws upon the men. None of them saw the dark haired, tanned skin man duck into the hospital.

# *Chapter Thirty-One*

Once again, Taylor found himself killing. As per Blain's plan, he was situated on the landing in the stairwell before the second-floor entrance. Blain had surmised they wouldn't use the elevator during their assault as it would be a kill box when the doors opened. So, while Blain and Samuel held the two halls leading into the main floor, Taylor had to hold the upper level.

They had fired gas into the hallway, which was supposed to be debilitating, or at least, that is what Taylor figured.

It had no effect on him.

He stood motionless at the top of the stairs as he could barely hear the men below. When they didn't hear any coughing or other sounds from above, they climbed the stairs. To their doom.

Taylor hated this, but he had a job to do, and Blain would punish him if he didn't do it. He always knew how to hurt Taylor the most. Oh, he wouldn't target Taylor himself. Not when any hurt or damage he did would repair itself. No. He would target innocents and force Taylor to watch or use his will to make Taylor kill.

*Fucking wanker.*

As soon as a decent number of men were on the stairs. Taylor launched himself downward, using his body as a battering ram. Screams and shouts of confusion broke out as Taylor came hurtling down upon them, smashing bones and breaking necks with the weight of his body.

The final man, who broke his fall, managed to grab his pistol and fired into Taylor, the muffled pop, as the gun was pressed against his abdomen, preceded piercing pain. Again, and again as the man grunted and strained to extradite himself from underneath Taylor.

Taylor bit down on the man's neck, before snapping his head backward, leaving a gaping hole fountaining blood, coating Taylor's fur covered face.

Smoke still billowed in the stairwell, making it next to impossible to see, which was an advantage for Taylor. Everyone else in the stairwell was an enemy. For them, they couldn't risk shooting, or they might catch a friendly.

Taylor rose and glanced over his shoulder. The men he had collided with were sprawled over the stairs; if there was movement at all, it was slight. None of them were a threat anymore, so Taylor turned his attention to the remaining men in the stairwell.

Static-filled calls for backup could be heard through the screams rising from one of the men's radio. Before he could respond, Taylor moved. Leading with a clawed hand, he barreled down the stairs. Taylor's claw buried into the face of the first man he met. His pointer finger dug into the man's eye socket. A viscous fluid spurted, and the man screamed. His other claws dug deep into the man's cheeks, ripping the flesh and tearing open the man's mouth. His scream was cut off in a choke as blood poured into his throat.

With one claw shredding the man's face, Taylor slashed out with the other to catch the next man as he moved in to investigate the sound. With his claws gouging the man's face, Taylor nearly ripped it off. He went down with a cry.

Thrusting out his hand, he tossed the other man down the stairs, knocking over the last two below. Taylor finished them off quickly.

The smoke had begun to dissipate, and Taylor stood in a stairwell full of corpses. Blood was splattered everywhere, especially upon him, his black/brown fur matted and clumped together with coagulating blood.

Taylor fought the rising bile in his throat.

Still, he knew what needed to be done. Calming his stomach, he grabbed the closest body and stacked it in front of the door. Then another, and another. At last, a barricade of flesh rested against the door. It would give him plenty of warning if they attempted a breach again.

Making his way back to the top of the stairs, Taylor shifted and sat, the wounds to his abdomen long since healed. It was like he hadn't even fought, apart from the blood now staining his skin where his fur had reabsorbed into his body.

Taylor studied the bloody stairwell. *What have I done?* He shook his head. *What will I continue to do?* He had no answer. Only tears as they fell, winding their way through the blood drying on his face.

Samuel unwrapped his tail from around the neck of the man whose neck he had crushed as he dragged his fangs through the neck of another. Eight men had entered this hallway and six had died already. The last two were backed against the doorway, one radioing for backup which apparently wasn't coming, and the other firing into Samuel's body.

After tearing through the man's neck, he held with his fangs, Samuel tossed the body aside, blood spraying from the ripped jugular, misting the air. Dashing forward, he halted the moment the men braced themselves and swirled around, lashing out with his tail, toppling the men.

With shouts they were knocked from their feet, and Samuel was on them in an instant. Burying a clawed hand into one man's abdomen, right under the armor, he felt the twisted mass of the man's guts and he tore them apart with his claws.

The man would die — slowly.

He bit the other man on his thigh, puncturing his femoral artery. With a twist of his head, he tore a chunk of muscle and skin out of the man's leg, leaving plenty of space for him to bleed out.

A mixture of copper and iron tinged the air and Samuel breathed it in. A strange odor struck him as well. Familiar, but different.

The door from the lobby opened and a man strode in.

He was a tall, muscular man, his brown skin corded and well defined. Slightly brown, curly hair reached right above his shoulders. His face was wide and slightly flat with coffee colored eyes.

The Latino froze upon seeing him.

Samuel smiled, the corners of his mouth pulling back and up. He sent out a forked tongue to lash the air before him. The odor. It came from this man. Was he a Were? If he was, he wasn't one of Sylvanis'. He knew all of them. If he was, he should be shifted if he intended to face Samuel.

It mattered not. Samuel stalked toward the man.

With an almost imperceptible movement, the man had a blade out and Samuel's froze.

The blade looked like nothing Samuel had ever seen before. Which, considering Samuel's long life, was surprising. With a blade nearly a half meter, it was too short to be a sword, but too long to be a dagger.

The blade itself was a dark green. Jade perhaps? Samuel didn't know. The blade met the handle with no cross guard. Instead, the handle was round and made of a brassy colored metal. It was difficult to see, but Samuel believed it had embossed pictures and symbols upon it, like his people's hieroglyphics.

The man didn't run. Of course, these agents hadn't run either, but they were wearing body armor and had assault rifles. This man had only a light flak vest and brandished a blade. *A unique blade, though.*

For the first time in a long time, Samuel felt trepidation. Not fear, but hesitation. Something here wasn't right. From the knife, to the scent, to this man with no fear in his eyes. He would need to be careful.

Samuel moved closer and the man dropped into a fighting stance, weapon ready, knees bent slightly as he bobbed. Samuel came in from the right and the man moved to cover him. Samuel stopped on a dime and spun, lashing out with his tail with the speed of lightning.

The man leapt over it.

His tail slammed into the wall, denting it from the impact. The man landed and moved in close. He was impossibly fast for a normal human and only Samuel's Were enhanced reflexes kept him from taking a slash to his midsection.

Tucking his shoulder, he fell back into a roll and sprang to his feet. The man had followed right after and lashed out with his blade. Samuel blocked the first swing with his claws. He was too slow when the second swing came, and the blade caught his fingers.

And sliced right through them.

Blood sprayed from his fingers and he sucked in a breath. Before the man could swing at him again, Samuel attacked. With his uninjured hand he slashed at the man, who moved with lightning grace to avoid the attack. But Samuel was relentless.

Slashing with his claws and striking out with his fangs, he had the brown skinned man on the defensive. While he attacked, he willed his body to regenerate his sliced off fingers.

His body did no such thing.

Samuel's attack faltered. His body wasn't repairing itself from the wounds of the blade this man carried. Shock stole his momentum, and the man didn't hesitate.

Slashing out with the blade, he cut across Samuel's arm and leg, tearing scales and scoring bone. Samuel went again on the defensive, wishing he had his own sword with him to counter these attacks.

Again, he tried to will his body to respond, to fix the damage done to it, to no avail. Cold dread seeped into him. His attacker was unnaturally fast and wielded a weapon stunting his healing ability. If he didn't drop this man soon, he might die.

The man jabbed at him with the blade and Samuel arched his body to the side, avoiding the attack. With his strike not meeting its mark, the man's arm extended past Samuel and he brought his own arm down hard against it and was rewarded with an audible snap of bone.

The man cried out in pain but didn't drop the weapon. Instead he rolled with the impact and spun his body around slamming his opposite elbow into Samuel's head, knocking him back.

Samuel staggered a few steps and the man took advantage and moved the blade to his other hand, the other arm hanging limp and angled awkwardly, much to Samuel's satisfaction.

His satisfaction was fleeting as the man spun the blade with his offhand, not seeming at all at a disadvantage using his left. Once again, his attacker moved on him and Samuel retreated.

As fast as Samuel was, he was on equal footing with the other man. The blade gave the man the advantage. Samuel's natural weapon attacks were at risk of being turned against him by the blade. Every strike he made he risked having something amputated, and it made him wary and on the defensive.

Not where Samuel wanted to be. At this point, he hoped to at least delay the man long enough for one of the others to arrive and together they could finish this assassin. For what else could the man be? An assassin sent to kill Weres. Who else would wield a weapon like this?

The assassin caught Samuel's glances at the doors behind him and must have realized his time was running out. If he meant to kill Samuel, he would have to do so quickly, or risk being trapped between two powerful Trues.

The man pressed his attack. The strikes were panicked now, quick and sloppy, and Samuel found them easier to counter. After effortlessly blocking one vicious strike toward his face, he managed to punch him hard in the chest, buckling the vest and shattering ribs. He staggered back, his breaths coming in pained gasps.

Samuel smiled. Now there was fear in the man's eyes. As there should be. Samuel launched into a fierce attack. Slash, slash, slash, strike. The flurry of blows came quick and the assassin could barely get the blade up to block, or to move out of the way.

He backed away, closer to the doors he had strode through. Samuel began to wonder if he surrendered ground on purpose. Getting close to the doors so he could make his escape, realizing now he would be unable to finish off Samuel before help arrived.

Samuel was tempted to let him go. But if he did, the man would be back. He would strike out at them again when they least expected it, and with that blade he could kill any of them.

The man retreated farther, and Samuel continued to press the attack. The man made a lunge for him and Samuel backstepped, but it had been a feint. Instead he turned and made for the door.

Samuel spun and lashed out with his tail, sweeping the legs.

As if gifted with preternatural vision, the man jumped up and came down upon Samuel's tail. The sudden tug, as the tail was yanked downward, sent Samuel stumbling forward, turning as he went.

As the man spun toward him, Samuel realized it had all been a ploy. The retreat, the attempt at an escape, all meant for Samuel to lash out again with his tail.

Before Samuel could stop his forward movement, the man, the *assassin,* struck. Extending his arm forward, he rammed his dark jade blade deep into Samuel's chest.

In all of Samuel's long years of life he had suffered many wounds. He was so in tune with his body. So familiar with every aspect of it, he had repaired almost everything at one point or another, so now, with every attack he felt precisely what damage it did.

So, when the blade pierced his heart, he felt every inch of it slide through his right atrium and ventricle. Could feel the organ flex once, bathing his chest cavity with blood. Blood meant to pass to his lungs.

There was pain. No. There was agony. Searing white hot pain lanced through not only his heart, but also his entire body.

With a roar, he slammed into the man with a powerful backswing of his arm, sending him flying through the doorway, the blade tearing its way back out of his body as the man refused to let it go.

Bones began to break all throughout his body, and he recognized the familiar sensation of his shift. A shift he had not initiated. His heart continued to coat his insides with blood.

With every ounce of his will he tried to heal his shredded heart.

Nothing.

He was fading fast. Returned to his human form, he felt frail. Weak. After all this time. Waiting so long for his mistress to return, only to die when she again walked this Earth. He dropped to his knees; head bowed.

For the first time in over a millennium, tears fell. He would not see Cirrus again. He had hoped. He had hoped that one day, when all this was over, he would be reunited with his son. Show him the world he had helped create. Help shape, with Kestrel.

He was not a sentimental man. And yet, he longed to hold his boy. Now that he thought about it, he had never embraced the boy. Not once. Never held him when he had skinned a knee or banged his head.

Cirrus had never truly known love. Samuel had never shown him any. He had never been a good father. Not even close. He had shown the boy how to survive in this world, but not how to care enough to try.

He hoped Cirrus would find someone to care for him one day. Care for him as Samuel should have done. He hoped Cirrus would never meet Kestrel. Would never experience this war or be forced to be a part of it.

He could feel his heart slowing, the blood which should have been returning to it no longer came. Thoughts began to turn sluggish, like being drunk or from a deep sleep.

He brought the image of Cirrus to his mind. His comely face and intense eyes. He focused on the image. Held it for as long as he could. Till it faded, as did Samuel.

# Chapter Thirty-Two

With his arm and body extended to make the killing blow, Hector had no way to avoid the devastating backswing. He felt more ribs break and the pain, a ravaging fire all along his chest. The impact from the Weresnake's arm sent him flying through the doors behind him and into the lobby.

The ground came up quickly to meet him and Hector found himself in a painful roll. He released the blade for fear he would stab himself, maybe kill himself as he rolled. The blade bounced and clanked across the tiles before disappearing behind a bank of cushioned chairs.

His body ached. Something had snapped in his leg when he had landed, and it hurt like a sonofabitch. He took a mental stock of his body. Ribs broken? Yep. Possible punctured lung? Judging from his labored breathing and pain in his chest. Check. Broken leg? Quite probably. He would have to take a better look at it to be sure.

He had other problems though.

His roll had taken him almost to the feet of the Wereboar who had made his way into the lobby. The beast was covered in blood. Red and dark black marred his coarse, bristling hair and he had a fevered look in his eyes as he stared down at Hector.

A sound from the hallway drew the beast's attention away and Hector managed to look as well. His flight through the doors had knocked them off their hinges and they each lay broken to the sides of the doorway. Lying prone within, was the body of the former Weresnake, unmoving.

A low growl emanated from the Boar as he turned his attention back down at Hector. Desperately, he tried to get to his feet, but the pain in his leg shot through him like lightning and he collapsed.

Large, beefy clawed hands grabbed him and lifted. As if Hector weighed no more than a sack of potatoes, the Boar raised Hector before him. The scent of blood and death wafted out from the creature's mouth to set Hector's stomach roiling.

"You killed Samuel?"

It seemed like more of a rhetorical question, so Hector didn't try to answer. Though he wasn't sure if he could talk right now anyway.

With a roar, the Boar threw Hector across the room. He slammed into a pillar, his body spinning from the impact. He landed behind a lounge sofa with a thud and all went black.

Samuel was dead. The idea barely registered in Blain's mind. Samuel was dead. The man had been alive for millennia. Had survived the first war and countless other dangers, and yet, somehow, this ordinary man had killed him.

True, Blain had never cared for Samuel, but he had respected him. Respected his power and cunning. His ability to survive. Now. Now he was dead. One more True gone. With Shae's supposed death, it left only Blain and Gordon to carry this war.

If things continued to go the way they were going, he wasn't sure they could succeed. They would need to stay safe, and that wasn't Blain's way. He was a brawler. A knuckle to nose fighter. Not someone who hid in the back to keep safe. That was more Gordon's way.

Speaking of which. Blain's attention turned to the battle occurring outside. Gordon tore through those agents, but blood seeped from multiple gunshot wounds all over the Croc's body.

Worse, there were more men coming. The only thing keeping Gordon from being lit up like a Christmas tree was being surrounded by friendlies. Once Gordon dispatched the last man closest to him, they would open fire on his fellow True.

He supposed he should help.

There was movement from where he had tossed the man who had killed Samuel. Surprise flitted across Blain's face for a moment. He honestly didn't think the man would get up after he had hit the pillar.

Blain moved to investigate.

He made it about halfway.

Leaping out from behind the sofa was not what Blain had expected. It was a large cat-like humanoid, tawny yellow in color with rosettes, rose-like markings spotting its body. White fur coated its front which could be seen through the ripped shirt and jeans.

Blain wasn't sure what kind of Cat it was and didn't have much time to contemplate it as it barreled into him, knocking him over. The Cat regained its feet long before Blain recovered and launched into a ferocious attack, raking, with sharp claws, the arm he raised to ward of the assault. Flesh and muscle parted, and pain lanced his arm.

With a lunge, Blain regained his feet, throwing a massive uppercut into the Cat's jaw, knocking him up and back. Like some sort of Circe de Solei entertainer, the Cat twisted in the air and landed facing Blain.

With a fur covered arm, the Cat wiped the blood leaking from his mouth from Blain's punch and growled. A low reverberation seeming to shake the air.

Blain brandished his tusks and readied himself.

358

With unbelievable speed, the Cat closed the distance, then darted right, broke left, before slashing out at Blain's unprotected side as he had moved to block the attack from the right which no longer came.

Blain threw a back handed swipe the Cat ducked under. Jabbing out with its claws, the Cat buried them into Blain's abdomen, slicing through thick muscle to wreak havoc on his insides. Blain felt the claws puncture his intestines and stomach, filling his insides with acid and waste.

Blain roared, spinning to pound down upon the back of the Cat, but it rolled out of his reach, taking with it a handful of flesh from his side. Willing his body to repair itself, it responded sluggishly. Slower than it ever had.

He grunted. He needed to end this. And quickly.

The Cat paced before him, looking for an opportunity to strike.

Blain charged him.

As he got closer, the Cat leaped Blain smiled. *Seems like you cats are all alike.* Blain managed to halt his momentum right under the leaping Cat. With nowhere to go, the Cat hung in the air above him. Blain reached up and grabbed the Cat's legs and brought him down in a swinging arc. Hard.

Body and head slammed upon the tiles and the Cat grunted from the impact. Blain reached down and grabbed him by the head and lifted him up. Turning he strode to the wall. He would bash this Cat like he had the Weretiger not long ago.

With a mighty swing, he slammed the head against the wall, buckling the drywall and showering them both with white powdered dust. Blain pulled the body back to slam it again, but the Cat had other ideas. With a quick swipe, he dragged his talons across Blain's face, tearing flesh and puncturing one eye.

Blain dropped the Cat with a growl, covering his face with his hand. Willing his eye to repair itself, he peered through his fingers with his undamaged eye, expecting to see the Cat launch another attack he would be woefully unprepared for.

359

The Cat was gone.

Blain dropped his hand and searched for any sign of the Cat. Nothing. There had been movement from the other side of the lobby by the now shattered front window, but whatever it had been, Blain hadn't been able to get a decent enough look at it to discern if it had been the Cat, or someone else.

Blain stood there. Unmoving. His body slowly repairing itself. *What the fuck just happened?* He again surveyed the lobby again. No sign of the Cat anywhere, and honestly, Blain was happy for it. *That Cat can fight!* It was a powerful Were. Worse, it had killed Samuel while in human form.

Blain couldn't ignore the fact his healing had been slowed, or at least, slower repairing the damage caused by this new Were. Kestrel would need to be told, and quickly, about this new threat.

Blain turned back toward the parking lot where Gordon hunkered down behind one of those black vans as bullets riddled it from the impending group of agents closing in.

Kestrel would have to wait. First, he needed to help Gordon dispatch this enemy. With a burst of speed, Blain launched himself through the broken window of the lobby and charged the nearest group. He couldn't take out his anger on the Cat, but he sure as hell could on these men.

Daniel sat panting at the side of the hospital, fear causing him to sweat and his heart beat like a war drum in his chest. He waited, not sure what he would do if the Boar came around the corner and found him. He had risked everything darting into the lobby, but he believed it had been worth it.

When Shae had told him to leave her, willed him to leave her. He had no choice but to comply. So, he had left her with the other woman, and instead, followed the other Weres from her group as they battled.

From his vantage point, he had witnessed the death of the young Werebear. He had not only witnessed it but saw who had done it. With nowhere else to go, and nothing holding him there, he had followed the man.

It had been easy to do. The man seemed unaware of the possibility of someone following him and so took no precautions. Daniel had followed him to New York and again when he came to Texas.

When the man left his hotel this morning and came here, Daniel didn't understand what to make of it. Daniel had sensed something was not right the moment he came into view of the object of the man's attention.

The hospital sat lonely on the corner of the block. Signs were posted claiming the hospital was closed due to quarantine. Yet, there were no news crews on site. In fact, there was no one around at all. The entire block was quiet.

He had recognized the man who had been part of the battle in Chicago, get out of his car carrying coffee. The Werecroc, Daniel remembered, though he was in his human form. When he went down and the crack of the gunshot reached Daniel, it became clear why no one was about, and what was about to go down.

Black tinted vans raced toward the parking lot and dozens of armed agents flooded out the back doors and the siege of the hospital had begun. Daniel watched as the agents ignored the fallen man, assuming him disabled from the gunshot wound to his head. *Idiots.*

Gas cannisters were fired into the hospitals. *Also, idiotic.* These men clearly had no idea what they were dealing with. Or at least, the extent of the danger. As the smoke from the cannisters began to dissipate, the agents rushed the hospital.

Shortly after, the killing began. Daniel watched as the fallen man had returned to his feet and shifted. There were no shots fired at the man, so Daniel could only assume the snipers had left their positions.

361

With amazement, Daniel watched the Werecroc overturn a van. *If I had one of these to study.* He shook his head. That life was over. He could never go back. Not now. He was tied to Shae. Controlled by Shae. She would never allow him to go back.

He disgusted himself. His . . . relationship with the girl left him with a mixture of anger, disgust, and dependency, and if he was being honest with himself, desire. She was barely into her teens. Not even a woman, and yet, she had used him. Sexually. And despite himself, he had enjoyed it.

When he wasn't hating himself — or her, he found himself wanting her. Wanting her to . . . use him. Again. He would never try to be with her. Never initiate anything. That would be too sordid. But if she forced him again. If he had no say in the matter. Was he truly in the wrong?

He watched as the Croc emerged from the van after dispatching those left inside, Daniel presumed. With a leap, he began tearing apart the agents who had remained outside to form a perimeter around the entrance to the hospital.

Daniel caught movement and saw the man he had followed duck into the hospital. Keeping low, Daniel crossed the distance to the hospital, wondering when he might be sighted. Thankfully, he made it with no one calling out to him.

Resting against the outer wall of the hospital, Daniel peered into the lobby. The window had been shattered and despite the smoky haze from inside, Daniel could see without difficulty.

A sizable half-circle welcome desk sat at the middle of the back of this room between two double door exits. Next to the doorway on the right sat another door marked with a sign posted above it, designating it as the stairs. Right beside it, sat the elevator doors.

With his acute hearing, Daniel could hear fighting coming from inside both doorways. The man he followed was nowhere to be seen. Daniel glanced behind him and watched as the Werecroc sliced open the guts of one man before snapping his jaws over the man's head. With a vicious jerk, he tore it from the man's neck. With disgusting irreverence, he spat out the head at a fellow agent, knocking him over with the impact of the flying cranium.

Daniel shuddered. These were the people Shae had aligned herself with. He needed to get her free of them. But she wasn't here. She was north, northeast of here. Had been since yesterday. He couldn't help wondering what she was doing. Well, nothing he could do about it. She had ordered him to leave her alone.

He turned his attention back to the lobby in time to see the man he had been following, fly through the double doors to land in a violent roll. Something flew from his hand, bounced and clattered across the floor to land behind a sofa.

What happened beyond that, was what actually caught his attention. Through the open doorway the man had been thrown through was a Were he had not seen before. Half man, half snake and . . . he was dying.

With painful slowness, the man shifted back to his human form. Every bone break, every reabsorption of cells and reformation of human attributes, painstakingly drawn out. Blood poured from a gash in the man's chest. The wound refused to repair as every other part of the man's body reconstituted itself.

When at last the man returned to his human form, having gone to his knees somewhere in the shift, Daniel watched as the light went out in his eyes. The man fell forward, no longer moving.

Daniel's eyes went wide with disbelief. The man he had been following had killed a Were. Killed him with his bare hands.

No.

Daniel's eyes flew to where the item the man had dropped had skidded to. Not with his bare hands. A weapon. A weapon which could kill a Were! And Daniel had been following the man around. *Idiot!*

A low growl drew Daniel's attention back to where the man had rolled. The Wereboar stood looking down at the man. Daniel ducked further behind the wall, making himself as invisible as possible. The last person he wanted to tangle with was this one.

The dead man came to the Wereboar's attention.

"You killed Samuel?" the Boar said. With a roar, he lifted the man and tossed him against a pillar. Daniel heard bones snap upon impact and doubted the man would cause any further trouble.

The Wereboar scanned the parking lot and Daniel stole a glance as well. The Werecroc had managed to kill all the agents who had been out there. Now bullets flew in from all around as more agents descended upon the hospital.

While Daniel watched, the Croc ducked behind one of the vans and waited. Ultimately, the agents would move in and he would dispatch them. Even worse for the agents, the Croc would soon be joined by the Boar and horror would rain down upon them.

A sound from inside the lobby drew Daniel's attention back, along with the Boar's. Impossibly, it seemed to be coming from where the Boar had thrown the man.

The Boar moved to investigate, and much to Daniel's surprise, and clearly the Boar's, a feline humanoid leapt out from behind a piece of furniture to attack the Boar.

The man had shifted! He was a Were, like them! He must be on the team of the other Druidess. Though, Daniel had not seen him in the last battle. Daniel studied the creature for a long moment, admiring the feline grace and lethality in the cat's movements. The markings which patterned its coat clearly marked it as a jaguar. He was extremely powerful, perhaps stronger than the Weretiger. He certainly seemed to be giving a good fight against the Boar.

Daniel glanced back toward the location of the fallen object.

If he was going to have a chance to retrieve whatever it was, the time would be now.

Dashing across the lobby, he ducked behind the sofa he had seen the object land behind. And there it was! *A knife?* But not merely any knife. No. This was something altogether more than just, a knife. The handle was made from some brassy colored metal and lined with rows of strange carvings, like pictographs or something.

The blade. Oh, the blade was beautiful. A dark green material. Jade perhaps. Over a foot and a half in length, a ragged edge lined one side of the blade from handle to tip. He had never seen anything like it, except maybe in some museum exhibit. Because that is what it looked like. Some weapon out of history.

Daniel wasted no time and went for the blade. The moment his hands touched the handle, they burned. Searing pain flared from his palms and he let the blade drop. Sucking in a breath he examined his hands. Red welts lined his palm. The markings on the handle had burned themselves into his skin.

He willed them to heal, as Shae had taught him. The pain receded, but the damage to his hands was slow to fix itself. He eyeballed the blade.

He couldn't let it stay here.

Tearing into the back of the sofa, he ripped the fabric in a long sheet, tearing it off. Wrapping the entire blade in the cloth, he gingerly picked it up.

Nothing.

The fabric offered him protection at least. Glancing up over the sofa, the Jaguar and the Boar were still fighting each other. Backing out the way he had come, he ducked around the side of the building and now sat gasping for breath, clutching the wrapped blade in his lap.

The blade. This blade could change everything. Whoever controlled this blade would be feared. Would be hunted. There would be no way Kestrel, or the other Druidess would want this to fall into the other's hands. Or worse, the government's.

He didn't know what to do. If he could, he would take this to Shae. But she had forbidden him from going to her. There would be too much of a risk for this blade to get into the hands of Shae's enemies. Ha! There was

too much of a risk for it to fall into the hands of Shae's friends.

Whatever happened next, he would need to be ready. He would need to keep safe. Without a backward glance, Daniel fled. He would stay close by. Just in case.

Eric Moran watched the battle ensue below him from a nearby rooftop. His spies had alerted him to this failed attempt by the DHS to attack these Were-creatures and he had jumped on a plane to ensure he would be there to witness the outcome.

The battle had, not to his surprise, gone poorly. Even now, the few remaining agents were being dispatched by the Boar and the Croc. The addition of the Jaguar had been unexpected. Especially since it had fled the scene.

It had been difficult to see what had been happening inside the hotel's lobby from his vantage point, but there had been an obvious scuffle and the Jaguar had left and had been followed outside shortly by the Boar.

Whomever this Jaguar was, he clearly wasn't with this group, nor with the other group. He had men still on them in Chicago. Watching very closely. He would have news when they moved.

He sensed a presence at his side.

"Gul?"

A grunt told him he had guessed right and had impressed the man with his ability to figure out who had approached him without looking.

"The man who ducked into the lobby and then left?"

"Daniel Mathias." He had wondered where the man had gone to. He and the girl, Shae, had all but disappeared. To have him turn up here was curious. As far as Eric knew, the man had never interacted with this group, though Shae had been involved with them, at least, at some point. She wasn't here though.

"If you say so, sir. We put a tail on him and are just waiting for your orders to take him down."

Take him down? Is that what he wanted? Eric wasn't sure. The man had gone in there for something. Gone in and fled and if his eyes had not been deceiving him, had smuggled something out from the hospital.

"Leave him alone. But keep an eye on him. I want to know where he goes and what he does."

"Of course, sir." Gul moved to leave.

"And Gul?" He said without turning.

"Yes?"

"If they can. Find out what he is carrying."

There was a hesitation as if Gul wanted to ask why but chose to keep quiet.

"Yes, sir."

Gul left him and he continued to stare down at the last remains of slaughter and peered back up at the hospital. He could see no movement coming from inside, but his agents had reported there were hundreds of people inside. Captives? Maybe, but Eric doubted it. He feared something much, much worse.

If he had the authority, he would order an airstrike on this building in hopes of incinerating everyone inside. They were on the precipice. A tipping point. He knew it in his bones.

367

They might well reach a point where they couldn't turn back the tide. If it happened before he was ready . . . Eric didn't want to consider it. He would be ready. Had to be ready. He may need to buy them all some time. He tapped a finger against his lower lip, thinking.

It might be time to talk to the Director of Homeland Security. Pool information and resources. It might be time for Eric to step out of the shadows. Or at least reveal himself a little.

He did not know the director personally, but his spies told him the colonel was an honest man. A practical man. He would understand the practicality of the things Eric had done. They had been necessary for them to understand what they were facing. To prepare for it.

He would leave Chad in charge down here — to watch the hospital. It was time he returned to DC and reach out to the colonel.

The last screams of the agents had died down and the Boar and the Croc had retreated inside the building. Eric wished he could get a blood sample from the jaguar, but it would be too risky.

He sighed. There was too much for one man to do, but he hadn't taken this job without understanding the burden and necessity of it. Keeping America safe sometimes required a hand in the shadows, so those in the light could sleep soundly. Eric was that hand.

# *Chapter Thirty-Three*

The sun rode high in the cloudless sky above the twist and turns of the hiking trail through the Appalachian Mountains. The bright sunlight warmed Cirrus' face, in stark contrast to the cold mountain air, as he gazed out over the lush forests carpeting the rise and fall of the landscape for as far as his eyes could see.

Much had happened to Cirrus these past few months. When his father left . . . no, abandoned him, he had struggled to make sense of the world and his place in it.

The man his father had hired to keep an eye on him and to manage his stipend cared little about what Cirrus did or where he went, so Cirrus spent little time at home. He had always been more comfortable in the forests and away from people.

People had never been nice to him. Cirrus held no illusions about how he looked. He knew with his broad forehead and puffy lips he had the look of a village idiot and less like the intelligent, one might say, genius, he was.

He had his father to thank for the last bit. If he had anything to thank him for at all. His father had been relentless in not only teaching him to value education but trained him in ways to retain as much as he learned as possible. Because of that, his ability to retain facts and information was almost flawless.

This, combined with the intensive physical and martial training his father had also expected of him, made him a formidable person. A formidable person who looked like a dumb Mr. Potato Head.

With a last look at the horizon, Cirrus began the descent on the forested trail. It wasn't steep so Cirrus could relax his normal vigilance and let his mind wander.

For a while after his father left, he kept an eye on the news for anything regarding his father, or the woman he had left him to serve. There had been nothing. Silence.

His handler had no information to give him either and grew irritated every time Cirrus asked him. Cirrus ground his teeth. He hated the man. He had clearly been siphoning off Cirrus' money and using it for himself. The expensive clothes, shoes and watches were a dead giveaway, but Cirrus didn't care about the money.

It was the theft which bothered him. His father, despite his faults, was generous when it came to those he employed. He paid well and if you did the job well, you were rewarded accordingly. There would be no need to steal.

Cirrus shook his head. He knew, when his father discovered the theft, Christian Haptil would meet an ugly fate. All for a little off the top.

The trail was empty, which it usually was. Few used this trail as it was not one of the popular hiking trails populating the Appalachians. The less people the better, in Cirrus' opinion.

Months had gone by after his father had left before Cirrus had decided he had enough. He would leave England and head for the States. He did not owe his father anything and if his father believed he would wait around for him to return, he was mistaken.

Though, if Cirrus was being honest with himself, he would admit to believing he would find his father somewhere in the United States. All signs pointed to him having left England and Cirrus believed he had gone to the U.S.

He had been here for weeks now though, and still, there had been nothing about his father's whereabouts. There was no indication as to what his father had been doing. There had been a report out of Chicago, and Cirrus had seen the internet videos showing the battle between the Werewolf, Weretiger and Wereboar, but no Weresnake like his dad.

He had been tempted to go to Chicago, but if he knew his father, any kind of exposure would have sent him back into a dark hole. He would be as far away from the situation as he could get.

However, the appearance of these Were-creatures could mean only one thing. The woman his father served indeed returned when Stonehenge fell.

He wondered if his father had mentioned him to her. Or, perhaps, he was too embarrassed by him to tell her? Would she call on him to serve her too? Would he get to fight alongside his father? Did he want to?

Anger flared in him and he cooled the fire immediately. Emotion was unnecessary and wouldn't accomplish anything. His father abandoned him to serve some woman whose only contribution to his father had been to turn him into a monster. A long-lived monster, but a monster none the less.

The trail began a switchback and the steepness began to increase forcing Cirrus to be more watchful of where he stepped. He had inherited his father's fast healing, but a fall from this height could still kill him.

Black vultures swam the updrafts created by the cool air and the warm sun, like dark twisters they circled lazily round and round. Mountain birds filled the air with their song. The 'drink your teaaaa' of a Rufus-sided Towhee and the 'what what where where' of the Indigo Bunting.

A perfect day for a hike, and the perfect place for one as well. He had never been more at peace with himself than he had since he had come to these mountains. Never felt so . . . at home.

He paused to take a deep breath when he felt his entire world break apart. Fiery hot pain flooded every inch of his body as every bone in his body began to break. His skin itched and burned, and he watched in horror as his skin turned from dermis to scales. He could feel his spinal column erupt from his lower back as muscle, bone and scales grew around it.

He knew immediately what happened and yet the knowledge didn't ease the pain now wracking his entire body. Stones bit into his knees and palms as he landed hard on the ground, panting.

He was shifting. He was shifting like his father had. Changing into a half man, half snake humanoid. A Weresnake.

The bones in his face and skull altered to accommodate the sweeping head and rounded snout. Fangs pierced his gums as they grew from his jaw. Their curved dagger-like projections recurved to fit snuggly inside his now widened mouth.

When at last the shift finished, Cirrus climbed to his feet. A forked tongue flicked out before him, tasting the air. It was like a whole new world of senses opened before him. Not only could he see clearer, but the scents of the world provided him with a spectrum of awareness he never thought possible. *So, this is what my father experiences.*

His father.

It hit him. Almost as hard as the pain gone from his body. The sudden realization of what his shift truly meant.

His father . . . was dead.


There was a blackness. A dark, deep blackness in Stephanie's heart. What she had done. What she had caused . . . it left her empty. Heartbroken. She had killed her best friend. Her big sis.

Beth had been so much a part of her life her at college. She had been Stephanie's rock. Her friend. In some ways, her mother, always looking out for her, worrying about her safety.

She had been so solid. So strong and fierce, and now . . . now she was gone. She would never grace this world with her presence again. Never grow into the amazing woman she had started to become. Never succeed in her career she had been acing all her studies for. Never be an amazing wife. An amazing mother.

And it was all Stephanie's fault.

She had trusted Sylvanis. Trusted her and put her friends at risk because of that trust. It was one thing to believe what you were doing was right; it was another thing entirely to drag someone else into it.

Her thoughts drifted to Jason. Another one she had dragged into it. He had come willingly, but truly, he hadn't been left with any choice. That could be excusable though. She had not known what was happening . . . what would happen to him.

She had known what could happen to Beth, though. Knew the risks and still dragged her into it. She couldn't forgive herself for it. Couldn't forgive Sylvanis for lying to her.

She had said if the person wanted to become a Were — if they were close to the person, they would be safe. *She never promised you though, did she?* No. She didn't. She had said she believed it helped in the survival rate. She had offered no assurances.

No. This all fell on her. She had known the risks and still presented the idea to Beth and Mike. Did her best to convince them to join them, and in the end, they had said yes.

In the back of her mind, she could sense the Mike's presence. She could go and find him. Tell him how sorry she was, but she knew those words would be hollow. She blocked his presence from her mind. He needed his space, and she needed hers. The wound was still too fresh for them to try and examine it together.

Jason was another story. He would go out daily looking for Mike. He would ask her to tell him where Mike was, but she refused. The look of pain in his eyes at her refusal cut her deep, but she would honor Mike's decision to be alone. When . . . if . . . Mike came back, it would be his choice.

She sat on the couch in the living room of Beth's and her apartment. Her refusal to leave her room had in many ways been because of her inability to look around the apartment and not see Beth everywhere she looked. Her bedroom had been a solace for her.

She had ventured out here, to the living room, but had gone nowhere else in the apartment. She certainly hadn't gone into Beth's room. Nor would she.

Beth's parents had come to take the body home and clean out her belongings. They had questions. Needed to understand what had happened. The doctors had been unable to give them any. Beth had a heart attack. There had been no drugs in her system. No indication of any injury except for a small laceration on her arm. Their little girl was gone, and they had no idea why.

Stephanie knew. Stephanie knew and yet, gave them nothing. They had left with a few boxes of memories and hearts full of loss. And Stephanie had given them nothing.

She pulled the blanket she had draped across her up further on her body and leaned against the side of the pillow and stared at nothing.

Jason had been gone most of the morning. Out looking for Mike, most likely. She hadn't had the heart to tell him stop, but maybe she should. Mike didn't want to be found and Jason needed to understand.

A soft sigh escaped her lips. Jason. The one man she loved with all her heart. He was being so amazing during this, so understanding. But she knew he was getting restless. Knew he wanted to go back to Sylvanis and fight. He still believed in the cause.

She did too. But . . . she . . . she couldn't. She couldn't trust to give lycanthropy to another. Not again. Maybe she could fight, but she couldn't help with raising an army. She couldn't lose another person. Be responsible for another death. Either way though, she wasn't ready. She was empty and she no longer cared.

374

The door opened with a crash and Stephanie bolted up. Jason came rushing in.

"Jesus, Jason. You scared me!" She had her hand over her heart as if pressing there would slow it down from its pounding.

Jason ignored her and went to the television, turning it on.

"Jason? What is it?"

Jason continued to ignore her while he frantically searched for the remote. The moment he found it, he wheeled on the TV and punched in the number for the news station.

Stephanie decided not to bother asking Jason what the hell was going on as she realized she was about to find out anyway.

The scene popping up on the screen was mind-numbing. The female reporter on the screen was talking, but somehow remaining calm as she explained what was being shown in a small window to the left of her head.

It looked to be an aerial shot, either from a helicopter or maybe a drone. Police cars were scattered around in a parking lot and there were dozens of sheets spread out in little rectangles all around. It only took a moment for Stephanie to understand there were bodies under those covers.

"We are getting mixed reports from people who were inside the refinery when the attack happened. According to several witnesses, and EMTs, three monsters attacked the refinery."

Stephanie was surprised the woman had kept a straight face. She could only imagine with so many witnesses collaborating the story, there could be no doubt.

"Witnesses say one of the monsters appeared to be a large humanoid crocodile, while two others looked like humanoid boars. Witnesses, including the EMTs, insisted they were not wearing masks or costumes, but were in fact actual monsters."

The scene in the little window grew and took up the whole screen. There were police officers and other men beginning to bag the bodies.

A scroll ran across the bottom of the screen stating there were over thirty dead and hundreds wounded. Among the dead were the police officers who were first on the scene, the president of the company and some of the upper management in charge of running the refinery.

"The attack has left many dead. Mostly it was the brave men and women of the local police department who were all killed. Their wounds, we have been informed by a source who wishes to remain anonymous, appear animal-like in nature."

The on-site scene reverted to a little window to the left of the reporter's head as she continued.

"The president of Yulchik corporation who had been visiting from Russia to inspect the refinery is listed among the dead. In fact, apart from law enforcement, the majority of the slain were part of the management team at the refinery. Authorities have not ruled out industrial sabotage."

She paused. "There has been no comment yet from the Yulchik company."

Jason turned the TV off and sank down onto the couch and turned to her.

"It's begun."

Stephanie stared at him. Her mind raced. Hundreds injured. Injured! Didn't they understand what it meant? There weren't dozens killed! There would be hundreds more! If not from their bodies rejecting the lycanthropy and dying, but when they shifted, and began killing.

"Jason . . . I . . ." She didn't know what to say. It was all too overwhelming.

He moved closer to her and took her hands into his, peering at them for a long moment before looking back up at her.

"Stephanie. I know you aren't ready. I understand. I do. But . . ." He glanced back at the now silent TV.

"I can't let this go on. How many more people are going to get hurt? Killed? How many are Kestrel going to force into fighting for her?"

His eyes met hers again and she saw the moistness gathering at the corners of his eyes.

"She has to be stopped. We . . . I, have to do whatever I can to stop her."

He glanced away and brought his hands to his eyes, wiping the tears away before they could fall.

"I don't expect you to come with me. You are still hurting. And know, that I love you, more than anything. And I hope you can understand that is why I have to go."

She knew this was coming. Had known for a while now. Had dreaded it. Had fought like hell to move past this grief, this agony of her heart, so, when the time came, when Jason had felt he had waited long enough, she would be ready. And now events had moved forward and the time was now.

And she wasn't ready.

"I don't want you to go," she said softly and saw him tense.

She realized immediately why. He was afraid she wouldn't let him. Was afraid she would use the control she had over him to keep him from leaving.

She reached over and this time took his hands into hers.

"I don't want you to go," she said again. "But I won't stop you."

Jason's shoulders relaxed in relief and he turned back to her.

"Will you come?"

She turned away. Here it was. The question she had been afraid he would ask. Since they had started dating, and more so since she had turned him into a Werefox, they had been inseparable. They hadn't been apart for more than few hours in a day. Didn't want to be apart.

And now, he would leave. He would leave her here. Alone. Or at least he would if she didn't go with him. Her thoughts ran back to Beth and her heart ached all over again. She wasn't ready to fight in this war which had taken Beth from her. Was she?

Jason took her lack of response as a no and pulled his hands away. They felt so empty now. Standing, Jason opened his mouth to say more, than closed it before opening it again.

"I'm leaving as soon as I can. I'm going to pack a few things. If you change your mind . . ." He didn't finish, stood there for a moment looking down at her before turning and going to the bedroom.

She didn't watch him go. Instead, she returned to staring at nothing. Jason was leaving, and she was staying. A sense of urgency in her mind blocked out all other thoughts. It sat there, in the back of her mind and try as she might, she couldn't quite grab it.

Jason returned from the bedroom with a small to go bag. Half full, it folded upon itself, pulled in from the handles.

"I will call you as soon as I get to Chicago. I don't know where we will be going from there. I guess it will depend on what Kestrel's next move is."

She nodded absently, not looking at him. She wasn't angry he was going. Only . . . numb. Numb everywhere. Except for the sense in the back of her mind. Like panic. Was she afraid she wouldn't see him again? She didn't understand what it was. Didn't get what was happening to her.

Jason stood behind the sofa. She knew she should say something. Say anything. Tell him it was fine. Tell him she loved him. Tell him goodbye. Anything. But she said nothing. She said nothing, while the sense of urgency trampled her thoughts.

Jason sighed and headed for the door.

She heard it open.

"Mike?"

378

Jason's question smacked her, and she twisted around and searched the doorway. Mike stood right outside the door. He looked in a bad way — gaunt as if he hadn't been eating well, or at all. His usual dour expression had been replaced by sorrow, tinged with . . . Urgency!

That was it. What she had been feeling. It hadn't been her sense of urgency. It had been Mike's! She had ignored his presence in her mind for so long that when it had intruded on her own thoughts, she had thought it hers.

"Can I come in?"

Jason turned his body to allow Mike to pass. "Of course!"

Mike swept in, striding right into the living room. He took her in, and his expression softened. Their eyes met and everything needing to be said between them was said in that moment.

A sob broke out between her lips. He had forgiven her. He had forgiven her and knew she hadn't forgiven herself. And she knew he felt the same.

Jason hadn't seen what passed between them, had only heard Stephanie's cry.

"Now, Mike . . ."

"It's O.K. Jason. I don't hold Stephanie responsible anymore."

Hearing him say it out loud made her cry all over again.

Jason dropped his bag and went to her. He wrapped her in his arms, and she cried against him.

For a long moment, no one said a thing as she bawled into Jason's shirt.

"Did you see the news?" Mike moved over to them.

Stephanie felt Jason nod.

"I hadn't known what to expect. And in a way, this was far worse than anything I had imagined." Jason stroked her hair as he talked. "And I'm afraid this is only the beginning. It will get a lot worse. And quickly."

Mike began pacing.

"When you two brought this to Beth and me. I really wanted nothing to do with it. Didn't actually take you seriously, in fact. Didn't see the whole picture, I guess."

He stopped before them.

"Beth had. She had understood everything. That was why she so readily volunteered. Why she didn't hesitate. She saw clearer than I did."

He paused. "I was a fool."

Mike bent down in front of them.

"Stephanie?"

She pulled her head out from where it had been buried against Jason's chest and wiped her nose with the back of her sleeve and sniffed.

Mike crooked a small smile.

"You look as bad as I'm sure I do."

She smiled a little back at him. "Yep."

He peered into her eyes, his darting a little, as if looking for something behind hers.

"Stephanie. I know you are still here, and not out there," he jerked a thumb back at the TV. She understood what he meant. "Because of what happened . . ." His throat bobbed. "Because of what happened to Beth. And I understand. Believe me. I understand. But . . . do you think this is what Beth would want you to be doing?"

The question hit like a punch to Stephanie's gut. What would Beth have said seeing her here curled up on this sofa, not moving for days? Not moving while a war she was supposed to be fighting in happened?

"No." She smiled thinking about it. "She would have already kicked my ass off this sofa and out the door."

Mike shared her smile.

"Exactly. She loved you Stephanie. You were her lil sis. She would be sad and hurt to see you like this."

He was right. Goddammit, he was right. Beth would be chastising her and would not have put up with the way she had been behaving. Grieving was one thing. Shirking your duty? Your responsibilities? Letting those who counted on you down? That wasn't Beth, and she sure as hell wouldn't have allowed Stephanie to be that way either.

She turned toward Jason, who held such a look of gratitude toward his friend she couldn't help but smile. He felt her look to him and turned to her, his eyebrows raised in anticipation of what she would say to all of this.

"Jason? Would you mind waiting a little bit while I pack?"

He offered her a broad smile in answer.

"No need to wait on me," Mike offered, "My pack is already in the car."

# *Chapter Thirty-Four*

Hank leaned against the far wall of the hotel room where, once again, Sylvanis held an impromptu conference. All the usual suspects were there; Kat sat perched on the dresser, her keen eyes alight with passion as she laid out what the man, Jessie Brumfield had told her.

Clint, eyes still haunted from all he had been through, and all he had done when he had lost control of himself, sat on the corner of his bed, staring at his hands as if they held all the absolution he needed.

Ben sat opposite Sylvanis at the lone table in the room. He stared out the window at the soft, gray clouds covering the entire Chicago sky. His brows were furrowed in thought and his fingers drummed in rhythmic cadence on the tabletop.

There was an absence here weighing heavily on Hank. In almost every previous meeting they had here, Sim had been present. He was always one to lighten the mood with a quick joke or a sarcastic comment which sometimes brought a disapproving glare from Hank. Which would only cause Sim to grin more, along with the rest of the group.

*Gods I miss him.* He wasn't a religious man, though he believed in God, and he prayed Sim knew how much he loved him. How proud he was of him for standing up to this threat, without any hesitation. He wanted to tell him so badly how he knew, with every part of his being, Jennifer would have been so proud of him as well.

His vision fuzzed a little and he, as nonchalantly as possible, wiped the tears forming in his eyes. *I'm not going to start crying again, dammit!* He remained leaning against the wall, waiting to see what Sylvanis would say of this new development.

It was good news — of a sort. Jessie, a former marine, had ties to countless others who he believed could be convinced to join the cause. It seemed too good to be true, which had Hank a little apprehensive.

The corner of his lips dipped in a frown. He was being pessimistic, he knew. Or realistic. But after everything that happened, it was too much to process. First, there was the loss of Sim, followed by the death of Stephanie's and Jason's friend, Beth and their decision not to return because of it. Followed by the news of not one, but three separate attacks by Kestrel's group, which meant hundreds would die or turn into Weres to join her army.

They were losing this war before it started. But perhaps, their losses needed to be realized before others would come to their aid. Hank didn't know. He hoped this Jessie could deliver on what he had promised.

"What is your take on the man?" It was Ben who asked. It was a measure of respect the lawman had for her that he trusted her instincts when it came to reading an individual.

Kat's shoulders rose in a hint of a shrug. "He seemed honest. Adamant he wanted to help, and he understood the risks involved."

Clint snorted.

It looked like Kat wanted to snap at Clint, but after a moment, she offered him a nod as if to say, 'You're right, he really has no idea.'

She turned back to Ben. "Regardless of his understanding of the risks, he seems to understand the threat Kestrel and her group holds for, not only America, but the rest of the world, and wishes to fight."

Sylvanis nodded and the group waited for her to respond. *Poor girl, she is barely a teenager . . .* Hank paused his thoughts. Once again, he let the way

Sylvanis look cloud his judgements. She wasn't a teenager. She was, at least, in her mid-twenties in life experiences. *Scratch that.* Mid-fifties in life experiences.

She had been to war. Fought and died in that war. Sent men and women to their deaths in that war. She was no child. These people had every right to show her deference. Sylvanis was their leader, and while she valued each one of their opinions, it would be she who would make the final decisions as to their course of actions.

"I have not lived in this age for very long," Sylvanis began, breathing out a short laugh and shook her head. "Not long at all, really. But what I have been able to learn in my short life here is that the men and women of the military in America are brave and would not hesitate for a moment to fight for their country."

She eyed each of them in turn. "The other thing I have learned in my short time is that the military is a branch of government and the government would not hesitate for a moment to try and subvert your powers for their own wishes."

Hank found himself nodding. She was right. They were all weapons. Weapons who could create countless other weapons. Worse, the weapons they created could create weapons of their own. Sylvanis impressed him with her understanding of the situation.

Sylvanis looked to Kat. "For now, we will explain to Mr. Brumfield the risks involved in becoming a Were. I don't want any confusion in his, or anyone he brings to us, understanding that this may end in their deaths."

Hank couldn't blame her for her being adamant. After the loss of Stephanie due to Beth's death, she wouldn't want a repeat of losing any other allies.

"We will, however, not tell them about your ability to control them."

All heads fixed on Sylvanis. Even Clint's who, as far as Hank had been able to determine, had shown about as much interest in the conversation as he would about a speck of dirt on the floor.

"Do you think . . ." Kat halted, as if searching for the right thing to say to that. "Do you think that is the right thing to do?"

There it was. The *right* thing to do. Hank waited with interest to hear Sylvanis' answer.

Sylvanis met Kat's wide eye stare. "No," she answered. "I don't think it's the *right* thing to do. But until we can be certain of Mr. Brumfield's intentions, I don't see any other course of action."

Kat continued to lock gazes with Sylvanis. Hank knew it wouldn't last though. Kat was too much of a pragmatist to not understand what was at stake here. That Sylvanis wasn't happy about making this choice would be enough for Kat to let it go, Hank believed, and was proven correct when Kat huffed, before nodding.

"Hank?"

He started, not realizing Sylvanis had turned her eyes to him.

"Yeah?"

"Your thoughts?"

She always did that. Included everyone. It was what he admired about her.

He cocked his head. "I think you are right. We would be an asset the government would love to get their hands on and that is not the war we were meant to fight. Mr. Brumfield has stated he no longer serves, but I believe the saying is, 'once a marine, always a marine'. Even if he doesn't report to the government, there is no way of knowing if at some point down the road the government won't come calling for his allegiance."

Sylvanis didn't offer a reply before turning to Clint.

"Clint?"

"Yeah."

He didn't follow up with anything else and Sylvanis watched him for a long time. He looked her way, before looking away again. At length, she turned to the rest of them.

"Then it is decided." She hadn't asked Ben his opinion. It wasn't as if she didn't value his opinion. Hank had noticed she had come to rely on the older man quite a bit. It simply wasn't a decision he could have a say in. He wasn't a True.

"Kat. Bring Mr. Brumfield in."

Kat hopped off the dresser and went to the door. A moment later she returned with Mr. Brumfield. He was a tall man, a tad taller than Kat, and broad of shoulder. He wore a tight-fitting shirt which did little to hide his bulk, his ebony skin lined with muscles. His marine tattoo, the eagle, globe and anchor were displayed prominently on his arm.

Kat led him to the center of the room before moving to regain her spot on the dresser, leaving the man, alone in the center of a room with some of the deadliest people on the planet.

Hank was impressed by the man's cool reserve. Or perhaps, Hank should be shaking his head at the man's ignorance to the danger he was now in. None of them were killers, but the truth was, up until now, none of them have had to make the, 'for the safety of the mission' call yet. If this man risked their mission, would they find themselves with no other option?

Hank hoped it didn't come to that. Never, came to that.

Sylvanis stood and approached Mr. Brumfield.

He offered her a charming smile and Hank felt a slight smile tug at the side of his lip at seeing Kat's roll of eyes.

To Hank's surprise, Sylvanis' faltered a little in her approach and Hank reevaluated the man. He was handsome, Hank guessed, in his own way. He had a confidence about him and bright blue eyes which he wondered if he had ever seen on a black man before.

Sylvanis regained her composure quickly and crossed the rest of the way to stand before Mr. Brumfield. She appeared small before the man, her petite, short frame, overshadowed by his height and bulk.

Though now that she had gathered her poise, her presence dominated between the two. It was uncanny. Mr. Brumfield became aware of the difference immediately and his smile fled as if realizing it had failed in its task and wanted no part of what came next.

"Mr. Brumfield . . ."

"Jessie. Please." He attempted another charming smile before deciding against it.

"Jessie. Kat here has explained your desire to join our cause and while we are indeed in need of people willing to fight, I wanted to make sure you understood the dangers in what you are volunteering for."

"Ma'am. I assure you that I do und—"

"I assure you that you don't, Mr. Brumfield," Sylvanis snapped and the man had the good sense to shut his mouth.

Sylvanis waited a moment to determine if he would keep with his good sense and when he didn't open his mouth to say anything further, she continued.

"What you are volunteering for could lead to your death."

The man opened his mouth again, but Sylvanis' hand shot out to silence him, and again he shut his mouth. Hank could see the muscles in the man's jaw bunch. Jessie was used to following orders it would seem, but it didn't mean he liked it.

"I know what you are going to say, Mr. Brumfield." She softened her tone. "Jessie. You would say something about how you would be willing to die in the service to your country and to protect those of this nation. Which is admirable and just the type of people we are looking for."

She straightened and stared him hard in the eye, which given the height difference seemed implausible, but she managed it.

"I am not talking about a death in the field, Jessie. I'm talking about the very real possibility of you dying before you ever see the enemy."

Jessie forehead scrunched and he made a face. He glanced about the room, looking for an explanation about what this woman told him. His eyes rested on Kat and he opened his hands, palms up in supplication.

Kat rolled her eyes again. "Why are you looking at me? She's in charge." She jerked a thumb Sylvanis' way.

He returned his gaze to Sylvanis is surprise, waiting for her to explain.

She sighed, turned and returned to her chair.

"What I'm about to tell you, is of utmost importance and can't be shared with anyone except those who have decided to become Weres." She halted waiting for his understanding and assurance.

After a moment, the man agreed.

"After the transmission of lycanthropy into the body, there is a point in which the body will reject it. The nature of lycanthropy however is so powerful the body cannot reject it and it will do the only thing it can think of to destroy it. It will shut it down."

Jessie frowned. "Shut it down? What do you mean, like knock you out? Faint?"

Sylvanis shook her head. "No, Jessie. You will go into cardiac arrest and if your body doesn't recover from that, you will die."

Jessie staggered a step back and looked at the ground as if expecting it to drop out from beneath him. Hank thought he understood. The man was a fighter. A warrior. To die on the battlefield, well, that was one thing. But to die before seeing combat? That was another thing entirely.

"That is the risk you take by joining with us. That is the risk your friends would take as well. I will be honest with you. Your desire to join with us, it being your choice and not one that is forced upon you will improve the chance your body will recover, and you will survive. But that is no guarantee."

Jessie ran a hand down his face and blew out a breath.

"I see," was all he said.

Silence hung in the room as no one spoke. It seemed everyone understood Jessie might need a moment.

Perhaps more than a moment.

Jessie tsked and shook his head and it seemed everyone in the room tensed. Hank began to wonder if this was one of those 'mission first' moments he had dreaded.

"Umm." Jessie still peered down, his foot dragging a line in the carpet in a half circle before him. This was doubtless the most uncertain this man had been since joining the marines, Hank guessed.

"I can't speak for the others as I haven't really reached out to them yet, but as for me . . ." He chuckled slightly and shook his head as if disbelieving what he was about to say. "As for me," his voice grew stronger and he glanced up at Sylvanis. "I would be honored to join your fight, Ma'am."

Sylvanis offered him a faint smile.

"Very well, Jessie. Welcome. Is there any particular animal you feel more connected to? The closer we get to your totem animal, the better for your body's acceptance."

"Totem animal?" Jessie made a face. "Like, my spiritual guide or something?"

Sylvanis smiled patiently. "Something like that, yes. I assure you; it is important to choose what feels natural to you. What you feel a connection to."

Jessie's pursed his lips, looking to Kat.

"Tiger," he said with a swagger.

Kat shook her head and rolled her eyes again, but Hank caught the twinge of a smile forming at the corner of her mouth.

"Very well." Sylvanis turned to Kat. "I leave you in charge of Mr. Brumfield here. Have him contact whomever he feels would be willing to join us and then cut him."

"Wait." Jessie held up a hand. "Cut me?"

Sylvanis raised an eyebrow. "You mean to tell me you are O.K. with dying, but a little tear in your skin has you running scared?"

"No. No." He shook his head. "I didn't say that . . . I just . . . you just . . . you didn't mention anything about cutting me."

Sylvanis smiled flatly, stood and crossed the room to him. When she got to him, she moved to step past him, but halted, placing a hand on his broad chest and stared up at him with a twinkle in her eyes. "That is the least of things I haven't told you about, Jessie."

She patted him on the chest and moved past him and out the door.

Hank concealed a grin and saw the others trying as well. Even Clint.

Kat slid from the dresser and moved up next to Jessie. "Come on big guy. I promise I won't hurt you too much."

Jessie shook his head, his mouth opening and closing. "That isn't what I was saying. I wasn't saying I was afraid of getting cut. It was just . . . you know. Unexpected."

Kat gave him a smug look. "Uh huh. Sure. Whatever you say."

"Seriously. It doesn't bother me."

"Oh, I believe you." Her tone made it clear she didn't, and she began to lead him out of the room.

"Oh, come on, man. I'm not afraid." Jessie pleaded for understanding once again as Kat took him out into the hall and closed the door.

Hank smiled ruefully and bid the others goodbye as he left the room. They were all flying out tonight to take Sim home. There was a small cemetery

390

not far from his property in Nova Scotia where he had buried Jennifer. It seemed only fitting to bury Sim next to his mother.

Entering his room, he tossed the keycard on the dresser and sat down on the edge of his bed.

He had thought to contact Sim's father and let him know Sim had died, but after the way the man had rejected Sim, Hank didn't feel like extending the courtesy. Sim would be laid to rest next to the woman who loved him more than anything by the man who loved him like he was his own son and the friends who had fought beside him.

What more could someone want?

*To still be alive, that's what!* Hank's hands tightened into fists as anger broiled through him. The worse part of it all was Hank had no idea who or what had killed Sim. No target for his rage.

If he ever found Sim's killer, there would be nothing or no one who could stop him from ripping them to shreds.

He closed his eyes tightly and unclenched his teeth. Deliberately, he relaxed his fists and let out a long sigh. He needed to right this. Somehow. And he would. But right now, they needed to take care of things. They had work to do, and he knew Sim would not forgive him if he shirked his duties to Sylvanis and the others.

He appreciated the understanding Sylvanis and the others were giving him. The world still turned and to spend time to fly home and bury Sim . . . well, it was almost more time than they could spare.

People were dying. Worse, people were being forced to become Weres. Once it happened in earnest, it would be a locomotive no one could stop. No one but them.

Hopefully.

With the attacks in Texas, there was a decent chance Kestrel had already increased her numbers by hundreds. When she turned her attention from specific targets and let her legions free. . .

Hank shook his head. It did no good thinking about what ifs and possibilities. With Jessie joining and bringing others with him . . . not merely others, but military men and women . . . people who knew how to fight and understood the risks.

They were much better suited than the rest of them. He huffed a laugh. The rest of them besides Kat. That girl was a fighter through and through. Down to her core. If one person survived this conflict, Hank would put his money on Kat.

Clint was a fighter too. But he had been through so much. Perhaps too much to be much use to them anymore. The loss of Sarah to the Boar. The loss of his control and what he did while lost in his animal instincts. The guilt. The fear. The anger. All warring inside Clint.

Hank hoped Clint would reconcile his feelings. They needed him. They needed all of them. And yet, tragedy haunted them. Sarah. Beth. Sim. All casualties in this war which, in reality, had not fully started yet.

With a sigh, Hank pulled off his clothes and climbed into bed. Tomorrow he would take Sim home. Take him home and say goodbye. Turning off the lights, he buried himself under the sheets, offering cool comfort against his warm flesh.

Sleep was a long time coming. When it did, images, like fleeting memories danced in Hank's dreams. Images of a beautiful woman and a young man standing in a forest, a log cabin behind them. They were holding hands, smiling. Sunlight dappled through the branches, and yet, it illuminated them fully.

Jennifer and Simon smiled at him. He watched, unable to step closer, though he desperately wanted to run to them. Embrace them one final time.

Together, they raised hands and waved to him, their smiles never faltering. They waved until the sunlight which had illuminated them so brightly before began to pass through them. Their bodies fading, the forest and the cabin could be seen beyond them.

Hank watched in utter sadness as they faded from view and he was left, standing alone in front of his home, with nothing but the trees to keep him company.

# Chapter Thirty-Five

Clint watched mutely as they laid the coffin which held Sim into the earth. Sadness was a palatable emotion riding the cool breeze of late morning. Kat stood next to him; her head bowed. She would occasionally sniff and wipe a tear from her eyes.

Hank stood at the head of the grave. He wore a suit, black over white. It looked odd on him. He was such a rustic looking man — to see him in such formal attire seemed unnatural.

Clint had not truly known Sim. They had briefly met several days ago at Sylvanis' home before Clint had lost control and left. By the time he had rejoined the group, Sim had been slain.

He knew Kat well enough to understand how heartbroken she had been when they had found Sim dead to believe he had been a decent person and someone he regretted not getting to know.

Sylvanis had been equally rocked by the death of Sim. She had cared for the boy. Or at least, it seemed as such. Clint believed Sylvanis cared for all of them, which made her different from Kestrel. Anyone who would surround themselves with monsters like the man who took Sarah, must be a monster themselves.

Kestrel viewed them all as weapons, and if one would break . . . oh well. Simply grab another. Sylvanis wasn't like that. They were not weapons to her. They were people, and she cared about them.

He glanced across at Sylvanis. She stood at the side of the grave, to the left of Hank. She wore a long black dress; her blonde hair fell past her shoulders in stark contrast. She made no attempt to hide her emotions. Tears fell from puffy eyes and her nose was tipped red. Clint could see her lips trembling which he knew was from more than the cold air.

She looked so much like a girl, barely into her teens. He knew she had been reborn in this body and her mind, far older than she looked, but given her manner, he wondered if the little girl her soul had taken over had some influence on her as well.

Three others had joined them this morning. Stephanie, her short tawny hair framed her pretty pixie-like face, stood stiff-backed and stone-faced. The funeral clearly much more than putting Sim to rest for her. Her eyes saw somewhere far to the south, where the body of her best friend now lay.

Next to her stood Jason. Stephanie was a short little thing and Jason, not much taller than she. He stood stooped; head bowed. Clint understood, though Jason and Sim had only interacted a little more than Clint had with Sim, the interaction had been bonding. Jason appeared like a man who had lost a friend. A good one.

His other friend, Mike, stood beside him, one hand resting on Jason's back making slow circular motions and occasionally offering a soft pat. Mike was one of them now. Stephanie had given him and her friend, Beth, lycanthropy. Beth hadn't made it, but Mike had.

They had all thought they had lost Stephanie and Jason. Clint wouldn't have blamed them. He often wondered, if it wasn't for Sarah, would he be here? Would he have joined Sylvanis' fight? He didn't know. He believed he would have, in the end, but he wasn't sure.

They were all together now. The four Trues and a couple of Pures. They would now take the war to Kestrel. Fight her and with a bit of luck, beat her and her Trues. In doing so, free Sarah.

Sim's coffin reached the bottom of the grave and Hank moved over to the pile of dirt and took the shovel from the caretaker. With a quick scoop, he hefted an enormous pile of dirt and tossed it down upon the coffin of his stepson.

Kat left his side and moved to take the shovel from Hank. She dug into the mound and sent her own shovel of dirt down into the hole. She stared down into the grave and sniffed once more before handing the shovel to Jason who had moved up beside her.

Jason poured his dirt into the hole and Clint heard him mutter, "Goodbye friend," before handing the shovel to Ben who had been standing next to Kat. Clint waited for Ben to toss his dirt before he, too, moved to take the shovel.

He felt uneasy about doing this, as if he held no right to offer up his contribution to the burial of Sim. They hadn't been friends. Hadn't really known each other. He did this because he felt he owed it to Sim. Like so many other things that had happened, this was one more thing Clint felt guilty for.

There was no way to know how the fight would have gone if he had been there from the beginning, instead of arriving near the end. There was no way to know if Sim would still be alive if Clint had not lost control of himself.

Yet, Clint still felt responsible. Still felt it had been his failure to master the beast within himself had led to Sim's death. The least he could do was offer up an apology. "I'm sorry, Sim." He tossed the dirt onto the lid of the coffin. "I'm sorry I failed you." The words had been almost inaudible. Would have been inaudible if he wasn't standing in a gathering of Weres.

Hank met his eyes from across the grave. He shook his head slightly indicating he did not hold Clint responsible for Sim's death. The eyes thoroughly catching his though, were Stephanie's. They held so much empathy and understanding.

He swallowed down his emotion and offered a sad smile to her. For the first time since she had arrived this morning, her face and posture were relaxed as if Clint now shared the burden she had been carrying alone since Beth's death. He could offer her that much.

Stephanie and Mike didn't take the shovel, each for their own reasons, Clint was sure. Sylvanis not taking the shovel surprised him though and he watched her intently.

She stood still; eyes closed as if she were the only one at the cemetery. With no one else coming forward to take the shovel, Clint handed it to the caretaker, who motioned for two others to take up the remaining shovels.

They made quick work, their arms and shoulders bunching and flexing as they quickly filled the grave. When at last they finished with it, they took their leave and left the eight of them standing there surrounding the grave.

Sylvanis stepped forward. At some point, she had stepped out of her heels and now walked barefoot. She stepped upon the fresh dirt of the grave. Clint frowned slightly and saw similar expressions from the others, who now fidgeted uncomfortably.

Most people feel uneasy around graves, especially fresh ones. One certainly doesn't walk upon a grave. It wasn't done. Kat seemed ready to say something, but Hank had caught her on the verge of the decision and motioned for her to hold.

They all watched in awkward silence as Sylvanis squirmed her feet in the fresh dirt till they were almost completely buried. She began to sing.

The song was unlike anything Clint had ever heard before. A song of a strange language, lilting and clear, like chimes on the wind. The cadence, so melodic, Clint felt his mind so utterly transfixed he became unaware of everything else but the song.

The song was both sad and joyful, like a dance where each emotion took turns being the lead. More, Clint felt a calling on his soul. A call to come. A call to share in this.

The song flowed through the morning breeze, which carried it up and down and through every living thing present. It flowed through those gathered here. It flowed through the trees, the flowers and the grass. It flowed through the squirrels, the birds and the butterflies.

Clint could sense, more than see, those gathering around them. He could hear the beating of wings, the strong flaps from birds and the whispered beats of butterflies, the chattering of squirrels and the chirps of chipmunks.

He was lost and yet, he was found. For the first time in a long while he felt connected to the others. His only connection for so long had been Sarah, but she had been lost. Now he felt a connection to all those here. An understanding. A part of something wonderful. Beautiful.

Tears flowed down his cheeks and he did nothing to stop them. He wanted their salted water to fall to the earth. To return to the world that had born them and from everything which had come before him.

Like an echo through the mountains, the song held onto a lone note for what seemed like an eternity before it faded into nothingness. Clint knew the song had ended, and yet, it still carried in his being. The song would never leave his heart. Nor his mind.

When his eyes, at long last, focused on his surroundings, he caught sight of Sylvanis, still standing upon Sim's grave. Clint's eyes widened at the sight. For now, instead of freshly dug dirt, there was a blanket of beautiful wildflowers. Red, purple, yellow and white. Glorious petals swathed in colors of the brightest hues.

Clint heard the other's gasp. A sob broke and Clint looked past Sylvanis at Hank, who had dropped to his knees before his stepson's grave, tears falling like heavy rain from his eyes.

Sylvanis moved forward and laid a hand on Hank's broad shoulder.

"These flowers will never die. They will never fade. If they are cut, they will bloom again. They will live on, much as Sim does in our hearts."

She turned to Stephanie.

"Did you feel it?"

Clint turned toward Stephanie as well, who stood wide-eyed, her mouth agape. She nodded.

"I'm sorry. Perhaps I should have asked first, but I used your connection to Beth to locate her final resting place. You will find similar flowers now rest upon her grave."

The wonder in Stephanie's eyes was mirrored in those around the gathering. They had seen power from Sylvanis. Power she had used to fight against Kestrel, but in Clint's eyes, this power far exceeded what she had displayed in Chicago.

She had won them all over again to her cause. She had solidified their desire to help her fight Kestrel, despite their personal losses and pain. Any resentment Stephanie might have felt for Sylvanis had fled with that gesture.

Clint believed Hank had already chosen to fight in this war, but if he hadn't been fighting this war for Sylvanis before, he did so now. And now, so was Clint. For better or for worse, this was his family now. He would fight with them and he would fight for them.

The group moved to their rented vehicles to return to the hotel and Clint sidled up next to Sylvanis as they walked.

"That was something. What you did back there. Really something." He gestured back toward the gravesite.

She glanced at him sidelong and offered up a small smile.

"It was the least I could do. Given their sacrifice. I just wish it had never been necessary."

Clint nodded his understanding. Regret was the one thing they all seemed to share.

"Will they truly never die?"

He caught her slight frown.

"Never? I truly don't know, to be honest. I do know they will be there long after we are all gone."

She shivered slightly, from the cold, or from the thought, Clint wasn't sure.

"I would imagine, that with my passing, the magic may fade. Eventually."

They walked in silence for a moment.

"How are you feeling, Clint?"

She cared. That was the one thing about her Clint liked. When she asked, 'How are you feeling?' it wasn't out of common courtesy. It was because she truly cared to know.

He sighed and scanned about as they all made their way to the cars.

"Better. There was something . . . I don't know how to explain it . . . something about your song. Something . . ."

"Healing?"

Clint turned his head to look at her.

"Yes. Healing. That's it. Was that your intent?"

She regarded him.

"Intent? Not really. It is just the nature of the song's magic. A by-product, if you will."

Clint grunted. "But you knew it would have an effect."

She nodded. "Not really on you, though. I knew Hank and Stephanie needed a measure of healing, which I believed the song would provide." She offered up a little smile. "You were just an added bonus."

He smiled back at her. "I'm not sure how I feel about having someone use magic to heal my emotions."

"Why, Clint? Did you really feel like you needed more time wallowing in self-hate?"

His face reddened at the rebuke. But she wasn't wrong. He did feel like he should be penitent for longer. Her tone made him feel he was being silly though.

"No. No. I guess you are right. I can't help feeling responsible for much of this. Sarah and even Sim's death."

Sylvanis snorted. Which seemed so difficult to reconcile with her primness.

"How do you think I feel, Clint?"

He stared at her confusedly.

She sighed audibly and pulled up short as the other continued the rest of the way to the cars. Clint stopped with her.

She waited for the rest to get out of earshot, which pretty much meant they were almost to the cars. Clint waited patiently for her to explain.

"All of this." She pointed to Clint and motioned toward the cars and back up toward the grave. "All of it, is my doing, Clint. Through my magic, I turned you all into Were-creatures. I brought you all into this conflict and in so doing, Kestrel sent the Boar to kill you, but he instead turned Sarah into a Pure. Our battle in Chicago with Kestrel and the others which led to Sim's death, all because my magic brought us together."

She gazed off toward the cars and the rest of the group. "My parents lost their only daughter when I 'confiscated' this body." The word was spoken with much disgust. "They almost lost their lives when Kestrel came for me." She turned her attention back to him. "So, you see. You are not to blame for any of this, because you would not be involved if my magic had not made it so.

401

"I am to blame for all of this. Because of a decision I had made in haste, and perhaps . . ." She paused. "Perhaps in error."

Clint reached out and touched Sylvanis arm, shaking his head. "You didn't have a choice, Sylvanis. Kestrel left you with no other options. I shudder to think about what would have happened if you were not here, and we were not given these powers to be able to stop Kestrel and her Trues."

He gripped arm a little tighter, intensity burning in his voice. "The only way Kestrel will be stopped is with your powers and knowledge, and our abilities. None of which would have existed without you making that initial sacrifice you had."

Sylvanis' bright green eyes darted back and forth as she searched his face. When she nodded, he let his hand drop.

"Don't ever doubt your reason or the necessity of what you did. It was the right thing."

She straightened at his words and raised her chin slightly.

"Thank you, Clint. You see. Even I have moments of self-doubt. So, the next time you are feeling them, come see me so I can return the pep talk."

He cocked a smile at her. "Done. Now let's join the others. We need to be finished here and back in the States as soon as possible. We don't know what Kestrel has been up to."

She gave him a quick nod and they hurried down the hill to join the others and return to the hotel.

Jessie was not happy to have been left on his own in Chicago. It wasn't that he was upset the others hadn't invited him along. He understood it had been something personal and private. It was he who had taken a huge leap of faith they would return.

It had been a matter of luck which had seen him at the battle in Chicago. It was true he had been there to try and find Kat and or Clint; he hadn't expected to find them. Their initial battle with the Boar had been a while ago, and no one had seen them since.

He had returned again and again to the site of the initial battle both during the day and during the night, and yet, nothing. When something had happened, it hadn't been what he had expected. The fight between Kat and Clint had been vicious and bloody.

When it finished, he had followed Kat to her hotel and waited for an opportunity to speak with her. When she had left the hotel with several others, Jessie had known something was about to happen. Something big.

The battle he had witnessed paled everything he had ever seen before, which said something after his tour in Iraq and Afghanistan. He had seen his share of death and destruction and fierce fighting, but nothing like this.

He had watched the entire thing unfold and had been horrified and amazed. The level of ferocity these creatures exhibited staggered Jessie. The sheer . . . brutality, especially among the other group, left Jessie speechless. It had become crystal clear what actions needed to be taken. Which was what he reported to his superior.

꒜

He had taken up at the same hotel as the group with Kat and the others. A generous distribution of cash had the staff as his watchmen, letting him know immediately when any of them were about to leave.

His room resembled most hotel rooms he had spent a great deal of the last five years in since leaving the service. It always amazed him hotels in Budapest appeared about the same in Boise.

The second he returned to his room, after following the group back here, he accessed his decrypted SAT phone. He knew it was late, but the decision needed to be made, and while he trusted his plan of action would be acceptable, he needed to get the O.K. from the big man.

The phone barely rang twice before it was answered.

"Director Simpson?"

"Go ahead, Brumfield. Report."

Jessie paused, took a deep breath. "The threat is very real, sir. There are . . . other variations, besides what you were aware of." He paused.

"Go on."

Jessie searched for the words. "There also appears to be . . . errr . . . witches?"

"I'm sorry, Brumfield, I don't believe I heard you right."

"Sir, I don't know how else to explain what I saw. There were two women who fought using . . . I guess you would say, elements. Fire, ice, wind, water . . . As far as I could tell, they were." He shrugged, knowing the director couldn't see it through the phone. "They were casting spells. Saying magic words. I don't know what else I could possibly call it, sir."

Silence on the other end.

It dragged on.

"Sir?"

"I guess it isn't weirder than anything else we have seen."

"No, sir."

"Continue."

"There are clearly two sides. As we saw with the previous fight here in Chicago, the Wolf and the Tiger are on one side and the Boar, on the other." He decided not to mention the fight between the Tiger and the Wolf, since what he had seen later showed some sort of reconciliation.

"However, they are not alone. Fighting alongside the Wolf and the Tiger were two Bears. Alongside the Boar, two other Boars as well as a Crocodile and a Rat."

"So, she resurfaced," the director muttered, almost inaudibly.

"Sir?"

The director ignored his question. "You say only one Rat?"

"Yes, sir."

A pause. "Go on."

The director was keeping something from him. Not that this was anything new. He was on a need to know basis, and as usual, there was more in the category of him not needing to know. At least, he hoped it was something he didn't need to know and not something which would later bite him in the ass.

"As to your theory that the Wolf and the Tiger were non-hostiles, it would seem to be correct. Their group worked with local police on the scene and even at one point, the witch attended to the wounded, using her . . . er . . . magic, to heal them."

"And did it?"

"I'm sorry, what?"

"Did her magic heal them?"

Jessie recalled the images of the men and women of the police as the boiling hot steam washed over them. The screams had given him flashbacks to Sayedebad. Watching humans being boiled is never a pretty thing. The quick transition from reddened skin to pus-filled blisters to skin sloughing off. Jessie shuddered.

"Brumfield? Did the magic heal them?"

"Yes, sir. It did indeed heal them."

"Remarkable."

"I agree, sir. She healed the damage caused by the spells thrown at them by the other witch. Their power is just as destructive as beneficial."

A pause. "Understood. Please continue."

Jessie related the rest of the battle with only a few interruptions. It was only when he related the last part the director became animated.

"What do you mean killed?"

"Exactly what I said, sir. One of the Bears, the younger of the two. Perhaps the other's son? I'm not sure. I didn't see what happened, but they were pitted off against several of the Boars. The Wolf, who had been absent during the beginning of the battle had arrived and began fighting with the larger Boar."

Jessie struggled to recall what he could of where the younger Bear had been and what he had been doing.

"The younger Bear had been thrown aside; it didn't appear to have been a killing blow, as far as I could tell. The next thing I know. The older Bear ran to where the younger Bear had fallen, and when I looked, he wasn't a Bear anymore, but a young man, maybe seventeen? Eighteen? I couldn't tell from where I was."

"So, you didn't see how it . . . he, died?"

"Sorry sir, I did not."

The director was silent for a long time.

"Thank you for your report, Brumfield."

"Sir?"

"Was there something else?"

Jessie hesitated. Here, on the ground, within spitting distance of the group who, he believed, would help battle the ones who appeared to be 'the bad guys' a leap of faith needed to be taken.

"Well . . . If I may make a proposal, sir?"

The director didn't answer him right away and Jessie decided he may be overstepping his place.

"What is your proposal?"

There it was. Permission. Now if he could frame this in a way which didn't make him sound crazy.

"I think I should join them."

"Excuse me?"

Jessie rushed ahead. "Sir. I am in a unique position to contact those who appear to be, if not on our side, at least against the side we are against. My proposal would be for me to contact them and integrate myself into their group. To become one of them."

"I don't think you understand what you are proposing, Brumfield."

"I do sir. I understand the risks. But . . . think of the benefits? I will be your man on the inside. I will be able to determine what their goals are. Whether they truly are on our side."

He paused a moment to let the director digest what he had said before laying the next part on him.

"Even better, if they are what we think they are, they will be able to make me into one of them. Then I will be able to make others into the same thing. Think of the military applications, sir. We will have a nearly indestructible and devastating fighting force."

Jessie had been to war. So had the director. They both understood what this could mean. The lives saved. The wars won.

"It is an interesting proposal."

"Sir, just say the word and I will make the approach." He dreaded asking this next part, but it was crucial to his success, not only his, but if he read the situation right, crucial to all their successes. "Sir, I will need a list of possible recruits."

"Recruits?" The word dragged itself unhurriedly out of the director's mouth as if hesitant to get an answer to the question.

"Yes, sir. I believe they will be looking for people to join them. They have set themselves against this other party and if I understand the lay of things, the other side will be recruiting heavily — through any means necessary."

He let the last part sink in for a moment.

"It would be to our benefit if we offered a means for them to combat the other group's numbers as part of why they should accept me as one of them. Also, if the threat is as bad as I believe it is, *we* will need the numbers as well."

Silence hang between them. Which didn't surprise Jessie. He had given a lot for the man to chew on.

"You will have your answer in the morning, Brumfield," the director said decisively.

"Thank you, sir."

The director had given him the okay and a list of names of retired and semi-retired military personnel his staff had compiled for him to approach about joining the group. After meeting with Kat and the others he had begun reaching out to those names on the list.

The director had given him clearance to 'read' them into the situation, along with security video of everything they had collected so far regarding these, 'Were-creatures'.

Jessie excelled at selling. He knew how to sell a mission, and he sold this mission like his life depended on it. Which it most likely did. Throwing out phrases like national security, doing your duty for God and country, a sworn oath to protect from both foreign and domestic. It didn't take him long to convince the majority of those on the list to join in the fight.

When the group returned from burying Hank's boy, he had over thirty recruits who would be joining them within a day.

"That is excellent news, Jessie," the girl Sylvanis told him. Jessie had difficulty thinking of this slim woman as anything more than just a girl, though he had seen her wield powerful magic.

"The moment they arrive, we will need to have them choose whom they would like to give them lycanthropy."

She glanced at one of the newcomers, a small chestnut-haired cutie name Stephanie.

"I understand if you do not want to participate in this, Stephanie."

Stephanie made a face, "I'm sorry. I can't."

Sylvanis nodded as if expecting the answer and turned to the two men who were also new arrivals. "Jason? Mike?"

The one called Jason glanced at Stephanie before answering. "I will do it."

The other one, Mike, nodded as well.

Sylvanis proffered them a smile. "Very well." She returned her gaze back to him. "Jessie. I will leave you in charge of your recruits and their choices but allow me to explain a few things that you will need to convey to them before they make their decision." She paused.

Jessie nodded for her to continue.

"First and foremost, reiterate the risk involved in the process. Do not downplay the very real chance that they could die. We have already had one loss due to this." She frowned and glanced momentarily at Stephanie who stared at her feet. It wasn't hard for Jessie to detect the quiet sniff as she stifled a cry.

"Second," Sylvanis continued, "affinity for their totem animal will greatly increase their survival rate."

"Their totem animal," Sylvanis searched for a word. "I believe some call it, their spirit animal. It is essentially the animal that one feels represents their personality more."

"Right. Okay." The dismissiveness was evident in his voice.

Sylvanis clicked her tongue at him. "Jessie. Whether you believe in it or not is inconsequential. You must relay this to your recruits if you wish more of them to survive."

She stared at him and he stared back.

Sylvanis cocked her head at him and frowned.

"Explain it like this. Tell them the animals they must choose from. The first animal they hear which interests them should be close enough. Their subconscious will have made the choice for them."

Once again, she glanced toward Stephanie, Jason and Mike.

She began to tell him something but changed her mind with a slight shake of her head. Instead, she turned to face all of them.

"We must do this as quickly as possible. Events are moving forward quickly. Whatever Kestrel is up to, it appears to be happening in Texas. The attacks on the refineries and the logging company set a clear line to Houston."

She turned as she spoke, taking everyone in turn. "That she is recruiting is obvious. According to the news, the attacks left hundreds wounded." She paused. "Hundreds," she reiterated. "Even at a fifty percent survival rate, we will be greatly outnumbered, though I suspect we will be looking at closer to a seventy-five percent or more survival rate."

"Shit," the man named Clint muttered, and frankly Jessie agreed. *Shit is right.* Here he thought bringing in thirty men a great achievement. It wouldn't matter.

Sylvanis looked at Clint and at the others. But not Jessie. "Yes, the numbers are not in our favor, but in the end, it really isn't about the numbers. You know this."

The group made slow nods to her. Jessie had been left out of something important here, he realized. But he was a soldier, and what the fuck else was new.

Hank shifted his bulk slightly and Sylvanis turned to him with an arched eyebrow.

"She won't wait long. Her man, Samuel, the one who has been around . . . since . . . before. He will have instructed her on what will be coming her way as soon as she is acknowledged as a legitimate threat. And after the other night and what happened in Texas, I can't imagine it will be much longer."

Sylvanis gave a nod.

"I agree. The government will make a move soon."

411

They had. Jessie already knew. They had and it had been a colossal fuck up. Despite everything he had told them, they had still gone in like they were going to fight normal bad guys. They had all been slaughtered.

"When they do, they will get a taste of what is to come. Between that time and when they decide to truly take things seriously, that is when Kestrel will strike. Change the focus from her and it will instead move to containment."

Jessie stared hard at this young girl. Her understanding of tactics and how the government worked, surprised him. There was something eerie about this Sylvanis which frightened Jessie.

"That will be our moment to strike at her and we need to be ready."

Kat spoke up. "I think I speak for everyone here when I say we are more than ready." Everyone either muttered their agreement or nodded.

Jessie studied her. She had so effectively overpowered him, though he topped her by a head and at least a hundred pounds. It had been at that moment he had fallen for her. There were strong female marines, but they couldn't hold a candle to Kat.

The nature of her strength, which came from her lycanthropy, allowed her to be unnaturally strong, but not have the bulk of muscles she would otherwise need. Which left her body trim, muscular yes, but more, defined, than large.

In other words, she had great strength, but still had a smoking hot feminine body, and it turned Jessie on immensely. Coupled with the fact she acted like she couldn't give two shits about him was like dangling a carrot in front of a rabbit.

She caught his eyes roving over her and hers narrowed. He smiled. His smiles always worked. She rolled her eyes and turned away. *Well. They usually worked anyway.*

"That is all for now," Sylvanis said after a moment. "Stay close, lie low and keep your eyes and ears open."

She stared out the window of the hotel room. "Something is coming." She turned back to them. "We need to be ready."

# *Chapter Thirty-Six*

Gordon and Blain climbed the stairs of the hospital looking for Kestrel. The last of the force which had attacked them had been eliminated, except for the mysterious Were who had fought and killed Samuel and fought Blain before fleeing.

*Samuel was dead.* It shocked Gordon. He hadn't cared much for the man, but he had been formidable. *Bloody oath, the man had been over two thousand years old!*

They reached the top of the stairs and Sarah, Blain's little plaything, the one who wanted to carve him up into little pieces if she had the chance, came out of the room in which Kestrel had taken up residence.

Blain stalked toward her and she froze upon seeing him.

"Where's Kestrel?" he demanded.

She glared at him. But she constantly glared at him.

"She is unavailable," she told him satisfactorily.

He growled at her.

To Gordon's surprise, she growled back.

"Get out of my way, woman."

Sarah held her ground, but Blain must have asserted his will upon her for she stepped aside.

"You can't go in there, Blain."

"The fuck I can't."

Gordon kept hot on his heels.

They didn't make it to the door before it opened, and Kestrel stepped out, absently unwrapping a bandage she had wrapped around her forearm.

He and Blain came to an abrupt halt.

Kestrel looked at them hard. She looked . . . haggard, her sweat-soaked hair clung to her forehead and face as if she had run ten miles. Kestrel's eyes went from Blain, to him and back again.

Tossing the bandage to the ground, she straightened, and she wiped the hair from her forehead.

"What has happened?"

Blain growled. "What's happened? I'll tell you what's happened. Your man is dead! Dead! And, we were attacked by an unfamiliar Were, who unfortunately, got away."

Kestrel seemed confused. "Dead? Who's dead?"

Gordon stepped forward bowing his head slightly in deference. Something Blain never did.

"Samuel, My Lady, killed by the Were that Blain just mentioned."

For the first time, Gordon saw Kestrel unnerved. She staggered slightly and reached out to steady herself with the wall.

"Impossible."

Blain sneered at her. "Well seeing how his lifeless body is lying in its own piss and shit downstairs . . ."

Kestrel had heard enough. With a shout and a gesture, wind stronger than any spawned from a tornado or a hurricane, slammed into Blain, lifting him up and throwing him down the hallway. With another word of power, flames roared to life within the gale, incinerating Blain's body.

His screams shifted to roars as he changed to his Boar form, his body healing as it burned. As the fires snuffed out and the wind died, Blain rose from the ground; pink skin burned by the fire, peeked through his bristling boar hair.

On unsteady legs, Blain began to stalk his way back toward her. Gordon looked to her and she regarded him. He knew what he had to do.

Shifting, he moved in front of Kestrel, blocking Blain's path.

"Get out of my way, Motherfucker!"

"Blain! Leave it! No one will win from this. We need to stay focused."

Blain didn't appear to be hearing him as he moved closer, glaring at Kestrel behind Gordon.

"Come on, Blain. This is stupid. You were being an insensitive wanker."

He kept coming and Gordon readied himself for the fight.

Blain pulled up short and took his eyes off Kestrel to look at him.

He snorted. "I was, wasn't I?"

"A bit."

Blain shifted back to a human and turned back toward Kestrel.

"My apologies, My Lady. And, my condolences."

His apology caught Kestrel off guard. It sure as hell caught Gordon off guard. He certainly wasn't expecting an apology for shitty behavior from Blain of all people.

Kestrel didn't immediately respond. After a moment she responded, "Apology accepted."

Gordon felt Kestrel's hand lay to rest upon his back, and he shifted back to his human form.

Sarah, who had been almost completely forgotten, stood open-mouthed and wide-eyed to the side. Whether from the battle which had almost taken place here in the hallway, or the sudden apology from Blain, Gordon couldn't be certain.

"You may go, Sarah. Please see to the others, the time of rejection for many will be soon."

Sarah glanced at Blain, who nodded that she was still under the command to do what Kestrel asked of her. With one last glance at Kestrel, Sarah departed.

Kestrel watched Sarah go, before turning her attention back to the two of them.

"Follow me." She turned and made her way back to her room.

The moment they entered the room she wheeled on them.

"Tell me everything. Now."

Fury burned so brightly in her eyes, Gordon faltered a step, but Blain had no such fear.

"As you had predicted, we were attacked. The battle went pretty much how we believed it would. They were unprepared for what they were facing and Gordon, Taylor, Samuel and I had no difficulty dispatching them."

Gordon could see the muscles in Kestrel's jaw clench and release in impatience. Blain knew what she wanted to know but took his time getting there. The bastard always liked to bait her.

"And?"

Blain offered a slight smile, reveling in his efforts to piss her off succeeding. "Oh, yeah. Then when we had the battle well enough in hand, I went to join with the others to clean up the rest. When I went to find Samuel, I found he had been killed by some sort of cat Were I have never seen before."

"It wasn't the Tiger?"

Blain gave her a look which clearly read, 'If it had been the Tiger, I wouldn't have called it a Were I hadn't seen before,' but didn't respond.

Kestrel's eyes narrowed on him, but she turned to Gordon.

"What did you see?"

Gordon hadn't seen anything. "I was busy fighting the last of the men. The Were fled before I could see it."

"Samuel is dead?"

417

"Yes, My Lady." Gordon rushed out before Blain could rile her up again with some pissy comment.

"Take me to him."

They led her back down the stairs and into the hallway where Samuel lay. Neither one of them had moved him. They passed Taylor on the way, parked in the lobby and keeping an eye out for any further attacks.

Samuel lay prone upon the floor. His face was frozen in death and held a look of sadness, an expression which seemed foreign to the man. Kestrel squatted beside him. With one hand she reached out and brushed his cheek, closed his eyes. She stood.

"Gordon? Please turn him over."

He moved over Samuel's body and reached down. With a slight shift of weight, he rolled the man over. A sick squelching noise assailed their ears as his body pulled free from the drying blood pooled beneath him.

With his body turned over, the wound which had sliced into his chest and from the look of it, cut through his heart, became visible. Gordon, no expert, believed the wound looked like a stab wound from a blade of some sort, not from a claw.

"He was stabbed," Kestrel said to no one in particular.

Again, she squatted down beside him and rested her palms on his chest. Gordon watched as she closed her eyes. Her breathing came in long, deep breaths. She stayed like that for some time.

Blain fidgeted with impatience and Gordon hoped whatever she was doing would conclude soon, otherwise Blain would likely say something offensive.

At last, Kestrel's eyes opened, and she took a shuddering breath.

"I've never come across anything like the weapon used to kill Samuel. But it is a weapon of great power."

She stood looking again at Blain.

"This Were, did he hold any type of blade?"

Blain shook his head. "Not that I saw. I arrived after he had killed Samuel. So, perhaps he had discarded it or secreted it away before I got there."

Kestrel frowned but said nothing. Gordon didn't think Blain's explanation made sense either. If the Were had a weapon which could kill other Weres, he would have used it against Blain, not hid it.

"This changes nothing," Kestrel said flatly. Gordon knew her better. Kestrel held no one as closely to her as Samuel had been. Whether through mutual like or shared experience, Gordon didn't know. But Kestrel reeled from this loss, though she hid it well.

*This changes everything*, Gordon thought, but he didn't voice it.

"Over three quarters of those from E.A.R.t.H have come through the rejection process already and we have only lost three. We will find out if the rest survive by the end of today or early tomorrow."

She looked at the them.

"Call the others."

Elias sat with a dozen others from the office, though they weren't in the office anymore. They hadn't been for several days now. After the horrific attack on Yulchik refinery by that . . . that . . . monster, they had initially been raced to the hospital. Though many of them had suffered only minor wounds, they had all suffered *some* wound.

That had been the deal. Let him wound you and they wouldn't tear you to pieces. Elias had seen him rip to shreds several people, so given the option, Elias had taken the wounding.

A good deal of them had only minor scrapes and after their initial treatment, most of them thought they were going home.

They couldn't have been more wrong.

Within several hours of arriving at the hospital, the place went into lock down. No one else in and no one else out. The ones who had tried to leave had been wrestled to the ground, handcuffed and locked in a room with an armed guard.

By the end of the day, they had all been loaded up into buses and moved to a huge warehouse, divided by long chain-link fences. Between the confusion, fear and recent trauma, most of them allowed themselves to be herded into what amounted to cages.

Elias saw several people with DHS jackets coming and going throughout the night. They had confiscated everyone's phones and tablets so there would be no communication with the outside world. As far as Elias could tell, they were prisoners at an undisclosed location, and no one knew they were there.

What this portended did not sit well with Elias.

The cages were equipped with cots and blankets and some had laid down either to fall asleep or lie in a fetal position and cry. Elias wasn't ready to do either. Something was happening here, and no one would explain what it was.

By mid-afternoon the next day, a dozen or so people had collapsed and had to be rushed out with a team of medics. There was no explanation, though the medics were peppered with questions. They had already given up asking the guards anything.

Those who had been rushed out began to trickle back in. More and more people were stricken down. Elias learned from one of the captives who had come back that they had suffered from some sort of myocardial infarction.

Every. Last. One of them.

Elias knew, before long, he'd suffer the same.

When the next group of buses arrived things went from bad, to worse. Scores of newcomers were pushed in among them. They were only given blankets as there were not enough beds to go around.

The newcomers were victims of a second attack. They had worked at a refinery as well. The details of the attack were eerily like what Elias and the others had suffered. Elias did his best to gather as much information as he could, though what he would do with it, he didn't know.

For some reason, others turned to him for guidance and he tried to keep everyone in high spirits, but he felt himself falling into despair.

"What are going to do, Elias?"

Reva sat next to him on his cot, barely concealing the panic in her voice. Across from him, Susan sat, and next to her, Sam. He had tried to keep the team together, but Matt had collapsed earlier and hadn't returned. Cynthia had collapsed yesterday and hadn't returned either. Elias didn't want to consider what it meant.

Elias scratched at the bandage on his arm from where the beast . . . man had scratched him. The others had similar cuts on their arms.

It was Susan who answered. "What are we supposed to do, Reva? We are here, surrounded by armed guards with no way to get out or communicate with the outside. All we can do is wait. This is still America; at some point they will have to release us. Family members will be demanding our return and they can't hold us against our will forever."

Elias didn't know about that. There were all sorts of scenarios Elias could imagine the government could come up with to justify keeping them here. Hell, they could deny they had us and stonewall whomever was trying to find them long enough . . . *long enough for what though?* What were they keeping them here for? Why were they systematically having heart attacks?

He realized Reva was crying, and he put his arm around her shoulder, rubbing her back softly.

"It will be okay, Reva. It will," he told her, not believing a word of it himself.

At that moment his heart stopped.

# *Chapter Thirty-Seven*

When he awoke, they had moved him into a white sterile room. He lay upon a gurney, wired to a heart monitor. The steady beep beep beep of his heart was the first noise he heard.

Sitting up, the hospital gown rubbed his skin irritatingly and he rubbed it against his bare skin to ease the itchiness. The fluorescent lights seemed extra bright in this room and he rubbed his eyes to lessen the glare.

He remembered little from what had happened. One minute he had been comforting Reva, the next, pain shot through his chest and he fell. Shouts, strangely distant, had been calling his name. Shouting for help. Then all had gone black.

The door on the other side of the room opened and a woman entered. A hefty looking brunette, she had her hair tied back in a tight ponytail. She wore a white smock over a blue blouse and khaki pants, and she carried a clipboard. A stethoscope hung tightly around her wide neck.

She offered him a smile as she entered. He wasn't in the mood to return it.

"Hello," she glanced down at the clipboard, "Mr. Tepper. I'm Dr. Hensley."

"Why am I here?"

She gave him a look of mild amusement.

"Because you had a heart attack." They both knew it didn't answer the real question he had been asking. "Now, I'm going to run some tests to see how you are doing, O.K.?"

He snorted. Like she was going to allow him to say no. He decided to push it anyway.

"And if I refuse?"

She smiled condescendingly and motioned with her hand. Two armed guards entered the room and took up position beside his gurney. Not surprising.

"Will you be cooperating today, Mr. Tepper?"

"Why am I here? Why are any of us here?" Anger overcame his reason. "You can't keep us here like this!" He swung his legs off the gurney and landed on his bare feet. The floor held no heat but felt like fire against the soles.

The two guards moved instantly, each locking their arms around his elbows, grabbing him tightly.

"Mr. Tepper," the doctor began curtly, "we can do this the hard way, or the easy way."

Elias had never been so angry in all his life. Heat rose within him making his face flush and his breath coming raggedly. He wasn't this guy. Never had been, this guy. He did not get angry at people. He was always the mild-mannered one. The one who diffused situations, not escalated them.

The guards had firm grips on his arms and for a moment, he ceased resisting. His muscles eased, but when he glanced at Dr. Hensley who wore a smug expression his anger came roaring back.

With a twist of his body, he tore one of his arms out of a guard's grip and used it to push the other guard away from him. To his amazement, the man sailed backward, stumbling over the gurney before falling to the ground.

Elias stared in wonder down at the man who stared back at him in utter shock. The other guard recovered quickly and wrapped his arm around Elias' neck in a choke hold.

The hold squeezed his neck and constricted his windpipe, his breath wheezed as he sucked in life giving air. In a desperate move, Elias pitched forward, tipping his shoulder downward. Lifting the guard from his feet, he tossed him over and the guard landed with a dull thud upon the ground.

For the second time in minutes, surprise struck him. He wasn't this strong. Couldn't be this strong.

*What the hell?*

The doctor screamed for more help, her voice sounding like an angry chicken, as she backed away from him. Armed guards flooded the room, quickly surrounding him. With both hands held out he warded them away. Strength and awareness coursed through his body. He could feel the blood flowing through his veins and arteries. He could feel the power of his body in a way he had never felt before.

When they came for him, they weren't messing around. Several guards physically restrained him, others had their pistols out and began striking him about the head and arms with the butts of their guns. He fought as best as he could, but in the end, he went down under a flurry of blows and the combined weight of four guards.

Consciousness returned gradually but return it did. Memory followed shortly after and he began to groan, only to realize, he felt no pain. Hesitantly, he opened his eyes and found himself lying flat upon the gurney again. This time, however, they had strapped him tightly to the bed. Leather straps dug into his wrists and ankles, while larger straps ran across his chest, his pelvis and his calves.

He strained against his restraints and they creaked with his efforts but did not relent. With a little more strength, he knew he could get free, but whatever had been the cause of his amazing strength from earlier had fled.

So, he lay there. Hours passed, or perhaps only minutes; it was hard to say as there were no indicators as to the passage of time in this room. It was the same sterile room he had been held in before.

His stomach began growling as the door opened and Dr. Hensley entered.

He growled at her, before catching himself. *What the fuck? Did I just growl?* He had. She faltered a step as she came in but straightened and continued toward him.

He got a decent look at her. Blue and purple stained her eye socket and her lower lip was split and swollen. Apparently, someone else took issue with being kept here and managed to get to her before the guards had gotten to them. Elias smiled.

She narrowed her eyes at him. "You're not so tough now your all strapped in, are you?"

He glared at her and fought his restraints again. They held tight.

"Why am I still here?" The words were forced out through clenched teeth and held all the vehemence he could muster.

She sniffed as she went about making sure all the straps were still tight. "We couldn't let you back into the general populace. Not with what you have realized."

*What had I realized?* Elias racked his brain, trying to figure out what she could be referring to. She began to examine him, touching his face and examining his head. "Remarkable," she muttered.

What had happened when he had been subdued came back to him; she was examining the areas of his head where they had hit him with their guns. The areas which didn't even hurt.

As nonchalantly as he could, he glanced down at his arms. The blows had hit him all over, but mainly about the head and the arms. And yet, he bore no bruises anywhere he could see.

Like sun gradually climbing above the horizon, it dawned on him. The increased strength. The healing. They were all the result of what that monster had done to him. Only, it hadn't manifested itself until after he had his heart attack.

He gasped, and the doctor looked at him sharply, trying to read him, but he made his face go blank. *If all these things happened to me after my heart attack . . . everyone else who has survived the heart attack must be the same!*

No wonder they didn't want him to return to the group. There had been dozens of men and women who had heart attacks and had been returned to the group. If they all decided to fight, there would be little the guards could do about it.

Oh, they might open fire and kill some of them, but the numbers would not be in their favor. And given the amount of hits he had taken from those guys the other day, a gunshot wound or two wouldn't slow any of them.

After a series of pokes and prods, and a battery of other tests, the doctor took a blood sample and left. No one else visited him. As time passed, lone guards would bring him meals, help feed him and leave. They never responded to any of is questions or demands to be released.

Elias had no idea how long he remained strapped to the table. Days maybe? At least two. For a while he yelled and screamed for help and all he got for his effort was a sore throat.

All he had was time, time to think. Clearly, they were afraid of him. For whatever reason, he was a danger. Yes, he had fought off a couple of guards, but did that make him a risk?

Keeping him from the others, he understood. If he hadn't fought those guards, would he have been aware of his extra strength? Yes, he felt amazing, and more alive than he ever had, but he might have chalked it up to surviving a heart attack.

But no. Something happened to his body, continued to be happening. He couldn't comprehend what it could be. He remembered the way the Boar had bashed in the door. *Such strength!* What had the Boar said? 'I can make you into someone like me. You will have power! You will have strength! No one will be able to hurt you. You will be unstoppable!'

By cutting his arm, he had made Elias like him somehow. Which meant . . . he could turn into one of those monsters! *But how?*

Elias didn't know. Didn't have a single clue how to make himself into one of those monsters. He blew out a breath in frustration.

The door opened, and a guard came in carrying a plate. The aroma of eggs and sausage reached Elias the moment the door had opened, and his stomach rumbled in greeting.

Pulling up a chair, the guard sat next to him. Elias didn't recognize this guard. A formidable looking man, like most of the guards, he had a broad chest and large, muscular arms. His left arm was inked with a picture of a dreamcatcher, the long, beaded tassels below the hoop trailed down the man's bicep.

With careful deliberation, the man scooped a spoonful of scrambled eggs and offered it up to Elias. The way he was strapped to the table made eating difficult. Straining his neck, he lifted his head up so he could put his mouth around the spoon to eat the egg.

*Shift!*

Egg fell from his mouth. The guard cursed and tried to catch the pieces of egg as they tumbled from his open mouth. He tried to shovel the pieces back into Elias' mouth, but Elias made no effort to receive them.

*Where had that voice come from?*

He knew he had heard it. Clear as day. Not from inside the room, but from inside his head. Elias became acutely aware of a presence inside his head. With shock, he realized the presence had been looming there, inside his head, for some time now.

With awareness of this presence, he could sense where in relation to him it was. Somewhere to the south and west.

*Shift!*

He strained viciously against the straps and the guard scrambled back from him, unsure of Elias' sudden violence.

Something shuddered through his body and instinctually, he clenched every muscle he could. It felt like everything in his body wanted to flee and it was all he could do to keep them from going.

*SHIFT!*

The compulsion overwhelmed him this time. The strength of will from the presence pushed away every other thought. With the command came instructions. A flood of images flitted through his brain and compelled him to follow them.

He remembered what that monster looked like. He pictured it in his head, somehow adjusting to make it more . . . him. The image solidified in his head and the pain came.

Like a torrent, it washed over his body. Bones broke, tore skin and reformed. He vaguely heard the guard yell and run for the door. In moments, he would bring back more guards.

In moments, it wouldn't matter.

Every inch of him broke and reformed. As these changes took place, he fought his restraints and they snapped in half or were ripped from where they were attached to the table.

When he stood, he towered over his usual height. He didn't need to see a mirror to realize he resembled the monster who had attacked the refinery. He had shifted into a humanoid Boar. Powerful and unstoppable!

*Good. Now come to me!*

Elias slammed into the door of his room, bursting it open as a half-dozen guards descended upon him. Like an avalanche, he rolled over them, slicing and shredding as he went. Blood and screams trailed him as he made his way through the building he had been held at.

When he began to hear other screams, screams from other areas, he realized others were escaping. Weres began to join him, and they tore their way out of the building. Several times he and the others were accosted by guards. He had been shot several times already, but to his amazement, his body healed itself, slowly, but it did heal.

They were in some sort of industrial park. Across from them, a huge squarish looking building sat. The rapid pop, pop, pop of gunfire could be heard from there. To the left lay an open parking lot which had been abandoned a long time ago. Cracks marred its surface and sprouts of grass had begun their long, slow war of reclaiming what had been taken from them.

The entire area was enclosed in a rusty chain-link fence fronted by a gate. On either side of the gate were wooden towers each standing twenty feet high or so. There were guards posted in each of them, pointing in their direction.

Somewhere, sirens began to whine.

As if the sirens were a summons instead of warning, the doorway to the squarish building blew off its hinges, striking the pavement, flipping over once and sliding to a halt a few feet away. Streaming out from the doorway came the most frightening and exciting thing Elias had ever seen. Monsters.

They came in a flood. There were ones like him, boarish, with huge white tusks jutting from their jaws and arched backs, and there were the Crocs. Huge beasts with long, jutting maws full of razor-sharp teeth and scaly hides, their ridged tails swishing back and forth as they ran for the gate.

Screams, shouts and roars were a battling chorus as Elias and the others with him joined the mass of beasts hurtling toward the gated fence and the two watch towers.

Gun fire began to rain down upon them, but as they struck across the front of the mass, they did little damage and were healed instantaneously.

Elias could hear gunfire from behind them as more and more armed guards exited the buildings they were posted at and took up the attack.

Bullets perforated his hide as he ran, but he ignored them. His only goal, to make it to the gate and get out of this area as quickly as he could. He needed to get to the one who summoned him, and he needed to get to him now.

More and more bullets struck him, and Elias realized that one guard had chosen him to concentrate his fire on. Elias broke from the pack and headed toward the tower. Fire and pain erupted from his side as the other guard upon the other tower had joined in the attempt to eliminate him. Bullets began to shred his right leg as he ran, closing in on the tower. His body fought to heal the damage, but the damage came too quickly for him to keep up.

The front of the pack slammed into the gate and it broke under their assault and they scattered into the surrounding industrial park, losing themselves from sight as quickly as they could.

When the bullets had ripped enough of his flesh away from his leg, they began chipping and shattering away at his femur. Near the foot of the tower, his leg broke under his weight and he went down.

As soon as he rolled to a halt, something slammed into his head, it hit him like a rock and his neck snapped sharply, his head knocked downward from the impact. Another slam, but this time from the side. Again, and again he felt the pounding against his head. Sharp pain and flares of white behind his eyes followed each hit.

*Their shooting at my head,* Elias realized, but found nothing he could do about it. His limbs didn't respond, except to jerk and shake like a seizure. He could feel pieces of his skull bursting apart and his vision left him.

His body fought to heal itself as it continued to take damage, like trying to patch up a leaky boat with paper. He was losing this battle, he realized. At some point, his body would cease being able to heal itself, and the damage would be too severe to heal anyway. The claim the man had made about being unstoppable had been a lie.

As bullets continued to perforate his skull, Elias felt life slip away.

Zach waited with the other members of E.A.R.t.H who had chosen not to become Weres but still wished to be a part the war. They waited outside an abandoned industrial park. Large, bulky buildings had been left idle from a time when this area had flourished. Now, with paint fading, and windows broken from an occasional rock throw, it looked run down. Zach frowned, *what a disgusting waste.* This had been, at one time, a lush forest with beautiful trees and thriving wild animals. Now it was a testament of what humans do, leave a blight upon the land.

He leaned back against the van they had procured for this mission. A dozen more were placed strategically around the neighborhood which rested outside the park. Tight, two story homes with faded siding faced off against the dying warehouses. The house across from him had peeling strips of siding from its façade, like lengths of banana peel hanging limp.

Weedy and sparse lawns and poorly cared for landscape spoke of the apathy of their owners, or, more likely, the overworked individuals with little time or energy to spend on caring for their home.

*More blight.* Zach tsked. He would see it all torn down if he could. A return to what it should have been. With Kestrel's help, it will at long last come to pass.

At the first sounds of gunfire, Zach straightened. Unhooking the radio at his belt he pressed the talk button.

"They're coming."

A series of 'copy' came over the radio as the other members checked in. Zach pulled his phone out of his pocket and called Kestrel.

"Yes?"

"Fighting has begun. We can't see them yet, but it shouldn't be long."

An alarm pealed in the distance. That's when the gunfire began in earnest. Zach went to the side of the van and opened it. They had gutted the thing and now, it was simply an open space. He figured he could fit maybe a twenty people in there, plus one up front. His would be the last to fill as he was closest to the park.

Gunfire continued to ring out and people were starting to emerge from the surrounding homes to look out over the park. Many of them gave him strange looks at his nonchalant demeanor. He ignored them. Zach saw phones come out and pressed to ears as they undoubtedly were calling the police.

Zach knew the police wouldn't come. The government had to have this place set up as their jurisdiction, not to mention, this looked like the type of neighborhood in which gunshots were a common occurrence. Just another Tuesday.

Zach admired their bravery though. The amount of ammunition being unloaded this close, should send most people into hiding, and yet, there they stood, on their porches, craning their necks as if they might somehow see over all those buildings to catch a glimpse of the firefight.

Zach knew their bravery, like paper, would shred soon enough.

A scream cut through the sound of bullets and Zach smiled knowingly. *They're here.*

The first of the Weres flowed out from around the buildings. Like souped-up race cars, they tore through the gaps in the buildings. Boar-like men and women intermingled with Crocodile humanoids. Zach's breath caught. It was one thing to see one Wereboar and one Werecroc, it was another thing entirely to see dozens of them. And they kept coming.

As they approached the outskirts of the park, Zach brought the phone back up to his mouth.

"They're here!" He tried to keep the fear from his voice as he told Kestrel before hanging up. Even knowing they were on his side he couldn't hide the terror at the sight of them. He could hear doors slamming, people screaming, yelling and running from behind him in the neighborhood.

Then it happened. Those Weres closest to him began to shift and change back to their human form. Zach turned away, feeling his stomach lurch and the tang of bile and acid rising.

Taking his mind from the screams of pain and the sounds of breaking bones, he brought the radio up.

"Be ready, they will be coming your way. Fill up as many as you can and go to the rendezvous."

He didn't wait for a response. Instead, he steeled himself to turn back around. Men and women flooded out from the park and into the streets of the neighborhood. Zach didn't understand how they knew where to go. As he understood it, a link existed between these new Weres and the ones who had made them, but he didn't understand it.

There were several vans within his viewing range, and he could see members of E.A.R.t.H helping the newcomers in. One van had already filled, and he watched it speed off.

More and more people and Weres came out from around the buildings. Kestrel had told him to expect many, but he had not expected this many. He felt a welling up inside of fear and excitement. *There will be no stopping us!*

He hadn't bothered counting but as the reports came from over the radio as each driver left, he began to get some inkling of how many new Weres were now joining their ranks. Six vans had already left. Six vans with at least twenty people in them. And more to come.

The sound of gunfire had moved closer. Soon, the last of the Weres would be emerging and entering his van. His heart started beating faster. When the last of them came, so too would the men with guns.

Zach moved around the van, got in and started it up. They wouldn't need him to show them where to go, so he needn't stand there waiting to get shot at.

At last, some of the men and women veered to his location. The last of them broke from the buildings, they were still in their hybrid forms. Three Boars. Men came behind them holding assault rifles. Gunfire ripped through the air and Zach could see blood spray from the bodies of those three.

*They're shielding us!*

Bullets continued to riddle the Boars as they came at the van. Zach couldn't help but wince as the bullets shredded flesh and muscle. He knew, even though they would heal from those wounds, it didn't make the pain any less.

They shifted as they reached the van and bullets began pelting its side. Zach didn't hesitate, he slammed on the gas. The Boars were now three men who dived into the open side door of the moving van.

"Close it! Close it!" he shouted at them as he banked the van onto the nearest side street away from the shooting men. The door slid shut, but Zach could hear the ping, ping, ping of bullets piercing the van's walls, followed by cries of pain as they found their marks.

Bullets continued to strike the van as Zach weaved around parked cars. He made another turn and the gunfire ceased. Gasping for breath as if he had been the one running through the industrial park, he spared a glance behind him.

The faces looking back at him held a mixture of fear, excitement and some confusion. He couldn't blame them. One minute they had were being held at some undisclosed facility by the government and the next they had shifted into Were-creatures and had broken out.

All because someone, in their head, had told them to.

Zach let out a little laugh, bordering on hysteria.

Someone else barked a laugh as well in response. Then, before he knew it, the rest of the van filled with laughter. He knew there wasn't anything funny, about any of this, but he couldn't help himself and joined in.

Since the attack on the hospital two days before, Kestrel had been filtering out members of E.A.R.t.H in twos and threes. As soon as they had survived the rejection process, Kestrel had given them instructions and money and they had left.

Samuel had managed to procure a generous plot of land, not too far out of Houston and they were each to make their own way there. That land is where Zach and the others were headed to now.

It would take them hours to reach there and he hoped his bullet riddled van would escape too much notice. He didn't wish to get pulled over.

Much to Zach's relief, the trip was uneventful. When they arrived at the property, the changes which had occurred since he had come here last, impressed him. What had once been an open plot of land, surrounded by forest was now covered with buildings.

Dozens of long rectangular buildings could be seen, which Zach knew from the plans were barracks for those who would come to join them. When they had entered the property, he had seen men and women within the forest itself, as sentries. And now, as they pulled into the clearing, he could see others as well, keeping watch on the surrounding forest.

The rest of the vans were parked and those they had help rescue were getting out and marveling at what they saw. Zach had spent the trip explaining as much as he could.

At first, he tried to sway them with the E.A.R.t.H mission and how they could play a part in that mission. There were some whom he saw nodded their head along with his impassioned speech. Others, he saw, frowned or listened with disdain clearly marked on their faces.

Once he had spoken to their hearts, he spoke to their heads. They were all now wanted criminals and threats to the United States Government. They would be hunted, and they would be killed, or captured, once again. Their only hope to survive and stay free meant joining with the others and doing what must be done. There had still been a great deal of uncertainty in the looks they had given them, but he could see they had begun to mull over what he had told them.

He knew, in the end, they would see the wisdom of his words. Not that it would make any difference. Those who disagreed or thought they would be better off on their own would be made to do what they wanted. They would not have a choice.

He saw those with him to their living areas and gave them a brief tour of the complex. There were still buildings being built and he explained to them they could use the help of any who were willing.

Over the next few days they would be given time to get used to the idea of being part of this organization. This . . . army. Then, Zach knew, Kestrel would arrive with the others and they would be getting their orders.

Zach already knew his. His involvement, they believed, remained unknown. E.A.R.t.H had been an early addition to Kestrel's war. Long before anyone understood the threat she posed.

The world would realize soon enough.

Zach bid the newcomers and the members of E.A.R.t.H who were going to stay at the property for now, goodbye and left. He expected Kestrel to arrive the following day or so. Once she did, those here would be taken into hand and made to understand their new roll in the upcoming conflict. In many ways, for those who didn't share Kestrel's beliefs, they had escaped one prison to only be put into a new one.

Zach needed to return to Houston. He had an interview to prepare for. He was about to announce the beginning of a new world.

# *Chapter Thirty-Eight*

Bodies lay sprawled out around Eric Moran as he surveyed the enclosed warehouse. The guards had managed to capture and detain most of the unchanged ones who had tried to escape.

Luckily for them, those who had yet to go through the process had been too frightened of their fellow captives who had shifted to follow them when they had made their escape.

Eric's team had been monitoring this little holding facility ever since the government had moved the victims of the attacks here.

There had been nothing he could do about those who had escaped. At least, not yet, anyway. These, he looked at the men and women, dead around him, he could do something about.

His experiments and observations had been right. None of these men and women had reached the point where their body had either rejected or accepted the, for lack of a better word, disease, which had been introduced into their body, and so, had been easy to dispatch.

Dozens of people and guards lay dead. The guards had been unfortunate casualties of all of this, but they had refused to admit his men onto the facility and his men knew their orders. To eliminate all of those who remained who hadn't changed. Kill them now before they could.

He had explained the necessity to Colonel Simpson.

He had surprised the colonel by waiting within his office when he had returned from lunch. Though he had surprised the man, he had recovered well, shut the door, moved around his desk and sat down, steepling his fingers and stared at Eric.

Eric smiled ruefully at him. "You don't seem surprised to see me."

The colonel frowned. "I had expected someone to show up at some point. I had hoped it would have been sooner than this, since, obviously, things are starting to get a little . . . difficult, out there."

Eric nodded slightly. "I apologize. We usually don't make our presence known. In fact, as far as I know, this is the first one on one interaction a member of my organization has ever had with the leader of the DHS."

"And which organization is that, exactly?" The Colonel did not seem at all pleased with this conversation.

"Who we are is not important. What we need to discuss, is . . ." Eric leaned forward in his seat. "You need to eliminate everyone you have at the holding facility. You need to do it now."

The colonel visibly reeled. The holding facility, of course, was top secret. Few people knew anything about it, let alone who it held.

It took a moment for the man to recover himself.

"We can't just kill all those people." His disbelief in Eric's suggestion evident in his voice.

"We can't afford not to, Director." Eric told him flatly. "Let us not dance around what we both already know. You moved those people there because you understand what we face is an epidemic unlike anything we have ever faced before. Those people will, in fact, become the next wave of that epidemic if they are not eliminated — now."

"Those people are citizens of the United States and they can't just be killed because of a perceived threat they might hold. We have laws. We have rules and regulations. We have morality." The man's face became flush, his voice rising as he spoke.

"Cut the bullshit, Director," Eric cut him off. "We also can't put people in holding sites without contact to the outside world or without charging them with something, and yet, you already did."

"That is very different from killing them."

"And yet, just as necessary." Eric sighed. "I don't like this just as much as you don't."

"I doubt that," the man said bluntly.

Eric ignored the jab. The director had a point.

"But don't be a fool. Every single one of those people is a threat to our national security. No. A threat to our very lives." Eric slammed a fist down upon the man's desk. "Think! How many people can each of those captives infect? How many can those infect? It will be exponential. We must do everything we can to stop this threat, Director!"

The director stared hard at him for a long time. When he spoke, the cold authority of one who has ordered men for most of their adult lives, crept into his voice. It brokered no argument.

"You listen to me, whoever you are. We will not kill civilians who have not committed any crimes. Those people are innocent, and while we are unsure of the possibility of the spread of the contagion they might be carrying, we can, under the law, quarantine them, which is all we have done."

He sat back and straightened his shirt with a tug. "I don't know who you report to, or under whose authority you operate under, but know this. Those people are under the protection of the DHS. I will not have any harm come to them. Do you understand?"

"You are making a mistake," Eric informed him.

"Do you understand me?" the director growled out.

441

Eric stood. "The men you have at that facility are as good as dead. And as far as I'm concerned, their death is on your hands. Good day, Director."

With that, he turned and left.

*Fool man.* He wished the director had listened to him. Now, he had been forced to eliminate the captives himself, and as he had said, the men the director had posted here were dead.

Eric turned to one of his men. "Download and wipe all of the computers. Then burn this place to the ground. Use an accelerant, I don't want the fire department to be able to recognize this was even a building by the time the fire burns out, copy?"

"Yes, sir." The man replied and left to see Eric orders were followed.

He scanned around one last time. The cat was truly out of the bag now. He had seen the news on the drive here. They were starting to report on this, though still hesitantly as if dipping a toe into a pool to check if it was cold or not.

There was plenty of video evidence out there. Videos of what went down in Chicago all those months ago. Videos of what happened in Sydney as well. Those had been isolated instances. Curiosities and most likely internet hoaxes. But now, they had become part of a larger story. Too many eyewitnesses. Too much devastation. Too much death to be ignored.

He had done his best to shelter the world from this as long as he could. He knew he could no longer succeed. The world would grasp this threat soon. Eric could not help but wonder how the world would react.

# *Chapter Thirty-Nine*

Stephanie brought her arm up to block Carver's swing. She took the hit on her forearm, deflecting the attack. Unfortunately, Carver brought his knee up to his chest and extended his leg out, planting his clawed foot to slam against her chest. Bones and cartilage snapped. Thrown backward she managed to roll over the matted floor before springing back to her feet.

Carver, one of the former marines Jessie had enlisted had chosen Wolf as his hybrid form. He outweighed her by a hundred pounds in human form but in hybrid form, things didn't equal out. For one, she was a True and he, a Pure. He was a Wolf and she, a Fox. For some reason, it worked out he had only two score pounds more than her.

Her ribs and sternum mended almost immediately.

He bared his fangs at her, and she peeled her lips back in a snarl and came at him. When she reached him, he swiped down at her and she swerved her body to the side to avoid the attack. He attempted another swipe and she swerved her body the other way, bringing her knee up this time to pound against Carver's midsection. She was rewarded with an oof as he had the air blasted out of him.

Before he could recover, she stepped behind the larger Wolf and raked his back, dragging deep furrows through his trapezius and latissimus dorsi muscles, her claws kicking up each time they struck a rib on the way down.

Carver howled, but swung a backhanded swing at her, but she sensed it coming and bounced back out of the way.

He rounded on her and stood there, panting for a moment. He relaxed his stance and she did the same.

"Good, good," he commended her. "You have improved much, Stephanie, in a very short time," nodding his canine head as he spoke. "You are using your quickness to your advantage. Keep it up. From our brief it is clear several of the other side will have a size advantage over you."

*You're telling me!* Stephanie thought back to her encounter with the Croc and the Snake, Samuel. While Samuel had been about her size, the Croc stood bigger than both her and Carver. The Boar she had only seen on video, but matching his size next to Clint and Kat, he stood bigger as well. As far as she had been able to determine, the only one she was bigger than was the Rat.

"Thanks, Carver." She offered him a smile, or at least, she hoped he knew it to be a smile. Those types of facial expressions didn't look right when you were a Fox.

With their bout finished, she became aware of the other fights going on around her. Kat had used her family's money to rent a gymnasium which had been seldom used. The idea had been to use this time while they waited for Kestrel to reveal herself, so they could strike, to practice fighting in their hybrid forms.

Jessie and Kat had arranged for his fellow soldiers to help teach those within the group who had no formal training in fighting, especially in hybrid form. Which pretty much meant everyone but Kat, though Jessie had assured everyone he was trained enough. Then Kat dropped him—hard. After that, he worked as hard as everyone else to learn what their new forms could do and how to incorporate fighting styles with their natural weapons.

Stephanie loved these moments as they allowed a certain blanking of the mind. An escape from thought. She needed these moments otherwise the hurt and shame would creep their way back into her thoughts. She didn't believe she would ever be truly free of them, but for a time, while fighting, they receded and let her be.

She gazed out over the paired off fighters and located Jason. She spotted him and winced. For some reason he had been paired off with one of the new Bears. She didn't know his name, but as she watched, he leaned back and rolled forward from his hips, crashing into Jason with his forepaws. The weight of the hit sent Jason flying, his ruddy colored bushy tail whipping around as he landed and bounced his way across the mat.

Jason got up unhurriedly. She watched as he rolled his shoulders and neck. It seemed such an oddly human gesture on a Fox.

She turned to Carver.

"Catch you later?" She tipped her head up in question.

He nodded and made a face. She had seen the expression on Clint enough that she thought she knew it for a smile.

"Yeah." He motioned with his head toward Jason. "Go save him."

She waved him off, turned and trotted toward the fight.

Jason and the Bear were squaring off again and they circled each other, looking for an opening. Jason spied her coming in their direction and changed his direction to ensure she approached from the Bear's rear. The moment she got within range, he feigned an attack and the Bear hopped back.

Stephanie took that moment to attack.

Ducking in low, she sliced at his hamstring, cutting through it.

He roared and Jason launched himself on him. Unable to sustain his weight on his one useful leg, the Bear went down under Jason's attack. Jason bit down in the space between shoulder and neck and savaged him.

The Bear roared again, and with an immense show of strength, tossed Jason off him, sending Jason and a solid chunk of his neck into the air.

Before he could regain his feet, Stephanie landed on him, punching with her claws extended, driving them deep into the Bear's chest. Before he could swing a meaty paw at her, she danced off. He rolled to follow her, but Jason pounced on him, landing with all four clawed limbs pointing downward to punch into his Bear hide.

He roared a third time and moved to strike at Jason, but he danced out of reach. Stephanie darted in, nipping at him and tearing at his shoulder with her sharp fangs.

"ENOUGH!" the Bear roared, and Stephanie immediately ceased her attack and joined Jason as the Bear regained his feet. Wounds closed on the massive Bear as he rose.

"Enough," he said more calmly. He looked them over as they stood side by side.

"You guys don't fight fair."

"Are we supposed to?" Stephanie's voice sounded sweet and innocent. She would have batted her eyelashes at him if she could.

He eyed her, and chuckled. "No. No you are not. You fight to win. If it means tag-teaming someone, well, then that is what you do. You guys seem to fight well as a pair. Use it."

She peered at Jason and peeled back her lips in her version of a smile. He did the same.

"Break?" Jason raised his eyebrows at his sparring partner.

"Sounds good to me, see you later, Jason."

"You too, Ed."

They nodded companionably to each other and Jason turned to her.

"I had him."

She patted him on the arm. "Of course you did, sweetie."

He chuckled but it died quickly. *He's thinking of Sim,* Stephanie thought. When they had first met Sim, he had saved Jason from the Werecroc. In the conversation that had followed, Sim had tried to help Jason save face by saying he knew Jason had the fight well in hand and hadn't needed his help. Jason, being the modest type, knew well enough he would have been dead if Sim had not intervened, had burst out laughing at the statement. Sim had followed suit and they had shared a good laugh over it and had bonded because of it.

Now, Sim was dead, killed in the battle in Chicago by some unknown assailant wielding old magic even Sylvanis knew nothing about. Jason hurt for the loss of his friend. As Stephanie did for Beth.

She looped her arm into his as they made their way to the lunchroom off the main gym area, shifting as they entered. There were several others in the room. All in their human form.

It seemed strange to have so many people here, not only aware of hers and Jason's lycanthropy, but also sharing it. They only had a few Foxes among the group. Stephanie would not give anyone lycanthropy. Never again. Jason and Mike had to step in if there were those who felt Fox fit them better.

Most of the new recruits had chosen Bear, Wolf, and Tiger. She wasn't offended. Not really. They wouldn't had gotten anyone at all if it hadn't been imparted on them how important it was to choose based on the animal they had more affinity with.

It was an easy test. You showed them a list of the four choices and asked them which one caught and held their eye. It was one of those things you had to simply do and explain afterward. Everyone has done it before on other tests. Your subconscious gravitates toward one thing and you fixate on it. It is your brain letting you recognize what it connects with.

Kat and Jessie were here and, as they approached, Kat roared a laugh at something Jessie had said. Jessie's mouth broke into a huge smile as he rocked back and forth with laughter of his own. Kat spied them and covered her mouth with the back of her hand in a failed attempt to cover her laughter. She waved them over with her other hand.

Stephanie and Jason sat at their table and Stephanie arched an eyebrow in an unspoken question. When Kat gained a modicum of control, she turned to them.

"Jessie was regaling me with stories from his time in the Middle East."

Stephanie regarded Jessie who was still chuckling. "I would think those stories wouldn't be all that funny."

"Oh, there are plenty of horror stories I could tell," Jessie nodded soberly. "But, when you stick a bunch of guys . . . well, mostly guys. But, when you stick a bunch of guys together for months on end, with very little to do, usually, well, we tend to find things to amuse ourselves."

Jason smiled knowingly. *Men!* Kat rolled her eyes at her and she responded in kind.

"How long were you there for?" Jason asked.

"I did a tour," Jessie responded, and she nodded her head along with Jason as if they knew what that meant.

"Yeah. I saw a lot of shit go down. But I find most people don't want to know about that stuff, you know? Or some do, but when you start talking about it, they grow uncomfortable and change the conversation. So, I just keep to the funny bits." He smiled. "Plus, I really don't like re-living it anyway."

Awkward silence followed, since no one knew what to say to that.

"Was it hard coming home?" she asked him.

He regarded her for a minute before answering. "It wasn't easy. I kinda floated around for a while. Unsure of what to do and how I would do it. Worked some odd jobs around, but never for long." He shifted in his seat. "I would get restless, you know?" He laughed. "It's funny, but all that time in the desert, unable to leave the base hardly at all and it never bothered me, and yet, when I came home, I couldn't stay in one place long at all."

Jessie turned away from them, rapping his fingers on the table. He turned to them abruptly. "Then I fell in with you guys, and now I feel I once again have a purpose and that helps. Yeah," he glanced off again. "That helps."

The table fell silent again. Then, to both Stephanie's and Jason's amazement, Kat reached across the table and took one of Jessie's hands and squeezed it. Stephanie caught Jason looking at her wide eyed and she could imagine her eyes were wide as well. Only a few short days ago, Kat was cold-shouldering Jessie, hard.

He hadn't let up though. She had to admire him for that. Wherever Kat went, Jessie would turn up with a smile and amusing quip or be there to assist her in whatever she needed doing.

Stephanie had been sure Kat couldn't stand the former marine, but apparently, she had been wrong.

"Kat, Jessie, Stephanie, Jason?" Clint stood at the doorway motioning to them. Kat let go of Jessie's hand immediately upon hearing Clint's voice and flushed, which showed bright on her pale skin.

If Clint had noticed anything, he didn't make a deal about it. They rose and approached him. As they reached him, he held the door open.

"Something is happening," he told them.

Clint didn't elaborate but led them to the back of the gym and into an office. Sylvanis sat at the desk, her face an unreadable mask. She wore a comfortable t-shirt, her blonde hair pulled back into a ponytail. On the desk in front of her rested a strange looking knife, long bladed and curved slightly. The hilt was made from some kind of antler. As strange as it was, it seemed an appropriate weapon for the Druidess.

Hank was there as well, seated at another chair in the room. His face made it clear something had indeed happened, and it wasn't good. Of Ben, there was no sign.

449

Clint closed the door after they entered and Sylvanis picked up a remote from the desk and pointed it at the TV which nested in the corner of the room by the ceiling.

Stephanie looked to the TV.

The screen sat frozen in pause, but the scene showed two people sitting. Their chairs were angled slightly toward each other, so they were facing the other person, but also facing toward the camera. A short square coffee table sat between them.

The woman in the one chair had blonde hair pulled back. She wore a dark red dress, pulled tight at the waist with a broad black belt with a golden buckle. With her legs crossed and her back erect, she had one arm resting on her knee and the other crossed over it, holding sheets of paper. An attractive woman, she had high cheekbones and a long chin. Her nose had a slight upturn to it, which left plenty of space for her full lips.

The man was a handsome man who looked like he took care of himself. His button-down shirt showcased his trim, solidly built body. Brown, sculpted hair framed his youthful, yet masculine face with a well-defined jawline and cheekbones. His frozen expression showed a friendly and inviting face. A tag along the bottom named him as Zach Van Stanley: Leader of E.A.R.t.H.

Sylvanis pressed play and the interview, which had already begun, began to play again. The woman spoke.

"So, Mr. Van Stanley, you requested this interview because you have claimed to have news about a new environmental movement which will change the face of global policy and save the Earth from its destruction."

Clearly while the woman might believe in the threat of climate change, she had doubts about Mr. Van Stanley's claim anything new would truly make a difference.

Zach Van Stanley offered an understanding smile.

"Believe me, Becca," he spoke using her first name with such familiarity it seemed to throw in the face of her formality in using his last name. "I know it is easy for anyone to come on here and make these claims, but I assure you, I am not here to offer up false promises."

He turned more toward the camera, to direct his next words at the audience at home. "We are on the brink of disaster. Organizations, like mine, have been warning of the calamity which faces us if we don't change our ways. We have marched. We have lobbied. We have sabotaged. All to no avail. The world continues to march to its inevitable end. We continue to pollute the land. To rape and pillage the Earth of her precious resources, without caring about the repercussions."

Stephanie found she could not look away from this man. His speech and his delivery were so captivating she found herself nodding in agreement with him.

"Well," he continued. "I say, enough is enough. I speak now to the government of this country and to the governments of all the other countries who have failed to do what is right for Mother Earth. You may have begun to realize now, there is a war going on. There have already been casualties and there will be more."

The interviewer lost her composure, unsure of where this interview was going now and wondering how she could stop it.

"We are not interested in your claims things will change. We are not interested in excuses. You have had your chance, and you have failed. You have not been part of the solution, and so that makes you part of the problem. And," he paused to make sure everyone listened, and Stephanie, like surely everyone else, was, "you will be removed."

"Mr. Van Stanley," the interviewer interjected. "It sounds like you just declared war on the government of the United States?"

He turned a wan smile on her.

"The war has already started, Becca. They just haven't acknowledged it yet." He turned back to the screen. "In the next few days though, they won't have a choice."

He stood up at that moment and Becca looked like a deer in headlights, as if she expected him to leap at her. Instead, he turned toward her, unhooked his microphone pack from his pants and slid the cord out of his shirt. He placed it on the small table which sat between them, turned and walked off the screen.

Becca watched him go, her mouth slightly agape. It took her a moment to remember they were live, and she turned back to the screen. The video froze.

Stephanie turned to Sylvanis. "What does it mean?"

"Do you think he is working with Kestrel?" Jason shuffled uncomfortably beside her, the idea worrying him.

Sylvanis tapped the remote against the desk and remained looking at the screen a moment before regarding them.

"I think, given what he said and how he said it, Kestrel has found her allies. I know a little about this organization. E.A.R.t.H. is a group which had caught my interest when trying to determine what Kestrel might be up to. They have thousands of members, worldwide. With that kind of membership, Kestrel would have an army of recruits for her war and she would have something she never had during the last war."

"Which is?" Hank asked.

"Willing people," Stephanie responded before Sylvanis could. The memory had jumped to her the moment Hank asked the question.

"You had said one of the reasons Kestrel had failed in the last war was because most of her army were people she had forced to be a part of it. That she could force people to fight, but if they didn't care about why they were fighting, they wouldn't fight well."

452

Sylvanis nodded.

"It's true. I'm afraid things have just gotten much, much worse. If they are stepping into the light and announcing, if vaguely, their plans to fight, she must have already gathered many people to become her Were army."

Silence fell on the group, no one sure what to say.

In the end, Hank spoke up.

"So, what are we going to do?"

Sylvanis looked pensive, uncertain. "I'm not certain. The ultimate goal hasn't changed and the means as to how we will win hasn't changed. If we take out Kestrel and her Trues, her army will disappear." She still appeared uncertain. "How we go about that, I have no idea."

"This, Zach Van Stanley guy," Clint began, "it said on the scroll that E.A.R.t.H. is based in Houston. Should we start our search there?"

"That would seem the best place to start," Kat agreed. "From the news of those other attacks, it would seem they were heading in that direction. It would be a safe bet to say that if those two monsters were going there that Kestrel will be there."

"It is not a safe bet," Sylvanis corrected.

"Kestrel is many things, but predictable isn't one of those. All of this could be a ruse. We might head to Houston to only find they had already left there, and the attacks are actually going to happen somewhere completely different."

She sighed. "However, it is the only clue we have as to where she might be, and we must take it."

She seemed to gain some measure of determination as she spoke. "Gather everyone. We leave immediately."

Stephanie and Jason left with the others.

"I'll go tell Jesse," Kat announced and headed toward the break area.

They watched her go. Clint had a sly smile on his face.

453

"What?" Jason eyed him.

Clint moved his head toward the direction she had gone. "For all of her tough talk and unapproachability, I think Jessie is wearing her down."

Hank grunted. "God help him."

They all shared a smile as they continued toward the gym.

"What do you think we will find when we get there?" Stephanie wondered at no one in particular.

Clint raised his shoulders in a non-committal shrug. "She'll either be there or she won't." He turned to look at them. "But if she is there, and that motherfucker Boar is there . . . I'm going to kill him. No matter what."

"I don't know if I'm ready for an all-out battle," she told them.

"None of us are, Stephanie," Hank grumbled. "None of us are."

They entered the gym to the sounds of grunts and growls as dozens of Werebears, tigers, wolves and foxes fought each other. No one turned as they approached as they were all concentrating on either kicking ass or not getting their asses kicked.

Before any of them could utter a word a loud, "Ten-hut!" came from the direction of the break room.

The entire room ceased their combat, turned toward the shout with arms at their sides and backs erect. Stephanie turned toward the command as well as Jessie and Kat emerged from the break room area.

Jessie addressed the group. ·

"It seems as if we got our orders, soldiers. We need to prep for immediate deployment. I'll need you packed and ready by 01300. Dismissed."

Everyone shifted almost as one. The collective sound of bones snapping, and bodies reshaping sounded like a dozen microwaves popping popcorn. It was a little unsettling. Quickly, the soldiers were out the doors and, Stephanie assumed, on their way back to their rooms to pack.

Jessie and Kat moved to join them.

"Sorry," Jessie murmured.

Hank shook the apology off. "No need. Sylvanis put you in charge of them. They're your men."

Jessie nodded his appreciation for their understanding.

"Where are we going? Kat didn't really fill me in on the details, only told me it was time to go."

For a moment, no one spoke, and Stephanie realized, without Sylvanis, there was no clear delineation of who was in charge.

Kat stepped up.

"Houston. We have credible intel that Kestrel might be there along with her flunkies. Either way, something is going to go down soon, and we need to be ready."

Jessie gave a curt nod of his head. "Sounds good. If you will excuse me," he reached out and touched Kat's wrist in a parting gesture that no one missed. "I'll go pack."

As Jessie parted, Kat watched him go for a moment before turning back to them. Stephanie, like the others of the group, were all giving her knowing looks.

"What?" she asked, not at all convincing on being confused.

Stephanie gave her a sly smile.

"Oh, come on!" Kat held her hands up and glanced skyward. "There is nothing going on!"

"I didn't say there was anything going on," Clint said with his half smile showing. "Did you, Jason?"

"Me?" Jason, with splayed hands and fingers to his chest in feigned shock. "I didn't say anything of the sort. How about you, Hank?"

Hank snorted. "Leave me out of this. I know better." He left them there.

Kat rolled her eyes and gave an exasperated sigh. "Very funny, guys. We are just friends."

455

"With benefits?" Jason wiggled his eyebrows at her, and Stephanie elbowed him in the ribs and gave him a warning look.

"What?" Jason gave her a confused look. He was undoubtedly still thinking they should keep prodding this, but Stephanie knew Kat better. She would only take gibing for so long before she kicked someone's ass, and Stephanie didn't want it to be Jason's ass that got kicked.

"We should go and get ready," she told him. He still gave her a questioning and somewhat hurt look for spoiling his fun.

"See you guys." She turned Jason around and led him off to go and pack. Not that they had much to pack. They had brought little since they had no clear idea about what they were to do or what would happen next. The one thing Stephanie did know — they were going to fight again. She hoped things would go better than their last encounter. Though she and Jason had not been there, they had lost Sim, and Kestrel and the others had escaped.

They were more prepared this time, but so was Kestrel. How many Weres Kestrel had at her side, no one knew. By Sylvanis' estimation it could be hundreds. Sylvanis believed she would use them soon and in so doing, would leave herself vulnerable to attack. Stephanie hoped so. If they had to fight that many Weres, though they would be mostly Pures and maybe Weres, those who had received lycanthropy from a Pure, they would still have the numbers.

When the time came, the fate of the world could well rest in the balance and that fate would be determined by whether they won or lost. If Stephanie was being honest with herself, she didn't like the world's chances.

# *Chapter Forty*

Kestrel came to the end of her ring of power and closed it. For several days she had encircled the city of Houston, laying down lines of power, while members of E.A.R.t.H. planted the seeds of her plan throughout the city.

She was about to attempt something no other Druid had ever attempted before. The power it would require would leave her drained, but she felt, necessary.

Standing straight, she brushed the hoodie back from her head allowing her midnight tresses to be caught by the midday wind. The beads woven in her hair made soft clicking noises as they bounced against each other.

Shielding her eyes, she looked back toward the Houston skyline. She had to admit, if only to herself, there was something beautiful about how the buildings rose high into the sky, like metal trees reaching for the sun's nourishment.

But they were not trees. They were an abomination, created my men who cared so little for the land they destroyed in order to leave their mark. They took from Mother Earth. They stole her life blood. Her tissue. All to create these monuments to their own destructive nature.

It needed to end. She, needed to end it.

Gordon stepped up next to her. He had been with her these past few days, shadowing her, much like Samuel had once done. He was not Samuel though. Samuel was dead. Taken from her by some unknown Were, wielding some unknown power.

She glanced at him sidelong. An impressive looking man, he had blond hair and bright eyes in a well-formed face. He had an arrogance to him she found attractive. A self-confidence from knowing he was likely the most attractive man in the room and the wealth he had accumulated from being a successful doctor made him more attractive. At least to many women in this day and age.

Where Samuel had a certain exotic look to him which had made him attractive, Gordon had manly perfection. While she could appreciate his beauty, she wasn't attracted to him. He was a tool to her. Someone she could trust to keep her safe and entirely devoted to her.

Unlike Blain.

She grimaced. Blain she could not trust. She could trust his motivations though. He wanted power and would do what needed to be done in order to secure it. He was wary of her, but he held little respect for her. As far as Kestrel could tell, he didn't respect women in general. Something had happened early in his life to create this predisposed world view. Frankly, she didn't give a shit.

Gordon and Blain. The only two Trues she had left. Well, besides Shae. She sighed and pushed the young girl out of her mind. Things were as they needed to be, no need to think any further about them.

She was glad for Gordon's presence though. Given the loss of their anonymity, a run into law enforcement worried her and it would be well to have a True here with her.

Blain she had left to orchestrate the rest of her plan. He would be meeting her and Gordon in a bit. She would need them with her when she enacted her plan because she would be vulnerable.

She turned and moved to the car Gordon had waiting for them. Gordon took the driver's seat. Though she had accepted this mode of transportation as a necessity in getting around in this era, she would not deign to drive them herself. It was a thing made from the guts of the Earth and used its blood as fuel.

They drove into the heart of Houston. They arrived at Sam Houston Park almost an hour later, a distance which, by horseback would have taken them twenty minutes.

Sam Houston Park, nineteen acres of green in an otherwise landscape of gray and black. The predominant feature was a small pond, and on this bright, sunny day, the park was filled with people, ducks and geese.

Blain waited for them. He stood within the open field which ordinarily would hold picnickers and people playing frisbee or flying kites. Blain's dominance of the space kept wary people away. No one wanted to try and have fun around the man who brooded darkness and menace.

He looked so out of place in the lush green, with his dark, slicked back hair. He wore bulky clothes these days, unlike the tight leather he had worn when Samuel had spied on him for her.

He flashed his gap-toothed smile at her, somewhere between lascivious and condescending. She ignored it.

"Is everything ready?"

"Everyone is in place." He indicated the radio he was using to send commands. He also indicated several others in the field. More Pures to help fight if need be. "Just give the word and the shit will hit the fan, lass."

She chose to ignore his lack of using, My Lady, when he spoke to her. Some battles weren't worth fighting.

Instead, she turned and took off her hoodie. She slipped off her sandals. She understood Blain would enjoy this next part, but she cared little for the man's perversions. Pulling her blouse off, she exposed her bare breasts to the hot, dry air. Her pink nipples hardened despite the heat.

She could sense Blain and Gordon's eyes on her back. She also knew there were others in the park whose attention she had now attracted.

Without any more consideration, she slid off her jeans. She hadn't bothered with any underwear, knowing she would be naked to be one with the Earth for this next part.

Blain whistled appreciatively from behind her. Gordon and the others said nothing. Gordon had already seen her naked before, the day she had approached him to join with them. Though she didn't doubt he examined her with as much lust as Blain.

She knew men wanted her for her body — long, shapely legs and a rounded, yet firm behind. She was shapely with wide hips and a thin waist. Her breasts were full and rounded and her dark tresses hung loose and shiny across her shoulders. Creamy alabaster skin, like milk, held not a single blemish.

Nestling her feet and toes within the soft velvety grass, she steadied her breathing. Closing her eyes, she sent her senses deep into the Earth, reaching out and connecting herself, bit by bit, with the nature which surrounded her.

Reaching out with both her hands, she angled them skyward and tipped her head back to bask in the sunlight. Its warmth, caressed her bare skin, and she drank it in.

The sense of the grass and the earth beneath her feet reached her first. She could sense the way the grass, its roots intertwined right under the topsoil, reached out and connected with the shoots around them. Worms dug tunnels, eating their way through, replenishing the nutrients into the soil as they went.

Shrews and moles moved tentatively about their underground homes, waiting for night where they would feel less vibrations above them, and they would be safer to explore.

Thin tendrils of tree roots grew thicker and thicker the closer they got to the base of each tree. Oak, Cypress, Walnut, Ash, Chestnut, Alder and many others. Young saplings and ancient giants all vied for the sun's life-giving rays.

The vibrant ecosystem of the small pond, filled with fish, frogs, insect nymphs, turtles, and water beetles, filled her senses as she touched upon each living thing. Cattails, lily pads, arrow leaf and other lake flora were tiny sparks, like constellations in the night sky to her.

She could sense the ducks as they skimmed the surface before diving below to snag at the underwater plants. The air around the park thrummed with the vibrations of hundreds of wings as starlings, bluebirds, and cardinals flitted from tree to tree.

Kestrel probed out farther, deeper into the city. Life grew thinner as she ventured out. Trees grew sparser. Songbirds were replaced with pigeons and doves.

She needed to strain to find what she searched for, but she found them. First one, and then another. One by one she found them. The seeds she had spelled and given to members of E.A.R.t.H. to plant all over the city.

All throughout Houston, they had planted those seeds. They had planted them in people's yards, in open spaces in front of the vast skyscrapers permeating this city. They had dropped them into shallow drainage sewers beneath parking garages and hotels. They had planted them all, for this moment.

As she touched upon each life within the seed, she gathered her strength. Thousands of seeds now awoke and teamed with life.

Kestrel began her spell.


Sylvanis sat with Kat, Jessie and Clint eating lunch in the small little restaurant in their hotel. They had arrived there the day before and gotten everyone settled. At her waist she had a deer-skinned sheath for her antler-handled knife. It had been hard to come up with the raw components for the knife, but she had managed. It gave her comfort to carry it. She had used her memory, as best as she could, to draw upon and re-create a knife like the one she carried during the war.

Her earlier self had been more proficient in fashioning weapons. The war had been a dangerous time and you never knew when your magic might not be enough, and you would have to defend yourself physically. She had carried it all through the war, until that fateful day she had used it to execute Kestrel before using it again to draw her own blood to create the spell which would see her reborn in response to Kestrel's reawakening.

Jessie had sent out many of his men to scour the city in the hope they might spot Kestrel or the others of her group but had yet to find them anywhere. Houston was a huge city and it seemed unlikely they would find them, but they were men of action and sitting around waiting for something to happen wasn't in their nature.

Kat, Jessie and Clint were engaged in conversation, but Sylvanis barely listened. They didn't exclude her, but when they attempted to draw her into conversation, she would respond with simple one-word answers, not wishing to be an active participant in the dialogue.

She had much to think about as she knew, once again, she would have to face Kestrel in battle. It wasn't something she relished happening again, but she knew it a necessity. She was the only one who could face her— should face her.

If she had been more suspicious of Kestrel that day all those millennia ago and had been able to discover her duplicity, she could have prevented all this from happening.

She knew all of this wasn't truly her fault. It was Kestrel's. But she couldn't help but feel responsible. She could have stopped it after all. But she had failed.

Clint's laughter broke her out of her self-recrimination, and she allowed a small smile part her lips. It was nice to see him laugh. He had been through a lot. Had lost part of his humanity. It was nice to see him get some of it back.

Picking up her spoon she dipped it into her tomato basil soup and brought it up to her lips.

It never made it there.

With a clatter, the spoon and its contents struck the edge of the bowl and spilled into her lap, the spoon bouncing once before falling to the ground.

The table went silent as Jessie, Kat and Clint stared at her. She sat, unable to move, her mouth open and her eyes wide as she felt Druidic power swell within the city. Not only in one part of the city, but everywhere. Sudden realization hit her and dread, like submerging slowly into a freezing lake, crept up her body as she realized what Kestrel was about to unleash.

"Dear spirits. No." she breathed out.

# *Chapter Forty-One*

Kestrel's power snaked out through the soil, surging into each and every spelled seed. Her voice sang out into the park, clear and crisp and full of energy. The power built and gushed into each seed, layered over and over again.

Kestrel sang into the air. A song of power. A song of magic. For what seemed like eternity she sang the same lines again and again. Building the magic into a crescendo.

With a shout, she sent out her command. *"FÀS!"*

With such power spelled into them, the seeds planted throughout the city surged. Roots spread out like lightning, plowing through the earth. Like some sort of time-lapse video, the seed parted, and a tiny shoot sprung forth climbing for the surface. As they broke through the soil, they expanded and grew.

Buildings had no protection from the destructive power of growth. Trunks and branches forced their way through concrete and blacktop. They entwined metal girders and supports, weakening them.

Seeds closer to Kestrel received the flow of power first and like a feral beast they tore and ripped their way skyward. All over Houston, trees forced their way skyward. With a staggering rapidity, nature attacked!

Kat, Jessie and Clint stared at Sylvanis, clearly understanding something was wrong, but not knowing what.

Before Sylvanis could explain what she was feeling, the ground began to shake. The building began to shake. Creaks and groans reverberated around the room as the floor bulged and cracked.

"Earthquake?" Clint's voice held a good deal of concern.

Sylvanis could only shake her head.

"We need to get out of this building. Now!" she told them.

Unexpectedly, a thick branch jutted through the floor, knocking a table over as it pushed upward. Screams and shouts of alarm began as more and more vegetation began to emerge from the floor and walls.

They all stared at the branch as it pushed against the corner of the ceiling and wall, plaster falling in chunks as it burrowed through.

"Yeah, I'm gonna agree with you there," Kat said, already moving as she spoke. Panic gripped the restaurant. Some people began hiding under tables, thinking it an earthquake. Others were already making their way toward the exit, while others were heading back into the hotel lobby, presumably to go back to their rooms.

Kat threaded through the disorganized mob of panicked people and Sylvanis followed, right on her heels. Clint and Jessie were right behind her.

As they broke out into the bright sunlight of the afternoon the full horror of what was happening hit them.

All around, trees were sprouting. Their tangled mass of branches and thick trunks were tearing up sidewalks and streets. Buildings surrounding them were under assault as their walls were no barrier against Kestrel's growth spell.

Far off to their right came a loud screeching and crashing sound. To Sylvanis' shock, a three-story parking garage tumbled apart. Sections, like cut pieces of cake, broke off and collapsed into piles of rubble.

From the sounds of some of the other buildings around them, including their hotel, it wouldn't be the last to collapse.

"What is happening?" Kat stared at her with wild eyes.

"It's Kestrel. She's doing this."

"How do we stop it?" Jessie peered up at their hotel. Many of his men were out in the city, looking for Kestrel and the others. She had no idea where Hank, Ben, Stephanie, Jason and Mike were. Sylvanis wasn't worried about most of them. A collapsing building wouldn't be enough to kill them. Ben, though . . . She pursed her lips. Nothing could be done about it. She could only hope whoever was with him would understand the danger and see to his safety. She had more important things to take care of.

"We can't," she told them flatly. "However, this use of power has revealed Kestrel's location to me." She looked at the three of them, fire in her eyes. "I know where she is."

Kestrel reveled in the power she unleashed upon this city. All around her, buildings had begun to succumb to the damage caused by rapidly growing trees. With her head tilted skyward she gave out a throaty, joyful laugh as the energy thrummed through her, pricking her skin.

She would do this to every city! She would turn nature into a weapon and civilization would fall! This, however, was only part of the plan. Turning her head, she peered back to Blain and gave him a curt nod. Immediately, Blain raised the radio to his mouth.

"Now!"

Corey Tay was a big man, broad of shoulder and tall. His jet-black hair lay tousled upon his head. Lantern jawed and hawk-nosed he had an impressive, if somewhat unpleasant facial features. His skin, dark from long hours working outside showed faint creases from too much sun. He had been a worker at T & G Logging, one of the largest logging companies in Eastern Texas. *Had* been a worker, because not long-ago, monsters attacked their establishment and turned his world upside down.

Now, he was under the control of the True Werecroc, Gordon. Corey had been at the holding facility outside of Houston when the shift had come upon him under the mental guidance from Gordon. He and many others had escaped their imprisonment and had been whisked away by members of E.A.R.t.H., the eco-terrorist group Corey had only passing knowledge of before this.

They had all been taken to a compound deep in a forested area somewhere miles away from nowhere. Over the next few days they were fed, clothed and were given their instructions. And while Corey had been thankful for being rescued from the government holding facility, he couldn't help feeling he had been moved from one imprisonment to another.

His instructions went against everything he felt strongly about and yet, he had no will in the matter. Gordon controlled him absolutely. He had railed against the control at the beginning. Fought with every ounce of strength, both physical and mental, to break free of Gordon's control, but it had all been for naught. Gordon had squashed his attempt, along with many others in those first few days.

Corey had at least something to be thankful for. He wasn't under Blain's control. Gordon seemed apathetic about his control. He used it as necessary tool to accomplish their goals. Blain, on the other hand, clearly relished in controlling others.

Corey had seen some of the more attractive, younger women being commanded to join him in the building he used for his living quarters. There had been little doubt in Corey's mind as to what Blain made those women do. He had seen them later, crying or staring off blankly as if their minds were now detached from their bodies.

Corey wanted to kill the motherfucker. If he could, he would rip his ugly, smug face right off. But he couldn't. Gordon wouldn't let him. Instead, he now stood outside the black iron fence surrounding the White House.

Gordon had made him group leader. Corey believed it a perverse joke to have done so, because after explaining their job, Corey had verbally defended his country. Now, he was here as the leader of a group of Weres that would attack the home of the leader of the free world.

There were twelve of them. It seemed ludicrous for twelve people to try an assault on the White House, one of the most heavily guarded buildings in the world, but they were not ordinary people. They were Weres. They were all but unstoppable monsters.

But they weren't. Corey knew. He had seen gunmen take out one of the Weres escaping from the holding facility. Concentrated fire at the head could cause enough damage to kill one of them. Somehow, those soldiers had understood. If so, there was a possibility the Secret Service would be aware as well.

Corey did not doubt the intelligence of those running the government. Well, maybe he doubted some in Congress, but the men and women of the intelligence community and the military, he didn't doubt. They would have come to understand the threat these monsters posed and would have figured out a way to deal with them.

He assumed that was why they had all been held at the facility. Not for the first time though, Corey wondered as to why they hadn't all simply been killed. True, he couldn't fathom the government ordering the murder of hundreds of innocent people. But, knowing what they would become . . . Well, perhaps they hadn't quite understood the threat after all. Corey had no doubt they would understand after today. He also held no illusions as to their fate. Twelve of them would be devastating. Disastrous on a scale not seen since maybe 9/11 or the Oklahoma City bombing.

But they were not meant to survive this. They would all be cut down. They were only a message. A warning about what will happen. A taste of the damage they were going to unleash as more and more Weres were created.

Corey stared at the stark white building. It seemed quite a distance across that lawn, a wide expanse of well-tended green grass and manicured trees and bushes. In many ways, it would soon be a killing field.

Corey caught sight of a pair of uniformed patrol officers watching him. He realized he had been concentrating on the White House for perhaps, a little too long. After all, he had no camera to take pictures. He wasn't eating or snacking on anything, only staring off at the building. It must have seemed a little suspicious. Not to mention, he had a radio clipped at his waist.

He saw they were conferring, and one brought a radio up to his mouth and spoke into it. The sounds of traffic and people made it hard, even for Corey's new enhanced hearing, to pick up what they said.

He decided it wasn't good, as the two men began approaching him. Blain's voice came over the radio.

"Now!"

Corey sent the men a heart wrenching look of apology for what he now had to do and shifted.

They had practiced shifting at the compound in order to master it and to shift almost instantaneously. The pain, still sharp, hurt, but Corey dismissed it.

Screams of those on the sidewalk next to him rang out into the air. Immediately, the two officers had their weapons drawn and were shouting at him to get down. One shouted into his radio for backup.

Screams and shouts began to echo up and down the long walk lining this side of the street as others of his kind shifted on his cue.

"Remain discreet until we give you the signal," Gordon's commands rang through his mind. "If, you are discovered or confronted in any way before, shift and kill as many people as you can as you make your way into the White House. It is unlikely the president will remain in the building once the attacks take place. If you can find him, cut him, don't kill. If not, injure as many office personnel as you can. Kill all opposition."

Corey charged the two officers. One of them turned and ran. The other opened fire, striking Corey twice before he attacked. Corey had little heart to kill anyone, but the pressure upon his will was undeniable. He would kill this man, but he would do it quickly.

With a swift slash of his claws, he opened the man's throat, cutting through the jugular, windpipe, larynx and the carotid artery, sending the man's life blood in cascading waterfalls down the front of his uniform.

Corey's reptilian hide healed quickly from the shots and he took a moment to look around. Pedestrians fled, though many were across the street, their phones out, recording or photographing what happened.

Sirens began to peel in the city, and another trumpeted from the White House. Up and down the sidewalk, his team made their way to where he stood. Four Boars and seven other Crocs moved toward him.

Without warning, a car popped the curb and careened into two members of his team. The attack had come as such a surprise, they had been knocked back and the car continued forward until it crushed them against the iron fence.

One Boar and one Croc were pinned against the fence, the hood of the car was buckled, and the aroma of anti-freeze poignant in the air. The rear tires of the car were spinning, burning the rubber tread as the car had nowhere to go.

For a moment, everyone stood frozen watching the tableau in shock. The two Weres caught were the first to recover. As one, they grabbed the front of the car, pushed back, causing the vehicle to lose ground, regardless of how much pressure the driver put on the pedal.

Then, with a silent agreeing look at each other, the two Weres heaved and tossed the car up and end over end to land on its roof. The Croc wasted no time. As the driver tried to open the wedged door, he leaped high and came down hard upon the undercarriage of the vehicle. With a crunch of metal and a shatter of glass, the car's roof caved in, trapping the driver inside.

The Boar followed suit, jumping onto the bottom of the car, smashing it further. The driver screamed for help. They ignored him and continued to slam themselves up and down on the car until the screams could no longer be heard.

Corey turned away in disgust.

His eyes trained back onto the Whitehouse. Even now, the grounds were a bustle of activity. Men converged on their side of the building. Corey knew his purpose.

With three full strides he launched himself at the iron fence, clearing it completely by turning his body lengthwise. Twisting in the air, he landed on his feet facing the people amassing across the lawn.

Thuds sounded all around him as the rest of the group made it up over the fence.

Bang, bang, clink, thunk. Someone shot at them from behind, but Corey ignored them. They would be irrelevant as soon as they moved closer to the House.

"Corey," came a warning from one of the Boars standing next to him. Lott, Corey thought his name was, pointed toward the House, but his arm angled upward.

Using his Were enhanced eyesight, Corey scanned where he pointed. Men were scrambling atop the building armed with long barreled rifles. *Snipers.* They needed to move!

Corey charged and the rest followed. They crossed the distance quickly in a thunderous charge, tearing up the ground as they ran. By the time they had reached the assembled Secret Service, the snipers were set and had begun shooting.

One of the Crocs had gone down, a sniper bullet had shattered his knee, causing him to fall and tumble. Corey knew he would be back up though. Those types of wounds, while slowing, were not debilitating. The wall of guns before them was a little more intimidating.

Two lines of gunmen faced them. Kneeling in front were men brandishing shotguns and handguns, while those behind had assault rifles. When they were no more than hundred yards away, the men opened fire. Corey felt aflame as bullet after bullet sliced through his hide.

Healing as he ran, he sent as many bullets back out of his skin as those that entered and knew the others were hurting under the same onslaught.

A bullet pierced his eye, popping it as it bored through into his brain cavity. That took a little more concentration to repair than the other wounds, but he willed his body to reconstruct his eye and before long, he regained sight in the previously damaged socket.

He felt a sense of pride and horrible regret at the unwavering wall of men facing them. These men knew they would die. They had to. They had unloaded a shitload of bullets into these creatures and other than the one who had fallen, and got back up, they hadn't slowed. Yet, they remained. They held their ground. All to buy time for the ones they protected to get to safety.

Corey crashed into them. He made his attacks quick and precise. 'Kill all opposition' had been the command and he would do it. But these men would not suffer by his hands. He knew others would feel the same and make quick deaths of these men. There were others in the group who enjoyed the violence or would be so riled up by the pain of being shot as to lash out at those who had shot them. Though they wouldn't have shot them if they hadn't been here in the first place.

Fifty men or so were dispatched summarily, but not cleanly. The snipers had begun doing what Corey had feared. Two members of the group were down. Their heads riddled with holes. Whatever process the body used to heal itself, whatever autonomic responses the brain made to enact those repairs had been stopped by the repetitive wounds it had received.

Corey wasted no time. Motioning to the others, he ran for the closest door, hurtling into it. It buckled but held. He moved aside as one of the Boars charged it, slamming into it. The door and the frame shook from the impact, bent from the collision, but still, it held.

They had been warned about the reinforced doors and already had a plan in place. The Boar who had hit it, quickly moved aside as another Boar threw himself at the door. At last, the door broke away from its frame and hung askew.

Lightning quick, they ducked into the building, knocking the door from its hinges. By the time the remaining ten had passed, the door lay upon the floor.

Upon entering the building, they split up into pairs. The man Corey had been assigned to pair up with had been one of the men killed outside. Instead, a Boar joined him, and Corey couldn't remember his name. In all honesty, he hadn't tried to get to know anyone at the compound. He hadn't wanted to be there and had seen no reason to socialize with the rest of them.

They turned a hall and ran into two more Secret Service agents. Before Corey could react, the Boar plowed ahead, goring one man on a tusk before slamming him against the wall in a sickening thud. Reaching out with a clawed hand, he dragged it across the man's abdomen eviscerating him in a gush of blood and entrails.

And like that, they were past them.

Corey felt sick to his stomach. Those men had died trying to protect the President and others here in the White House. They didn't deserve to die.

The Boar took the lead and after turning down another hallway, they entered a long one which held dozens of office doors. People were milling about in the hallway, looking one way and another. They knew there had been a threat to the White House, but Corey doubted they believed it would ever get this far.

They were wrong.

One man turned in their direction when they came around the corner and yelled, "What the fuck?"

People turned to look at the man, and in doing so, got a decent look at what he saw.

That is when the screams began.

With a growl, the Boar took off down the hall. Like a stampeding bull he barreled into the fleeing people. Corey followed, somewhat slower. If the Boar wanted to do as they had been instructed, Corey would leave him to it. He wasn't actually refusing the commands, because he couldn't. But there seemed to be some gray area which allowed Corey to not try hard complying to those commands, and since the Boar preceded him, Corey could avoid hurting anyone.

The Boar whirl-winded through the panicked crowed. He slashed out with his claws, cutting and slicing. With quick thrusts of his head, he jabbed others, puncturing them enough to injure them but not kill them.

Men and women reeled away from them, bleeding and crying out as they went. The hallway was narrow, leaving them nowhere to go.

They passed by an office and Corey made the mistake of looking inside. Two people were huddled there, backed up against the corner of the room. The Boar had already passed. They had been commanded to injure every civilian they saw.

Corey couldn't ignore the command.

Reluctantly, he entered the office. The two women cowering inside desperately tried to move farther away from him, though they were as far away as they could.

Corey closed on them. They scrambled away, pushing at the floor with their feet and flailing at him with their hands. Tears flowed down their cheeks. The older woman shook her head in disbelief, mouthing 'No, no, no."

His heart broke for them, but he could do nothing. While they flailed at him, he took the opportunity to strike out with his claws, cutting them. They were small slices, barely breaking the surface of their skin to draw blood. It was all that was necessary. Or so he had been told.

Drawing himself up, he stared down at the two women who were now crying audibly, holding their injured arms.

"If I were you. I would kill yourself as soon as possible. If not, you will end up like me."

He turned and left them there. Nothing in the commands given to him, prohibited him from telling them the truth. He would tell them all, though he doubted any would listen.

Najeen Swat sat with her friends at a table in the food court of the Mall of America. Becky spoke to Amber about Chad Kartner, the blond-haired cutie who sat next to her in Chemistry.

Najeen barely paid attention, since this was Becky's fifth crush in almost an equal number of weeks, and instead watched the people in the mall. The mall, as per usual at this time, was packed. It always seemed crazy to her how many people spent their days at a mall.

*You mean like what you are doing?*

"Have you seen his butt, though?" Becky closed her eyes tight and tilted her head back with a serene smile on her face. "It is sooooo perfect!"

Najeen shook her head in amusement. She had seen Chad's butt and she had to admit it was pretty fine.

An interesting grouping off to the side of the food court caught her attention. A dozen people, mainly men, were clustered around each other, but weren't engaging with others in their group. Instead, it looked like they were all waiting for something.

She frowned. *Maybe it will be a flash mob? Wouldn't that be something to see?* She had never seen a flash mob. She wondered if they would do some sort of song and dance.

One of the men, she noticed, had a radio clipped to his belt which he kept fiddling with nervously. She smiled slightly. She would be nervous to perform in front of all these people too.

Suddenly, the man started and peered down at the radio. When he glanced back up, impossibly, his eyes met hers. Even across the distance she could see the emotion carried there. Sadness. Resignation and maybe — horror?

Goosebumps rose on her skin and the hair at the nape of her neck rose. This was no flash mob.

The man turned away from her, then looked back at the rest of the group he stood with. Then something happened. The bodies of the men and women began to alter, contort, shift and reform. The people sitting closest to them stood and staggered back from them in alarm, knocking over chairs and tables. Within moments, a dozen humanoid looking beasts stood in a cluster within the food court.

What happened next became a nightmarish tableau. The monsters separated, attacking anyone in sight. Screams and yells of fear and alarm permeated the food court. Becky and Amber had already jumped up. Amber screamed, 'Oh my God, oh my God' over and over. Najeen sat, frozen.

She couldn't believe what she saw. It was all so unreal. These creatures couldn't exist. It had to be some kind of stunt, or prank. Somehow, those people had used sleight of hand or visual tricks to put on monster outfits.

She knew it wasn't true, but she couldn't mistake what she was seeing, and her brain worked furiously to come up with something which made sense.

One of the creatures made its way over toward their table. Becky grabbed her arm, trying to get her to move, but she was leaden. Becky pleaded with her, begging her to go. Her voice sounded far away, distant as if down a long tunnel. All Najeen could focus on was this thing . . . this monster slicing its way toward her.

Remotely, she realized Becky had let go of her arm and she could no longer hear her. In a fog, she looked around, but Becky and Amber were nowhere in sight.

*They left me.* She couldn't blame them. Any sane person should be running away right now. Instead, she sat there, waiting for the beast to arrive.

When it did, it was like standing right next to the road, or beside a railway track. The creature hurled by her, sucking the air out of her lungs as it passed. It didn't even acknowledge her. It only reached out as if by instinct and dragged a claw across her bare arm.

It burned and she gasped. Warm fluid ran down her arm while her shorts became soaked with the release of urine as she peed herself. Death had come for her. Then passed her by. She lived. Everyone lived. Those monsters had weaved their way through running and screaming people and had hurt them all. Had hurt them, but like her, had left them alive.

Najeen peered around. People were clutching bleeding arms, legs, scratched torsos and abdomens, and while there was plenty of blood, no one lay unmoving.

Nervous laughter crept up on her. First a little, then more. She began to laugh hysterically, while tears ran down her face in a steady stream. Others joined her. The laughter sounded maniacal and yet so needed.

In the coming days, news spread of countless other attacks perpetrated like the one at the Mall of America. There had been an attack on Wall Street leaving hundreds of brokers injured. Dozens of these monsters appeared on the streets of the Las Vegas strip, killing dozens of police officers and security guards and injuring hundreds of tourist and street workers. Even the Kennedy Space Center had been attacked! Many NASA scientists had been wounded, but none killed.

There had been rumors of an attack on the White House. The White House had been circumspect about confirming the attack and how successful it had been. However, there had been plenty of internet videos showing how successful it had been.

Najeen couldn't watch them. Not after what had happened to her. So many people hurt, but not killed. It made no sense to her. She had gone to the hospital of course, but she had lied about how she had gotten cut. She had told her parents it had been on a sharp piece of metal she had accidently dragged her arm across while walking next to an old fence.

She didn't know why she had lied about her injury. Becky and Amber had made it out of the mall safely and their parents had called her parents. She had told them she had fled immediately after Becky and Amber had left her and she had hurt her arm as she had run.

If her parents had been suspicious of her altered story, they didn't press her. They had doubtless been so relieved she lived; they didn't want to interrogate her.

*I'm alive!*

The next day, Najeen died from a heart attack.

# *Chapter forty-Two*

What should have been an easy route to traverse had since been made almost impossible for the four of them. Streets were clogged with abandoned vehicles which had nowhere to go now buildings had collapsed all around them.

Clint couldn't help but marvel at what had once been a road clustered with shops and high rises now appeared decimated and replaced with towering oaks, cypresses and walnut trees. It reminded Clint of those pictures he had seen in grade school of the mighty sequoias in California. With trunks wider than an average home, these trees could match the highest skyscraper.

If it wasn't for the devastation they had caused to Houston, they would have been beautiful to behold.

Their decision to forgo the car had been the right one as massive root systems had fissured the asphalt, leaving many of the roads undrivable. It meant going on foot, but they would have had to anyway.

People were still running around in panicked frenzy. Looting had begun as shops were in ruins, so their wares were taken without difficulty. Clint had to fight the impulse to shift and run the fools off. It was always a shame people reverted to acting like this in a crisis. They should be helping each other, not ruining people's livelihoods.

In the distance, deep rumbling sounds and earth trembles could still be heard and felt as Kestrel's circle of power worked its way farther out, destroying buildings as it went.

Ahead, a veritable forest had sprung up, clogging the way. Pieces of debris clung to branches high above. Metal girders created twisted ornaments hanging from outstretched limbs.

Screams for help came from inside broken buildings as they made their way. As much as Clint knew they should stop and help these people, they would be helping more people in the long run if they stopped Kestrel. Pained expressions grew on the rest of the groups faces as they left people to their fates and he knew they mirrored his own.

After what seemed like an eternity, they arrived at a park. If there had been other people in the park earlier today, the madness surrounding the park had driven them away. Calls coming from loved ones trapped in buildings, or those at home wondering where their loved ones were, had emptied the park.

Sylvanis drove them on, deeper into the park. The sureness of her strides told Clint all he needed to know, and he didn't bother asking if she knew where they were going.

At last, they entered a clearing and Clint felt his rage flare up immediately.

Before them, in its center, waited Kestrel. She stood before them, naked, her arms held up toward the heavens. Her alabaster skin held a sheen of perspiration and she swayed slightly.

Behind her, the source of his rage. The man he knew to be the Boar, and another who, from Kat's descriptions would be the Croc. There were others in the clearing as well. Four other men roamed the edge of the forest. They had yet to see them.

Kestrel's eyes sprung open and she spied them across the clearing.

"No!" She pointed towards them and collapsed, falling to the soft grass.

Everything happened in an instant. Clint shifted, his Wolf hybrid form replaced his human form and he shot off after the Boar. Kat and Jessie shifted as one and moved to intercept the Croc.

481

Across the field, the Boar and Croc shifted and stepped between them and Kestrel's fallen form. The Croc motioned to the other men in the field and two of them shifted, both Crocs to attack them. The other two, a Boar and a Croc, went to stand over Kestrel.

The two Crocs were smaller than the True, but not by much.

Clint didn't care. The Croc set between him and the Boar and Clint would not be stopped. As the Croc came to him, Clint knew immediately this person was not a fighter. Maybe he didn't even want to be there but had been controlled to fight. While Clint felt pity for the man, it didn't change what Clint needed to do.

As they closed together, the Croc thrust out with his jaws to snap at Clint's head. Clint moved aside and thrust his claws upward burying them into the soft underside of the Croc's throat.

With a pivot, he pushed his back against the Croc's body, his hand still deep inside the beast's gullet. With a powerful thrust, he pulled the Croc over his shoulder as he bent at the waist, tossing him back the way they had come.

As the Croc flew away from him, Clint had managed to grab hold of the Croc's windpipe and esophagus in his claws, tearing them from its body as it sailed away from Clint. It wasn't a wound that would kill him, but he would be some time to heal.

Then the Boar slammed into him.

Jessie darted across the field, keeping pace with Kat. He marveled at his new body. In all his years in the corps, he had handled all manner of weaponry, some of the most powerful weapons mankind had invented even. And yet, they all seemed to pale in comparison to the weapon his body was now.

He could feel the power pulsing through his body as he ran. His clawed feet dug into the earth as he propelled himself forward. The bunching of his leg muscles with each stride made him think of nothing short of perfection. He didn't wield a machine for killing. He was the killing machine.

They barreled toward the two Crocs. The smaller one lay between them and the bigger one. Jessie would let Kat handle that one while he tackled the bigger one.

"I've got the big one in the back," he told her.

She growled at him. "No. You will attack the one in front."

Jessie found himself lining up with the smaller one.

*What the hell?* He tried to alter his course and found he couldn't. He wanted to. He tried to, but he still found himself moving to engage the smaller Croc.

He growled this time.

"What the fuck!"

"Just do it!" Kat commanded him again and he launched himself at the Croc. Anger clouded his mind, his thoughts a tangle and he attacked carelessly. As he collided with the Croc, he grabbed Jessie's arms and yanked them out wide. Lunging forward with his mouth he bit into the spot between Jessie's neck and shoulder, crunching down hard.

Jessie could feel his clavicle snap under the intense bite of the Croc. Terribly sharp teeth ripped into his fur covered skin, shredding as the Croc began to thrash his head, whipping Jessie around like a ragdoll.

Wildly, he began raking the Croc's underbelly with the claws on his feet. He could feel the hide parting as he tore into the beast. With one vicious thrash, the Croc released him, sending him flying to tumble across the ground, bouncing as he went. His shoulder joint jarred out of its socket as he hit. He came to a stop twenty feet or so away.

He hurt, but he knew his body would repair itself in time. He didn't heal as quick as Kat. He had observed that much in the time they had spent together. There was a definite difference between the level of power between

483

them which bothered Jessie. It bothered him more now it appeared Kat had some control over him. Somehow.

Pushing himself off the ground, he turned his head as a scaled-covered clawed foot slammed into his face. His mandible shattered and knocked loose. Pain seared through him as his nose broke. His sharp fangs were shattered and rocketed into the back of his throat.

Spinning away from the force of the blow, he immediately cleared his mind of all thoughts of pain and willed his body to heal as quickly as possible. His head lay turned away from the direction of the Croc, but he could feel the tremors of the ground as it closed on him.

This fight was not going well.

Kat knew Jessie was pissed. She had never intended to use her will on him. Wasn't supposed to, in fact. Sylvanis had wished to keep it secret from the new recruits. Though Sylvanis trusted them to help them win, she didn't truly trust them.

It seems she had learned a lot of this day and age in the short time she had been here.

Dismissing Jessie from her mind, *a problem for later,* she stared at the Croc she had fought before, its mouth agape, knife like teeth lining its long maw. Saliva dripped from it. *If there is a later.*

She couldn't let Jessie fight this monster. For one, she owed it a rematch. For another, Jessie would have been killed. From the corner of her eye, she saw Jessie launched into the air, tumbling across the ground as he hit. *He might still get killed.*

Focusing back on the Croc, she slowed her approach.

"Ah, I see . . ." he began.

"Shut the fuck up!" Kat cut him off.

He chuckled in wry amusement and moved on her.

She forgot how quick the bulky creature was. It came at her like an avalanche of scales and claws.

She leaped back to avoid the slash of his claws, but as it brought his claw around to swipe at her, it continued in its pirouette and whipped its longer tail out at her.

It collided with her side with an audible crunch. Her ribs snapped and she could feel their sharp ends dig into her internal organs. As surprised as she had been by the move, her instincts had still kicked in and she moved with the impact, lessening the damage. Somewhat.

With a roll, she hopped back on her feet and moved.

The Croc finished his turn, ready for her. She darted in so quick his attempt to swipe at her this time met nothing but air. Instead she was inside his reach. He was bigger than her. Taller. And she found herself under his jaw.

Bending at the knees, she jutted her hands straight out and dug into his underbelly as she launched herself upward. Slicing as she went, her head slammed into his throat. The impact jarred her head and neck, but she could hear the crunch of his esophagus as it collapsed in his throat.

Staggering back, the Croc reached up to grasp at his throat, making wheezing sounds as he drew air in and out. As his throat repaired itself, a deep growl reverberated from him and the glare he sent Kat's way made her a little weak in the knees.

Steeling herself, she waited for his attack. He didn't charge her like she thought he would. No. He stalked toward her. Holding his arms out slightly, claws bared, as he tipped his head down slightly so his eyes were focused on her face.

485

Like rolling waves, his muscles rippled under his scaled hide. The dark green scales reflected light from the sun overhead, giving them a glistening darkness.

Lashing her tail around behind her, she crouched and waited for him to close the distance. His hulking shape came closer and closer. She knew there was no backing down. No backing away from this fight. She had chosen to meet this threat head on, and she would. He needed to be stopped.

She wasn't sure she could do it.

# Chapter Forty-Three

Watching everything unfold before her, Sylvanis kept her eyes focused on Kestrel. Still lying naked on the grass, she began weakly trying to rise. She was weak. It didn't surprise Sylvanis. The amount of power Kestrel had unleashed on Houston would weaken any Druidess.

The two Weres stayed guarding her, though they appeared eager to join the fight.

Well, she would oblige them.

*"Talamh nathair"*

Reminiscent of her first battle with Kestrel, a column of earth rose from the ground. Dirt, stone and roots climbed upward right behind the two Weres. The sound of its rise caused them to turn.

Ten feet. Twenty feet. The earthen snake rose, twisting upon itself and fell with alarming speed toward the Boar guarding Kestrel. Barely jumping aside, the Boar missed being crushed as the snake battered the ground.

It did not stop though. Instead it lashed out to the side, crashing into the Croc who stood there, jaws opened in surprise. He was even more surprised when it hit him. The Croc went soaring through the air.

As quickly as it had struck the Croc, it darted back toward the Boar, who deftly sidestepped the attack. With scant concentration, Sylvanis kept the snake on the attack, keeping the Weres at bay.

She began to cross the field, intent on Kestrel, who had seen her now, still trying to stand. Sylvanis pulled out her knife. It reminded her of the time two thousand years ago when she believed she had ended Kestrel's life and the threat she represented.

Instead, she had caused the chain of events which had led to Kestrel escaping death and coming back here and now. In response, Sylvanis had taken steps to follow her. It had been a desperate move, but one she had believed had been necessary. She wasn't so sure now it had been.

Yes, Kestrel had already caused great suffering, but what had Sylvanis done to stop her? She had tried, of course, but Kestrel had always been one step ahead of her. Thanks in large part because of Syndor, Samuel now. She gave a passing thought as to where Samuel might be. It seemed odd he wasn't there at Kestrel's side during her weakest moment.

She could end this, now. Kestrel was so weakened by her spell; she could not draw upon her magic to protect her. She wouldn't be capable of putting up much of a physical fight either.

With a grim determination, she weaved her way through the fighting Weres, hoping they would at least buy her time to get this done.

Clint felt the tusks of the Boar pierce his back, one puncturing his kidney. The blunt force trauma of the Boar's head broke his back as it hit. And he sailed through the air.

He focused his mind immediately on healing his back and almost had the concentration jarred from him as he landed. As feeling came back to his lower limbs, he rolled on instinct.

With a crash, the Boar landed in the exact spot his head had been. The hooves would have caved in his skull if he had landed on Clint. Bouncing back to his feet, he wheeled toward the Boar who sneered at him.

"I've enjoyed your girlfriend, you know? She has the nicest ass I've ever had the pleasure of buggering."

Clint growled feeling the fury build inside him. He could feel the animalistic hunger to kill rise. It took all his will to stamp it back down. He would not let himself become lost again. Never again. Too often he had allowed his rage to cloud his thoughts. He knew the asshole baited him. Clint wondered if he could get as good as he gave.

"Really?" Clint cocked his head. "Even better than your mom's?"

Clint got the answer he was looking for, but perhaps not the answer he wanted as the Boar roared with furious anger and launched himself at Clint.

By now, Clint's body had repaired itself and he was ready to fight.

The ferocity which the Boar came at him frightened Clint. It reminded him of how he had been when he had gone wild. When he had lost all control over the Wolf inside and let it control his thoughts and actions. Remembering those times brought a strong sense of guilt which threatened to overwhelm him.

He had no time for guilt though as the Boar was upon him in seconds, lashing out with his claws. One raked Clint's abdomen, slicing through skin and muscle, but Clint had arched his body back to avoid being eviscerated.

As the other claw came in, Clint met it with a claw of his own, slicing into the Boar's wrist tendons, cutting them cleanly. The Boar roared again, this time in pain.

Clint didn't let up. Snarling, he bit down on the bicep of the same arm, his fangs ripping into flesh, muscle and scoring bone. With a yank, he ripped his head back, pulling off a meaty chunk of the Boar's arm muscle.

The Boar pulled away from him, grabbing his arm with his other hand to staunch the bleeding. Clint spat out the disgusting piece of flesh and renewed his attack.

Darting in, he slashed and cut with his claws, raking this way and that across the Boar's exposed flesh. With one arm useless for the moment, the Boar could do little to fend of his attacks. Which Clint had counted on.

Again, and again he struck, laying bare and flaying the Boar's skin and muscle. The Boar would heal, but if you damaged enough of him, he would be slow to heal everything. If you kept up the attacks, you could overwhelm the body to the point it would become vulnerable to more powerful attacks.

Muscle began rebuilding itself in the open wound of the Boar's arm, so he charged the Boar who continually gave ground beneath Clint's attack.

The Boar, intent on stopping Clint, reached out to grab at him. Clint went low, slicing the femoral artery in the Boar's leg as he ducked past, almost running on four limbs, then turned and snapped out with his jaws, closing on the Boar's hamstring. His sharp teeth sliced through it, and the Boar screamed and fell, losing the ability to put any weight on that foot.

Clint bounded up once again and rounded on the man who had taken his love from him. The beast who had done untold horrible things to her while Clint could do nothing to stop him. He would stop him today. He would free Sarah from this creature's control. Free her from being a Were in service to that bitch Kestrel and this monster.

Once again, instinct saved him as he hopped back from the attack from the Croc, now recovered from Clint's initial attack.

Clint roared. This fucker would delay him long enough for the Boar to heal. He couldn't let that happen. Clint leaped upon the back of the Croc as he passed by in his attempt to gore Clint.

Reaching up, he dragged his claws down the sides of the Croc's head, cutting through scaled hide and tearing open its eyeballs. The Croc thrashed around to rid itself of Clint, but he dug his claws in deep and all he managed to do was damage itself further.

As the thrashing slowed, Clint reached forward again and grabbed the Croc's upper jaw and he began pulling back with all his might. He could feel the Croc's maw fighting to close, but he leaned back and pulled harder.

The Croc staggered around, blind and in pain as it tried to figure out a way to free himself of Clint. With a violent roar which pierced the surrounding forest, sending birds squawking into the air, Clint put all his weight into a bone and tendon ripping pull.

With a snap, Clint felt the upper jaw pull lose from the lower one and he twisted and threw himself to the side. It made a disgusting tearing sound when the tendons and muscle ripped apart as Clint yanked the upper half of the Croc's face off.

With a crash, Clint fell backward, and the Croc collapsed on top of him, showering him with blood. Releasing the Croc, Clint scrambled out from underneath the massive weight of the Croc.

He didn't know if the Croc would heal, but for the moment, it lay there unmoving.

Turning, Clint glanced back to where he had left the Boar, hamstringed and prone.

He was neither now. Back on his feet, the Boar sized him up, growled and started forward.

*Oh, for fuck's sake.*

# *Chapter Forty-Four*

Kat tumbled to the ground, bleeding profusely from the severed forearm the Croc had just got done sending down its gullet. She was in a bad way. She had done little to the Croc. Mostly minor wounds which it had long since repaired.

Willing her body to repair the arm, she could feel the warmth as her body responded by first shunting off the blood and rebuilding her forearm. Stem cells flowed through her body to form bone cells, muscle cells, tissue and blood vessels. It was the most grievous wound she had ever received and while she believed she would heal; she hadn't needed to heal something so severe in previous fights.

The Croc dropped his gaze back toward her after tilting his head up to swallow down Kat's arm.

"Mmmm, yummy."

Kat didn't have it in her for some witty banter. She needed to bide some time while her arm healed.

The Croc must have sensed her plan as it began stalking toward her.

"Now, for the rest of you," he mused.

Kat scrambled back, trying to keep some distance between them, but the Croc continued to close the distance.

Snatching out with his clawed hand it grabbed at her ankle, dragged her closer and lifted her up into the air. She swiped at his arm but was unable to put enough power into the swings to do more than merely cut him superficially.

Instead, she went limp and poured every ounce of her will into her arm. The burning feeling of rapid healing, like a balm to her, confirmed her arm would heal. It simply needed to hurry the fuck up.

Lifting her high, he brought her almost to eye level so he could stare into her eyes. She watched in horror as first the sides of his mouth peeled back in a frightful smile, before he opened his jaws and tilted his head.

She got feeling back into her once missing hand and with a hard swing she lifted her upper torso up and latched onto the underside of the Croc's mouth. At last having something to use as support, she pulled down, hard on her leg, yanking it out of the Croc's grasp, and she could feel the ankle bone slip out of its socket as she did.

Letting go, she dropped down and tried to throw herself free.

It was too late. With a twist of his head, the Croc brought his maw down and around her midsection, biting deep into it. The power of the Croc's jaws closing around her, crushed her ribcage, and punctured her stomach and intestines. She could feel stomach acid leaking out into her body.

He continued to bear down on her with his jaws and she could do little but cry out in pain. Despite being used to having her body transition from Tiger to human and from human to Tiger, this pain was excruciating in comparison.

Pain lit up her insides as the bones of her ribs were squeezed into her lungs, punctured and deflated it. It was only a matter of time before her heart was crushed as well.

She would die. She had failed. All her training. Everything her parents had tried to prepare her for had all been for naught. She would die here in this park, eaten by a humanoid crocodile. If she could have laughed, she would have. If she had been told this would have been her fate a year ago, she would have died laughing at the ridiculousness of the notion. And yet, here she was.

The pain lessened now; she could feel her body losing the battle of healing the damage quicker than she received it.

Then everything went sideways. Trees, sky, ground, she hit the dirt with a groan. She could hardly move, but she managed to tilt her head enough.

The Croc fought someone else. *Jessie?*

$$\text{இ}$$

Lying on the ground with his face battered and broken, Jessie could do little but wait for the inevitable as the sounds of heavy footsteps came for him.

*What the fuck are you doing, Jessie? You have never given up this easily. Are you a marine or a fucking pussy!?* He recognized the voice in his head. It was the voice of his drill sergeant in the Corps.

He had been right though. Jessie always fought. He fought till he had nothing left. And that wasn't now.

Rolling farther away from the oncoming Croc, he managed to get his legs under him and stood, turning to face the Croc. He could feel the bones in his face knitting up and he peeled his lips back in a snarl.

Crouching, he waited for the Croc to come to him. The longer he had to heal, the better.

With measured steps, the Croc came at him, wary now Jessie had managed to recover from his initial attack.

"Come get me, you ugly motherfucker," Jessie taunted, waving him forward with his hand.

The moment the Croc started to charge him, Jessie darted forward, getting in close before the Croc could get ready. Ducking low under the Croc's grasp, he crossed his arms and brought them back out in a crisscross slash, digging deep into the softer underbelly of the Croc.

Tearing open the skin and muscle, Jessie was greeted with a pouring out of intestines, their reek accosting his keen sense of smell. Not wanting to lose his momentum, he choked back the bile rising in his own belly and snatched at the grayish twisting snake of the man's guts and sheared through them, leaving them in tatters.

The Croc roared and reared back – a mistake as it left its torso at Jessie's mercy.

He didn't show it any.

In what was without doubt the most disturbing and disgusting thing he had ever done, he reached into the Croc's torso and grabbed anything he could get his hands on and ripped it out. Stomach, liver and a few other things Jessie couldn't identify were dragged out and torn asunder by Jessie.

Wailing, the Croc swiped at him with a back hand, knocking him away. Jessie staggered, reeling from the blow. Recovering he readied himself for a counterattack, but instead the Croc fled, trailing pieces of his insides as he ran.

Spinning, he searched for Kat.

He gasped when he saw her being crushed in the mouth of the larger Croc. Without a second thought, he moved.

He crashed into the Croc at full speed, knocking the bigger beast over, and sending Kat flying. He pounced on the prone Croc, slashing and biting everywhere he could reach.

With no doubt in Jessie's mind he could stand up to this Croc alone, he attacked with everything he had. If it had beaten Kat, the strongest and ablest fighter he knew, as much as it hurt his ego, he knew he would fare no better. His best chance was to last long enough to do enough damage, or at least take as little damage as he could and give Kat time to heal.

With a powerful thrust, the Croc threw him off and Jessie managed to land on his feet and throw himself back on the Croc before the beast could fully rise. He managed to once again knock the Croc down and he launched his offensive all over again. Biting and clawing.

He tried to tear off a piece of flesh with his teeth when he felt enormous hands grasp either side of his head. Bit by bit, the hands pulled his head away from where they had been biting and Jessie could only watch in amazement at the power of this creature as he climbed to his feet, still holding Jessie's head between his massive claws.

His head ached with the intense pressure the Croc put on his skull. He didn't know how long his head would hold up to the crushing squeeze.

Snarling, he reached up and grabbed the wrists of the beast and punched his claws in between the tibia and fibula bones, twisting he snapped the smaller bones in each arm.

He felt the pressure release on his head, and he dropped to the ground, staggering. The Croc moved away from him, creating some distance so he could heal his broken bones. Jessie couldn't give him the chance.

Charging, he launched himself at the Croc, claws out. The Croc grappled with him and Jessie used his weight to push back, snapping the healing wrists further.

The Croc snapped out, and Jessie had to duck and dodge to avoid getting his head bitten off as he forced the Croc back. With a sweep of his leg, he knocked the Croc off his feet and Jessie went down with him, landing with a heavy thud on top of the Croc.

This close to the Croc's body, he couldn't snap at Jessie with his mouth. Jessie continued to yank and twist on the Croc's wrists, breaking them again and again as they repaired themselves.

As much as he incapacitated the Croc, he wasn't doing much of anything else. He couldn't further damage him from where he was, but if he released the Croc, he would be giving him a chance to heal.

For the moment, it was all he could do.

Then the Croc managed to get his tail under him and leverage himself over, tossing Jessie off, before landing on him. The only thing saving him was

496

the Croc could not support himself with his arms as his wrists were still broken, but now he was on top and Jessie's hands were pressed to the ground, unable to twist his hands to keep breaking the Croc's wrists.

Soon, his wrists would heal, and he would be in a position to bite Jessie. Jessie did not want to be there when that happened.

# Chapter Forty-Five

Sylvanis flowed across the plush grass as she went to Kestrel. Kestrel's bodyguards were now preoccupied with trying to survive against a twenty-foot column of stone and dirt which attacked them with the quickness of an adder.

Kestrel watched her approach with murder in her eyes and perhaps, a little bit of fear. She had managed to rise and now backed away from Sylvanis.

"You have failed, Kestrel. All your threats. All your plans have failed." Sylvanis shook her head. "What a waste. You had such potential to do good. To really make a change."

"I have made a change!" Kestrel spat at her. "Look at what I've done!" She motioned to the city which surrounded the park. So many of the city's skyline were gone now, the tall buildings nothing more than rubble and instead, mighty trees had taken their place.

Sylvanis stared around at the devastation. "Yes. Look at what you have done," she replied with scorn. "You have used your magic to raise mighty, majestic trees, the likes of which no one has ever seen before. You raised them, and now, when you are gone, they will cut them all down and build their city once again." She shook her head again.

"You have wasted your magic. You could have used it to create marvels in places which had already been set aside for the appreciation of nature. But instead you used it to destroy something which will only be built again. It is what they do. This is their home." Sorrow tinged her voice. "Can't you see that? You destroyed their homes and they will not let that stand."

"They won't have a choice. This is only the beginning. I will move to city after city and nature will rise again and again to take back what they stole from nature in the first place."

Sylvanis continued to stalk Kestrel. "There is no going back, Kestrel. Humans are animals too. They are part of nature. What you are doing is tantamount to destroying a beaver's den because it killed trees to build it. It is not our place to decide which animal to condemn and which to embrace. Either they all have their rights, or they don't."

Kestrel sneered at her. "You are a fool, Sylvanis. You always have been. All humans do is destroy. They have no respect for the world around them."

Sylvanis cocked her head and offered a small nod. "Some don't. That is true. But many, many others do." She realized she was back to this same old argument she had been having with Kestrel since before the first war. It was circular and pointless. They would never agree.

"This is done, Kestrel. You haven't the strength to fight me." She moved forward with her knife. *"Ruemhach trahb."*

Roots sprung up from beneath Kestrel, snaking around her bare ankles and wrapping up her calves and thighs. Kestrel yelled and tried to pull at the dirty, hoary roots holding her fast, but she hadn't the strength.

"It doesn't matter what you do to me, Sylvanis. My followers will continue to do what needs to be done!" Kestrel remained defiant. She ceased fighting and stood tall.

Sylvanis couldn't help but admire the woman, so strong-willed, so sure of herself and her purpose. If only she had been on the right side.

"With you gone, Kestrel, it will only be a matter of time before your people evaporate like morning dew, just like they did the last time. They have no heart for this war. They only fight for power, or money, but they care little about what you believe."

She caught a flash of uncertainty in Kestrel's eyes.

499

"Yes. You know it to be true. Syndor may be the only one who truly believes as you do."

The uncertainty fled, instead, Sylvanis caught a hint of pain in Kestrel's eyes.

*Had something happened to Syndor?*

It would be useful to know if they still had the Snake to deal with, but she doubted she would get any confirmation from Kestrel. That she had shown even a hint as to Syndor's fate surprised Sylvanis.

Stepping up to Kestrel, Sylvanis looked her in eyes.

"For us, it hasn't even been a year since I killed you. I have already used my magic to determine if there are any spells lingering on you like the last time. I will not be fooled again. This last spell required too much of your power, and so, you have not cast a contingency spell on yourself this time. There will be no resurrection for you."

Sylvanis steeled herself for what she was about to do. Again.

"This time. When I execute you, you will stay dead."

With a quick motion, Sylvanis brought her knife up and plunged it into Kestrel's heart.

Clint stared at the Boar and the Boar stared back.

Resigned, Clint extended his claws and moved to engage the Boar. His fury had abated and now he was simply tired. He had been so close to beating this fucker. So close and now, he would need to try and take him out again.

When they came together, neither one held back. Tooth, claw and tusk. Clint slashed and snapped while the Boar bashed and jabbed. It all became a blur as they each tried to cause as much damage as they could.

At length, they broke apart and Clint staggered back. His left ear had been ripped off and the side of his skull gleamed pale white from where the flesh had been torn. His right thigh had been ripped to shreds, the left side torn into tatters, strips of flesh and muscle hung like streamers at a party.

The Boar fared little better; Clint had somehow managed to rip one of his tusks out, leaving a gaping bloody hole. His left arm clung to his shoulder by mere tendons causing it to flop and spin around, tangling up the thin threads, before unravelling in a quick spin.

Panting, they faced off against each other again. Clint could feel his ear growing back and the muscles in his leg begin their repair. As he watched, a new tusk began to emerge from the face of the Boar and his arm began to knit.

Movement off to his left at the edge of the clearing caught his attention. Figures began to emerge. Crocs and Boars, and Clint's heart sank.

With a snort, the Boar bared his teeth.

Jessie lay pinned beneath the Croc, his arms out wide, held there by the sheer weight of the Croc's body. When at last, the Croc could put weight on his arms, he rose up, his snout inches above Jessie's own nose.

Spittle dripped down onto his face and mouth and he turned his head to avoid its foulness from leaking inside his mouth. The Croc's maw parted, and Jessie saw dozens of razor-sharp teeth like sentries guarding a dark and fetid cave.

"I kind of like his face, so leave it the fuck alone."

As one, he and the Croc turned their heads. Kat stood there, claws on hips and her tiger tail slashing angrily back and forth in the air. For a moment, the Croc eased up on the pressure and Jessie slammed his head forward, taking the beast right the base of his snout.

With the impact, the Croc reeled back, and Jessie used that moment to push the Croc off him.

Scrambling to his feet he tottered over toward Kat.

"You like my face?" He gave her an awkward smile.

She gave him a withering look.

"More than I like his." She jerked a thumb at the Croc who, now back on his feet, faced them warily. Alone, they had given him trouble. Together, he must understand, he didn't stand a chance.

Figures stepped out from the trees behind the Croc. It took Jessie a moment to realize they were more Weres, and not one of them was on their side.

"Shit!" Kat said perfunctorily.

Jessie couldn't agree more.

# *Chapter Forty-Six*

"*Fuasgail.*" With that command, the roots released Kestrel's body and she collapsed to lay on the soft earth. Sylvanis sank to her knees beside her. Kestrel had a faraway look in her eyes, as if she was no longer there, but instead enjoying a vista of some far-off place.

Reaching out, Sylvanis clasped the hilt of her knife in her right hand. With a quick yank, she pulled the knife from Kestrel's bare chest. Blood bubbled out of the wound and ran in rivulets down Kestrels chest and side.

"I'm sorry it has come to this again, Kestrel. I wish . . ." she faltered, hanging her head down, her blonde hair cascading around her face, tickling against Kestrel's skin. "I wish things could have been different between us. I wish you had never forced me to do these things. I was not made for killing. I was made for growing things. For living things."

A tear formed in the corner of her eye, pooled and fell to the earth. A deep sadness fell over Sylvanis. Sadness, and relief. She had been reborn for this, and now it was done. Now she could rest. Maybe. Just maybe, she could return to her parents and try to be the daughter they had wanted.

She knew, even as she thought it, that it would never be. They should have a little baby girl to grow with, to teach, to discover with. Not a grown woman two millennia old.

What she would do with her life now, she didn't know. Well, the rest of the Trues still needed to be dealt with — the Boar, Croc, Rat and the Snake, though she wondered if Syndor had already been dealt with. She couldn't imagine any other fate for him that would have caused Kestrel to have shown any pain.

She sighed. The war was not over. Not really. Merely a battle won.

Laughter startled her, and she glanced up.

Kestrel stared right at her, an amused smile on her face.

"What?" Sylvanis began and watched in horror as the wound in Kestrel's chest closed.

Bones broke and Kestrel's body began to alter.

Sylvanis tried to climb quickly to her feet, but a clawed hand shot out and grabbed her wrist. The skin of her arm parted as a sharp talon dragged a furrow through it.

Sylvanis stared at the hand holding her arm. Pink-skinned fingers ended in sharp claws. Brown fur covered the arm from the wrist up. As Sylvanis' eyes moved up the arm, she met Kestrel's gaze.

Beady black eyes stared back at her. Gone was the alabaster skin. Gone were the high cheekbones, the full lips and slight upturned nose. Now, it was a rat's face looking at her.

*No. It's not possible.* In no scenario did Sylvanis ever believe Kestrel would allow someone to have control over her as she would have to in order to become a Were. She would never trust anyone that much. It just wasn't possible.

Only it was. The proof was staring back at her. Worse, Kestrel had cut her. Had infected her.

Kestrel's rat face parted in a wicked, needle-like toothed grin.

"Got you."

# *EPILOGUE*

Not for the first time the rage overtook her, but she had little to destroy anymore. The bank of monitors which had been set up for Shae to watch the news had long since been smashed. Shattered screens and consoles still buzzed with power, but they held no windows to the outside world. There were no windows anywhere.

After Samuel had left her here, she had reveled in having a place of her own. There were TV shows and movies to watch, so much of which she had been unable to see while she had been held prisoner and experimented on by Daniel and the organization he worked for.

There was plenty of food as well. Microwave dinners, frozen meats, instant potatoes and other instant meals. Hundreds of packages of powdered milk and fruit drinks, cases of soda and gallons of coffee grounds.

She spent a day or two getting comfortable with being in the bunker and spending time just . . . doing nothing. Oh, she spent time watching the news for hours on end waiting for any reference to Kestrel and the rest of the Weres. Afterall, she had been brought here to do just that.

Eventually though, she got bored and went to go outside to get some sun. Only, the door would not open. She pressed her hand against the identification screen, and it beeped angerly at her and turned red. Again, and again she put her hand on it, and again and again it refused to identify her as someone the door would open to.

She immediately tried to call Kestrel, but her phone had no reception. She knew that of course. She had discovered that the first day, but she had thought nothing of it because if she needed to ever make a call, she could go up to the surface and call from there.

Only she couldn't.

She wasn't worried — at first. She thought it must be a computer error. Some technical issue as to why the scanner didn't recognize her. Everything would be taken care of as soon as Samuel came back. Or better yet, when Kestrel came to visit her.

Days went by. Then more days passed, and no one came. No one attempted to contact her. No checking up on her. Nothing.

Still, she tried not to panic. They were busy. Kestrel fought a war. Shae couldn't expect her to drop everything and come and visit her. She would have to be patient.

After two weeks, she didn't believe there was anything wrong with the scanner. A dark realization crept up on her. She fought against it. Denied it. Kestrel was her friend. She had told Shae she had been like a daughter, or a younger sister she never had. They had shared so much.

A month went by and Shae knew she had been betrayed. Worse than betrayal because not only had Kestrel betrayed her, but she had trapped her here in this bunker. And though it was far more comfortable than her last prison, it was a prison, nonetheless.

Even after knowing what being imprisoned had done to Shae, Kestrel had still done it.

She tore apart her room in a fit of rage. Shifting into her hybrid form, she smashed the TV monitors, shattered the table and broke the chairs.

When her anger at long last simmered down, she had gone to work on the door to the outside. With her enhanced strength she hammered the door,

506

again and again. With all her strength she battered at it, breaking her hands and wrists, healing, and punching it again until she broke them all over again.

It remained undamaged.

Whatever metal had been used to create the door remained impervious to her attacks, even with her increased strength.

She gave up on the door and moved to the walls and ceiling. For days, she tried everything to open a hole in a wall or the ceiling. And for days, she failed.

At last, she resigned herself to her cage. There was no escape. She was trapped here, in this prison and she could do nothing about it.

Kestrel had used her and discarded her as her real mother had. Just like Anne had, just as George had. Kestrel had befriended Shae. Treated her with kindness and caring and Shae had grown to care for Kestrel as well. For so long she had been devoid of real human interaction. Real caring interaction, and so Shae had let her walls drop.

She had begun to trust for the first time in years. Not only trust, but care about someone. The more time she and Kestrel had spent together, the closer they had become. They had sat up late into the night and did things Shae believed actual girls did when they hung out together. It had been the most normal her life had been since those early days with Anne.

It had been one of those nights Kestrel had told her what her important job would be. Kestrel knew she hadn't wanted to be a part of the war and had told her many times she had a different job for her.

When she told Shae all she needed to do was give her lycanthropy, Shae had been relieved. Despite the new trust she had felt for Kestrel, she still feared the woman would ask her to do something she knew Shae didn't want to do but would leverage their friendship so Shae would feel obligated to help.

Instead, she had asked for something simple, though Shae knew it would be dangerous for Kestrel, Shae certainly could do it.

507

After she had cut her, Kestrel had told her she had one other task for her. That she should leave with Samuel who would take her somewhere safe and would have something she could do to help the war effort without doing any fighting.

She had happily agreed.

Now, she was here. Trapped in this bunker, with no way out. She could sense Kestrel, somewhere to the south and west. Most likely still in Houston. It was maddening to be connected to someone who had betrayed her so completely.

Sobs wracked her and the tears flowed like the hope draining from her life.

It seemed her fate in life was to be linked to those who had hurt her the most. Kestrel. And Daniel.

*Daniel?* She sent out a mental call toward the presence in her mind she knew to be him.

The presence answered.

Cirrus arrived in Houston the day before all hell broke loose. It had been somewhat difficult to track where his father had gone to when he had died. Fortunately for Cirrus, he had paid attention to many of the things his father had done in his presence.

It wasn't often his father had conducted business in front of him, but when he did, Cirrus remembered everything. It was one of those things he could do. Names, places, people his father had dealt with on regular basis, banks he had transacted with, passwords he used, Cirrus remembered it all.

Using what he knew, he had tracked his father first to Chicago. He learned much about what had happened there, but consistent with his father's manner, he had managed to not be openly involved with the events.

From Chicago, he tracked him to Houston and arrived in town and went about trying to find where he had taken up residence. Through his father's contacts he learned about the battle at the hospital and figured out it had been where his father had died.

His arrival at the hospital had been unproductive. The government had barricaded the place off and wouldn't allow anyone in. If his father's body had been recovered from there, Cirrus had no way of knowing.

He realized the only place he would find answers for his father's death was from the woman, Kestrel, to whom his father had pledged his loyalty and service. She would have knowledge of what happened.

According to his sources, she still operated in Houston somewhere, Cirrus had no way of finding out. He wasn't the only person looking for her and so he guessed she might be laying low.

He couldn't be more wrong.

The second day in Houston, nature went on the attack. Trees began erupting from the Earth, destroying everything in their wake. Stuck on the tenth floor of his hotel, Cirrus knew he was in trouble. The building began to shake, like some giant shaking a fruit tree to see what would fall out.

Desperately, Cirrus raced down the stairs, but when he reached the fifth floor, the stairwell, a huge tree bole blocked the way. Backtracking, he climbed back to the sixth floor and exited the stairwell. On his left, a floor to ceiling window.

A roaring sound from outside sent Cirrus to the window to see what caused it. Two buildings away, a parking garage collapsed around shoots of branches which had torn through the support braces.

Dread washed over Cirrus as the building he stood in continued to shift and shake. It was only a matter of time before it went down, like the parking garage. He turned back to look down the hallway.

Panicked people scrambled around the hallway, some pushing past him to enter the stairwell. He didn't bother to tell them they were wasting their time. He had to think.

The chances of using the elevator were slim to none. They were already in heavy rotation and waiting around for one to open on his floor and having enough room to fit him in seemed unlikely. Especially given the pile of humanity already pressed into the little off shoot hallway holding the elevators.

Which left one other option.

Looking back out the window he checked below.

Nothing but concrete and asphalt.

None of the tree branches had broken through this side of the wall which may have given him something to catch on the way down. Or better yet, something to climb.

Cirrus knew he had increased healing, but a fall from the sixth floor?

A loud cracking sound cut through the chaos and Cirrus wheeled around. The far side of the hallway sheared off and fell away from the building. Screams of panic came from those still clustered into the hallway and those unfortunate to still be on that side of the hotel. People began to press themselves into the tight area of the elevators, crushing those before them.

Cirrus turned back and slammed his fist against the window, shattering it.

Closing his eyes, he focused on an image of himself in his hybrid form and felt his body shift. The pain hurt less now he had practiced it since that fateful day his father had died, and he gained the power which had once been his father's.

There were different shouts of alarm from behind him, but he ignored it. Moving to the edge of the open window, he glanced down again. Nope, the scene hadn't changed. It still looked painful.

Sighing, he jumped out of the window. Wind blasted past him as he fell, a roar in his sensitive ears. When he hit, he tried to turn it into a roll, but one leg snapped and he pitched forward, slamming his head against the ground.

Things went black momentarily and his head throbbed in time with the painful throb in his leg. Warmth spread through his body as its healing powers began to fix the damage incurred from the fall.

A deafening snapping sound followed by a sound like a fast-moving waterfall rumbled toward him.

As his vision returned, he was greeted by the unwelcomed sight of the hotel building collapsing on top of him.

☒

Days and nights melded for Hector as he did his best to gather his sanity back and come to grips with what had happened. One minute he had been fighting the Wereboar and the next he had found himself blocks away, his clothes in tatters and his knife missing.

Fragments of memory crept up on him and refused to go like some unwanted guest who wouldn't get the hint, regardless of how many times he slammed the door in their face. Memories of him fighting against the Wereboar, but not fighting with his knife, instead, fighting with claws, covered in tawny fur.

It was impossible. His purpose, his mission, had been to kill all the Were-creatures, he couldn't be one himself, *could he?* He thought back to that day when his grandfather handed him the knife, how it had flushed him with heat. The power of a God, he had believed, and now, it seemed likely.

The Werejaguar. The god who had come to defend his worshippers from the were-creatures the other gods had sent. By taking the blade, he had allowed that God to infuse Hector with his abilities.

Hector went cold with realization of what his grandfather had surrendered to him when he gave him the knife. He remembered how hale his grandfather had seemed. Young, even. Certainly not like someone should be at his age. And yet, the day after he had given Hector the knife, his grandfather had died.

That morning, Hector had found his grandfather at his desk in his study. He had looked to have aged considerably since the day before. Hector had taken this as a symptom of his death. But now. Now Hector realized it had been the knife all along which had granted his father unnatural vigor.

Part of the healing ability granted by lycanthropy had kept his grandfather alive longer than he should have been. When he had given the knife to Hector, the power transferred to him and his grandfather was now bereft of its gifts, so his body could no longer sustain him.

Hector stumbled through the city looking like a beggar as his mind reeled from all he now understood. His grandfather had known. *Of course, he had known!* His grandfather had willingly given his life so Hector could do what needed to be done.

But his grandfather had been wrong. Had not truly understood the dynamics of this new group of shifters. There were heroes among them. Heroes . . . and he had killed one.

He would not do so again.

A war was coming, and when the city of Houston was attacked by Mother Earth and people were terrorized all over the country by hordes of Were-creatures, Hector realized the war was here.

Now he must choose a side.

# THE END

The saga will continue in the third and final book of the Lycan War Saga

# "The War"

The Gathering

Copyright © 2019 by Michael Timmins

This is a work of fiction. All of the characters, and events portrayed in this novel are products of the author's imagination.

Michael Timmins lives in Toledo, Ohio with his wife and two sons. His inspiration for writing came from his many years making modules to run for his D&D group. It has been a dream of his to one day get his work published, and now with ease of self-publishing he has made his dream come true.

CPSIA information can be obtained
at www.ICGtesting.com
Printed in the USA
LVHW040948151019
634129LV00022B/3590/P